TOWERS ABOVE

by

Buck Brannon

To Randy,
Hope you enjoy
this – you'll recognize
the VENUE!
There's A sequel coming

Buck Brannon

AKA
Dr. Bob Gaulden

Disclaimer

Towers Above
is a work of fiction. Names, characters, places, and
incidents are the products of the author's
imagination or are used fictitiously.   Any resemblance to
actual events, locales, or persons, living or dead, is
entirely coincidental.

CHAPTER 1

The first week of October in the Midwest is usually warm, with a welcome hint of an Indian summer in the air – but not this year. An early fall cold snap changed my thoughts of wearing a short sleeve shirt today. It was Friday, and the day when I would meet up with my long-time friends for our annual fall get-together. Although we'd be more warmly dressed in Oxford shirts, ties and blue blazers, the four of us would also be wearing our lucky tee-shirts, emblazoned with the farm's signature logo – The Four Horsemen – on the back.

I entered the gate of the Thoroughbred racetrack where we always kicked off our annual adventure, nodding "hello" to the security guard. As I handed my ticket to the attendant, another track patron rammed his portable chair-in-a-bag into the back of my right thigh. I wheeled around to see what had happened.

"Sorry about that," was all the man could muster.

Pausing just past the turnstile to massage my thigh, I saw at least a dozen other patrons pass through the turnstile without anyone bothering to do a look-see in their bags either. I couldn't believe that in this day and age, security would be so lax.

I mumbled to myself, "What world are these folks living in? Jesus, any of those people could have an assault rifle in their bag! Terrorism isn't limited to New York City or Washington, DC. Hell, it wasn't that long ago that Colonel Hassan did his Allahu Akbar thing at Fort Hood. They've got more Arab horse farms in this state than anywhere else in the country. Who can say some nut case isn't going to get even?"

Finally shaking off my paranoia, I bought a program before heading up the steps to the roundabout between the paddocks. I paused by the majestic 'Clock Tower' and the cluster of Pin oak trees in the center of the circle. Woodlands Park, constructed in the early 60's and located a few miles east of Corbin Kentucky, was nestled in the foothills of the Appalachian Mountains.

If imitation is truly the the best form of flattery, then Woodlands Park was a fraternal brother of Central Kentucky's hallowed race track that was built during the Great Recession. Woodlands Park, being the newest track in the Commonwealth, was assigned racing dates that proceeded the Spring and Fall racing 'Meets' being held in the mid-state region.

"The leaves are huge and still so green – in four weeks they'll be brown and down," I said, laughing at my attempt to rhyme. As I always did for luck, I put my hand to my lips, then reached out and touched the trunk of the largest of the three trees. Taking the elevator to get to our reserved seats, I realized that I was the first to arrive.

Friends since our early days in college, we had been blessed in having successful lives and careers: I, Rob, became a dentist; Donnie followed in his father's footsteps as a Thoroughbred trainer and Mark became a geneticist. Mike opted to be a veterinarian. By any measure, we all were successful in our respective fields. Before finishing undergrad and going on to our next life experiences, the four of us had made a pact to get together every fall for the last two days of the 'Meet'. These annual outings were generally social in nature – a chance to reminisce and catch up with the latest events in our lives.

Today was going to be more than catching up on the events in our lives over the past year, though. I had a proposition for my friends, and needed their commitment to make it work. While I had already talked to Donnie and knew he was on board, I was pretty sure that Mike and Mark were going to be more difficult to convince.

"Do I look too much like I'm trying to sell these guys

something?" I wondered as I sat there holding a portfolio filled with contractual prospectuses. "This sales persona just isn't you," I reminded myself. In all my years as a dentist, I never felt that advising patients what they needed for good oral health was a sales pitch. I simply presented the facts and what the expected financial obligations were – and let each patient make up their mind. It was their mouth, not mine, after all – I was their servant.

I smiled, recalling the time I'd been handed a prospectus – it was back in the '70s –when a neighbor tried to get me to buy into his friend's oil well business. Skeptical from the get-go, I remembered his pitch was, "The previous dozen wells had 'come in' – except for one." After reading all the legalese within his prospectus, I came upon the small print … a clause that included a demand option for an additional amount equal to my initial investment. I called it a "just-in-case" clause, as I had no idea what would trigger the demand for further investment monies. I should have known better than to entertain the thought of buying into an oil well from a neighbor whose main source of income was bookmaking!

Reminiscing aside, I turned my thoughts to today – when I was going to ask Mike and Mark to listen – and to be a part of my dream – a dream that would require a huge leap of faith on their part, along with commitments of their finances and time.

Suddenly hearing their recognizable voices, I was jarred out of my reverie and saw Mike and Donnie coming towards our seats. Donnie with his usual exuberant greeting, called out, "Hey Mikeee ... delivered any fillies today?" It was the same every year – with Mike exclaiming back, "Damn Donnie, you know full well most of them are born in January and February" ... bear hugs and laughs were springing forth from all of us.

It was great to see Donnie again. He'd returned to the Kentucky a couple years earlier to finally fulfill his dream of being a successful horse breeder. He knew the profession as well as anyone and realized that if he was ever going to be a big-time horseman and trainer, it wasn't going to happen in Montana. He was savvy enough to accept that "Big Sky" doesn't necessarily translate into "Big Success." You had to be where the action is.

I turned to greet Mike next – he'd pulled up short of giving me a hug and was looking at me with obvious doubt. "Rob, what the hell ... did you bring patient charts to the track today? You know that work is forbidden for the next two days!" We all laughed, and Mike quickly added, "So, I'm not the last one to arrive today. Mark is ... and he's buying the first round." Mark, who had been standing slightly behind Donnie, retorted, "The hell I will ... I saw you slip the security guard a 'Lincoln'."

"Oh sure, Barney Fife was going to pat you down … my ass!" I blurted out.

Six eyeballs were trained on me … each friend wondering what had caused my outburst. I was unwilling to confess, though, that the earlier security-lapse incident at the track entrance had really spooked me.

"Just kidding, guys. Look around – tell me this track's security guards don't resemble Barney Fife. They couldn't protect a piggybank." All four of us laughed at that image … and I quickly buried my fears in the deepest recesses of my brain. "Another blowup like that last one and this plan will go down in flames," I thought to myself.

But still, everything wasn't right in Southern Kentucky.

Sitting down next to me, Mike whispered, "Becker, what ya' got in that satchel?" He wasn't laughing and I squirmed in my seat as I said, "Let's grab some lunch before the first race and I'll give all of you the new tee-shirts." A smile slowly stretched across Mike's face. He'd bought my explanation – and besides, who doesn't love getting a gift when it's not Christmas or your birthday?

* * *

"Hey guys, Rob has new T-shirts for us but he's holding onto them until we eat," Mike yelled out. "I don't know about you, but I'm real hungry . . . now that I know I'm having a delicious cotton shirt for lunch."

Now that Mike's attention was no longer directly on me, I took several deep breaths to slow my heart rate down. I really believed in this dream and wanted my best friends to become part of it, not just for my sake, but their sake as well.

In the meantime, we indulged ourselves with bourbon, beer cheese, hot browns, bread pudding – and then more bourbon. Kentucky traditions are priceless!

I waited until the cocktails and beer cheese were finished before handing out the T-shirts ... and then the packets. Donnie looked passive, but Mike and Mark both had the quizzical look I had expected. I blurted out, "Mike and Mark, I need to be upfront with you. Inside these packets is a synopsis of a dream I've had and if it comes to fruition, it will be the most exhilarating venture you'll ever participate in. Donnie already knows about this hair-brained idea that I'm talking about – and is on board with it. I'm going to leave you guys alone for a few minutes so you can skim through the packet. Donnie can answer any questions for you."

"I don't expect a Yes or No answer today, but if you decide not to partner with us, the venture will die this weekend."

I paused to let my words sink in, and as I was heading towards the door, I reminded my friends why we were together now. "We're here to bet on the ponies and have fun. After dinner tonight, go to your room and read it in more detail – and talk about it with your wives. Without their support, there's no reason to move forward. Tomorrow after the race card is finished, hopefully we sign the agreement and we'll open a bottle of bourbon to celebrate. Otherwise, we'll just promise to get together again next year."

Adding one further point, I told my friends, "Oh yeah. Marty's responsible for putting together this synopsis. She said if I tried to explain it to you verbally, we'd be here till midnight. I'll be back in a bit, and no matter what your decision is, I love you guys. You're my brothers!"

I got up and didn't return until thirty minutes later. I knew when I got back to the table, I would be answering questions during lunch – and I was sure the first would come from Mark.

CHAPTER 2

The questions began to fly once we were all seated at the table again. It was obvious there'd been some early discussion among Mark, Mike and Donnie – and as I expected, Mark led the pack with the first question.

"Rob, Donnie explained to us where he got the lock of Secretariat's hair, but do you really believe that the lock of hair you bought on eBay is also from Secretariat?" Mark asked.

I could tell that there were questions racing in his head, and that I needed to give Mark much more information. I chose my words to explain the background of this venture to him as technically as possible. After all, he was a geneticist.

I started by saying Donnie was fully convinced of the authenticity of the hair sample – that indeed it was from Secretariat, affectionately also known as Big Red – and that it had been in Donnie's family for years. The sample had been securely locked away in his father's safe deposit box. I continued to explain the family connections: that the hair came from a stablehand – that worked at Meadow Stable.

"The other lock of hair I bought on eBay. Its authenticity can be easily verified, Mark, you do a genetic analysis with Donnie's sample and the eBay hair. If they match, we know it's legit – then it's up to Donnie and me."

I went on to explain to the guys that Donnie and I would get hair samples from mares and stallions that were actively breeding in Kentucky. Donnie would do his homework on the bloodstock, and narrow down the choices for a potential breeding of the two best Thoroughbreds ... using the DNA sample information derived from the hair clippings.

"Mark," I went on, "as you analyze the samples that we collect and decide which sample is closest to matching Big Red's DNA, well ... that's when we decide whether to try and coax the owner of the mare to sell or breed her. We'll have to pay a stud fee once she's bred and successfully delivers a foal. Mike, you'll be responsible for verifying that the stallion is fertile when you do your examination of him."

Continuing, I said we wanted a mare that has as close a DNA match to Secretariat as possible – adding that some divine intervention wouldn't hurt. "We pray that a stallion is born with those same traits that will produce a Triple Crown champion. In case Donnie didn't tell you, most of Secretariat's stallions didn't achieve much on the track. It was his female progeny that were responsible for any significant success."

Going into more detail, I explained that the mares carried a supposed genetic X factor – and that this was why they were responsible for bringing in a significant majority of the race winnings. Looking directly at Mark, I said, "It's going to be the result of your findings to determine if we even have a chance in hell of pulling off this genetic wonder."

It was important that Mark know how important his role in this venture was – and that his expertise in genetics was going to be key behind it all. "What we need you to do is the most critical part of this adventure. I know your company is doing some cloning stuff – and of course, the Jockey Club isn't going to accept the registration of a horse created in a test tube. I have no clue as to what you do in your laboratories, but if anyone can pull this off, it's you."

Changing direction, I told Mike, "Your responsibility lies in the birthing of our champion, as well as its health and welfare as he grows. Right before his birth, you'll take up residence at Donnie's farm – and we'll need you there 24/7. We don't want to lose this colt during its delivery."

"Look guys, I hate being negative, but you all know that anything can happen in the Thoroughbred business. I'll never forget that couple from Florida who brought their horse here to Kentucky to race on this track. Their horse's record was four races and four wins. Yet it took only one misstep on the home stretch when suddenly, both were down on the track with their horse. The stallion was loaded into the horse ambulance – on its way to be euthanized. I'll never forget their heartbreak," I told my three friends.

It was time to remind them that we all want to experience our dreams. "We've all accomplished a helluva' lot in our lives. And every year when we get together, each of you light up, just like I do. I see the gleam in your eyes! Each one of us has said more than once how much we envy these owners and trainers. Just look at Stan Kersey. He's had two epiphanies in his life. His first one was the telecommunications business and the second was Thoroughbred breeding. That guy is one of the happiest individuals I've ever met. I don't need to use any more clichés. The bottom line is, Stan had a dream and he fulfilled it."

I pointed out that we all want to be remembered for

something special after we each take that final breath. "Every week, the newspaper includes an obituary section of notable deaths. Well, I want a chance to be 'notable.' We've been serving people our entire lives and now, we're living out the short end of the straw. Is it really selfish to do something for ourselves? Just one time? If we do this, my life will be complete. So will yours."

I could tell that I was pushing too hard and losing traction. Donnie could see it in Mark's face – and took action, breaking the tension by slipping the new T-shirt over his shirt and tie.

As always, his timing was impeccable. In Kentucky Big Blue Nation lettering, the back of the shirt pronounced the birth of a new Bluegrass horse farm, the Four Horsemen Farms. That brought a smile to everyone's faces again.

"Guys, it's almost post time for the first race and we don't have our bets down. Let's get to work because the one that wins the least money today buys dinner tonight," Donnie proclaimed.

* * *

I believe it's all about handicapping. My mantra in life was and still is, "If you don't ask the question, you will never get the answer." If anyone had asked for my prediction as to whether Mike or Mark would sign on first, I would have said the odds on Mike would have been four out of five.

Mike has a Type A personality. As a veterinarian, he'd created a large-animal, predominately-equine group practice from scratch. It rivaled the most historic Thoroughbred veterinarian practices in the Commonwealth ... but he'd been pushing papers for the last five years and now felt a need to return to veterinary basics again. My challenge was just the kind of venture that could shake him out of the doldrums.

Good thing nobody asked me to take those odds on Mike ... it would be Mark who actually was the long shot. As Friday's Race One horses broke from the starting gates, I felt that Mark's odds couldn't have been better than twenty-five to one. Mark wasn't a risk taker and that was a plus, in my opinion. I liked that in him. If he signed on and had to make a tough decision at crunch time, I knew he'd tell me "No" if he was uncomfortable. He'd say, "This isn't good enough, it won't work."

No more talk of business – or worry over who would sign on or not. Now it was time to enjoy the races. I finished my bread pudding and headed down to the riders-up paddock and watched

Race One's horses proceed through the tunnel and onto the track. The first three races were usually Claiming Races … and I did my handicapping for these races the night before. The horses broke cleanly from the starting gate and the best sprinter grabbed a three-length lead. By the time he'd rounded the turn for the homestretch – and if past performance held true – he'd look like he was running in place, and the rest of the pack would catch and pass him. Sure enough, two of my picks battled for the win and the long shot finished third. I really didn't care which horse won, because my bet was an exacta box wager.

Claiming Races offer some of the best returns at the track. Not only does an owner come away from the track with an addition to his or her stable, but bettors can expect some really bizarre results and good payouts. I always paired the two favorites with another horse with long odds. I smiled, knowing I was off to a good start.

The next two races were almost mirror copies of the first race. I barely missed out on the exacta in the second race, but scored big in the third. Two of the favorites wore themselves out in the paddocks. One horse spent his energy battling his handlers as they tried to saddle him – his actions caused his main competition to suddenly break loose, bolt and head for the entryway. By the time both of these horses crossed the rotary into the second paddock and waited for their jockeys to get a leg up, they were washed out, which meant they couldn't work up a good sweat anymore … even if they wanted to. I bet the best long shot and paired him with my two new favorites, then upped my bet and boxed it. By the time I cashed in the winning tickets from the first and third race, I was six hundred dollars to the good.

I was waiting for the horses in the fourth race to enter the paddock when I realized I had company.

"Hey Mike, picking any winners?" I asked.

"Rob, I haven't bet a race yet. I called Jill and explained your plan. I've got to tell you Rob, she never said one negative word and I don't know why. I started to repeat everything and she interrupted me and said she wanted me to be happy. She said I've been … well, let's just say I've been difficult to be around for almost a year. She said if this venture 'is what it takes to get me out of my funk,' then she was in favor of it. I have been walking around for over an hour since we hung up. Rob, you're right. You didn't use a cliché but I will. I want a chance to grab the proverbial brass ring before it's too late. So count me in with you and Donnie. Now what's it going to take to convince Mark?"

My reply was instantaneous. "I've been in Mark's office once. He must have twenty plaques hanging on his walls. They're copies of patents he holds that are now registered with and owned by the government. I asked him what they were for and he said, 'If I tell you, I'd have to kill you.' Mike, I'm telling you – even though he smiled, I honestly don't believe he was kidding. I've read about his company's business profile, and half of their income is government contract money." I paused so Mike could take all this government intrigue in, before going into more genetic detail.

"Secretariat's supposed X factor is the key, and I suspect that would be Mark's first challenge. I don't believe anyone has ever bothered to genetically unravel the factor's secret. When Sham died, they weighed his heart and it was monstrous. Many horsemen believe he also had the genetic X factor. The speculation was that Secretariat's heart weighed over 20 pounds. Imagine in the same year, there were two Thoroughbreds competing against one another and both of them were genetic freaks."

"Sorry, if Marty was here she would have interrupted me five times by now," I apologized.

"It will be a major coup if we walk away from here tomorrow with Mark on board, and we both know that once we part ways, the odds of him signing on will incrementally decrease."

"Damn," was all I heard as Mike walked towards the betting window.

CHAPTER 3

"Rob, Rob, wake up! Answer, damn it," Mark shouted into the phone.

I'd stopped using wake up calls years ago. I just didn't trust them anymore, even though they'd become automated. Then I realized – this wasn't a wake-up call.

"Mark, what the hell time is it? Is something wrong?" I wiped the sleep from my eyes and glanced at my iPhone to see what time it was, realizing that it wasn't much after midnight.

Not answering my questions, Mark said, "Meet me downstairs in the lobby in twenty minutes. I'll drive."

We were now on our way to the local pancake house for a late dinner or early morning breakfast – depending on your point of view. As we made the ten-minute drive to the restaurant, I tried to gauge Mark's demeanor, but deciding it was not the time for small talk. I kept my mind on bacon and eggs instead. Once inside, Mark headed for two empty seats at the far end of the counter. The waiter handed us menus, but I waved mine off, giving him my order of two eggs over easy, crisp bacon, whole wheat toast and coffee with cream and sugar. Mark asked just for black coffee.

"What! Wait a minute. You drag my ass out at 1:00 a.m. in the morning for coffee only? You're shitting me!" I laughed. Mark put up his hand, stopping my frivolity.

"Janie and I are getting divorced. I've tried for the past six months to turn things around, but I've lost her. Maybe there's someone else, but the private detective I hired came up with nothing. I still love her Rob, but she wants out and I just can't fight anymore. I've got nothing left in me … no more energy." I glanced at him, stunned by his revelation and saw a tear begin to trickle down his cheek. I grabbed a napkin and put it in front of him, but he dismissed it like he was swatting a fly.

"I'm sorry, Mark," I told him – my laughter now replaced by silence. I was no longer hungry but forced myself to eat because there was nothing else to do or say. I downed my cup of coffee and motioned for a refill.

"What's the name of your future Triple Crown-winning horse?" Mark asked.

"Huh?" I blurted out. He had totally disarmed me and I said again, "Huh?"

"C'mon Rob, you've got a name. You and Donnie have this venture mapped out far more than what the prospectus shows. Count me in, but you better lay it all out. Everything – and now!

"Towers Above," I answered. "And no, I don't mean his height. You know how much I was affected by 9/11 – Marty's brother worked in the World Trade Center's Number 7 Tower." It was my turn to blot my eyes with a napkin. "He didn't work in the North or South Tower. No plane flew into it, but Tower 7 collapsed just like the Twin Towers. The experts basically said the building was collateral damage, that fire caused it to collapse. Really? I mean, c'mon … you tell me how that happened!"

"Collateral damage?" I repeated angrily. "Bullshit!"

"Marty figures he went to help in one of the main towers. I've read everything, from the Commission Report to the 'truther' stories. There are too many questions that still beg answers. Bush classified at least twenty or more pages of information as Top Secret and the government won't undo W's decision. Some or all of the documents have to be about the Saudis who were in the U.S. on

9/11. Can you or anyone tell me why this stuff remains classified?"

Now well into a pent-up diatribe, I continued, "Those folks who died deserve more than the 9/11 Commission's explanations. There needs to be a new investigation. The classified materials need to be released."

"For Marty, naming our horse Towers Above is my tribute to her brother and a tribute to all the others who lost loved ones that day."

Pausing a moment to regain my composure, I elaborated a bit more for Mark. "Donnie and I have been researching this project for over two years. When Big Red retired to stud, he stood at Claiborne Farms. The way we figure it, the mares he was bred with were, for the most part, Kentucky bred. That narrowed the equine version of ancestry.com legwork considerably. Donnie and I think that two-time Horse of the Year, Wise Dan, is carrying Secretariat's X factor. We've got some of his mane clippings, and also have hair clippings from his brother Successful Dan and their sister – even from the mother, Lisa Danielle."

I went on to tell Mark about a discussion I'd had with a guy who worked in Wise Dan's' stable … and while he wasn't sure about the size of the horse's heart, he said Successful Dan's heart was very large. However, Successful Dan was not as great a Thoroughbred because of health issues. "Wise Dan was great because of his attitude and it didn't hurt that he usually had a Hall of Fame jockey on his back controlling the reins," I added.

Going further into the lineage, I told Mark that Wise Dan's grandmother, Askmysecretary, was born in '82, and carried the genetic anomaly from Secretariat's breeding with Laquiola. "That's where you come in. We figure if anyone can verify this X factor trait, it's you. It all starts with the hair samples that Donnie's father had secretly stashed away."

Continuing on, I told Mark what we had for control subjects. "We've got hair samples from California Chrome, Curlin, A.P. Indy and probably the best two-year-old Thoroughbred that's racing now, American Pharoah. We also have samples from Pharoah's father, Pioneer of the Nile and his mother, Littleprincessemma. So, Mark, now that you have the whole story, tell me what you can and cannot do."

"Rob," Mark asked, "just how tight are you with Donnie? Well, maybe I should reword that question. Do you trust him with personal information?"

"Yes, I do Mark. Why are you questioning his integrity?" I replied.

"If you want me to be a part of this business venture, I need you both to understand how much the government 'owns' me. You probably already figured out when you came to my office a while back that my company has some federal contracts. A few years ago, I wanted to take the company public. The government came to me and made an offer I couldn't refuse. Now, there's not a single moment that I don't regret that decision."

Mark went into more specifics, telling me that there were no public records indicating that federal contracts were ever awarded to his business anywhere in the system, or that his company even existed. "You can't even find an appropriation in the government budget that references my company. I suspect my corporation is now a Department of Defense expense. My independent business no longer exists and I have no sales staff because everything we do is secret. I don't pay any taxes or Social Security, and the employees receive their paychecks from the government. I can't ever retire. The only way it ends is when I die; I'm certain they've already identified the next person who will take my place."

"Take a look at this."

Mark took off his watch – I thought I knew what he was going to show me. In our undergrad years, we each had tattoos inked on our wrists ... tattoos easily hidden by the faces on our watch. Mark's was slightly faded but still looked like the university's logo of yesteryear. "What am I looking for? It looks a little faded, but so does mine," I said.

"Look closer," Mark ordered. There was a slight scar not much larger than three millimeters in length.

"So it's a scar? If you hadn't picked at it ..." I pointed out.

"Damn it, Rob. I'm serious. They placed a GPS Radio Frequency Identification Device chip in my wrist. Don't be obvious, but when you get up and go to the bathroom, take a look out into the parking lot. I'll bet there's a government agent eavesdropping on us right now, smart ass."

"Mark, you're creeping me out. What kinda' stuff do they have you doing?" I stammered. He didn't answer.

Getting back to the matter at hand – horse genetics, I said to

Mark, "OK, I'll give you the scenario. What if … and that's a big if, the genetic X factor exists? What I'm trying to say is that the X factor is responsible for Secretariat and Wise Dan being several hands taller and stockier than most others. The factor also caused their hearts to be enormous and weigh over twice that of a normal Thoroughbred's heart." I explained to Mark that nonetheless, the real reason for the success of both horses was something intangible – and genetically impossible to control. "The presence of the X factor might also determine the horse's ability and drive to not just compete with – but dominate – an opponent. The result is a freak of nature. All the tumblers align to unlock the perfect specimen of horse racing flesh." I was done talking … for now.

"Rob, I'll be able to determine if the X factor exists," Mark answered back. "What scientists haven't been able to determine until just recently is how to control those intangibles that you might call miraculous. This type of science is what my company has been under contract to try and develop. It's all about genetic engineering."

With that last comment, Mark deliberately spilled creamer on the countertop. Dipping his finger in the spill, he spelled out "new guy" with an arrow pointing to a different server now behind the counter. Then he took out a pen and wrote on a napkin, "I have the genetic answers but they don't know it yet!" Just as quickly as he wrote it, he grabbed another napkin and wiped up the spilt cream. Then he wrote, "Do you realize what the possibilities are if we could do this and who would benefit?"

Again the creamer spilled onto the countertop and Mark spelled out "military" and then, "so wrong!!!" He rubbed the napkin into the spill, the ink smearing into a blue blur.

"Hold that thought. I'll be right back," I told him. I headed to the restroom … not quite believing what I'd just heard and seen, but slowing down enough to pause and look out into the parking lot before opening the bathroom door. Sure enough there was another car in the parking lot, but no other customer had come inside since we'd arrived. When I returned to the counter, Mark was no longer there and our dishes had been cleared. Heading to the car where Mark was already in the driver's seat, I saw him put his fingers to his lips, making the zip-it gesture to me. We headed back to the motel in silence.

We walked back into the motel lobby, continuing an uneasy silence as we entered the elevator, both going to our respective floors and rooms. I assumed I would receive his signed contract later in the day.

My head spinning from what I'd learned over the past two hours, I found myself looking over my shoulder as I left the elevator and hurried to my room. Once inside, I couldn't help but wonder if it had been entered and violated during the time I was away – and surely I wasn't going to stay there any longer. I showered, dressed, packed and left my room and the motel . I couldn't get away from there fast enough, and headed for the track's kitchen to grab a second breakfast and start handicapping that day's races.

The only constant I was certain about now was the sunrise.

CHAPTER 4

Mark was still wide awake at 4:30 a.m. that Saturday morning – unable to sleep after the excursion with Rob. He'd been busy researching and reading. It had been quite a while since he'd read anything about Secretariat's historic Belmont Stakes feat – and how the horse's anatomically-large heart had supposedly allowed it to carve out a stunning and record-setting time for the mile and a half race. Mark surfed the Internet, pulling up a YouTube video of the 1973 Belmont Stakes event. He replayed the video five times before he stopped watching – at the same time shaking his head in disbelief at what he was again seeing – and what he had forgotten.

"Jesus Christ … wouldn't it be something if we could duplicate that? Damn you, Rob Becker," Mark caught himself thinking and laughing aloud to himself.

For the next couple of hours, he researched horse genetics and made notes. Most of the information he already knew, but nonetheless bookmarked specific web sites for future reference. He skimmed through the basic genetic information, already planning to have some of his government lackeys hack into the websites when he got back into his lab office. If the websites didn't provide the information he was looking for, then he'd have them hack deeper into the author's records within their respective university facilities until they found it.

After a cursory examination of over thirty websites, Mark reached a preliminary conclusion ... that the X factor is a genetic reality. He learned that historically, the trait extended as far back to Thoroughbreds that were bred in the 18th century. The consensus was that Eclipse, a European Thoroughbred, was the first documented horse of significance that had both the X factor anomaly and the associated large heart anatomy.

Eclipse's offspring, Glencoe, was shipped to America and stabled in central Kentucky. Years later, her presence eventually led to several progeny that American horse racing fans watched and grew to love. Included in this group were Man o' War and War Admiral, along with everyone's favorite top Thoroughbred, Secretariat and his arch rival, Sham.

Mark wasn't convinced, though, that the genetic trait of a huge heart in a Thoroughbred could be responsible for twenty-five percent or more of any horse's racing success. If the horse didn't have a pulmonary system capable of handling the increased efficiency of a massive pumping system, then the resulting delivery of oxygen to all the muscles would be no different than a horse with a normal-sized heart. He also knew that conformation defects, like a bowed leg, a crooked hoof – these types of physical imperfections could neutralize any positive effects the X factor contributed to a Thoroughbred's potential.

X factor or not, the only constant was that dams – brood mares that produce foals – historically contributed the most, both genetically and environmentally, to a foal's success on the race track. It was known that the large heart gene factor was handed down by the dam and that this factor literally was a part of her X chromosome. However, Mark was certain that there also was some connection with a stallion's Y chromosome. Genetics was Mark's forte and using this expertise was how he would help his friends.

Still awake, despite spending hours researching online early that Saturday morning, he now believed that there were rare instances when the X factor would emerge during breeding – and that an equine freak of nature such as Secretariat would be the end result. Instead of a rare, naturally-produced large-heart champion Thoroughbred bursting on the scene every fifty years, it would fall to Mark to make that happen sooner than later. He would have to find a dam with the dominant X factor and then a suitable male to mate her with – this would be a stallion that carried the yet to be discovered mini-X factor within his Y chromosome.

What Mark was developing for the government was classified, and involved the genetic engineering of messenger RNA and its potential emerging capabilities in saving lives and limbs. Giant strides in decreasing battlefield morbidity had been achieved in the new millennia, with some new technologies still in the experimental stages. Mark's research facility was one of several tasked with developing a new clotting technology – one that could help the country's military warriors who were injured on the battlefield. Theoretically, if a wound that occurred on the battlefield could instantly be closed by an accelerated clotting mechanism, then limbs would no longer require amputation, organs would remain almost whole and viable, and lives would be spared. Our military, being all volunteer, is often hamstrung by a limited number of soldiers – and this technology could conceivably help return a soldier to duty more quickly.

Early in the design phase of his lab's clotting program, Mark's geneticists had determined that Thoroughbreds were among the best candidates for testing of new techniques because of their propensity to bleed when racing. If these research scientists could genetically modify the horse's clotting mechanism by speeding it up, then the use of drugs like Lasix would no longer be needed.

Mark suddenly realized that the clotting technology could be a boon to their venture. If the clotting mechanism could stop bleeding at the capillary level in the alveoli at the deepest depths of a Thoroughbred's lungs, then there was no reason their technology couldn't extend to larger arterioles, arteries and veins.

Mark couldn't believe his good fortune. He felt like a god, with a destiny of greatness in his own hands.

Just as Rob had withheld information from Mark, Mark also had secrets he couldn't reveal. Questions and concerns were swirling through his mind.

"Is this fate or am I just blessed – and why on this particular weekend? Why have I stumbled onto all of this?" Mark asked himself. "Rob can't possibly know that an integral part of my research involves horses. Did a special operative tell Rob what my lab is working on? If a government agent tipped Rob off, then he's in danger and has no idea what these people are capable of, or what they'll ultimately do to him and his family! I've got to warn him."

Mark's mind was swimming in a sea of paranoia. Finally, he collapsed on his bed, fast asleep.

On the desk across from the king-sized bed was Mark's packet of information and the prospectus from Rob. Other papers he'd been working on, marked *Confidential* and *Project Withers,* were also strewn across the desk,.

Several paragraphs within the *Project Withers* pages bore Mark's orange highlighted markings, with asterisks and additional notations in the borders. Triple underlines seemed to indicate specific topics of importance. One of the highlighted paragraphs discussed how sixty percent of a horse fetus' growth occurs in the last three months of the mare's eleven-month gestation period. In capital letters above this particular paragraph was a scribbled sentence that read, "High doses of modified messenger RNA should be administered in this time frame …" An asterisk at the bottom of the page was followed by a line and arrows at both ends, and next to the asterisk was a sentence stating, "Administer high levels of my modified RNA until the foal is weaned, four to eight months after birth."

The last two pages of Mark's papers contained the government's summary of *Project Withers* … "In conclusion, with the commencement of the next World War …

• We must take into account that anything operating on the

grid will be neutralized for unknown periods of time.

- This includes mobile transportation not shielded from an EMP attack.

- Civilian technology will be rendered useless for varying periods of time.

- (Temporarily) Any form of long distance travel will revert to animal-assisted transportation.

- (It is) Imperative that these animals be healthy with no immunological issues.

- *Project Withers* will become justified and implemented by Homeland Security.

- Breeding increases when hostilities begin!

- A cover story will reference an *Unmanageable Equine Virus*."

Mark was in deep REM sleep, experiencing a recurring battlefield dream. It was not all that dissimilar from some of the battle scenes in the movie *Braveheart*. Only this time, genetically-modified war horses and their genetically-modified mounted warriors were galloping across the battlefield.

This recurring dream was subliminally inspired by what Mark had learned of future military actions – specifically that the government intended to reinstate a Calvary into its future war plans.

It wasn't a big leap from Thoroughbreds to Quarter Horses. Every species of horse would become an asset; even mules, which genetically are not much different from their four-legged horse cousins, would be M-RNA inoculated for battle.

People's memories are always short. Most had forgotten that during America's initial invasion in Afghanistan after 9/11, many of our Special Forces were engaged in battle on horseback. The Afghan Mujahideen that battled the Russian troops to a stalemate in 1978-1992 utilized mounted warriors as well.

Mark's phone alarm went off and he got out of bed, collecting his papers. As often happened after a short snooze, his mind was extremely alert – and driven by a sense of fear – he was now uncertain about joining with his friends in the venture.

"There's no way I can partner with these guys," he told himself. "I can't jeopardize them because of my activities and work. But I can't pass on this opportunity. Finding two Thoroughbreds – a mare and a stallion, then breeding them – how can I turn this windfall down?" Mark thought about this for a moment until he was interrupted by a female voice.

"Honey, do you have to leave so early? Come back to bed for

just a few minutes."

Mark was tempted. She could always be counted on to start his day right – something his wife was never able to do. It was also one of the innumerable reasons why Mark had begun searching for a new partner in his life. "Not this morning. We'll have a ton of time tomorrow. Love ya' … gotta go," he told her.

Mark left the room, his mind still racing. "She'll have to remain a secret – the guys would never understand about her. Brother, I hope Rob is not disappointed in me for backing out of this deal."

It was time to head to the racetrack and get the day started … again.

CHAPTER 5

The day was already off to a scrambled start. Since I never ate my entire breakfast at the pancake house, it only made sense to have some of Kentucky's best breakfast eggs … those made by the cooks at the track's kitchen. I was glad that I made the decision to leave the motel and come here early. Although still dark, there was a hint of the coming sunrise – and enough daylight for the first of several horses to begin their day's workouts.

Standing by the rail, I could hear the horse's hooves pounding against the dirt before catching sight of the magnificent animals making the noise. The most fun for me was closing my eyes and listening to the pounding of the hooves. First hearing the sounds of a trot, then a cantor and a gallop, followed by a quickening pace that meant a horse was breezing … running easily on its own momentum. Perhaps, mixed in would be the sounds of the horses doing a "bullet workout" – if there was already enough daylight for track officials and handicappers to start their stopwatches and time the horse's performance.

I was ready to go get that breakfast, when a tap on my shoulder interrupted the first peaceful moment I'd had since 4 a.m.

this morning.

"Rob, did you see those Navy F-18 Hornets doing their touch-and-go routines yesterday?" I thought I recognized the voice, and before turning to confirm, said, "Jack, that's got to be you." Sure enough, I was right – it was Jack who'd arrived early for work. We shook hands.

Jack worked in the track's grandstand, seating patrons during the meets. He'd been retired for years, and along with most other track employees, worked the two annual events for a pittance of what they'd earned during their careers, simply because they loved it. "What brings you out so early?" I asked.

Ignoring my question, Jack brought up the F-18 Hornets again. "I bet they're here in preparation for next year's Owner's Challenge Cup races," Jack said excitedly.

The Owners Challenge Cup was the Super Bowl of horse racing. There are several races during the two-day period, with the climax of the Cups' race card being a mile and a quarter dirt race – and a purse of five million dollars.

"I actually didn't see them, but I sure heard their

afterburners. What makes you think they were here because of next year's Cup races?" I replied.

"Rob ... c'mon, they were Navy planes. There's no salt water or aircraft carriers in Kentucky. The paper said they were here for refueling. Fat chance! Louisville's Bowman Field is only a few minutes away from here, if they go supersonic. They've got the same jet fuel as our airport."

"They were here to practice air coverage for next year in case some crazies decide to do a repeat 9/11 airplane attack. Homeland Security already knows those fighters have enough operating runway length. Hell, even the sheikhs from the Emirates can land their 747's, if need be. Yesterday was Homeland's test run for them and also for the track. I bet track officials wanted to see how much those fighters would spook the horses."

I hadn't thought about it that way, but Jack was making some sense – even if it was in a conspiracy-theory sort of way.

"So, what else do you know about next year and the security here?" I asked him.

"This goes no further than you and me, OK?" Jack said.

"Promise me," he added. "Sure Jack. Who else am I going to talk to?" I said back.

"I know some of this is … well, you're just going to have to take my word for it. They're supposed to adopt the NFL-type container rules. That means nothing bigger than a one gallon see-through container, or you know … those plastic zip-lock bags, gets through the gates. Everything you want to carry in here will have to be in that kind of clear container or bag."

Continuing on, "Right now security officers basically just do a cursory peek into people's bags and purses. Occasionally one will take a stick and poke it into the bag … like that is going to do anything. They don't even check everyone's bag. It's a here and there type of search. I also don't think that people will be allowed to carry in those folding chairs that are in a long carry bag. If they do allow those chairs in, people better expect an extensive search and long waits. Hell, someone could bring in a disassembled weapon – nobody would know the difference, the way security screens people now," Jack told me with a sound of disgust.

"I also heard a rumor that they're putting in some state-of-the-art metal detectors. And I've seen bomb-sniffing dogs here too, usually before May and the Derby. Supposedly they're just getting in some practice. I've been told that the dogs and their handlers will be here every morning, sweeping the grounds for explosives.

The Challenge Cup officials will literally take over these facilities. We'll become their employees. I've even heard we won't be parking on track property, which probably is a good idea."

Now my curiosity was thoroughly aroused. "Why's that?" I asked, prodding Jack for more information. I wasn't disappointed.

"Rumor has it, we'll park off-site and get bussed to the track. Right now, we get a parking pass that we're supposed to show as we enter the employee parking lot at the end of the property. Well, guess what? I just wave my pass at the security guard … and he just waves me through. Getting in is too easy!" he said in a worried tone.

"Rob, I could go on and on. In my opinion, this track is an open book. Oh, and get this, the horses running in the various Cup races will be in the barns on Clay Road. You know, at the backside of the track. I understand there will be Cup guards down there 24/7. Their people don't mess around," Jack explained.

I was truly amazed at what he'd told me. "Jack, I don't know what to say. I know Homeland has a list of facilities that they consider at the highest risk for a terrorist attack. Those events and venues get the best bang for the limited security bucks. Obviously if you're right, the only explanation is this track is not considered a risk unless it becomes the host for an event like the Challenge Cup," I haltingly stated.

"Bingo, Rob Becker! Hey, I've got to run. I have to go collect money from the patrons that get here before the gates even open. Say hello to Marty for me." Jack was gone.

I was sorry now that Jack had found me. He just added another layer of stress and an additional budget expense to our group's future venture. I had no clue how much security would cost. I certainly didn't want or need an unknown expense that might give my future partners an excuse to delay their commitment to the venture today. No breakfast for me after all – the eggs would have to wait until next spring now. I decided to do a walk-about and see for myself just how weak the current track security was.

I saw other patrons arriving early, just as Jack said. These were folks like me – out to enjoy the early morning quiet and solitude of the track. I never thought about others just wandering around or the lack of security before today, but now that Jack had raised the point, I wondered – about many things.

Sure they would eventually have to pay the admission charge and receive an appropriate tag to wear that indicated that they had paid. But would they be challenged to show what they brought onto the grounds or had in their possession? Had they brought some contraband in, conveniently hidden – without even a cursory security check? I proceeded to the barns and walked up and down the rows of stalls, sharing pleasantries of "how you doing?" and "good morning" as I walked, acting like I was track savvy and supposed to be there.

Most likely, I was being videotaped by a security camera … but was I being watched at this very moment, or was the video merely a documentation tool that would aid in my prosecution in case I made a poor behavior choice?

An hour later, I was tired of walking – and somewhat disappointed in myself. I took pride in covering all the contingencies, whether it was performing a routine dental procedure for a patient or planning for the eventuality of racing a champion Thoroughbred. I returned trackside and began handicapping the day's races … and figuring in my head how high our security expenses might be.

Jack seemed to be right. This quaint and beautiful horse

racing venue would never be able to, or want, to adapt to the evil happenings in the world – except for a couple of special days. Then they'd be willing to shake things up.

I had some serious thinking to do.

CHAPTER 6

I had no idea how much the cost of security would add to each shareholder's financial obligation. Certainly expenses would be in correlation with just how famous our horse would become – and the caliber of the races he competed in. I figured there'd be an accountant under the employ of one of the more-recognized horse farms nearby who could probably give me the figures I needed. However, as a neophyte horseman, I hadn't yet made that particular connection.

I texted Donnie. "Are you at the track yet?"

"Down here at the rail watching the horses work … what's up?" was his reply.

"Stay there, I'll come find you," I texted back.

I was at the rail in five minutes. "I had no idea you were on the grounds. I was down here earlier talking with a friend," I said, knowing I possibly had some unexpected news to share.

"Donnie, I screwed up. I totally forgot to include a line item in the budget that covers security expenses ... and I have no idea what the costs might be. The last thing we need right now is a deal breaker."

"Rob, slow down ... take a deep breath and slow down. What the hell are you talking about?" Donnie asked me. I told him about the conversation I'd just had with Jack.

With his usual aplomb, Donnie managed to calm my hysteria. "Rob, no one is going to know about Towers Above until he starts winning races. When he wins some graded Stakes Races, his winnings will easily cover any security needs we'll have. Until then, he'll be stabled at my farm and will be safe."

He paused, giving me a chance to let my brain process that information, adding, "Rob, just be open and upfront with Mike and Mark. I'm sure they'll understand. I'll grant you, it is something we're going to need to address eventually."

"Hell, I know security is more important than before. I was coming out of the men's room this morning and there was a father and his twin teenage boys going in. They looked to be of Middle Eastern descent and reminded me of horse sale events up at the track in central Kentucky." Donnie went on to tell me that while the Arabs don't usually have a visible presence at race events, they are definitely present for the horse selling.

"They can stare you down in a heartbeat. Maybe that wasn't the way they acted before 9/11 but now it creeps me out. One twin had braces on his teeth, so he wasn't quite as imposing" he said, trying not to laugh.

"Damn you, Donnie!" I replied. His attempt at levity worked and had somewhat eased my tension, although I had some comments of my own.

"I also saw that father. It was before sunrise and I couldn't see the boy's features as well as you did. With all that's going on in that region of the world ... hell, now we've got homegrown jihadists. Donnie, you just never know what's going down on any given day."

Since my day was pretty much trashed already, I figured it was time to share Mark's early morning revelations with Donnie. When I finished telling him all that Mark had said, I could tell by Donnie's gaping mouth and full-moon eyes that he was about to say, "You've got to be shitting me!" I intercepted his comment, interrupting with my own assumptions.

"Once he partners with us, you can pretty much expect the government will lump all four of us together. By default, that would also include our significant others. I've messed with some powerful people in my life, but to my knowledge, none of them were associated with any government research project or agency. Even if the President of the United States gave us a written pass, I still would have doubts," I said seriously.

Driving home my most critical point – a fear that Mark would not be able to ensure our safety – I stressed my concerns to the hilt with Donnie, "I'm not really sure I want to spend the rest of my life wondering what's around the next corner. Somehow Mark has to find a way to assure all of us that his involvement in our venture will never jeopardize any of us … and that includes our families."

Donnie had nothing to say at first, and gazed across the dirt track for a good minute or two. "There is a way out." Another thirty to forty seconds passed – and I could see the wheels turning quickly in his mind. "When you file the paperwork to form our LLC, only list three officers. Mark can't be a part of our group. He'll have no shares in the corporation ... he won't attend our annual meeting and he can't receive any distributions from the corporation. We can still call our entity The Four Horsemen Farm – even though there would only be me, you and Mike. Mark will truly be a silent partner."

It was my turn to stare and say nothing.

Donnie was right. It was the perfect escape from what I feared was going to be a dead-end situation. I just kept looking at Donnie, who could tell my brain was focused on which of us had to tell Mark he was out – and how we would do that.

"Oh no, you don't. Don't you put that on me! Mark's closer to you than to any of us. You're going to have to deliver the bad news to him," Donnie said.

"I know, Donnie … I know."

* * *

I waited for Mark by the Clock Tower. He hadn't responded to my text yet, but I knew he'd find me.

"Morning, Rob. I figured you didn't go back to bed this morning. You look exhausted," Mark mumbled behind me.

"Christ, Mark. Don't do that," I shouted, jumping in nervous fear.

"Sorry about that, brother. Let's walk, I'm sure someone's eyeballing us right now." I followed Mark as he headed toward the barns.

"Don't talk, just listen," Mark told me somberly. "This morning was a test. I wanted to see just how tight a leash I'm on with the Feds, and I got my answer. Rob, there's no way I can be a partner with you guys. God knows I really want to be included, but I might as well be radioactive. My involvement will endanger all of you … and your families would also be in jeopardy."

Looking directly at me and trying to be more reassuring, Mark continued. "C'mon Rob, don't look so dour – you can't get rid of me that easily. I plan on leaving here today with the hair samples. It shouldn't take more than a couple weeks to determine the DNA match and then another couple weeks to determine whether the X factor exists, and if so, where it is located in the genome. If you and Donnie have been holding out on anything else, I need to know about it now, because it's going to be difficult to meet with you after today." He waited for my response … but I was at a loss for words.

After a few seconds of silence, Mark continued. "I won't be able to contact you if and when I've got a match. You're going to have to handle that part somehow … but without coming directly to see me. You've been at my office before and they know who you are. It would also be difficult for me to get anything out the door."

Mark had apparently been thinking about this, and went on to give me specifics about how we could communicate in a code that made sense to each of us. "I've written a timeline of events for you, Rob. The Thursday before Thanksgiving, e-mail me and ask if I'm going to my parents for dinner. If I answer that I'm staying home, that means that the eBay sample and Donnie's Secretariat hair samples are a match. A week before Christmas, e-mail me again and invite me to dinner on Christmas Eve. If I reply, 'I'll try to make it,' that means I've got the X factor isolated."

I couldn't believe what I was hearing. I was off the hook – and I didn't have to hurt Mark or our friendship. My legs half-buckled under me, forcing me to stop and steady myself against the side of the barn. All that built-up adrenalin in nervous anticipation of a possible confrontation was quickly dissipating. Taking a deep breath, I motioned with my hand for Mark to pause a second.

"Too much excitement for ya'?" Mark asked, laughing. He was relishing my obvious angst and even more apparent relief. "C'mon Rob – just give me the two, three or four envelopes with hair samples of the mares and the stallions you already selected to create our wonder horse."

"How … just how did you know?" I blurted out in shock.

"Jesus Rob, how many years have we known each other? All those poker games we played in college – you couldn't bluff worth a shit! Everyone knew your 'tells'. Didn't you ever figure out why we always had a card game after you received one of those care packages from your parents? We all knew you had some extra spending money … Mike and Donnie were just as eager as me to win it from you!"

Mark started laughing; I tried to resist, but it was futile. I reached in my sport coat and removed the hair samples I'd brought to the track, along with the Secretariat samples he knew about from our earlier discussions.

Passing the samples to him, I said, "That's all of it, Mark. You've got everything Donnie and I collected. I need you to promise me something, though. If you're putting yourself at risk at any time by doing this, e-mail me and somehow put the words 'no joy' into the message. That way I'll know you've done all you could. Okay?"

"Okay Rob," Mark promised, putting his arm around my shoulder and pulling me close. I already had an older sister, and at that moment I realized what it felt like to also have an older brother.

And then there were three.

CHAPTER 7

It was the fall of 2014. Ben had no idea in that pre-dawn morning that the man who was standing at the rail just twenty yards to his left shared a profound heartbreak as a result of the attacks of 9/11. The horrific losses in each of their lives occurred in different settings and at different times, both during and following that tragic day.

On this Saturday, Ben's job was to continue his twin nephews' equine education. It was hard for him to believe Ahmad and Jamil would be fifteen years old in another month. Their Saudi father had left the boys and their mother when the twins were barely one year old. The father didn't abandon his family over domestic issues – he left to fight with other Saudis and was supposedly in Afghanistan fighting with a group known as al-Qaeda.

The twin's mother emigrated to the United States when her sons were very young, knowing that they would easily be granted asylum to live with her Uncle Ben. He'd left Saudi Arabia to live in the U.S. decades ago, settling in southern Kentucky.

Ben was honored to serve as a surrogate father to the boys.

After all, who better to know what it was like to be an identical twin? He also had an identical twin brother – Omid – and despite being identical twins, their lives were drastically different.

Ben left his native land in the early '70's – years of watching the increasing foment of terrorism and religious conflict in the Middle East convinced him it was time for a new homeland. For many years, though, he continued to go by his given birth name, Ahmed.

His twin, Omid, remained in the Middle East ... he was a Doctor of Veterinary Medicine. With Omid's studies and expertise in large animals, it made sense for him to stay there with their father, where he could manage the royal family's Thoroughbred operations.

Ben's mind wandered back to that fateful day in September.

* * *

Omid flew into Central Kentucky a few days before 9/11 to visit with his twin brother and prepare for the annual yearling horse sales at the nearby track. Omid and his brother left for the track at sunrise on that fateful day, but Omid's boss, a Saudi sheik, was nowhere to be found. While waiting in the track rotunda and reviewing his notes on the bloodstock, Omid couldn't help but notice the turmoil and hushed conversations going on near him. He asked one of the track staff what was happening and the woman, in tears, informed him that the towers at the World Trade Center had been attacked.

Shaken, Omid looked for his brother – but Ahmed wasn't part of the Saudi group that was there to buy horses. Seeing his brother sitting in the back of the auditorium, Omid went up the walkway of the amphitheater and frantically told his brother he would be back in a bit.

It was obvious to Ahmed that something was amiss … he went looking for a television monitor and with others, watched in shock and horror as the news stations reported on the tragedy in New York City, and the other terrorist attacks unfolding throughout the United States. He was sickened by what he saw and his stomach began cramping. Finding a restroom, Ahmed went into a stall to compose himself.

The door to the men's room opened while he was still in the stall and Ahmed heard a man speaking in an Arabic dialogue … the words coming out of the man's mouth sent shivers up his spine. He was certain that it was Omid's superior speaking

"I knew it was going to happen today ... I just didn't know when," Ahmed heard. "I figured they'd go after the Twin Towers and Washington. Call the embassy and tell them the sales will probably be postponed until tomorrow and that we'll need safe passage home as soon as possible after," the man said.

The next voice Ahmed heard was his brother Omid. "You knew ... you knew and didn't tell anyone? Why? The Americans have been good to ..." There was no response, other than the apparent sound of flesh striking flesh. It was obvious that Omid had been silenced – and the next words Ahmed heard were not his brother's.

"You will never question me again! Do you understand?" the angry voice exclaimed in Arabic. Again, there was no reply, just the sound of a door opening and people walking out of the restroom.

"What has Omid gotten himself into?" was all Ahmed could think.

As with the rest of the country, it was not life as usual once the news about the attacks broke. The horse sales were postponed until the next day. Ahmed waited for Omid in the pavilion well past lunch time, calling him several times from his phone … but getting no answer. When Omid didn't return by dinnertime, Ahmed went back to the track to search for him.

He knew something was wrong. Twins, even when they're separated and perhaps more so during times of stress, can always tell. It's a telepathic thing. The brothers had experienced this phenomena more than once growing up – if one was under duress, the other was aware of it. After a useless search, Ahmed returned to the motel and a restless night's sleep, worried about his brother. He was back at the track before sunrise.

Ahmed waited in the back of the Rotunda and finally saw Omid and a bloodstock agent enter and go to their designated seats. Omid had told his brother that there were three or four horses that the Saudi family intended to place bids on – but the actual bidding process was considered too menial for the Saudi ruling class. The Royal Family members were tucked away in a private room, while Omid did the scut work.

The bidding signs were obvious to Ahmed – he could tell the auctioneer knew that the bloodstock agent's tug on his right ear lobe meant Omid wanted the agent to place a bid. He could also see his brother elbow the agent in the side just before the ear tug. Ahmed wondered why the agent didn't simply raise his hand. By the time the morning's stock had been auctioned off, the House of Saud had spent $1.2 million dollars – and was now the owner of two stunning yearlings.

There was a set protocol to follow after each yearling's sale: first, a track official brought paperwork in triplicate for Omid's agent to fill out. The agent kept a copy with his receipt of sale, then went to the sales office to get a copy of the yearling's health history and other pertinent papers. After, the financial transaction was taken care of. The final piece of paperwork was a ticket that would be presented to track security guards to show valid ownership before the horse could be trailered off the grounds. The Jockey Club also had offices on the track premises, with standing orders to mail the registration papers to the Royal Family.

After the second purchase, Omid stood, telling his agent that he would take care of the paperwork this time. Omid prayed that his brother was watching as he proceeded to the sales office.

Ahmed was.

Ahmed quickly sprang to his feet to follow his brother. Omid sensed his presence without turning around; he stopped suddenly and bent over pretending to tie his right shoelace.

Catching up with Omid, Ahmed slowed down just enough to drop a piece of paper on the ground next to Omid.

The note stated, "I was in restroom … heard everything. Don't leave – stay here. Asylum will be easy. Do it for your grandchildren."

Omid scooped up the note, read it, and continued on his way.

That was the last up-close exchange Omid had with his brother. No hug, no goodbye, no "I love you, brother." They both knew they would never see each other again.

The horses were loaded into a trailer, with Omid accompanying them in the cab of the truck as they most probably headed to an Arab holding farm before flying to the land of Saud.

* * *

Ahmed knew Omid was still somewhere in the states, probably in Kentucky. There were still no commercial flights in the air anywhere in the United States. For days after 9/11, the skies were contrail free.

On the morning of the fourteenth, Ahmed received a letter with no return address. He immediately recognized the handwriting and ripped the envelope open. Omid's words brought him to his knees. Omid apologized for not staying. He had to return to take care of their father who was turning ninety-seven in six months. He promised to try to emigrate once their father died. He detailed his boss's close ties with friends of al-Qaeda and stated that several members of the Bin Ladin family were in the United States on the eleventh. Omid made his brother promise to never reveal his involvement with the Saudi family because he didn't want to disgrace his own family name. He ended the letter with what Ahmed knew essentially was a goodbye.

"Brother, you have no idea how much I've missed not being with you these past years. Please watch over my grandchildren. I beg you ... do not let them follow the radical Wahhabi path. There has to be a better way. There is a Heaven and you and I will be as one again – someday. I love you brother. Goodbye."

Ahmed sobbed.

The anger and hatred he had for the theocracy in the Arabian Peninsula surfaced anew. Ahmed hated what he was and what he'd been taught to believe. He knew that hatred of any kind destroyed oneself from within.

He didn't care!

At that moment, Ahmed promised himself that if his nephews ever followed their father's ideology, he would channel their Wahhabi fundamentalist Islamic beliefs to his advantage. He would not debate or fight with them.

After finishing dinner on the sixteenth of September, Ahmed nodded off in his recliner. Around ten that evening he suddenly woke up, his body stiffening and ramrod straight in his chair. He couldn't breathe. He tried gasping for air, but his chest wouldn't move. It seemed as if he was drowning. And then he realized what was happening … and began to scream Omid's name.

* * *

Earlier in the day, at 4:00 p.m., a tricked-out 727 took off from a Central Kentucky airport. The manifest included a dozen or more Middle Easterners, mostly Saudis, along with Omid's boss, the Royal Family entourage – and Omid. The first leg of the flight was bound for Newfoundland, Canada. The plane would refuel there and then fly on to London.

Upon leaving Newfoundland, the plane climbed to an altitude of five thousand feet. It was 9:55 p.m. in Central Kentucky. At the back of the 727, Omid's boss ordered the rear cabin stairway unlatched and lowered. The nose of the 727 lurched upward and the cabin instantly depressurized. A bodyguard was ordered to move Omid to the stairway.

Omid did not resist.

He walked to the exit and down the steps.

He would not jump. He wasn't going to commit suicide. Someone would have to push him!

The bodyguard took three steps down the stairway, extended his right foot and planted it squarely in the center of Omid's back. Unlike the famous Boeing 727 hijacker, D.B. Cooper, Omid had no parachute. Mercifully, his neck broke immediately upon impact with the water.

* * *

Ahmed slept intermittently, in between shedding tears over the death of Omid … even thinking briefly about ending his own life to be with his brother. Then hatred welled up within him and extinguished that thought.

By morning, hate was the victor.

During breakfast, he began to formulate a list of possibilities and immediate realities. His first call was to his attorney.

"Ahmed, why are you calling me so early?" his lawyer asked.

"I want to change my name. I assume there are legalities," Ahmed replied.

Ahmed's lawyer began laughing and Ahmed cut him off sternly. "I'm serious! If you won't do this, then I'll find someone who will. Is that understood?"

"Certainly Ahmed, I'm sorry. I have to ask, does this have anything to do with what happened last week – ya' know … 9/11?"

"It does."

"Well, I need to know. What would you like your new name to be?"

"Benjamin A. Slaughter, no middle name just the initial – and I want to be known as Ben. And oh, Carl, I want the boys' names changed too. I'll e-mail you the names I've selected."

"Okay Ben, I'll start drawing up the paperwork for everyone and get back to you."

Two weeks later, Ahmed was in county court with his attorney, filing for his change of name. After that was finished, he took his new documents to the Social Security office … waiting for four hours until they finally found an administrator who knew how to process a name change … but not change the Social Security number. His final stops were the regional Medicare office and the local license bureau, both of which required his legal change of name papers. One week later, Ben received his new Social Security card in the mail.

The following month, his nephews had their new identities.

By the end of 2001, Ahmed no longer existed and Ben had

begun the process of narrowing his list of payback options.

The first thing he did every morning was to read letters he'd received from his brother's fiancée. She wanted to know where Omid was. He had not returned from the United States … and she alone was caring for Omid's father. Of course the words "send money" were not written, but that was an obvious message within the tone of the letters. Ben knew these letters might be a trap to find out how much he knew – and he also knew that any money he sent would end up in the wrong hands. Not only had he lost his brother, he now had to accept that his father was also a casualty of fanaticism. The sad fact was that the fiancée had never lifted a finger to help any of Omid's family.

Once the fire of passion is lit, it needs to be fueled on a constant basis. The same applies to hatred.

* * *

Ben had decisions to make about avenging his brother's death, and over time, went through a process of elimination. The first option he considered then discarded was a return to his homeland. Even though Ben had dual citizenship, he knew returning to Saudi Arabia would be a one-way trip. If he was going to die, he preferred it be in

America.

He also quickly realized that any attempt at direct confrontation with the Royal Family that had murdered his brother would be futile.

It wasn't until 2002 at the race track that Ben had his epiphany. What did the Saudis value more than their plentiful economic commodity of oil and their religion? They loved their Thoroughbreds.

Time was on his side.

Ben knew that every year, the Saudis made a visit to Kentucky. Knowing that they'd be on his turf was the best advantage Ben could ever hope for. The only question that remained was … what could he inflict on them that would produce the most lasting pain?

It was going to happen … he could feel it. Ben told himself that he just had to remain patient.

CHAPTER 8

Mark's response was what I'd expected. He "would be staying home for Thanksgiving," officially verifying the credibility of the sample from Donnie's father. It was the eBay hair samples that I worried about. It would be a few weeks yet before his response to my Christmas invitation – and that would determine how we would proceed.

It was the week before Christmas – and according to our "code," I emailed Mark, inviting him to dinner on Christmas Eve – fully expecting an immediate reply. Twenty-four hours passed with no response – my spirits began to wane. I knew with certainty that Mark wasn't purposely messing with my head – he knew how much everything hinged on this research. Marty tried to lift my spirits, but to no avail. Finally at 1:00 in the morning, I decided to check my e-mail one last time before heading to bed. Yes! There was a message from Mark in my inbox … I was hesitant to open the message for fear of what it said. I forced myself to move the cursor and open the e-mail, delaying a bit longer before finally reading his response.

"Rob, I wasn't sure until now if I could come, and had planned to at least try to make it – the good news is that I'll actually be there. I should arrive late Wednesday afternoon, Christmas Eve."

"Now what the hell does that mean?" I thought. "He did write the key code words 'try to make it,' but we never mentioned an actual visit. Is there a glitch? Do we need to get more hair samples? Arghhh!" I screamed at the iMac screen before returning to my recliner to pout – no longer tired enough to sleep. Marty walked into the room, opened the DVD player, inserted a movie disc and pushed the play button. My favorite film started and I slowly settled further into the recliner's cushions.

"If you build it, he will come," was the last thought I remembered during the remainder of that early Tuesday morning.

* * *

Christmas Eve for Marty and I is always an event steeped in tradition. Our daughters, along with their spouses and kids, fill every room in the house with sounds of laughter. Preparations for Santa Claus' visit includes milk and Marty's orange cookies. The holiday season was the only time when these family delicacies actually make it to a cookie plate.

When I told Marty that Mark was going to be a guest on this

Christmas Eve, an early winter chill descended upon our home – and it wasn't from the weather. Not only was Christmas sacred family time to her, the last thing she wanted was my attention focused on business instead of family. I awoke each day, determined to ease the situation … and every day an argument ensued. Tylenol and Rolaids became a staple on the weekly grocery shopping list. I finally gave in, and e-mailed Mark to say that I reserved a room for him at a motel five minutes from our home. Again, I received no immediate response. However, two days later, Mark responded with two words, "No problem."

I had no idea Mark had already made a motel reservation and that he wasn't coming alone. The same companion he had a few weeks earlier was accompanying him.

Thankfully, I had underestimated Mark's intuitiveness. He knew Christmas Eve was for family and by the time his headlights switched from high to low beam coming up the driveway, everyone was already tucked in their beds – and gifts were neatly arrayed around the Christmas tree. The security alarm was off in case Santa couldn't get down the chimney. I greeted Mark with a hug and a cup of hot black coffee. On occasion, my intuition could match his.

Wasting no time with further pleasantries, we headed for my

office.

"Rob, you might want to get your tablet and take some notes," he told me. "The X factor is real. It took the lab only five days to locate it on the genome. I was pretty surprised that the eBay sample matched Donnie's sample – and I'm sure you thought the same."

Mark explained that he'd asked the lab techs if there was a way to identify which horses presented with a more prominent X factor, and then going into specifics, told me, "Based on Secretariat being the benchmark, I anticipated this would be difficult to determine because without any body parts, there was no way of measuring Secretariat's heart size, lung capacity, brain size, or true stature – all physical indicators that a good bloodstock agent might immediately recognize. Wise Dan caught our attention first because he's got the factor. We worked through his genome and fed that data into the super computer for analysis. Comparatively, Dan is genetically about two-thirds the horse Secretariat was. Believe it or not his half-brother, Successful Dan, is a better match with Big Red."

"Are you with me so far? Now it really gets interesting!"

Elaborating more, Mark said, "Of the group of samples you gave me – specifically the American Pharoah sample – it's amazing! I'm convinced that this stallion is about as close as you're going to get to matching Secretariat's DNA, as well as matching the levels of influence of the X factor. I'm telling you Rob, barring any catastrophe, he could very well be a Triple Crown Winner. These are double blind studies and I'm the only one privy to this final information. I intend to bet this horse during his three-year-old campaign. He's going to be my retirement meal ticket. Since I won't be a member of the partnership, I figure I deserve a bone thrown in my direction."

"C'mon Mark … you aren't serious are you?" I asked.

"Gotcha' Rob," was Mark's reply. I assumed he wouldn't make any bets, but that didn't mean others wouldn't.

"Sorry for messing with you. Okay, for fun – let's assume I'm right and this horse, Pharoah, is the real deal. You were the one that said the X factor was predominantly a female trait – and it is! That makes his dam, Littleprincessemma, that much more valuable. There's no way you guys can afford to buy her – assuming she would even be up for sale. As that's not very likely, I did an online search of her ancestry – specifically looking for fillies and stallions of Grade One winners with Secretariat ancestry."

"Did you come up with anything?" I asked Mark hopefully.

"There is one broodmare that just might meet your needs. I also found a stallion with a genome, that when combined with this prospective mare's DNA, would achieve everything you're looking for. His stud fee is reasonable."

Mark cautioned me that there was confidentiality involved. "You can't ask how I came by this information – but know that none of it was acquired illegally. Let's just say that my resources are immensely more extensive than any handicapper you may know."

Knowing that it all sounded too good to be true, Mark let the other shoe drop. "Now for the bad news. Statistically, everything I've gathered for you, including all of my research, amounts to about half of what you need to get that Triple Crown Champion. I will give you information about vitamin supplements and the types of feed that in proper proportions will generate maximum performance. But I can't help beyond that. I can't let you use any of the performance-enhancing products that we're developing – and you won't be getting any of the genetic modifiers we've created either. They inventory everything going in and out of the facility – and security couldn't be any tighter. I'm truly sorry, Rob."

Tapping nervously on my notepad, I said, "Fifty percent – no different than a coin toss. Heads we go forward, tails we end this dream – my dream – right now on Christmas Eve." The dour look on my face couldn't be more obvious.

"Jesus Rob, I didn't drive this far to attend a wake. You have more information than any breeder in Kentucky. Everything meets your budget. What the hell else are you looking for?" Mark looked at me with surprise, and reminded me of the gambling spirit I had in college.

"Have you forgotten that Knute Rockne speech you gave us two months ago? Rob, these animals aren't robots and even if we could clone Secretariat, the horse would still have to run on the track. He could still get his heels clipped coming out of the gate, step in a hole, or get a bad batch of feed." Mark was silent ... he could tell I clearly needed to digest all I'd just heard.

* * *

Mark was also thinking, recalling in his mind events of the last few weeks that led to this point. "What else can I do?" Mark asked himself. "I'm ready to press this case with additional facts and finish my presentation with as close a guarantee as possible … if that's what it takes. I have access to the finest IT folks the government employs; this gives me an advantage far superior to any horseman or bloodstock agent in the world," he said to himself.

Mark's mind drifted back to the Monday following the group's last get-together and the subsequent business proposition.

* * *

Upon returning home after the annual fall weekend outing with his friends, Mark gathered his computer technicians together and presented the facts concerning the X factor and its transmission progression. He tasked them to develop an algorithm which would take into account that some Thoroughbreds never race. Some of his staff members were skilled computer hackers … easily able to get into the Allbreedpedigree.com computers, as well as the Jockey Club's database listing all Thoroughbreds ever registered. Included in the club's database was information on the DNA of any Thoroughbred's parents, along with the DNA sampling of any specific registered Thoroughbred.

This type of data is collected through a specific registration process which requires submission of a hair sample – roots and all –

collected from the horse's mane. This information, including the X factor historical data, was translated into computer code and subsequently, the creation of a computer program by Mark's IT associates.

It took the computer geeks, with the assistance of the most sophisticated super computers, only a week to generate their findings – producing everything Mark was looking for.

The number of active mares and stallions worldwide was narrowed down to twenty-three. Twelve were standing in the United States.

Mark could just imagine the looks on the faces of the Jockey Club officials when operatives showed up, dressed in pin-striped suits, flashing IRS badges and demanding to see the files of the twenty-three Thoroughbreds. Caught off guard, the club officials provided the files – while simultaneously placing calls to their lawyers. By the time the lawyers arrived, the operatives were gone – carrying hair samples in their briefcases. The government credo post 9/11 had become "just don't get caught" – and these operatives hadn't.

It was from that heist that Mark got his DNA samples.

Once narrowed down from the domestic and international samples, three mares and four stallions were identified as meeting the criteria for creating another Thoroughbred superstar. One pair was in America. The other mares and the remaining stallion were standing in Europe and the Middle East.

The pair of American horses was still breeding, but never yet with each other. They were a possible solution for the quest of four dreamers.

* * *

Both of us were masters of the pregnant pause – and an eternity seemed to pass before I looked directly at Mark – only to read the disappointment in his eyes. Everything he'd said was right. Nobody guaranteed I'd be a successful dentist. I was trained and licensed, then released into society to practice. I performed the best I could, albeit with an occasional misstep. But I always finished to the best of my abilities.

"Give me the information Mark. It's time to get this process started!"

Mark smiled. He didn't have to lay down his entire hand – or even bluff. Nor did he have to reveal how easily the deck had been stacked in his favor.

CHAPTER 9

It was 2002, one year after 9/11, when Ben decided to again drive up to Central Kentucky and attend the track's annual yearling sales event. This would be the first time he would wear a disguise, but not the last.

He believed a goatee and glasses would be enough to change his appearance. This time, Ben didn't confine himself only to the auction arena – he wandered around outside. Every now and then, he'd ask an attendant to bring a horse from its stall for viewing. The attendant would walk the horse back and forth, and Ben would do his best bloodstock agent imitation. Mixed in with the crowd of buyers were trainers from all parts of the country. Notebooks and reams of reports with statistics and computer print-outs were cradled in every agent's arms. Their hands blanched from the heavy grip on their paperwork. Ben would have to kill them before they would have let go of their valuable data.

He could have given a rat's anatomy about these people. He was looking for Arabs.

And he found them.

Dressed in Levi jeans, cowboy boots and Oxford shirts, they blended in with all the other buyers and horsemen. The only indication that they were outliers was their Mediterranean features.

Most folks, when looked at directly, turn their eyes away in a second. Ben knew the Arabs were different when it came to stare-downs – even more so since 9/11. Their eyes would remain affixed on anyone whose glance lingered. It was their method of intimidation and was the new normal for them. They were silently saying, "I know you're profiling me, go ahead and give me your best look." If a Western woman was caught staring, their gaze took on an even angrier edge … in the Arab culture, women were expected to be subservient and considered second-class individuals.

Ben rather enjoyed these types of confrontations. But he was more interested in following the Arabs and eavesdropping on their conversations whenever possible. Because they were dressed in a Westernized mode, Ben had no idea if they were from the Emirates or Saudi Arabia. The Arabs from the Emirates always parked their Boeing 747s where they were visible from the track. After 9/11, Ben wondered if the Saudis had hitched a ride on the UAE 747s in order to maintain a low profile.

He played detective for three straight days and watched as the Arabs purchased their new yearlings. Never once did he get a sniff as to their citizenship. No one that he recognized from the previous sales event had returned this year; it was obvious the Arab world was keenly aware of the distrust that had developed since 9/11. The Arabs knew they would be categorized, and they were determined to protect their identities.

After the first two days, the most expensive horses had either been sold or their reserve hadn't been met. The 747s had disappeared and Ben figured their precious Royal Family cargo left with them. If there had been any royals in attendance, they were well-hidden from the general public.

The wounds from 9/11 were still fresh, at least in middle America.

As Ben left on the last day of the event, he resigned himself to the fact that he would most likely not be able to exact his revenge at any future sales events … it was time to move on to a different venue … one that would attract the Arab family he wanted to hurt. But he couldn't rid his mind of one thing – the lack of track security. "I can't believe I wasn't challenged by anyone. All of that expensive horse flesh, all of those multi-millionaires walking around like they're at a church festival. The security at this track is a joke," Ben said to himself.

* * *

As the plane was climbing to its cruising level, Ben looked down at the architectural footprint of what once was the foundation of the Twin Towers in New York City. History books would come to blame Osama bin Laden, his al-Qaeda leaders and other followers for the carnage, but the true blame should have fallen on the leaders of the Ottoman Empire and their alignment with Germany prior to World War I.

Calling upon his knowledge of history, Ben said to himself, "They befriended the wrong people."

It was May 2003, but Ben was deep in historical reverie … his mind in another time and era of discontent. European leaders never seemed to understand Middle Easterners and more importantly, their driving force, the Quran. With the demise of the Ottoman Caliphate and Empire, which was overseen by the League of Nations, the seeds of turmoil were planted for the remainder of the 20th century and into the 21st century. The ultimate divisive decision, the Balfour Declaration, permitted the Zionist leaders to begin the creation of a Jewish homeland in Palestine.

"I wonder how the people in the Texas Panhandle would like it if the Congressional leaders in Washington D.C. voted to establish a Nation of Islam for Louis Farrakhan. They'd carve out the boundaries from the Oklahoma border and extend them just south of Lubbock, Texas. On January 1 – pick any year – America would hand over the territory," Ben thought, amusing himself with his historical reverie … briefly envisioning the strong reaction from Texans whose ancestry was strongly rooted in the region.

The European leaders also had the audacity and stupidity to start carving out the boundaries of their new protectorates. France acquired Syria and Lebanon, while Great Britain got Iraq and Palestine. Saudi Arabia evolved from a Sultanate and the states along the Persian Gulf – Kuwait, Bahrain and Qatar were also claimed by the Brits."

During World War II, most Arab leaders doubled down, and this time sympathizing with and supporting Nazi Germany. Undoubtedly their feelings were stimulated by Palestinian leadership which had increasingly observed an influx of Jews from Europe. "The Nazis were doing a good job solving the problem with the Jews, so why not throw their support behind the Third Reich's efforts and spare the Palestinians any future headaches?" Ben finished his train of thought.

He glanced over at his niece Nona, the twin's mother, already deep in slumber. She had taken an Ambien as soon as her seatbelt was fastened – and her eyes closed even before the plane's take-off instructions were displayed on the video screen. Ben knew there was no way the medication would work for the full eleven-hour flight, but at least there'd be no arguments for a few hours. She wanted to bring the twins, but Ben had firmly told her no. She had no clue that Ben knew she intended to ditch him the next day so she could catch a flight to Damascus and reunite in Iraq with her husband – or that emails on her Blackberry had been easily deciphered.

There was no way his nephews were going to become religious zealots. He owed that to his brother Omid. Ben left the boys in the care of his farm manager while he was away, knowing they'd be safely taken back and forth to school and home. Ben had even booked Nona a return ticket so as to not draw government attention. That wouldn't prevent a lengthy interrogation when he returned without her, but he'd deal with that in a few days.

As he looked out the window at the approaching dusk, Ben's

mind wandered back to the previous spring when he began in earnest to find a way to pay back the Royals.

* * *

He'd had a pilot's license for years, and in March, took off a couple of hours before sunset in his single engine plane to do a flyover of the Saudi's horse farm in Central Kentucky. He saw that the farm had two training tracks – one was a turfed oval and the other was a synthetic surfaced oval. The property's entrance was heavily surrounded by hedges.

The next week, Ben attached a bike rack on the back of his car and loaded up his ten-speed. He parked the car at a nearby volunteer fire station, having received permission to leave his car there for a few hours. With the fireman's nod of approval, Ben began a healthy morning ride intended for more than exercise … he was going to do an exploratory search of the farm from the ground. Some horse farms in Kentucky border main roads and Thoroughbreds often like to graze very close to the roadside. One could easily stop for a few moments and pull up some fresh bluegrass, and walk over to the horse fencing, and quietly stand waiting. Sometimes the horses don't have full bellies and when one approaches the fencing, several others might follow … hoping for an additional meal. That's exactly what Ben was hoping for as he turned onto the road that passed the Saudi farm.

Ben came to a stop and dismounted from his bike, intending to walk the rest of the way, looking for openings and to catch a glimpse of grazing mares and stallions. It was everything he had expected. The frontage of the Saudi farm was a groomed wasteland; the farm's steeds were kept deeper and further back on the property. The fence was intact; the gates were electronic and everything was camera-monitored. As Ben mounted his bike for his return trip, he suddenly slammed on the brakes.

"Damn, just last week I flew over this place. Why not attack it by air? Now I just need the right weapon."

His journey that day hadn't been wasted. He'd satisfied his curiosity, but also discovered a new obstacle to be conquered.

It didn't take much thinking that night to come up with his next plan. The Saudi King was untouchable. Ben highly doubted he ever visited his Kentucky property, but other sheikhs had … and would visit again. In his mind, they were also untouchable. But the Thoroughbreds couldn't hide in their stalls all day. He didn't want to harm the horses, but their expendability was all that was left for Ben to use as punishment for what had happened to his brother.

What kind of ground disaster could he deliver from the air?

In a few hours, perhaps his old friend Hamid would help Ben with the critical components needed to implement the bizarre plan he'd devised.

CHAPTER 10

Hamid was an entrepreneur. He didn't have patience or tolerance for those with religious inflexibility. If a business deal meant traveling to Israel, he went. As a commodities dealer, that meant he made frequent trips to the Jewish state. On this Monday morning, he and Ben were taking a commuter flight to Israel. They'd depart for the farm from the airport, and then finish their day's journey at a processing plant.

One of the few medications Ben hated was one he'd been force-fed as a child – castor oil, which came from the medicinal plants cultivated in the farm fields he was about to visit. Upon arriving at the farm, Hamid was greeted warmly by its owner … and after a short conversation in Arabic, Hamid introduced Ben to Aaron. The two talked a bit about America, Ben's heritage, and about Kentucky basketball – a "who would have guessed?" kind of discussion. Aaron then invited Ben out into the field filled with rows of Ricinus Communis, better known as castor bean plants.

Today, the plant is largely grown in China and India, although it is indigenous to the Middle East. It is known as a healing plant – its oils, the dreaded castor oil, used in the treatment of arthritis and to relieve constipation – and also used in skin oils, soaps, perfumes, bio fuel and even as a jet engine lubricant.

Aaron's plants were well irrigated in loamy soil and the plant's stalks were staked to prevent collapse. The flowers were red and the seeds that would soon be ripe contained the castor oil. Aaron reached in his pocket and pulled out several Castor seeds to show Ben and Hamid. They were mottled with dark spots, while the bulk of the seed's color was brown.

"The only thing they don't come with is a warning label of skull and crossbones and the words *Do Not Eat,*" Aaron said. For an adult, several seeds chewed and ingested, would be lethal.

It's from these seeds that Ricin is made.

Ben had decided this was going to be his weapon of choice – he recalled reading somewhere that Ricin was six thousand times more toxic than cyanide. Ben was determined to learn the manufacturing process before he returned home – he'd already researched its toxicity when incorporated into horse feed. Ben guessed that two ounces of Ricin would be a fatal dose for a Thoroughbred.

Ben, Hamid and Aaron rode together to the factory where the plants were processed. It was more like a pharmaceutical factory than a manufacturing plant. Everyone was in sterile uniforms and wearing hair nets, gloves and facial filtration masks. Eye protection was mandatory.

The process was extensive … the castor beans were washed several times before they were pressed. The extracted oil was funneled in one direction for further processing, while the pulp waste went through further oil extraction. Finally, after every possible ounce of product was extracted, the waste material exited the main facility and entered a secondary facility.

Aaron nodded to Hamid, who taking his cue, headed for the staff breakroom to enjoy several cups of coffee. Ben followed Aaron into his private office.

"Alright Ben, Hamid told me about your interest in the plant and that it isn't commercial. Level with me. Tell me what your intentions are or we'll end this meeting right now." Ben proceeded to give Aaron all the details of what had happened to his brother.

"So you intend to use the plant as a weapon?" Ben confirmed that with a nod to Aaron.

"Unless you have unlimited funds to create a top-notch laboratory, you should focus on the plants' by-products. You could easily grow the plants and harvest thousands of seeds. It shouldn't be difficult or expensive to come up with a press. Extract the oil and save the mash," Aaron suggested.

"Heck, the entire plant contains some level of Ricin. From this stage, you can go the fertilizer route or the feed route. My suggestion is to concentrate on incorporating the mash into the production process of a food additive. When you mill it, keep in mind that excessive heat will neutralize the toxin. Once you've got it ground up, throw it in with some flaxseed and you'll be in business. Remember, it only takes about eight castor seeds to kill a horse!"

Aaron couldn't resist the thought of sticking it to the Royal Family.

The two men rejoined Hamid and all three continued their tour of the facility. The finished product at this factory was an organic fertilizer which underwent extensive toxicological testing to make sure it was safe.

The business was over, and the three men went to Aaron's

home for a dinner feast, after which they spent time sipping wine and talking global politics – including a discussion of the Iraq war. As the evening was coming to a close, Aaron ended the conversation with an eerie prediction of the war's outcome.

"The Americans will prevail. If they remain as occupiers, peace will return to the region. They'll insist the new Iraq government be representative of the Kurds and Sunnis. Having a neighborly presence next to the Iranians will quiet the region," Aaron predicted.

"Hell, I want the Americans to hint at the threat of possibly using nuclear weapons. They could station a couple B-52 bombers in Iraq and not say a word. The threat would be implied. Unfortunately, I believe the American press and public opinion will prevail. The American public will do a three-sixty, adopt an attitude of 'this war is hopeless' and demand that the troops be extracted from the region.

"There will never be another Korean type of settlement – very few even know that the war there has never ended. There's an armistice, but a peace treaty was never signed," Aaron pointed out.

"Once the Americans leave Iraq, the real war will commence.

Mark my words, Iran wants to turn Iraq into a Shia partner and the Sunnis will not let that happen!"

The following morning, Hamid and Ben said their goodbyes to Aaron and boarded the shuttle back to Cairo. The short trip was a silent journey, with Ben speculating to himself whether the information he'd shared would remain secure. He even had some apprehension that Hamid might give him up.

After disembarking the plane, Ben bid goodbye to Hamid. One last look into Hamid's eyes reassured Ben that his secret was safe. He and Hamid embraced a final time, both realizing they'd never see each other again.

The cab ride back to the hotel seemed like an eternity. Ideas about his payback to the Royal Family and the expected expenses were swirling around in Ben's brain. He'd need to build a greenhouse for seedlings in order to get as much product out of a growing season. He'd need a press and milling equipment. His mind was still only scratching the surface of his scrambled thoughts when the cab stopped at the entrance to the hotel, the driver turning to get his fare.

Back at the door to his room, he inserted the keycard and turned the door handle. The beds were made, looking as if no one had ever been in the room. As he walked past his twin bed, he noticed an envelope placed neatly against the pillows. "One last parting shot," he thought.

"Dear Uncle, I'm sorry things didn't work. You're right, the boys are far better off staying with you. I have to be with my husband. I know you don't approve of his actions, but he believes they are righteous and I also believe the same. There will come a day when we will ask our boys to join us once again. Don't try to stop them if they believe it is the right thing to do. I know you won't believe me when I write this – but I do respect your right to your opinions and I do love you just as I loved their grandfather. We will meet again hopefully in the next life. Praise be to Allah! Sincerely, Nona

Ben wheeled around and surveyed the room for luggage. The only thing missing was the backpack Nona had brought on the flight. Her suitcase was still in the same place. He lifted it up on the bed and carefully examined the latches. Ben then retrieved his portable hand-held suitcase weighing scale and lifted the bag. It was five pounds heavier than the weight that registered on the airport scale in New York. Ben sat down and did the math. She took the same back pack, but there's more weight in the suitcase!

Beads of perspiration began to form on his forehead. Ben's paranoia had kicked in … nervous thoughts were swirling throughout his head.

"Nona had no idea when I was returning, so the suitcase's contents probably aren't on a timer. That has to mean the suitcase is rigged to trip on opening. My flight isn't taking off for another six hours – but if I call the front desk and alert them, I could be detained for who knows how long."

Ben quickly packed his bags and prepared to leave for the airport. He hid Nona's bag in the bathroom and placed a call to the bell captain. Five minutes later, he stood at the front desk to check out. Ben had the bellboy take his bags to the first available cab and started to get in. He quickly hesitated, saying "I'm sorry, I'll be right back, I left something in my room." Using the keycard that Nona left with her note, he opened the door to the room, thankful that front desk hadn't yet changed the code on the lock. Going to the bathroom where he had placed Nona's bag, Ben wrote a note on hotel stationary and stuck it onto the soft-sided bag, spearing it in place with a hotel pen.

The note, in big letters, read, *"Tick Tock."*

Going to the elevator with the bag, Ben waited for the elevator door to open, put the bag inside and pushed the button that went up to the highest floor. Strapping his carry-on bag over his shoulder, Ben took the next elevator down to the lobby.

In a few moments, he'd be back in the cab and ready to head home.

"Hey mister, do you speak English?" "Yes," Ben nodded. "Well, you can stop turning around 'cause no one is following us," the cabbie said. "What did you do – steal the bathrobe or something?" The cabbie broke out laughing and Ben couldn't help but do the same.

Deep down, though, he was seething. Two more people had just joined the Saudi Royal family on his retribution list.

CHAPTER 11

The task of growing a plant is the easy part. The harvest – and how the end product is delivered and used – can be the challenge.

Ben was in uncharted territory and he knew it. He'd received zoning approval from local officials to erect a greenhouse on his property. During its construction, Ben physically divided the greenhouse in two, with one half serving as a laboratory for his experiments. Now months later, his first crop of castor beans had ripened … and was ready to harvest.

The first piece of equipment he'd installed was an industrial-grade press – and his first experiment was with a hundred pounds of oranges and the press. After loading the oranges into the chute, it seemed only an instant before the juice was harvested into one portal; the pulp was repeatedly rotated and pressed again and again before dropping into a waste container. Cleanup was tedious – but thankfully easy.

The first harvest produced about twenty pounds of castor beans and it was time for Ben to process the first batch. It performed flawlessly and as Ben had hoped … the castor oil poured easily through one portal and into a five-gallon bucket. As with the oranges, the pulp from the beans continuously rotated through the process until no more oil could be extracted. The pulp was not discarded, but carefully gleaned from the flutes of the press, and placed in a container. Ben added a small amount of distilled water to keep the pulp moist before tightly sealing the container. Removing his gloves, Ben walked a few feet to the rodent cages.

He planned to start with mice.

Ben was not one to consciously kill anything. He'd never hunted in his life – and still had unpleasant childhood memories of neighborhood bullies pulling the wings off insects – and laughing hysterically when the insects were unable to take flight and escape. He especially abhorred how these same boys would hold an insect down by piercing its body with a pin, and with a magnifying glass, reflect the sun's hot rays onto the insect's body to fry it unmercifully.

Yet he was going to kill a group of mice that were blissfully unaware of their impending execution.

Perfectly measuring and weighing a small amount of the

castor pulp product, Ben added a drop of molasses to make it more palatable for the rodents. He placed one of nearly a dozen mice in a small cage by itself, giving the mouse time to familiarize itself with the new surroundings.

Ben knelt down and bowed his head. He prayed for God's forgiveness, telling the Almighty that what he was embarking on was for the greater good.

Carefully, Ben placed the food in the cage. The mice hadn't been fed for three days and not unexpectedly, the mouse devoured every bit of the pulp in fifteen seconds. Ben then placed a small thimble of water into the cage – that too was consumed quickly. He started his stopwatch, not knowing how long the gruesome process of death by Ricin would take.

The first sign of any abnormal activity from the mouse was it frantically running from wall to wall. Ben theorized that this was a flight or fright reaction – natural among animals when they are in distress. Suddenly the mouse stopped running and had a runny bowel movement, quickly followed by vomiting. Both bodily discharges were blood-filled. This continued for another half hour until there was no further movement. Ben recorded the time of death.

Repeating the experiment in an identical manner two more times – and with the same results, he upped the dosage, doubling the amount of pulp with the next three mice and also experimenting with increased amounts of water given to the mice. Theoretically, twice the dose should have shortened the killing time. Ben looked at his watch, suddenly realizing that he had pulled an all-nighter. Downing a fourth cup of coffee, he returned to the house to wake the twins and get them ready for school.

After dropping the boys off at school, Ben hurried home and entered the greenhouse lab. The stench of death immediately overwhelmed him. Rushing out into the fresh air, he began to dry heave. After five minutes or so, the queasiness subsided enough that he could go back inside the lab. He quickly gloved up and removed the mice, placing them in a plastic trash bag for burial. In preparation for his experiments, Ben had fenced off two acres of land some fifty yards north of the lab weeks ago. Now heading to the graveyard area with the bag and a shovel in hand, Ben proceeded to give the mice a proper burial.

Ben knew that well before all the experiments were done, he'd need a Bobcat to dig the burial pits.

Over the next weeks, Ben repeated the same experiments

three dozen more times with additional research animals. At the conclusion of each experiment, he entered the data into his computer. This helped him calculate an average amount of time it took the creatures to die, based on the amount of product ingested and the weight of the animal.

The second phase in the process was to dry out portions of the pulp end-product – and he devoted two hours every night for "mortar and pestle" time. During this process, Ben slowly pulverized the material into a fine powder, and then conducted his round two experiments with a liquid/powder combination formula on the same number of mice. This data was also entered into the computer. The proper amount of bulk pulp was compared to the powder product's weight and volume. Ben was trying to determine which product sample resulted in the quickest mortality and what the proper amount was.

"If they're going to die so miserably, it might as well be quick," Ben murmured to himself.

CHAPTER 12

The experiments continued for almost a dozen years. He believed time was still on his side.

The twins hid their iPads from Ben every evening – but had no idea that the next morning after they left for school, he retrieved the computers from their not-so-secret hiding places.

He'd suspected that the twins' parents would try to contact the boys – and he easily hacked their passwords in order to access the iPads – hoping to find out for sure. Once in, it didn't take Ben long to realize that he was right. The boys were not only in regular communication with their father, they were learning the ways of ISIL from him every week. The routine was that there was no routine – and the given day for the lessons varied from week to week. When it was time for a new lesson, the boys simply logged onto a link their father had sent ... instantly connecting all three in direct communication.

Ben learned that the father could be in Northern Syria one week and in Iraq the next, and that he'd even been in several skirmishes in Libya. This week, Ben gleaned that their father's teachings were about the religious righteousness of rape – proudly sharing with his sons that during raids of Iraqi villages in late summer 2014, he and his men had murdered the male villagers and enslaved the women for sex. Apparently, their God approved of the rapes since the men prayed every time, both before and after raping the women. According to their father, these actions only brought them closer to the true teachings of the Quran.

The online training included graphic videos of the rapes, with their father encouraging both boys each week to be ready to come join him in battle … when it was time. Even though teachings of the Quran faith would consider the videos as pornographic, the father knew at their ages, he was preying on their prurient interests.

He was goading them, too, telling them that if they insisted on staying in America, it was then time to fully commit themselves and their actions to their faith and to Allah. In short … perform jihad in America or come and join him.

The morning had turned dismal after reading the chat session from the night before … Ben realized with despair that there was no longer any chance of saving his nephews from their father's radical beliefs. The inherent evil intent of the father's teachings, coupled with the metamorphosis that too many insurgents in several Arab countries had already undergone, was by any civilized measure insurmountable and serious. More serious, perhaps, than the atrocities the world's citizenry had witnessed or experienced during and after the end of World War II, courtesy of the Third Reich.

Ben had tried and failed.

Over the years, he had discussions with the twins about the evil that was consuming the land of their birth. But it had become increasingly obvious that his message was falling on deaf ears. The Takfiri way that the twin's father was teaching them was like an incurable cancer. The twins argued incessantly with Ben during dinners, always aligning with their father's beliefs that the Shias had never accepted the Quran in its true form, and therefore they were apostates that needed to die.

Ahmad and Jamil embraced the concept of enslaving converted non-believers – and even more – the crucifixion and beheadings of apostates. In their minds, Shariah law was the only law to be followed. The caliphate of medieval times had returned and the apocalypse was the end goal of ISIL. The boys truly believed that someday they'd be among the last soldiers fighting in Jerusalem against Dajjal, the anti-Messiah – and that they would then witness the return of Jesus. After all, Jesus was destined to kill

Dajjal – and those remaining Muslim soldiers who were still alive would witness and share in the final triumph.

Ben poured himself a bourbon on the rocks, collapsed in his recliner – and cried for fifteen minutes. He missed his brother's Omid's guidance.

The twins would soon be eighteen. They'd told their father the first thing they would do to celebrate their birthday was to apply for passports. Ben had squashed their previous attempts with a promise that as soon as they finished their education and turned eighteen and if they still wanted to travel, he would begin their passport application process. Everything he did until that day was a delaying tactic.

For years, Ben rationalized away Ahmad's and Jamil's beliefs – but now he could no longer deny their madness. Ben was a believer in a higher power – and his religion had become a composite of all religions. His core beliefs revolved around the Commandments – but he refused to acknowledge these rules were delivered by a Jew – and the name Moses never crossed his lips. Indeed, many of the Commandments, if violated, had consequences that were a part of Sharia law. If one stole, the hand that committed the theft would be amputated. If one committed adultery, the adulterer would be stoned. The consequence of murder would be a beheading.

Another shot of bourbon was added to his glass.

"They're not going to Damascus and they're not going to commit Jihad in America, or anywhere. They may think they are and that's fine by me. My agenda and theirs are entirely different," Ben thought to himself.

It's amazing how alcohol can cloud and justify one's actions.

It was time to incorporate their fanatical beliefs into Ben's plans of retribution by making them believe they were striking a mortal wound to the enemies of ISIL – and he had to be quick about it.

All three had now crossed an invisible line that set in motion the final stage of their lives. The only one who realized this inevitability at the moment, though, was Ben.

CHAPTER 13

Hurry up and wait – that's all we could do.

Our mare was pregnant and each of us was acting as if we were expecting our first child – again. Instead of our usual early October get-together, we decided instead to purchase box seats for the Challenge Cup races and meet up there. It was the second day of the Cup races. Before the others arrived, I called my friend, Len, who is a track employee, inviting him to join me for a pre-dawn breakfast at the track kitchen. He accepted.

Len had been working around the track's Clock Tower location for years and we'd become close friends. I remembered another track friend, Jack, and his predictions from the previous year and his thoughts on how security would be increased for the Fall Meet and Challenge Cup. I was anxious to learn from Len what changes had taken place, and perhaps see a few of the world's best horses in their early morning loosening up exercises. Hopefully, that would be a part of their race day protocol today.

Entering the track grounds was the first test of security. I had a parking pass and wondered if anyone would be at any of the track's entrances to challenge me at 5:30 in the morning.

There was – and that was a good sign, I thought.

Even at that early hour, the track's kitchen and dining area was filled with people: horsemen, horse valets, grooms, jockeys, workout riders and Kentucky Highway Patrol officers – lots of them. I had never seen so many patent leather shoes in my life. I couldn't help myself – I approached a table with several troopers eating, and addressing no one in particular, said, "So, tonight about 5:00, if I hop on I-75 north at the Florence ramp and head south, I should be able to reach the Tennessee border in a little over an hour ... hmm?"

Big smiles broke out on the faces of the troopers and one said, "I don't think I'd try that, there's not even a full post of troopers on duty here this weekend. Someone would nail you," was his reply.

So much for my trooper analysis.

Len was crouching in his seat, laughing and pretending he had no idea who I was. "Gotta' push that envelope, don't ya'?" he said. I just nodded vigorously and sat down.

"So now that I've made an ass of myself, tell me what's

changed for the Cup races?"

"Lots of things and nothing," was Len's reply.

"C'mon Len … don't mess with me," I begged.

"Okay. You saw one positive change with the entrance passes. We employees also have to wear badges now – just like you do – to get on the premises. And yes, we're being bussed in and out. Our usual employee parking lot is now used for parking patron's cars, I guess," Len told me. He then told me about the dry run held just two days ago.

"I walked up to one of the entrance gates to see how patrons are checked. I expected to see each woman's purse checked thoroughly. I was wrong. Security is doing the same shit they always did – a cursory look into the purse before waving the patron on to the next security guard to have a wand check."

"Huh?" I said quizzically.

"That's what I said! Look, I was up in Cincinnati this past summer for a baseball game. Remember, this was the first year the Great American Ballpark made people pass through metal detectors before they could get to their seats." He reminded me that the MLB organization had scheduled the annual All Star Game there in July, which is why the Reds' management team upped their security profile at the stadium.

"And I'm telling you Rob, the detectors were every bit as sensitive as TSA's airport detectors. I'm talking about belt buckles and other crap that made the detector go off. There were no metal objects going through that stanchion that weren't detected. When I went to a regular season game after the All Star game, the metal detectors were still there and they were being used. Management decided that they weren't going back to their old ways of handling security – not with what's going on in the world now."

Changing direction and getting back to security at the race track, Len again said, "So down here, our security guards are doing a wand check, but that's only a half check."

"Huh?" I said again.

"You heard me right," he said, explaining that a wand check is done between mid-torso and the knees and that full bag checks were conducted on only every fourth or fifth person carrying a bag. "Do you think someone might be concealing a gun at ankle level?"

Len asked. He said that upon asking the guards why every bag wasn't checked, he was told that it was a management decision, because they don't want to create delays and subsequent backups of people trying to get in. "So the patron holds the purse or bag out to the side while a security agent wands their torso. Again, do you think a weapon could get past them? I will say on a positive note that no one is bringing in those folding chairs like they do during our regular meet days."

"Are there any bomb sniffing dogs?" I asked.

"I didn't see any yesterday or today, but that doesn't mean they aren't here," Len stated. "And there are a couple other security guys on the grounds that I've never seen before now. They're in uniform, and the shirts have a logo printed on the back identifying them as part of the Joint Emergency Services. I asked them what their job is and who they're affiliated with – I got this vague response ... something about being deputized under the Federal Marshall Service."

Going into more detail, Len said he then asked if they were with Homeland Security, and their response was again somewhat vague – not quite a confirmation or a denial. "One of them is armed and the other one isn't – and their belts have all kinds of gizmos and tools attached. These tools include some kind of measuring instruments. I asked what they were for and was told, 'radiation detection, Co2, carbon monoxide, and O2 levels,' ... and then he tells me the state of Kentucky has an active RED unit – some kind of mobile radiation detection vehicle that is circling the track 24/7 right now. Apparently it's one sensitive mother."

"Well that's interesting," I said to Len. "Anything else?"

"Yeah, the F-18s were here last weekend, buzzing the track and making their presence known. I'm sure they're above us right now but you can't see or hear them. They could respond in a heartbeat, if necessary. And there was a flock of military helicopters that did the same type of fly-by last week. The FBI is here – but I haven't seen any of them. When we had our general meeting, the Challenge Cup staff showed us the insignia the agents are wearing on their lanyard badges. And in case you didn't know, the Cup staff working in the paddocks – they're all former cops, state troopers and law enforcement folks. They're the ones responsible for deciding who gets into the paddocks and winner's circle. They're the equine security team."

"Really?" I replied, trying to coax more information out of Len. I wasn't disappointed – Len was in a talkative mood.

"Hell, yesterday one of the Cup officials wanted to know how some guy got on the roof by the south entrance. In fact, I always wanted to go up there to take some pictures and was told 'no way.' My best guess is a food prep guy takes smoke breaks on that roof. It wasn't more than five minutes later when I look up and see that security dude standing on the roof. So, it's not all bad news – apparently there is some improved security in place. Hell, if nothing else, the sheer numbers of security people seems to have increased by fifty percent or more for these two days."

"So you'd do what to improve things?" I asked, digging deeper.

"Rob, don't get me wrong, I'm no authority in security matters. I'm guessing that the wands will be used again in the future. I've watched the Cup folks come in here, telling all of us that this place would be tightened up for the Challenge races. Yesterday the newspaper reported that there were forty-two thousand people on the grounds. Today we'll probably top fifty thousand. When the Challenge Cup is over, do we return to the former security protocol? Do the wands disappear? Will people be allowed to bring chairs in a bag again next spring? What inspires those who make decisions about security to believe that this place is immune from terrorism? I think I know the answer, but what the hell … "

"C'mon Len, don't leave me hanging – finish what you were gonna' say, damn it."

"Promise me you'll never tell anyone what I'm about to say."

"Len, you have my word."

"Rob, I believe some time ago, even before 9/11, representatives from the Arab horse farms and their respective sheikhs promised the officials who govern all of the Kentucky Thoroughbred venues that every one of them would be immune from any attacks. I also think our government knows about this agreement. The Sport of Kings takes place all over Kentucky … that includes these very grounds. How naive can people be? Jesus Rob, who would've ever thought that schools, theaters, military recruiting facilities, and marathons – I could go on and on – would become fertile killing grounds for evil individuals?"

Len stopped talking. His hands were shaking. I couldn't even muster a reply. We just sat at the table staring at each other. Our minds were spinning out of control and there was nothing left to say.

I promised myself to file everything that Len had just told me away in the recesses of my mind, in the eventuality that Towers Above was successful and lucky enough to run in a Cup race.

CHAPTER 14

Once we had the vehicle, we knew we needed to find a competent driver.

Donnie knew from the beginning this was going to be his responsibility. It didn't mean anything if we owned the best Thoroughbred – but didn't have a savvy jockey to guide him around the oval track. That was a huge priority.

Donnie had been watching a young female jock for over three years. She'd been an exercise rider at the training center, just west of the main track, for two of the last three years – and the chatter around the barns was that she had the ability to make it to the next level. It remained to be seen if she had the gumption to make that jump – and mix it up with the men in a race. That's what really mattered.

Towers Above would soon draw his first breath and Donnie needed to close the deal.

It was Monday, immediately following the end of Central Kentucky's Fall Meet and the Cup races. The fall's annual horse sales had begun and most of the trainers and owners were occupied, scouting for and buying new stock. Joey, short for Joanna, was cleaning tack at the training center when Donnie approached her.

"Joey, hello … I'm Donnie from Four Horsemen Farms – do you have a minute?" Joey extended her left hand, firmly shaking Donnie's hand.

"That's even better – she's a lefty – an out-of-the-box thinker," Donnie quickly mused.

"Hi Donnie, it's a pleasure to finally meet you."

"Come again?" Donnie replied.

"You've been stalking me for over a year," Joey retorted with a smile. Donnie's face began to flush with embarrassment.

"I didn't think you noticed. Are you ready to take the next step?" Donnie blurted out, while quietly wondering just how intuitive she was.

"It depends on what you're offering," she replied in quick order.

"Checkmate. She's sharp, might as well cut to the chase – there's no bullshitting this one," Donnie thought.

"A stallion – our group's Thoroughbred – is about to be born and I want you to be there when it happens. I want you bonding with the foal from the get-go. Besides his mother and myself, I want our boy to think of you as family. You'll fondle him, love on him every chance you get. When the time comes, you'll break him and finally, you'll ride him – not just exercise riding, but in graded Stakes Races. When he races, you'll be aboard."

Donnie stood there staring at Joey. She had a slight smile on her face and just stared back. Donnie wondered if she was an epileptic. She was catatonic … or so it seemed to him.

A stream of questions finally spewed forth.

"What's your horse's name? What makes you so sure about Stakes Races? Can I ride other owner's horses? Where's your farm? How much are you willing to pay me?" Suddenly Donnie knew he should have brought someone along to take notes.

"Whoa, Joey ... slow down. Have you had breakfast yet this

morning? Tell you what … why don't we go to the track's kitchen and at least have a coffee and I'll answer all of your questions." Joey nodded yes and both headed to the kitchen in separate trucks.

Donnie told Joey about the group's history and the X factor theory. He didn't tell her about Mark. Luckily, she didn't ask how we determined the selection of a mare and sire for Towers Above. Donnie promised Joey that we'd never interfere with any other rides that she picked up and agreed that she could contract with other stables if she wanted. However, when Towers was in training for a race, our group had first dibs on her.

Joey wasn't stupid. She realized that barring injury or Towers being a dud on the track, ninety percent of her time would be devoted to the Four Horsemen Farms. Instead of telling her what she would be paid, Donnie asked her what it would take financially to make her happy.

"Why me, Donnie? If you're right about the research, why don't you get one of the top male jocks – a Hall of Fame jockey? I'm a nobody right now!" Joey stated.

"Joey, I've got a daughter and a grandchild. Dr. Becker and his wife have three daughters and a handful of grandkids. Rob and I raised our girls to believe there is absolutely nothing a man does that a woman can't also do … and do it well. You called it stalking, I call it research. I've watched you on the track, performing all the scenarios that jockeys do on tracks all around the world … every day. I've watched you come up on another horse's rear and in an instant swing outside or inside, switch leads and not skip a step. I've been there when you've clipped heels and almost went down. I was there when you took that spill six months ago – and you tucked and rolled for twenty yards – then got up and ran to the horse to comfort it," Donnie said, finally pausing to take a breath. "Now ... will you answer my question?"

"I want a bedroom, access to a video room, a fully equipped workout room and two hundred dollars a day per diem. That per diem doesn't include masseuse fees. I get thirteen percent of winnings. I want a disability insurance policy that will pay me the maximum benefits in case I can no longer race … and I want gold level health insurance. Also, licensing fees and any membership dues are your responsibility. And, I want a 401K plan. There may be other items I'll need – we can negotiate on those as they come up."

The light bulb suddenly went on in Donnie's head – realizing that he was the one who had been stalked. He looked at Joey and started laughing.

No longer appearing catatonic, Joey reached across the table and extended her hand once again to Donnie. Donnie looked into Joey's eyes and realized he had a winner. He latched onto her hand and another Kentucky handshake deal was consummated.

CHAPTER 15

It was late May, early in the pre-dawn hours. She was pacing and had vaginal drainage … it was time.

Now the strange thing was, our group had decided to breed her in late June, four full months before the Challenge Cup Races – and later than the norm. Generally the majority of breeding activities in the Kentucky Commonwealth are completed in the months of February and March. Similarly, most of the yearling foals had already been born this year.

Mark was the one who gave us the huge tip about breeding later in the year. His statistics – and he had a wealth of them – indicated that if Towers Above was foaled in May, it would provide him the best odds of winning the Kentucky Derby as a three-year-old.

The reason horse farms artificially brought their mares into heat at the beginning of each year is purely based on economics. A Thoroughbred born in February is a one-year-old until the clock turns midnight on December 31st of that year. At 12:01 a.m. on January 1 of the incoming year, each one-year-old becomes a two-year-old. The same age determination process would then occur the next December 31 – when all of the two-year-olds turned three – and would be ready to enter and race in Derby-qualifying Stakes Races.

Now, if we had wanted to sell Towers Above at the yearling sales in September with the "older" horses, it was doubtful that anyone would consider buying our puny horse. When compared to the other yearlings that had a two to three month advantage in development, Towers would be woefully deficient in all distinguishing Thoroughbred categories.

Confirmation issues that might disappear with further development could de-value Towers. A bowed leg at six months might not exist a half year later.

Mike did a wonderful job preparing for the birth. Our horse was positioned properly in the birth canal and his mother's labor didn't last long. Once Towers' feet hit the ground, we all felt as if the young horse had already bolted from the starting gate. He stood up in what seemed to be record time to Donnie, Mike and myself. He was accepted on the teat immediately – and what all three of us had secretly worried about throughout the past eleven months would become no more than a faded memory three years later.

For the remainder of the day, we stood around like proud parents, finally giving in to Mike's encouragement to leave.

"Guys, the hard part is over. Go home ... the best days are ahead of us now," he said.

I left first and Donnie returned to the farmhouse to catch some shut-eye – he'd been awake since midnight. Mike also left the stable, his body telling him that a short stint on a Tempurpedic mattress was in order. Donnie left Juan – one of the farm's stable hands – to mind the stall, making sure he was armed with his nine millimeter Glock. He had a list of instructions to follow – one of which was highlighted and in all capital letters: NO VISITORS ALLOWED.

It was nearly 9:00 p.m. when headlights appeared on the dirt road heading towards the stable. Juan awaited the uninvited visitor.

Mark stepped out of the car ... recognizing the face, Juan approached, extending his hand. Mark returned the courtesy and offered his own hand containing five crisp hundred-dollar bills. "Thanks for the call. Even though I'm not an official co-owner, it's still nice to be recognized off the record. Where is he? I need to check him out." Mark and Juan had become tight as a result of the numerous Ben Franklin's Mark had dispensed his way over the past months. Mark had also convinced Juan that TA needed some specific therapeutic products during his last months of gestation as well as his first six months of life.

Juan led Mark to the stall where Towers was separated from his mother, and now taking his first nap.

Mark had a couple tiny sugar cubes in his palm. Towers was about to get his first taste of sugar from Mark's open palm. Distracted by the treat, TA didn't notice the syringe Mark had pulled from his coat pocket. The syringe cap was loosened and easily discarded – Mark completed the injection in an instant. Towers Above flinched and gave out a frightened whinny.

Mark grabbed a couple more sugar cubes – and TA's distrust faded – like an infant child.

The continued reformation had now begun post utero. "Hopefully Donnie or Rob won't ever realize I've been here," Mark said to Juan before driving away from the farm.

"See ya' next month, Juan," were Mark's parting words. As he drove down the road he exclaimed, "Hi ho RNA ... away," he said laughing.

Over the next five months, Mark made monthly surreptitious visits to the stables – and Juan's net worth increased each time. During the final visit, Mark gave Juan a note and a duffel bag containing one hundred thousand dollars – a total of one hundred parcels, packed in ten one-hundred dollar allotments.

Mark's note read: *"Juan, don't go crazy and disappear. I'm using my money as gambling money. Remember the word gambling! Remember this phrase too: easy come, easy go. I – and I can't emphasize the word "I" enough – intend to bet a considerable amount of money on Towers Above's first Stakes Race! Why you wonder? TA's' odds will be high. It will be a huge pay day!!! Juan, 1 can't tell you what to do ... but choose wisely."*

Suddenly Mark had become Yoda.

CHAPTER 16

It was Friday in the Middle East and Thursday night in central Kentucky. Less than 48 hours until the attack.

Muhammad wasn't totally disappointed. At least something and somebody was going to be attacked. It wasn't the target of his choosing – but it would suffice. He wanted the target to be flipped. Ohio State's Horseshoe Stadium would be too well-protected.

The track had been scouted by several ISIL soldiers who were already embedded in the area. An air attack coming from an undetectable sport plane would offer his sons a higher chance of survival and escape. Either way, another chink in the armor of the infidels would be exposed. It wasn't a coincidence that bit by bit, the economy of America had declined since 9/11. The impending attacks would add further stress, uncertainty and chaos in America.

"Soon, very soon, America will experience a revolution and the Islamic faith and its followers will rise to power. Sharia law will rule," Muhammad thought, as Friday ended and Saturday began for him. He was no longer physically able to fight on the battlefield – his field of combat now originated in his home in western Pakistan.

His waking hours were devoted to cyber terrorism and spreading the Caliphate's propaganda. His wife Nona, the mother of his twin sons, had died in a Russian bombing attack in Syria three years earlier, but he knew she would be proud of her boys on this day.

Muhammad, once an al-Qaeda operative, had established contact with his boys when they were of middle school age – their first computers were his gateway to re-enter their lives. Sympathetic Islamic contacts in central Kentucky had provided him with the IP address to Ahmad's iPad and he slowly began their fundamentalist training. However, what usually took only a few months, stretched into years. He had no clue that Ben was aware of his indoctrination lessons.

ISIL recruits were a conglomeration of losers from all over the world. For whatever reason, they were individuals who had been shunned by their respective societies and cultures. Low self-esteem was exhibited by most of them. ISIL provided them refuge from rejection.

The hierarchy of ISIL was led by the true Salafists – and then there were the worker bees. It was Muhammad's job to make the losers believe that each of them was special – that each of them was the winner of a King of the Mountain contest.

A subliminal mental chess game of sorts was taking place between Muhammad and Ben as a result of the cyber teachings from Muhammad to the twins – teachings that were immediately and continually countered by Ben.

Over time, the boys began to surrender to Muhammad, drinking his poisoned Kool-Aid and bonding with their father. Their online conversations revealed that they no longer questioned the propaganda they'd been fed over the years. Ahmad was the first to ask about traveling to meet up with Muhammad, who felt the time wasn't yet right. He wanted the twins to be totally devoted to the Caliphate and put any travel plans on hold until he was convinced they were ripe to commit murder.

It was no coincidence in Muhammad's mind that the pornographic videos of rape were a major factor in his sons' conversion and allegiance to the cause. The twins were fast approaching the height of manhood hormonally; however since puberty, both had been fully rejected by their female classmates. If the Caliphate had created a standing university that included doctoral programs, then Muhammad would have garnered a PhD in Psychology from ISIL-U.

Ben, too, would have earned the same degree – with honors!

Ben remembered his oft repeated words to the twins … words that he believed now won the day for him as he began to further prepare each twin for what would most likely happen after their respective acts of terrorism on Saturday. He chose his words carefully … speaking in a tone of warning … and religious zeal.

"My nephews, I'm proud of you – you have been like sons to me. If your father is still alive, I'm sure he would praise you. After this day is over, if you choose to join him, I will not stop you. You both are now of legal age and can make your own decisions. Everything that we've planned can easily be modified and I can act alone," he told both. However, Ben needed to be sure the twins understood the consequences of their actions.

"After Saturday, both of you will be hunted relentlessly. Your actions over the past few years will be unraveled … your terrorist footprints will be exposed. With all the attacks that have occurred during the past few years, there will be zero tolerance for your plans and for your cooperation with me. If you are caught, you'll serve multiple years in a federal prison – at minimum. I don't need to tell you how that experience will be. If you join with me and we die – both of you will have a seat next to Allah in his kingdom," Ben said.

A resounding "Allahu Akbar" spilled forth from the twin's lips.

It was 12:00 a.m. somewhere in Pakistan.

In the early Saturday morning hours, Muhammad reflected on his two decades of battle. Even though his first terrorist allegiance was with al-Qaeda, when the Caliphate was formed, it was an easy decision for him to switch his alliance. The reason he was still alive was because he didn't make stupid cyber mistakes – but that would soon come to an end.

Five kilometers away, atop a two-story Pakistani home, was an NSA Stingray listening device mounted on a tower. The residents had been turned two years earlier with American tax dollars. Following their NSA training in Virginia, they returned home, constructed the listening structure and began monitoring terrorist chatter. As Friday turned into Saturday, a message destined for an IP address in Saudi Arabia was intercepted. The message read:

"So many horseshoes to choose from ... can't decide which ones to nail on first. I've searched north and south for these brands. Think I'll try the northern ones first and later in the day, if there's

any signs of discomfort, switch to the southern brand. Pray to Allah
for a great outcome."

The message was instantly forwarded to Virginia and then re-forwarded to the intended IP address. Hussein, Muhammad's most trusted lieutenant, relayed the information up the chain of command, with ISIL's hierarchy anxiously awaiting and preparing for the events that were going to unfold in America on this early spring day.

Almost immediately – and after a short moment of glee – Muhammad realized that he had fucked up. The message he sent had been attached to an unencrypted app. Sweat began to form on his forehead and upper lip.

He began praying for Allah's forgiveness and help.

CHAPTER 17

The rehearsals were over and done ... it was now time to put events in motion.

Ben's final plan, one of at least a half dozen or more schemes he'd previously considered then discarded, hadn't jelled until a month before this first Saturday in April.

He realized that the plan's success was far too dependent on the habits of Rob Becker's pre-race routine. However, he also knew there wasn't a casino immune to Becker's usual "Night before Towers Above runs in a Grade 1 Stakes Race" gambling habit. Becker had stated as much in a *Wall Street Journal* article. Besides, Ben had hired a courier who was carrying a letter addressed to the Athletic Director at The Ohio State University – it would arrive on campus by Friday afternoon. The letter read:

Dear Buckeye Nation,
BOOM!
Enjoy.

Enclosed in the envelope was a tiny bag of Ben's finest Ricin

… personally harvested and refined.

The twins had no inkling that Ben had sent the letter, but he was certain it would trigger the same events that a Rob Becker casino scenario would set in motion. The fact that the courier would be traced to Southern Kentucky – which in itself was a demographic mismatch – would also draw Homeland Security's attention to the region south of the Ohio River. If for some reason Becker failed to show up, Ahmad would accompany Jamil on his Saturday flight. Of the two, Jamil had better piloting skills, leaving Ahmad responsible for handling the payload.

Ben had managed to keep control of the twin's radicalization from their early teens up until the last couple of years – and the boys still had no clue that Ben regularly hacked into their personal computers and cell phones. He was still keenly aware they were being coached and cheered on from afar.

As the commercial flight made its way to Springfield, Missouri that Wednesday morning, he looked over the paperwork faxed to him the day earlier. The auto dealership received the money he'd wired, and the Toyota Camry had a hold sign on its windshield. The sales manager expected the deal to be completed no later than that afternoon.

Settling into the airliner's faux leather seat, Ben began to recall memories of his years with the twins. After all, Ahmad and Jamil would be dead in three days.

The boy's infant and toddler years were wonderful. They had no memory of their mother and neither one asked about their father. Ben was pleased he'd become the twin's surrogate mentor and wanted to believe he could continue his success in integrating them into the western culture. In hindsight, his one regret was the religious affiliation he'd thrust upon them. Even though he was no longer a practicing Muslim, he still felt obligated to introduce them to Islamic teachings.

That upbringing was a family tradition he felt he couldn't violate – but now the error of this theological decision had come full circle to haunt him. As young boys, they were innocents. There wasn't anything they didn't share with him – but as they matured, they became more free-thinking. The boys could no longer be sheltered by him from world events and opinions, or biases from others which began to influence their thinking. Having had no children of his own, the benefits and curses that accompany the rearing of 21st century adolescents soon ensnared Ben. It was a trap he couldn't escape.

Ben sipped his Makers on the rocks and yearned for those early years prior to iProduct technology. Hell, it was companies like Apple, Microsoft and Qualcomm that helped Ben become a multi-millionaire. He, unlike other visionaries, had invested in technological companies that at the time were still start-up businesses and small cap investments. He had bought shares of stock and ignored the risk of their purchases. The twins and their generation only confirmed his clairvoyance. For those in their pre-teens, it was all about iPhones and subsequently iPads.

It was this technology that began a game of cat and mouse once the boys started communicating with their father. The boys would hide their electronic devices and late each evening, Ben would find them and review their online activities of that day. Even though they thought they were savvy, they still were kids. Their passwords were easily deciphered.

Also unknown to Ahmad and Jamil, Ben had installed surveillance equipment throughout the farm's confines. When deliveries arrived, Ben knew exactly which company, UPS or FedEx, had dropped off packages.

It was six months earlier that year when a package had been

delivered while Ben was away on business – and it was unaccounted for when he returned home. Ben knew the delivery men by name and always tipped them generously – so it didn't take him long to get the tracking number and with a little more financial incentive, Ben learned that two CryptoPhone500 cell phones were somewhere on the property. Ben was aware of this type of encrypted mobile phone – and knew that they were modified Samsung Galaxy S-3 phones.

After all, he had purchased a Blackphone for himself the previous year, wanting the same level of secure conversations and data exchange that the more expensive CryptoPhone provided.

It was obvious to Ben that the twin's father had just upped the terrorist ante. Ben knew that these phones, besides costing thousands of dollars, were top-shelf in the encryption world. The phones were also equipped to detect Stingray cell towers. Since Edward Snowden had revealed the existence of NSA's network of cell towers across America, designed to re-route cell phone traffic and enable NSA eavesdropping, it was apparent that Ahmad and Jamil could now choose to go totally rogue.

Ben was no longer able to restrain the twins – and he couldn't afford for them to take direction from their father. He knew they'd shared a series of plans with him and it would come as no surprise that their father would try to redirect the boy's efforts and the plan's payload to another target of ISIL's choosing. Ben knew that with these mobile phones, the twins could communicate directly and not through an application on their tablet. Just like their tablet's encryption app, their mobile phone's messages would self-destruct via a pre-set timer.

Luckily, Ben was always one step ahead of the twins. He figured he'd start the search in the barn with a metal detector and then proceed to the stable.

"Where would two teenagers hide something and yet be able to easily recover it without detection?" he wondered. It took Ben only fifteen minutes to find the phones in the barn. He replaced their cache with new iPhones and enclosed a note.

"My sons, these new phones are as secure as any other sophisticated cell phones you could purchase. Turn off their GPS tagging feature and download the MAPR application. Your location will be anyone's guess. The other app already loaded is Telegram Messenger. Please trust me – now let's finish our tribute to Allah. I love you. Ben."

Ben was pretty sure he'd re-tightened the boy's reins and had also finally tweaked their father who hopefully was now relegated to the role of observer. His only chance of successfully interfering would be by entering the country for a face-to-face meeting – an occurrence Ben highly doubted would happen since Homeland Security had a million dollar bounty on his head.

After landing at the airport and heading to the dealership, Ben finalized the paperwork around 3:00 p.m. and drove the car with its temporary tags back to the airport. He parked the Camry in the airport's long-term lot and boarded his return flight to Kentucky.

He was asleep before the landing gear retracted upon takeoff.

* * *

Ben awoke to his phone alarm at 5:00 a.m. Friday morning. The rental car office he was headed to didn't open until 8:00 that morning, giving him time to drive Ahmad to a dealership in Louisville where he'd taken another car he'd purchased – ostensibly a gift for a granddaughter in college – for a new paint job. The real purpose, though, was to finish up a business transaction with Jimmy, one of the guys in the sales department.

With the keys to the newly-painted 1990 four-door Honda

now in hand, Ben stopped by the sales office. Jimmy wasn't there, but he'd left an envelope for Ben on the desk – the envelope contained a second temporary tag – this one a forgery. Ben slipped two crisp one hundred dollar bills under the blotter on Jimmy's desk and left. He had what he had really wanted – another temporary tag – but was out the cost of a paint job.

After spending less than thirty minutes at the dealership, Ben and Ahmad drove to the rental car lot.

By 1:30 that afternoon, Ben in the rental car, and Ahmad, driving the Accord, were headed toward the Horseshoe Casino in Indiana.

Both drivers pulled into a convenience store gas station, Ben parking by the side of the building and Ahmad topping off the gas tank in the Accord before moving the car next to where Ben was to transfer some things. Ben had already put items from his own vehicle into the rental car, and now began moving these same items into the front seat of Ahmad's car. Everything Ahmad would need for his cross country journey was now in the Accord. Ben took the temporary tag out of the envelope and replaced the Accord's license plate with the tag. Ben asked for the keys to the Accord and gave the rental car keys to Ahmad.

That task accomplished, they continued in the direction of the casino, both driving along the route leading to an American Legion building just west of the Horseshoe Casino – this was their first destination. They pulled into the parking lot of the Legion building, where Ben got out, pretending to stretch his legs ... while checking the parking lot for other people. Seeing none, he walked behind the Accord, intentionally dropping his phone. Bending over to pick it up, Ben quickly and carefully put the keys to the Accord in the hot exhaust pipe, motioning for Ahmad to climb into the passenger seat of the rental car so he could drive them back to the rental dealership to pick up Ben's car.

"Your father is going to leave us alone – he knows we're acting on Saturday, right?" Ben asked Ahmad out of the blue.

Ahmad's head nearly twisted off his shoulders – a contortionist movement unlike any Ben had ever seen.

"Huh? What ... what are you talking about?" Ahmad stammered.

"C'mon son," Ben stated with emphasis on the word son. "You really think I didn't know your father has been chatting with you boys these past few years? Look, he's not here and it's easy for him to pick random targets. He has no understanding of how much money, time, effort and research this venture has required. I refuse to take orders from someone who abandoned you and your brother years ago, and then suddenly decides to re-enter your lives – fully expecting both of you to follow his orders. My plan is solid and nothing your father has contrived compares to what's going down on Saturday."

Ben hoped he'd been convincing. He sat quietly, determined not to say a word. Whether he worked alone on Saturday was now squarely in Ahmad's lap. Jamil always followed Ahmad's lead ... possibly because Ahmad was the first-born twin, although only by a few minutes.

"Pull over!"

"Why?" Ben answered.

"Please. Just pull over somewhere," Ahmad pleaded.

It took Ben a couple of minutes to find a safe place to stop on the road, and he finally was able to slow the car to a halt. Ahmad, still not admitting a relationship with his father, exited the car while pulling his new iPhone out of his pocket.

"That's it, give your brother a call and tell him everything," Ben mumbled to himself, somewhat agitated. "I'll be damned if he gets back in this car – not until he gives me an answer. I can't move ahead without knowing one way or another. Either they're in or they're not. If not, Ahmad can walk back to the Legion building. If either one of them comes home to the farm after saying no, they'll just have to die a little earlier than planned," Ben told himself, his thoughts now clear.

After several minutes, Ahmad returned to the passenger door to get back in the car. He pulled on the door handle a half dozen times in quick succession – the door was locked.

"Open the fucking door!" he screamed.

Ben rolled the window down partially. "What's the decision? Are you and Jamil on board or not?"

There was no verbal response – only an affirmative nod. Ben opened the door and Ahmad got in, collapsing in the passenger seat. Ben had won and he knew it. He took his right arm and gently placed it around Ahmad's head, moving it to rest on his shoulder and giving him a slight squeeze of love.

It might as well have been a dagger. Ahmad had a momentary pardon.

They finally arrived at the lot to retrieve Ben's car and said their goodbyes. Ben would head home and Ahmad, driving the rental car, would go to the casino and await his prey.

CHAPTER 18

The car was zipping past the broken white lines on I-64W when Marty finally spoke to me.

"Okay, you haven't said one word since we left – are you mad at me?"

"No, I'm not, please believe me!"

"Then tell me what's bothering you or I'll start pinching," Marty laughingly warned. Marty and I, ever since we said our vows, enjoyed the silly games we played. More than half were somewhat juvenile – but they made us laugh – and laughter is important when you're trying to reach the Golden Anniversary. The pinches that she intended to inflict would be to my right side, in the rib cage area where the flesh is thin and a pinch – well, let's just say, it's no fun.

"This is their first race against each other," I caved, saying "Uncle" much earlier than usual.

"Who are you talking about?" Marty replied impatiently.

"This is the first race that includes a Saudi horse by the name of Nidalas."

I knew my answer had just released a tsunami of questions. "Open the flood gates," I wanted to scream – but started talking calmly instead.

"Mark told us about this Arab Thoroughbred last year. He'd been tasked with analyzing all of the Thoroughbreds born throughout the world that were registered with the Jockey Club the same year Towers was born. So he fed the data for every one of this year's three-year-old class registered with the Jockey Club into his government computer. All of their ancestry was included – Mark was specifically looking for any X factor genetic connections. He was able to determine that Nidalas seems to be a carbon copy of Towers Above. Nidalas' sire and dame have the same ancestry and genetic X factor traits that Towers possesses – this horse will be a real threat to us in achieving our goals."

I went on to tell Marty that Nidalas had torn a suspensory ligament in an earlier race – and the four of us hadn't heard or read anything about him during last year's two-year-olds' racing campaign. I pointed out to Marty that I had actually forgotten about Nidalas – but Donnie hadn't.

"Then Donnie reads in the *Bloodstock Journal* that Nidalas was going to be shipped to the states this year, preparing to run at the Risen Star Stakes Race in New Orleans in February. Donnie then went down to watch his workouts and the race."

I paused a moment to take a sip of coffee before answering questions I knew she was going to ask – before she had a chance to ask them.

"So after the Risen Star race was over, I get this call from Donnie – and he's frantic. He hadn't bothered to call me anytime during the week leading up to the race, but after the race he's in a panic. He tells me, 'Rob this horse is a clone of Towers Above. He's got identical confirmation, his weight can't differ more than twenty pounds either way from what Towers carries and his stride ... I filmed it and compared it to Towers Above stride length. There can't be more than a half-foot to a foot's difference'," he told me.

"Marty, that night I pulled up the race that's now posted on YouTube and Donnie was right. Their horse smoked the other entries by ten lengths. He went wire-to-wire. God, he's a beauty, just like Towers." I explained that as of this very minute, that race has given the owners enough points for the horse to enter the Kentucky Derby.

"Donnie and I believe the only reason he's running tomorrow is because the Winner – and for that matter the Place points – that he'd earn would guarantee him a post position in the Derby field."

"So, you're telling me this race tomorrow is going to be TA's first real test after all the races over the past two years?" Marty asked.

"No shit Marty! I even called Mark about a month ago to see if he could get me a supply of the secret supplements that he's come up with. The government has been experimenting with and using them for at least a year."

"What did he say?"

"He said 'No,' but was actually pretty gentle in his refusal. Mark told me that the ingredients they were feeding their horses is classified information and if I gave even the most minute amount of these supplements to Towers Above, the ingredients would show up in the required post-race blood tests which, by the way, are drawn by the track veterinarian. He also reminded me that TA has been on a specific regimen of hay and grains, along with select vitamin supplements for his whole life – and it's the same diet that the government uses with their research horses."

With no more questions left to anticipate, I admitted to my wife that Mark seriously doubted the Saudi Thoroughbred's trainer had any idea about his studies, but nonetheless, he had one more caution for us.

"Rob ... this is going to be one hell of a race. Your jockey better be on top of her game because there's no room for error in this one," is what Mark said to me.

"And that's what I've been holding inside me for the last month."

"I'm sorry. I wish you'd shared," Marty admonished, turning her head to stare out the passenger window.

"Way to go asshole! How many times have you done this in your lifetime?" I said to myself.

Marriage is a 50-50 proposition, but my entire life with Marty has been more like a 60-40 equation, in my favor – and I know Marty hates and resents my acting that way. I shifted focus and asked Marty to check the weather app on her iPhone to see if anything had changed in the forecast for Saturday.

"God Rob, it's worse now than this morning's forecast. The National Weather Service has almost every Midwestern state in the tornado and severe thunderstorm warning box. I'm not talking about weather watches – they're all warnings!"

Now somewhat worried, all I could think about was that TA is not a fan of sloppy tracks and during the drawing for the starting post positions, we were placed in the worst possible spot, drawing the number one post position. If Towers broke poorly and was trapped on the rail, his odds of winning on a sloppy track – and with all that sandy mud flying up into his face – were slim. Donnie had purposely trained him in simulated horrible track conditions with mixed results. Once TA simply quit trying, but other times it was like he'd get so pissed off that he'd explode and accelerate – flying past any horse kicking debris on him. Donnie had no idea what to expect if there was a deluge on Saturday. He called before Marty and I hit the road to head to the casino – reassuring me that Joey fully understood just how imperative it was that she and TA broke well coming out of that position.

"I've never understood why the number one post position is such a bad draw," Marty suddenly said.

I should have expected this comment – knowing that after nearly fifty years together, she could easily read my mind.

"Marty, I don't know if you've ever really looked at the surface of a horse track. It's crowned in the middle. When it rains, the water soaks straight down as well as laterally. Close to the rail, it can be sloppier," I said, explaining the physical impact of heavy rains. "On top of the physical condition of the track, when horses break from the post, all of the jockeys steer their horses toward the rail because that's the shortest trip around the oval. Some of the greatest Thoroughbreds were vanquished very early in the race because they had a bad start … and were then trapped behind several horses. Maybe you remember American Pharoah's second place finish in the Travers Stakes Race in Saratoga?"

"No, I don't remember and you know damn well I don't!"

"Whew ... it's going to be a long night if she keeps up with this attitude," I thought, before responding.

"Serious race fans believe Pharoah was not rested enough and that's why he finished second. I think there was some questionable gamesmanship going on too. Frosted, the horse everyone expected to be the rabbit, kept Pharoah pinned to the rail. Hell, Frosted's trainer even said afterwards that he didn't tell the jockey to run that kind of race. Now assume Frosted keeps Pharoah pinned at the rail – but Pharaoh finally rallies and grabs the lead. His jockey is so focused on breaking out that he doesn't notice Keen Ice is closing and coming up the middle of the track until it's too late."

Taking my theories one step further, I said to Marty, "You know, these jockeys share the same dressing room. Who's to say that the jockeys riding Frosted and Keen Ice didn't have a plan of their own to bring down Pharoah? And people wonder why horse racing always has the shadow of doubt – this cloud – hanging over it. Well, it's no wonder for me, huh?"

"Always the conspiracy theorist, aren't you?" Marty said, smirking at me.

"Yeah, well that's why we're going to win at the table tonight. I've got to cover all of tomorrow's exacta bets that I made," I answered with my own grin.

An hour later, Marty and I checked in at the Horseshoe Casino's reservation desk.

* * *

Rob and his partners weren't the only ones aware of Nidalas' prowess. It was late summer when Ben read about the Saudi horse in *The Blood-Horse* magazine. The article said that the two-year-old had suffered an injury and would not begin training until later in the year. An interesting quote in the article from the trainer stated, "We have every intention of shipping Nidalas stateside, perhaps the first part of next year. Our goal is to qualify for the Kentucky Derby."

Ben, as he always did when it came to considering important life decisions, sat down with a yellow legal pad and vertically divided the page into two columns. At the top of the first column, he wrote Pros – and titled the second column Cons.

He immediately made several entries in the Pros column, more thoughts than complete sentences:

- Twins turn eighteen next year. Totally devoted to their father. Both absorbed with fundamentalist Islamic ideals. They are radicalized beyond hope and I can't prevent them from joining their father.
- I must NOT allow them to disgrace my family's good name in my homeland.
- This horse Nidalas must be a special horse! Did not race

155

anywhere as a two-year-old – but he's coming to America. Obviously confidence level of Saudi family is high.

- Saudi family rarely brings horses to campaign in America.
- Easy to scout Derby-qualifying tracks. Observe and probe each track's security.
- Nidalas will likely train at the central Kentucky Arab farm, and perhaps also train at the main dirt track or training center.
- Need some luck! Nidalas enters the Derby Qualifying Race – here in central Kentucky – a month before the Derby

It took Ben very little time to create his Pros list … it wasn't going to be as easy to come up with a list of Cons. He stared at the Cons column, deep in thought, before finally adding just one item:

- Convincing Ahmad and Jamil that it is far better to martyr themselves by killing Americans in their homeland versus fighting with ISIL in some Middle Eastern country.

He was done with the list.

It was time for contingencies. Even if the twins were ready and willing to die in the name of Allah, he knew if they thought there was a chance to escape after their terrorist attacks, they'd take it.

Ben ripped the Pros/Cons sheet off the notepad and wrote Escape at the top of the new page. He was pretty sure the twins had no idea what he was plotting. Hell, he didn't even know until now, but could sense now that things were coming together. Ben had told the boys he'd act when the time was right. He knew he needed a secondary target and a place for both of them to hide. Then he remembered an earlier stay with his friend Hussein in a remote cabin in Colorado.

"And – I've got a plane that's invisible and two nephews who can fly it!" Ben shouted out loud.

From that day forward, everything came together in the plan … Ben couldn't help but believe that there was divine intervention involved. He was truly blessed.

The meet at the track was now just a couple of weeks away – Ben needed to focus on tying up loose ends.

Ben felt it deep inside. He visualized being with his brother again. It had taken nearly two decades – now his journey was almost over and he'd end it with the special blend of Ricin cakes, an injection or a bullet.

CHAPTER 19

The Wall Street Journal profile article's headline read: *Dr. Blackjack's Safest Bet is Tower's Above*

Kennedy half-dollars ... do they really serve a purpose? Except for birthdays and a little reward from the Tooth Fairy, a fifty-cent piece has no value other than its equivalent of fifty pennies, ten nickels, five dimes, or two quarters – except in Las Vegas – and specifically when playing Blackjack. An ace in combination with another face card or a ten of any suit results in winning one and a half times the amount that is bet. A dollar bet earns a gambler a buck and a fifty cent piece.

That's the first rule of thumb Dr. Rob Becker learned when he sat down at a Blackjack table in Binion's Horseshoe Casino in the 1980s, he told The Journal.

"Playing Blackjack at Binion's was no different than playing at my kitchen table. My wife, Marty, would deal several hands to each of us over the course of a few hours. We discovered that if we played long enough, the game was pretty much evenly split as far as winning a hand," Becker claims.

"In Nevada back then, a cheap date cost fifty dollars. I would sit at a table for two hours, bet the minimum of a dollar a hand, ride the roller coaster of card games and still leave with my original stake," he added.

"Gambling money has no home," said Becker's fellow Thoroughbred owner, Donnie Long.

Becker responded, "These trips are never just about money. I love to people watch. Gamblers let their inner self, their true personality, reveal itself when at the tables. Here's an example."

"One night while we were waiting for a table for dinner at Hugo's Cellar in the Four Queens Casino, a cowboy approached an empty blackjack table. He pulled out a wad of cash and peeled off fifteen hundred-dollar bills, lining them up in an orderly manner on the blue felt tabletop. He watched the dealer shuffle two decks of cards, then say quite audibly, 'money plays,' before dealing the cowboy and himself their first two cards. The cowboy waved off another card and the dealer flipped over his hole card – and drew another for himself. The three dealer cards now totaled twenty. He flipped over the cowboy's hole card, swept up both of his cards and his row of hundred-dollar bills, which he folded and pushed into the

table's bank. The cowboy turned around, expressionless, and left as quietly as he had entered the blackjack area. I walked over to the empty table and excused myself for prying – but I was very curious about what I'd just seen. The dealer said, "Oh the cowboy ... he's a regular. Once a month he comes in, and always plays the same amount of cash – and win or lose – he always leaves immediately after."

"That's what I love about blackjack," said Becker.

"I've experimented with my playing positions at the tables. At First Base, I get the first play whether the table is full or not. The beginner sitting two chairs to my left – or the player half stoned on booze, pot, heroin or Oxycontin – can't mess up my first two cards.

I then decided that I liked Third Base even more, and it became my preferred gambling spot. If there's one seat at the table to people watch, Third Base is the best. Everyone plays their hands before me, with the exception of the dealer. There's an advantage at Third because you get to see the cards that've been played. I'm not a card counter, but from this vantage point, you can't help knowing when a lot of face cards haven't been played. I love it when it's my turn to take a hit ... or not. If I don't hit and the dealer draws out for a win, others at the table are sending invisible daggers of death in my direction. Yeah, Third Base is my stage – a casino domain. I'm in *total control and nobody at the table can do anything about it – until I lose my stake – or let those daggers of death mess with me enough that I give up my throne. Sometimes it's just too much fun messing with people's minds. Marty and I take these casino trips before Towers races. It's like a Disney World distraction for adults," I said, ending the interview.*

I thought the profile piece was well-written – but Marty was livid, because I'd broken a promise. My ego had prevailed and that mistake would haunt me. Nowhere in the profile was the origin of TA's name, along with my feelings about 9/11 and its aftermath.

* * *

TA was ready, and Donnie said he was in the mood for a run. So I suggested to Marty that she and I head up to Indiana for a quiet dinner and some playtime at the blackjack tables in the Horseshoe Casino. It was ironic that after all these years traveling to Las Vegas, Jack Binion's namesake would become our favorite local casino getaway.

After dinner, I settled into my preferred seat at Third Base for an evening of relaxation, patiently waiting for the gentleman playing directly opposite the dealer to finish out the remainder of the double deck. I had two hundred-dollar bills ready to convert into eight green chips, when I looked up at the player.

"I've seen you before," I said to myself. You're him. Damn, it's got to be him," I thought.

"Think – was it that flight to Phoenix back in 2001, after 9/11, to visit Annie for Thanksgiving?"

It was that same black hair, the same coal black eyes that stared at me as he boarded the plane more than seventeen years ago. He begged   no   dared me or anyone else to challenge his right to be a passenger on that plane. Suddenly, my heart was racing.

Oh, I had seen him for sure, but it was post 9/11; he was that kid with braces then, about five years ago, standing at the rail of the track not more than thirty feet from me. On this day, though, my sense of recall was not working … I couldn't make the right connection.

It was Ahmad – and he too was watching. He watched me out the corner of his eye and saw how agitated I'd suddenly become. A half-hour earlier, he'd watched Marty and I check in at the reservation desk – that was his cue to head to the twenty-five dollar double-deck Blackjack table.

"Damn adrenalin. Not now – look down or look away – but get it together Rob! He can't be the Phoenix guy," I tried to convince myself. Looking up once again, I saw him get up from the chair and walk away from the table. "Good, he's gone – no, he left a marker. He's not done playing. Jesus, those are black chips he's playing with. What the hell have I gotten myself into?"

I took my two one-hundred-dollar bills from the blackjack table, left my seat and went looking for Marty. I found her three tables away. "He's here," I stammered. "What?" she muttered with that irritated tone in her voice that was all too familiar. "That guy from the Phoenix flight." She threw in her bust hand and wheeling around with a scowl said, "what the ... what are you talking about ... what Phoenix flight?"

"You remember – the flight after 9/11. It's the Arab guy that scared the hell out of us. He's here, or it's his twin – damned if I know. Cash out and come look. I'm telling you – I've seen this guy before!"

"Ouch, you're hurting me," Marty said. I hadn't realized the vise-like grip I had on her upper arm was so strong. I relaxed my hold a bit, and hurried her to the table to confirm that the pit in my stomach was justified.

I couldn't look at him again, and stared instead at Marty, watching her face slowly pale and go ashen. I could feel the weight of her body shifting with my hand – she not realizing I still had a grip on her arm. This time I could tell she was grateful for it – that's what kept her from falling.

"You're right ... maybe?" was all she could muster. "What do we do?" Marty pleaded.

"Look, we can't do crap. He's not doing anything wrong. Let's just watch ... I don't know."

We watched in stunned amazement. For a while.

His playing was eccentric, if not downright stupid. Now I was in my blackjack zone. We both slid to a position slightly beyond the back of his left shoulder to observe his cards and playing pattern. The dealer showed an eight ... Ahmad had fifteen and waved off another card. The dealer turned over a Jack of Hearts and swept up the five black chips. Ahmad pushed out another five blacks and took a hit on his hard seventeen against the dealer's Queen up card. Sure enough, he busted.

"What kind of game is this guy playing?" I whispered to Marty. She shrugged.

Out came another five blacks and then another five – over and over again. Then the marker went down and I watched his actions. He got up, walked a few yards away to an empty table, lit a cigarette, pulled out his cell phone and appeared to make a call. A minute passed … seemed like an eternity and then he was back, peeling off three thousand dollars' worth of paper. Of his thirty new chips, he stacked ten blacks in the betting circle. "Now he's chasing," I quietly said to Marty. Damned if he didn't hit a Blackjack. "Maybe I'm wrong, maybe he's a pro, playing a game I've never seen before," I said, once more speaking in a hushed voice. And then damned if he didn't stand when he should have taken a hit.

We weren't the only bystanders watching the theatrics that were playing out at the table. By now, fifteen or more people were gathered – every one of us exchanging quizzical looks with each other after every rookie play. And then out would come the marker, another walk, another cigarette, and another phone call – followed by more insane play.

A half hour turned into forty-five minutes of Blackjack Hamlet and now no longer mesmerized, I tugged on Marty's sleeve and said, "Come on, we've got to get out of here. Let's go."

Even though I was walking, it felt like I was sprinting. My mind was racing even faster. "Think damn it! Do I go to the cashier's window?" Marty pulled me to a halt. "What the hell is going on? Are you going to explain?" she asked.

"Marty, you remember about 9/11?" Her eyes had that blank look which meant I wasn't making sense. Things were just moving too fast, I told myself.

"Jerry, my FBI patient – he and I were talking about 9/11 a year or two afterwards, before the commission report came out. I asked him why there weren't any tells that would have given the authorities a heads up. He told me that the only hint of something amiss were the terrorist's actions the days and nights before the events of 9/11. At that time, none of the agents had any idea that jihadists would act the way they did."

Still stopped about a hundred yards from the table Marty said, "What are you thinking?"

"Well Marty, it's not exactly what Jerry said. This isn't a strip joint or a brothel! But his gambling antics are certainly just as bizarre as the 9/11 hijackers actions were prior to that terrible day. I've never watched anyone throw money away like that – and you know we've seen about every type of strange play that's possible in a casino," I said. I was hyperventilating and had to bend over to catch my breath.

Again Marty said, "What are you thinking?" this time in a more demanding tone.

"Well, I can't go back and say anything to the pit boss. I guess I'll go to the cashier window and ask for the casino manager and tell him about my fears."

"Like hell you will," Marty interrupted. "Look, this is 2018 – 9/11 was years ago and you're not getting us sued for slander. Don't you think this casino has knowledge about what happened back then? Don't you understand they've probably already forwarded his picture from one of their cameras to authorities? Who made you Jack Bauer?"

Pausing to catch her breath, Marty appealed to my sense of logic. "I'm willing to bet that the NSA is watching his play, live ...

right now as we're speaking. Don't you dare make a fool of us, especially the night before TA runs. We don't need to be the lead story all over the Internet tomorrow."

As we headed to our room, I had no idea just how right Marty was.

"I'm still going to call the office and get Jerry's number, then give him a call … just for my peace of mind," I said sheepishly.

"You do that," Marty answered, even before I could finish my train of thought.

CHAPTER 20

As Ahmad was continuing to violate Blackjack rules at the table and the Horseshoe Casino was getting rich, live video was indeed streaming to an NSA facility at Bolling Air Force Base in Washington, DC. The casino had absolutely no clue as to the identity of the erratic player, and Einstein, situated several miles east and one of only three top-level supercomputers in the world, began to analyze Ahmad's actions. The facial recognition program was one Einstein's core software programs – and a basic function. Everything about Ahmad would soon be identified since Einstein had profile photos of millions of Middle Easterners throughout the world. Every individual not fully vetted and who had stepped foot in a mosque in North and South America in the last forty-eight hours was also in the database.

It was precisely one hour and thirty-four minutes after Ahmad began playing at the table when he abruptly stood, started to put his marker down and then withdrew it. He exchanged his green chips for blacks, picked up his remaining black chips and headed to the cashier's window.

It was a race now. Would Einstein be able to make an ID

before Ahmad left the casino? The cashier raked in and stacked the black chips, and reached into the money drawer, pulling out forty crisp hundred-dollar bills, counting them out in rows of ten. Einstein purred away at a steady pace, not aware his subject was about to exit the building. "Thirty-five, thirty-six, thirty-seven, thirty-eight, thirty-nine and forty. Thank you and come back again," the cashier said.

Ahmad casually headed for the Horseshoe parking garage, glancing every few steps over his shoulder to see if he had company, taking one last look before opening the driver's door. Once inside, he again checked his mirrors and started the car … it appeared that there was no one following him. "I guess my behavior at the table wasn't that strange after all," he thought.

Einstein was drawing a blank. It had completed multiple analyses of its internal database. A huge portion of this database used Interpol's facial recognition program which had been in operation since early in 2015. Einstein's software included twenty-seven basic head shapes with the inter-pupillary distance measurements of every individual in the database, as well as other recorded facial landmark measurements. Einstein even had a secondary program which stripped away mustaches and goatees, along with any other facial hair adaptations, to help determine an identity.

Like a siren warning of an emergency, red lights were flashing within the computer – indicating that a human being would now get involved. Humans had no semblance of Einstein's IQ – and for Einstein, being identified as the most elite computer in the world – not finding a match was embarrassing. Einstein was the closest creation and precursor to what would qualify as Artificial Intelligence. Perhaps if he had been AI, the computer would have said, "Just give me three more minutes and I'll have an answer." Einstein finally came to the same logical conclusion that its human handler had already deduced – Ahmad was home-grown.

A flash message had just been received at the Horseshoe security office.

Detain this person of interest immediately. Hold for interrogation!

Attached was a picture of Ahmad from earlier in the evening when he was seated directly across from the dealer.

Ahmad pulled up to the garage's exit gate, which opened after a two-second pause generated by the sensor in the concrete. A photo was taken of him, and also of the car's license plate.

He was out of there.

Ahmad glanced back at the gate and saw that the BMW behind him in line waiting to exit was still sitting at the gate. He silently counted, one thousand one, one thousand two, one thousand three. He mused, "I must have broken it,"... or had he?

The husband and wife in the BMW looked at each other, wondering what the problem was. Another fifteen seconds passed and the husband put the car in reverse, backed up a bit and then pulled up to the gate a second time. A Horseshoe security guard stepped out of the darkness. The driver rolled down his window and was about to yell at the guard, when he noticed the guard glancing at a paper in his hand and then back at him. He said, "Sorry for the inconvenience, thanks again for visiting the Horseshoe Casino. Please come back soon."

Ahmad, who was driving the rental car, turned onto Highway 11 and headed west. He knew attention would be focused on the interstate roads – and that time was short. It was just a matter of time before the vehicle's GPS computer chip was identified.

Ahmad turned onto Highway 211 and then back onto

Highway 11 again, heading now towards the city of Elizabeth. A quick glance in the rear view mirror showed nothing. He slowly approached the American Legion building, coasting past to see if the Honda was still there – it was.

A few miles to the east and flying at three thousand feet, a Homeland Security drone completed a series of ever narrowing circles, searching for the signature of any rental cars within seventy-five miles of the Horseshoe. Its camera was clicking every minute or so, relaying information back to the same building Einstein was housed in. But this information went to one of Einstein's sister computers, a Cray XK7 hybrid supercomputer whose functions included mobile identification.

Ahmad turned the car around and headed back to the Legion building. Pulling into the parking lot, he turned off the headlights and parked next to the Accord – scanning the lot to make sure no one was there. He then began to go through his checklist – a To Do list of things intended to confuse those who found the rental car. After putting on gloves, he lit a cigarette and took a long draw on it. Once the filter was brown, he put out the cigarette and tossed it on the ground by the car. Next, he grabbed a plastic bag which held almost a dozen smoked and extinguished cigarettes – all Marlboros gathered from different locations – and put them in the ashtray. Each one had a different DNA signature on their respective filters – one even had lipstick on it.

"That ought to throw them off," Ahmad laughed.

He then used Wet Wipes to rub down the steering wheel. Opening the door, he also wiped down the arm rest and door handle, closing the door only enough to trip the dome light.

Heading to the rear of the Accord, he reached into the exhaust pipe and pulled out the car keys. Once inside the car, he waited a few seconds for his eyes to adjust to the darkness. He could've been blind and still would have known where every compartment was in the car, because he'd practiced this routine many times before. He retrieved a small LED flashlight from the ashtray.

On the passenger seat was his travel bag. He grabbed a pair of shoes identical to the ones he was wearing out of the bag. However, these shoes had been soiled north of the Ohio River, not south. He got out of the Accord and went back to the rental, where he tossed the shoes onto the back seat. He also threw in a set of clothes that matched what he'd been wearing at the casino earlier that evening.

"Shit, the outside mirror." He'd forgotten to wipe it down. "Slow down," he reminded himself. After pushing the door closed with his knee, he wiped down the outside door handle. One more trip to the Accord to check his list one last time ... and he'd be on his way.

Unknown to Ahmad, though, was that the Life section of the previous Sunday's *Columbus Dispatch* was in driver's side rear storage pouch of the rental car.

Back in the Accord, he turned the ignition key and all four cylinders responded. "No keyless remote on this baby," Ahmad snickered as he shifted the car into drive and headed west.

Over an hour had passed since leaving the casino – this included the ten minutes since he left the rental car in the Legion's parking lot. In those ten minutes, the Homeland drone received a notification ... immediately changing course and heading for the target and the rental car, where it began to snap photos in rapid-fire succession. Two seconds later, analysis of the information had begun.

Einstein was now starting the third recognition program –

this one would take more time. It processed the NSA photos that had been taken of children of Middle Eastern descent post 9/11. The software was designed to morph the images into a semblance of what the individuals might look like at the present time. These were composite photos that had not been updated in many years – and somehow these individuals had gone off the grid.

Einstein's sister computer finally had an unidentified hit that might be what they'd been searching for. All the other hits had been identified by photos secretly taken as other rental cars left the rental parking lot ... their drivers had been pulled over by sheriff deputies inside the seventy-five mile radius of the Horseshoe Casino. However, while this particular car wasn't moving, they knew it had been because an infra-red signature of a still warm engine was beamed up to the drone.

It took twenty-five minutes before the first FBI vehicle pulled in next to the rental car.

CHAPTER 21

Ahmad had made this trip once already in the past month, the first time, driving with his brother to check out the route – both on the lookout for potential detours or road work that would affect drive time on the actual day. Now he was solo. Shining a penlight into the travel bag on the floor of the passenger side, he pulled out the first set of printed instructions Ben had given him.

- *Go north on Route 11.*
- *Head west on Highway 62.*
- *Continue to Evansville and cross the Ohio River.*
- *Get on US Route 60 and continue west.*

Coming down from the adrenaline high he'd been on since leaving the casino and ditching the rental car, Ahmad reached into the bag again, this time grabbing an energy drink, downing it in two gulps before tossing the bottle onto the back seat. Wondering again if anyone was searching for him yet, his mind started to wander back to the high school years – a time when he just wanted to be a part of the group – a group nobody would let him join.

Anger began to rise up in him. Why hadn't he been accepted?

After all, he'd hung out with a few of the popular students. His grades were good – he was in the top ten percent of the class. He had lettered in soccer all four years of high school.

But each year that he matured was another year that his Middle Eastern- Mediterranean features became more prominent. His beard was heavy and by noon every day, he looked like he needed a shave. His hair, was now jet black. As he stood at his locker, he couldn't help glancing at the girls across the hallway, giggling and every now and then peeking in his direction. The "with-it" girls automatically turned down any of his flirtations or attempts at a date. Occasionally, he'd score a date with a girl who wasn't in with the most popular group. These girls, the second tier, went out with him on a first date, but there was never a second. He could see it in the parent's eyes when he went to pick their daughter up for the date. The parents never smiled – and wouldn't even look directly at him. They'd talk to the door or wall – anywhere but to him.

There were many times when Ahmad wanted to scream, "Look at me … I'm an American just like you. I'm no different. I respect your daughter." He eventually came to the conclusion that he'd never be accepted into American society. His uncle, well aware of his nephew's increasing anger and withdrawal, encouraged him to take out this girl ... or that girl. Ahmad knew these girls his uncle suggested. They worshipped at the mosque, just as he had when he was younger. But he had stopped going to the mosque – and would worship his God in his own way – and on his terms.

Ending the not-so nostalgic reverie, he stopped to stretch his legs and relieve himself. Only ten minutes more and he would cross the Ohio River. It was time for the first item on the list.

Easing the car into an area that truckers had used as a rest stop for many years, Ahmad gulped down a second energy drink. He was fighting exhaustion and needed to regain his composure before he could stop and rest. Checking his watch, he discovered he was fifteen minutes ahead of schedule. "Too much of a lead foot," he mumbled. With gloved hands, he opened the cell phone and took out its SIM card, closed it and grabbed a rag from his travel bag, using it to wipe the phone clean. So much for that dinosaur, he thought. He counted down until it was time.

Taking a new phone from the metal Faraday bag in his travel satchel, Ahmad placed a call – assuming that the conversation would be encrypted. While all the mobile phone manufacturers guaranteed privacy, Ahmad knew that every time a new operating system or update was developed, NSA's cryptologists would subsequently attempt to crack the codes for the new software or update. It was like a Tom and Jerry cartoon – every tit was met with a tat. Even though the lag time between the introduction of a phone's new operating system or update did create a slight window of secretive opportunity, back doors were eventually opened – often by patriotic nerdy insiders who were well compensated. "They'll get access even if they have to get a court order," Ahmad thought.

"I'm here," he said to the man on the other end of the phone.

The voice replied, "Are you on time?" "Yes," Ahmad said.

The voice responded back, "Take your time with the drop."

Ahmad answered, "You know I will."

And the voice once again answered, saying "Praise be to God," in Arabic. The phone connection went dead.

Rubbing his face, Ahmad realized that he'd almost forgotten the fake facial hair. Slowly he peeled away the goatee – rubbing for another minute as more glue rolled off his face. It was like rubber cement and the last thing he needed was gook that looked like snot stuck to his nostrils. Turning on the dome light, he looked closely in the rear view mirror. He was clean … and ready to get back on the road.

Just across the Ohio River was a Pilot gas station with a large rest area for truckers. Entering the parking lot, he stopped just short of the area where many big rigs were parked. Walking towards the restroom to freshen up, he stopped first to attach the now SIM-free phone to the flatbed of one of the trucks. After leaving the restroom, he attached another phone – the one he'd just used – under the left front fender of a Zaia truck. It could have been a ConWay or Arkansas Best eighteen-wheeler – the only thing that mattered was that it would be traveling somewhere.

The likelihood was high that the smartphone's mapping app was already communicating its location via GPS to Einstein's sister computer. Hopefully the truck's driver would climb aboard and get underway soon.

The voice Ahmad had talked with earlier was his uncle's – and Ben was ecstatic. The first smartphone call would be the tripwire to Ahmad's demise. If the discussion in Arabic hadn't convinced the NSA that Ahmad was a threat, then Ben was overestimating America's intelligence agencies.

Ben would not be disappointed.

He had personally packed Ahmad's travel bag. It contained four new smartphones and a car charger, over a dozen energy drinks, a fully-charged electric razor, two cyanide pills, and a loaded nine-millimeter automatic with four additional loaded clips. In the backseat, there was a winter coat, wool hat and gloves, along with a snow shovel, boots, a cooler filled with orange juice and a couple dozen Smucker's peanut butter and jelly Uncrustables. Ahmad also had several more sequential sheets of printed instructions.

One printout stood out from the others: *Do Not Take Any Phones Out of the Main Bag Until It is Time!!!*

This was the most critical thing Ahmad needed to heed, especially given the properties of the Faraday bags. These bags are basically metal – made of copper, silver or anything that can serve as an electrical conductor. Any signal emitted from the activated phones couldn't pass through the metal. If Ahmad wanted to live, he would obey this rule.

But Ahmad had no idea his gun's clips were filled with blanks. His uncle had made sure he would die … one way or another.

CHAPTER 22

We know it as Homeland Security, but many agents of Homeland don't hesitate to go off record and anonymously acknowledge that this agency, charged with protecting America, is ripe with turf battles, staffed by control freaks and filled with inefficiencies.

The FBI crew on the scene at the American Legion building was nearly finished with their preliminary investigation of Ahmad's rental car when a black Prius entered the parking lot – its driver was one of those control freaks.

The Homeland agent – one of the agency's lead operatives – stepped out of the hybrid and flashing his badge for everyone to see, came to an abrupt stop in front of the FBI agent in command. This agent wasn't attached to the DIA, NSA, FBI, or CIA – although his pay checks were government issued – budgeted through the Department of Defense, and considered to be part of the DOD's Black Operations.

During the Cold War, the Army Security Agency – a subsection of the NSA, complemented our nation's security forces.

Perhaps this agent was a remnant of that past era and truly a Man in Black.

"We'll take over now. Leave the evidence and pack your stuff," he tersely ordered. It was short, sweet and condescending to his fellow federal agents.

The agent first on the scene started to object – and was immediately dismissed by the "badge" with a backhand gesture. "Oh … and please leave your notes. Thank you," he said in the same terse tone.

The FBI agents had been on alert since Friday afternoon – from the time that the President of Ohio State University had reported the threatening letter to the FBI. The chief agent was also running point on the drone's positioning in the Midwest and wasn't taking the dismissal well.

Standing next to the badge were three other agents – none of which had any visible credentials – and wouldn't show them even if asked. They were CIA and by rights, shouldn't have been there. They looked like misfits, except that their khaki pants, Columbia shirts and lightweight coats would readily fit in with many different Hollywood movie profiles.

"Probably ex-Seals or Rangers," the admonished agent thought to himself. He wanted to flip them off.

The senior Homeland agent gathered his team together to review the notes the FBI team had compiled. He read aloud, "popped hood … engine still warm" – then reaching into a duffel bag, pulled out the newest model Exergen temperature gun. Just like a major league baseball scout aims a radar gun to catch the speed of a pitch, he aimed the temperature gun at the car's engine to gauge how long the car had been idle.

Taking into account humidity and the ambient temperature around the engine, the unit instantly displayed a reading that showed the time lapse since the ignition was turned off. The data was entered into a laptop sitting atop the hood of the Prius, and within seconds, the information was under analysis by an Appro supercomputer at NSA headquarters. Thirty seconds passed and in green boldface type, the laptop flashed out a text message.

"Radius 175 miles."

He nodded to one of the CIA agents and said, "Text Olympus. Give them the data and tell them to direct the flock 360

185

degrees – 250 miles. We better add a fudge factor, just in case." The agent stepped away and pulling out his mobile phone, began to type a message.

In just a few minutes, a trio of Boeing's latest drones would begin circling from the center of the radius, which was directly above them.

The agent then read the next FBI entry. "Several Marlboro cigarette butts outside and inside vehicle. Lipstick on one."

"Everyone agree he might have an accomplice?" The other agents all nodded up and down in unison, like robots. "Tell Olympus 'plus one'." The same agent stepped back from the group and added a second text.

The agent started to read from the notes again but suddenly stopped, his attention directed to a loud distraction in the sky, coming from the southeast. The noise steadily grew louder and closer – it was a chopper that hovered over the Legion parking lot for fifteen seconds before beginning to descend for a landing. When the rotors finally came to a halt, out came two more khaki-clad agents, each carrying duffel bags.

The two men joined the group. "Okay, listen up, the initial wipe down was negative for prints. Clothes and shoes were on the back seat … any comments?"

One of the two agents who'd arrived by helicopter suggested that they could be the clothes worn at the Horseshoe but his partner, who was examining the trousers chimed in with an observation. "These pants still have a perfect crease. If the pants had been worn, there would be wrinkles and the creases wouldn't be this perfect."

"Okay, assume the pants are decoys. What about the shoes?"

A third agent chimed in on this. "The shoes are dress shoes. If he's on a road trip, well, I wouldn't wear them – they're too uncomfortable."

The lead agent paused for a half minute and made a judgment call. "Assume these are the shoes he wore" – and into one duffel bag they went. The clothes went into the other duffel. "We have a section of last Sunday's *Columbus Dispatch* – the Life section and a separate section on Events occurring this weekend. What do you guys think?"

There was total silence. "Well ...?"

Again there was silence. "Why the clippings and what events are so important this weekend?" the Homeland agent wondered aloud – coming up with even more questions. "What assets do we have in Columbus? Has there been any chatter about Columbus or anything that might reference the ancient explorer? There's too much uncertainty and no real concrete evidence. Maybe I'm just shadow boxing," the lead agent speculated.

"Okay. Sum it all up and text the information … we'll let the tech wonks sort it out," he started to say … pausing mid-sentence because of another interruption. This time, it was a civilian's car pulling into the Legion parking lot. The driver started to get out of the vehicle, suddenly pausing with one foot still in the car when he saw the group that was assembled.

"It's alright, we're the police. What's on your mind?" the agent shouted towards the driver.

"My name's Eric, Eric Johnson. I'm the executive director for the Legion. This is my building. I work here," he stammered. Now, if you'd asked Eric, he would have admitted that at that very moment, he could have peed himself. The agents were that intimidating!

"Mr. Johnson. Step over here … c'mon, we're not going to hurt you." Eric felt his legs move even though he hadn't ordered them to respond, or so he thought. "Eric – it's Eric, right? Have you seen this car at any time today or even before today?"

"No. No, I haven't," Eric was nearly stuttering now.

"I tell you what, take a deep breath and relax. Now you say you haven't seen this car – so how about any other strange activity or cars yesterday or today?"

Eric paused. "Well … yes, yes. There were a couple of cars, come to think about it. It was today and I was wrapping up my work when …" his sentence unfinished as he was again interrupted by the lead agent.

"Joe, take him inside and get the details and … hey, Mr. Johnson, do you have any cameras aimed towards this lot? I didn't see any when we pulled in here."

Eric, now less intimidated, answered. "Yeah, yeah we do. They were installed just last month. Our members take pride in this country and no socialist piece of crap is going to mess with us.

They're inside and let me tell you ..." his thoughts yet again interrupted – this time with the realization that there was a tight pincer grip on his upper right arm – and he was being led, no, pushed toward the entrance of the American Legion building.

"Danny ... go with them and download the film if you can and forward it to Olympus. And damn it, calm the guy down. If you have to, take him back to Louisville, along with the two duffel bags. The rest of us are heading to the casino."

Perfectly on cue, a tow truck pulled into the parking lot at that moment, maneuvering into position to retrieve the rental car. Fifteen minutes later, Eric and the entourage of agents emerged from the building, pausing only to lock the door. In five minutes they were airborne and headed to Louisville's Bowman Airport just a few minutes away – with Eric having no clue he wouldn't make it home that evening.

CHAPTER 23

In less than twelve hours, Towers Above would answer the Call to the Post – in front of an anxious crowd of more than thirty thousand patrons – with the majority placing bets. Millions of dollars would be wagered at the track and via simulcasting.

I hadn't slept one minute. My usual bedtime cocktail of two extra-strength Tylenol and two twenty-five milligram Benadryl tablets didn't do the job this night … and my mind was racing. I knew I'd seen that guy before, but I still couldn't remember where! There had been too many trips since 9/11, I thought to myself.

I knew I wouldn't leave the Horseshoe Casino until I'd talked with someone about what had happened at the blackjack table. Since Marty was still asleep, I convinced myself that there was no better time than now.

Throwing on some comfortable clothes, I headed back to the casino at 4:30 in the morning, still pitch black with no hint yet of sunrise on the horizon.

As I approached the row of blackjack tables, I could tell

something was off. There weren't as many tables, I thought, or the spacing was different … or maybe I was just plain tired and confused. I paused at the spot where I thought everything had gone down and then stared at the dealer. The dealer, wearing his "Hi, I'm Steve from Cincinnati" name tag, wouldn't look at me, pretending instead to do an inventory of his chips. Then I glanced down at the base of the blackjack table and saw that the table was askew. It wasn't seated on its carpet imprints. Either the table I'd been at earlier had been moved or a new table had been put into its place.

"So, Steve from Cincinnati, how long have you been working this table tonight?" I asked. Steve half smiled and replied, "Sir, this is the sixth table I've worked tonight. I've been at this table for the past fifteen minutes."

"Well Steve," I said in a confrontational tone, "I think you're a liar because this table has either been moved or this is a different table from earlier tonight. Look for yourself at the imprints in the carpet. They don't match up! So why don't you just tell me the truth?" I couldn't keep my agitation from rising.

"Sir, would you like to talk with someone else?"

"Damn straight, Steve."

"Oh hell, I've stepped in it now," I thought. The Pit Boss came over to Steve's side.

"Can I help you, Sir?" the Pit Boss asked.

"Okay Rob … tone it down a notch," I told myself. "Hi, I'm Rob – and let me start over. I played blackjack at this spot earlier last evening. I can't tell if this is the same table or not, but I suspect it isn't because it's obvious something's changed. This table isn't sitting in its imprints in the carpet. The table has been moved or it's another table. Look, I'm not a trouble maker, but there was some crazy blackjack play last night and frankly, there was a player here that frightened the crap out of me!" Out of the corner of my eye I could see a couple men approaching me and … suddenly, I was out.

When in twilight sleep, one moment you're conscious and next thing you know, you're in a state of "where am I and what just happened" form of disorientation. I heard someone calling my name, but had no clue who was asking for me.

"Dr. Becker, Rob Becker … can you hear me? Open your eyes, Dr. Becker," the agent said while gently shaking me.

"What … what time is it? The race! I've got to get to the track … where am I?" I stammered, according to Marty.

"Hold on, Bud. Slow down … your race can wait. There are more important things we need to talk about. Now," the agent said to me firmly.

I turned to my right and then to the left before I spotted Marty. She and I were nearing almost fifty years together and the only other time I had seen that look of apprehension was when we walked in on burglars robbing our house. "You can't hold us. We've done nothing wrong. I have rights and I want to talk with my lawyer …" I tried to say when a hand clamped over my mouth.

It had been a long time since someone had purposely smothered my voice – the memory of my Dad's corporal punishments flashed briefly from the depths of whatever portion of my brain holds those unpleasant memories. He slowly removed his clammy hand while whispering in my ear.

"We are going to do this my way, aren't we?" I wanted to continue to protest – but my head was nodding in the affirmative.

"Okay, you told the Pit Boss you witnessed crazy play last

194

night and that you had seen the player before. Would you please elaborate?"

"Look, I have no idea who you are, but just for my wife's sake as well as mine, I'm going to assume you are good guys. I told my wife I recognized the guy. I've been up all night and hell ... I can't remember anything. I'm just a dentist and maybe he was in my waiting room, or maybe on a plane. I just don't know," I said to him with apparent frustration.

"And yes his behavior bothered me a helluva' lot. I'm not stupid. I know what the terrorists did before 9/11. His behavior was not normal. Look, I've got a stake in a horse that's running today, Towers Above. Perhaps you've heard of him. He's our tribute to those people who ..." This time the hand stopped just short of my lips, indicating it was time to shut them once again.

"Dr. Becker, we know who you are – and we know about Towers Above – and you're right. The man playing blackjack here last night is a problem. If this was any day other than today – and having read how close you owners all are to that horse, well let's just say we know how much that horse means to people in this country. If it wasn't for that, horse racing wouldn't be part of your itinerary today."

Having said all that, the agent then informed me that Marty and I would have company throughout the weekend. "Our man Tommy is going to accompany you for the remainder of this weekend. We need your eyes and your focus at the track today, for your horse's sake as well as for the patron's welfare. We don't have an ID on this guy as yet. If any thoughts, location, or flashback occurs – tell Tommy. Nothing is insignificant. Do you understand?"

"Yes," was the only word I had left to say.

And then the room was empty. I got up … Marty was already in my arms when I felt a slight tug on my arm. I suddenly remembered we had a new companion for the weekend, Tommy.

"Dr. Becker, we have to leave. We need to get to the track."

I learned from sources later that day that I was right about the table and workers who were in that area so early in the morning. The table where Ahmad had played was gone. Steve from Cincinnati was an FBI agent, and the Pit Boss worked for the CIA.

Tommy drove across the Ohio River at Louisville. Marty sat in front and I fell asleep on the back seat, still trying to remember where I'd seen the mysterious blackjack player. Tommy didn't need to hear what was happening from his agency's Virginia office. Although he'd remained silent in the Legion's parking lot, he knew about the OSU threat. It was just too damn obvious. He'd remain a good soldier for a while, but in his mind Towers Above was the epicenter of the chatter coming out of the Caliphate in the Middle East, which he also knew about. He truly wanted to confide in me about the intel that his agency had, but was prohibited from doing so.

CHAPTER 24

The alarm went off at 3:30 a.m., Central Time. Ahmad groped clumsily in the darkness for the glove compartment latch. Finding it, he reached into the compartment, grabbing the clock. "Where the heck is the snooze button?" he said in a fog. Finally, after pushing and pulling every toggle, button and switch, it stopped ringing. Clearing his eyes, he grabbed a penlight to look at the contraption his uncle had thrust upon him. He'd never seen anything like it – but then most millennials wouldn't know what to do with it because it wasn't an i-This or i-That. It was an old Bulova wind-up alarm clock that folded like a woman's make-up compact. He put it in the bag and grabbed the next sheet of instructions.

- *When you reach Springfield, take exit US 60.*
- *Head north to the Springfield-Branson Airport.*
- *Enter long-term parking.*
- *Search for a silver Toyota Camry four-door sedan with an Obama for President logo on the left rear bumper.*
- *Keys in the exhaust pipe.*
- *Wipe down the Accord.*
- *Put the Camry's sun visor down – the parking ticket is there.*
- *Hand attendant cash $$$.*

- *Cover your face – use your hand.*
- *I will call at 9:00 a.m.*

Entering the airport's long-term parking lot, Ahmad took the parking ticket from the automated machine, and drove up and down the first two aisles looking for the designated car. Rounding a corner into Aisle C, he spotted the Camry. Two spaces away was an empty parking spot, and he eased the Accord into it.

Taking a deep breath, he got out of the Accord, and approached the rear of the Camry. Pretending to drop his keys, he quickly reached into the exhaust pipe to retrieve the new set of car keys.

It took fifteen minutes to empty and sanitize the Accord before settling into the Camry's driver seat. This time his exit would be more challenging. Visor down, he started the Camry, heading to the exit and cashier booth. Straightening himself up in the seat, he tried to cover at least part of his face. Ahmad handed the parking ticket and a hundred dollar bill to the attendant.

"I haven't seen any of these today – you got anything smaller?" the attendant asked. Ahmad, shielding his face with his left hand and elbow, shook his head "No."

"Okay man … give me a minute. How was your flight?" The attendant was now in small talk mode. What seemed like an eternity took only about a minute – but was long enough for front and lateral cameras to capture photos of Ahmad's car and his face before he exited.

Finally, Ahmad was on his way back to the highway. He planned to take 60 to U.S. 160, before heading west toward U.S. 281 – and then finally go north.

As he headed south, a Delta regional jet crossed the highway on its approach to the airport – prompting Ahmad to wonder how his counterpart was proceeding with his instructions. He'd done all the heavy lifting so far and felt he had passed with flying colors – no pun intended – as he laughed to himself. Would his best friend and brother be as lucky?

The horizon had a light orange, slightly purple tinge. It wasn't a "red sun in the morning, sailor takes warning" type of sunrise – and Ahmad was driving blind as far as weather was concerned. But his twin wasn't handcuffed in the same fashion and in fact, had just printed out the aviation maps for Kentucky and Ohio for that Saturday.

Ahmad's uncle had cautioned both boys that there was one intangible they couldn't control – the weather. Ben knew the weather could possibly delay and disrupt timing of their plan – and that was why they had to be flexible with their actions. Delays might happen, but ultimately the events planned for that day would take place.

None of them took into account the weather events that happened on a spring day in 1974. It was the worst outbreak of tornadoes ever recorded – and the brunt of the carnage took place in Ohio and Kentucky. That day, out of a total of one hundred forty-eight tornados, thirty were classified as F4 or F5. More than three hundred people died.

This day's NOAA/NWS maps were mirror images of the 1974 historical maps. The storm prediction center in Norman, Oklahoma had already issued tornado warnings for the same states that had been hit in '74.

All their trips, meticulous schedules, and training were now threatened by Mother Nature. Certainly their God wouldn't interfere with this righteous mission.

Ahmad's best friend, his twin brother Jamil, was physically

shaken.

He had flown in almost every type of weather, but never in the conditions he could possibly face this day.

Frantically, Jamil pulled out his cell phone and called his uncle.

"Why are you calling me?" was all Jamil heard. Not a hello, but a why – and he knew he was in trouble.

"Have you seen the weather forecast?" Jamil replied.

"Yes I have … I'm monitoring it. We're still a go. It may affect our timing and if that happens, I'll contact you with any changes. Now get off your phone and don't call me again until you're on your way. Do you understand?" Jamil meekly answered "yes" before hanging up.

Looking up at the sky, he shook his head, mumbling aloud, "perhaps it's not to be." Getting in his car to make the drive to the airstrip, Jamil wished it had been two out of three instead of just one when their uncle did the coin toss. Ahmad and he had both been trained to fly the plane – and they had cross-trained in all facets of the plan.

"Why didn't I call heads?" he screamed – with no one to hear – at the same time beating the steering wheel with his fist.

CHAPTER 25

The angle of the sun was just high enough on the horizon that its bright light was now blazing through the back seat window. I found myself squinting at my watch while shielding my face with my right hand. The time indicated that I'd slept for only an hour – but I felt refreshed. For a retired man, that's all that's needed, I thought.

"So Tommy, how much can you share with us about this guy at the casino and what your people think is going on? I mean … maybe it might help nudge my memory."

Sitting up straight now, I looked ahead into the rear view mirror, staring at the reflection of Tommy's sunglasses. He didn't move his head one iota, but started to summarize for me the information they had – and more importantly – what they didn't have. Then he brought up the section of the *Columbus Dispatch* that had been in the rental car. "So what's going on in Columbus this weekend?" I asked.

"Nothing out of the ordinary. A soccer game on Sunday, a concert at Nationwide on Saturday night … and the spring football scrimmage at the 'Shoe," Tommy replied.

What happened next I can only describe as one of those moments of a sudden epiphany. Everyone has them. It's like someone or something hits the flush handle on a certain part of our memory centers. You know, when tons of information and thoughts come flooding back into the conscious part of our immediate thought processes. "Whoever this guy is, he's playing all of us. It's like *that Die Hard* movie – was it the second or the third one?" I told myself. "Think Rob. Wasn't it the one with the Simon Says character – the Riddler guy? That's it … it was Simon Says! Damn, this guy is messing with all of us," I thought again.

And suddenly I blurted out, "It's the 'Shoe' … it's got to be! Don't you get it? First it was the Horseshoe Casino and now it's the Horseshoe in Columbus. It's Ohio State's spring scrimmage and there could be close to one hundred thousand fans there. It's not a real game but …" In less than four seconds, we were off the road. Tommy did his best Superman imitation – he was out of the car and on his cell phone in what seemed like a nano-second to me.

Marty's head jerked, and she quickly turned around, staring hard at me. Perhaps her brain was in replay mode?

It was.

I'd seen that look on her face before.

It had to have been the Ohio State/Purdue game in 1968 … the first game we attended at Ohio Stadium. OSU's Rex Kern, Jim Otis, and Jack Tatum were pitted against Purdue's Leroy Keyes, and the place was rocking. Marty and I had never been to a football game where people went that crazy for their team. And the game wasn't the best part. Nobody left their seats at half-time – everyone wanted to see the band perform. They called themselves the Best Damn Band in the Land, and the halftime show always included a special routine called Script Ohio. We both got goosebumps watching it. We were definitely hooked.

Hell, I hadn't been to a game since the early 2000s. The stadium, I'd read somewhere, now accommodates over one hundred thousand fans. What was once the open end of the stadium is now closed. The last time I was there, everyone sat on one butt cheek for one quarter and shifted to the other cheek for the next one. And everyone stood for the halftime show. Going to the men's restroom was like a cattle call. Nothing could compare to hanging my anatomy out in front of thirty other guys at a trough with others lined up ten deep behind each of us. The guy behind me was mumbling something about why I was taking so long.

I chuckled out loud and Marty poked me.

"What are you thinking?" she asked.

"I wasn't thinking, just remembering old times. I tell you what, I think I must be onto something because he sure pulled over quick. Maybe OSU's security is similar to what it is at UC's Nippert Stadium. Perhaps they do a cursory check of bags and wand people. For sure no umbrellas are allowed – but since it's a spring practice game, I'm guessing their attention level won't be as high as it would be for a regular season game."

Marty nodded her head, agreeing with me. "Tommy's coming back. Let me do the talking," I said.

Tommy got back into the seat behind the wheel, continuing in the same direction we'd been going before the abrupt stop. I figured we had maybe a half hour before we reached the farm.

"Well … what did they say?" I asked.

Again I found myself looking into the rear view mirror for a response. "C'mon man. You didn't stop to call some chick," I said sarcastically.

This time his head jerked around instantly … I knew I'd crossed an invisible line. Slowing the car down, he turned to me and said, "You do want to go see your horse perform today, don't you?"

"All I'm asking is for you to share," I told him. "Look, I know I'm right. It's got to be the stadium … something's going to happen today. I feel …" before I could get the "it" out, we were off the road once again.

"Dr. Becker, or should I say Rob Becker, there are certain things you don't need to know. Yes, your thoughts were very helpful and I shared them with the proper individuals. Your job is to focus on where you saw our John Doe before your casino encounter yesterday. You do your best and we'll do ours." Tommy was done talking.

And we were back on the road again.

I knew I'd helped and took solace in that fact. The frustration of not remembering where I'd seen this terrorist was wearing on me. Until someone told me differently, that's what he was – a terrorist –

and no amount of political correctness would change that.

Tommy's call wasn't about my sleuthing abilities and my intuitive powers. He simply wanted to tell his superiors what I now suspected … and to get guidance on how much additional classified information I was entitled to know.

The moment NSA headquarters became aware of the *Dispatch* connection, assets within three hundred miles of Columbus were notified and already on the road or in the air on their way to Ohio's capital city. Web chatter that week had also referenced Ohio's capital and that helped trigger the immediate response from federal agencies.

Everything was going as Ahmad's Uncle Ben had planned.

CHAPTER 26

Donnie was downing his second cup of coffee and it was only 5:30 a.m. "Would the weather wreak havoc with today's race and mess up the results?" he worried. Post time for the Stakes Race was 4:35 p.m., but the forecast made the late afternoon start time a moot point.

Using the weather app on his phone, he was watching where the storms were and how fast the front was moving. You could see him calculating when they'd arrive in central Kentucky. He'd already watched every weather forecast on the television news with their predicted time of arrival of severe storms – but Donnie liked doing his own math.

He'd grown up in the west. He'd seen his share of forest fires and learned their patterns. In the evening, with cooling temperatures, a fire would lie down, but with dawn, it would strengthen and grow. It was the same with severe weather. The sun comes up, air temperatures and humidity rise – and storm energy increases.

It was going to be a long day.

Lance spent the night inside TA's trackside barn – armed with a nine millimeter handgun, and his conceal and carry permit. The group had decided to supplement Lance's regular earnings on the farm by paying him what they'd shell out for a security guard. If the track administration had a problem with that arrangement, they'd deal with it then ... if challenged. In their eyes, there could never be too much security before TA's big race days.

The horse had quickly become very special to his fans. Every day, over a thousand pieces of mail arrived at the farm, with people wanting a lock of TA's hair or asking to have a photograph taken with him. You name it, folks requested it.

There were also the evil notes, threatening harm if this or that happened. Donnie and Lance were amazed at how many individuals were mentally unhinged. They would try to hide the haters and their messages from Mike and myself, but I received my own disgusting fan mail – and most of it was from the same individuals.

"Lance, after TA is done with his light meal, would you take him out to the paddock and school him one last time?" Donnie asked, approaching the stall. On race days, TA got half his usual feed early in the day, and then fasted four hours before his race. TA always knocked his feed pail around when he finished the half meal because he knew what was happening. It was time to run.

"Sure will boss," Lance replied. Lance had worked for him ever since Donnie bought the farm in Paris, Kentucky; he'd left Montana right after his divorce. The divorce and death of his father quickly severed any binding ties Donnie had to the west – and when I came up with our *"things we'd like to do if there been a genie to grant our wish"* list, well that only cemented Donnie's decision to move back to the Heartland.

In his younger days, Lance had been an exercise rider and knew Thoroughbreds as well as anyone associated with the track on any given day … at least as far as he was concerned. If Donnie had asked him to, Lance would have saddled TA and taken him out for a breeze that very moment. Right now, though, he could tell that Donnie was the one saddled – with worry. Besides the weather, TA hadn't been at ease during the past week.

The unease started the previous week when Towers Above took up residence in Donnie's barn at the track. Lance had breezed him on the Saturday prior to the start of the track's Spring Meet, and three days later, took him out for schooling in preparation for his upcoming race.

Schooling a horse familiarizes the Thoroughbred to that particular track's environment and the routine that's followed on a race day before proceeding onto the track's surface. Two-year-olds are usually the most skittish about this undertaking, occasionally needing several trips to both paddocks before race day to be more at ease.

It was nearly noon on Thursday when they entered the gate, emerging onto the pathway of the saddling paddock. TA had bells on so he couldn't clip his heels; they walked towards a mature maple tree with the numbers 1-2 posted on the each side of the tree.

Lance's assistant, Juan, carried a blanket, pad and saddle and stood nearby while Lance, leading TA, circled the tree three times. Halfway around the fourth circle, TA dug in his heels, refusing to move any further. Across from the paddock, behind the low tan colored pipe rail and shrubs, stood an elderly man dressed in the standard employee track garb. His eyes were focused on the most beautiful horse flesh he'd ever seen. And the only one that noticed him was Towers Above.

Among the hundreds of others watching TA at that moment, the horse noticed only that one man – and for him – the man represented danger. Sensing the horse's nervousness, Lance didn't force him to move, instead reining him closer, gently patting his neck and whispering some calming words. But TA was having none of it. Lance could tell he was frightened, but of what?

Lance motioned for Juan to come and take the strap and as soon as he grabbed hold of the halter's lead, Lance stepped away and began sweeping the paddock grounds with his eyes. Usually something falls, like a tree branch. "Maybe it's a woman's flashy attire or her latest Michael Kors purse with its bright color that caught TA's eye," Lance thought.

The watcher saw Lance give up the horse's lead and observed as Lance scanned the crowd. The man decided it was time to move on – however, he would be back again. He'd been present last year when TA ran at the track as a juvenile Thoroughbred … the man needed to watch him as much as possible now, because the horse had matured.

TA pawed the soft tiles encircling the tree as Lance took the lead back from Juan. Together they placed the blanket, pad and saddle on TA, then cinched up the saddle. After the national anthem was sung, they proceeded around the rotary to the second paddock where, had this been a race day, Joey would have been given a leg up. The workers at the crossover between the paddock arenas pulled the tan straps, so no patrons could spook TA as he crossed. He proceeded to do three turns around the paddock oval before gracefully exiting the same gate he'd entered.

On Friday, as they did the day before, the schooling was repeated and went off without a hitch. Donnie figured Thursday's incident was a fluke.

At 9:00 a.m. Saturday morning – race day – Lance put the halter on TA and led him toward the track once again. For some reason, even though Friday's schooling had been unremarkable, Donnie felt compelled to walk along. The beautiful morning sky made Donnie forget for the moment what the vivid colors portended.

"Don't trust me this morning, boss?" Lance said half laughing.

Donnie needed the jab and returned the sarcasm. "After this race you're done. No sense in taking you to Churchill for the Derby …"

Passing through the entrance gate, which they had to open themselves, the two headed with TA for the 1-2 marked maple tree when TA stopped suddenly. Saturday became Thursday all over again.

"What the hell?" Lance stammered. Then TA began tugging and backing up simultaneously.

There's no way to stop a horse when they move that quickly. A human just doesn't have the strength to combat an unexpected move like that. Lance moved in sync with TA, doing his best to wrest control.

"Try to calm him, Lance … turn him out. He's spotted something." Donnie was shouting now. Donnie eyeballed the paddock and spied a single track employee standing thirty yards away. He had a cap on and the unmistakable tan all-weather coat that was standard track-issue to employees. He was turning and starting to move away.

"Hey you … hold up there … please stop. I want to talk with you," Donnie shouted. The stranger ignored his plea and began moving away faster. Donnie broke into a run, heading towards the rotary. There was no way he could successfully hurdle the hedge and tan rail. He turned in the direction of the grandstand and track – but the stranger was gone.

"What the ...? Did he go upstairs to the grandstand seats? Damn it," Donnie grumbled to himself. "If that employee shows up at post-time, he'll spook TA! That's all we need, some guy freaking out our horse," he thought.

Bent over, trying to catch his breath, Donnie heard his cell phone begin to bugle – his ring tone was a rendition of Boots and Saddles.

"Donnie, it's me. You're not going to believe what happened last night and early this morn...."

"Rob ... stop just a second. We've had an incident here in the paddock," Donnie interrupted Rob.

"Is TA alright?" I asked.

"He's spooked and probably a little washed out, but otherwise as far as I can tell right now ... he's okay, I guess." Donnie headed back towards Lance and Towers Above.

I began to tell Donnie about my evening and the new best friend I'd be bringing to the track. The more I talked, the more I

217

spooked Donnie.

"Rob, listen up … what just went down here and with what you've just told me, there's something going on and I'm really … ya' know. First you, then this morning and this past Thursday – we've never had a problem anywhere that TA has raced," Donnie said.

"Slow down Donnie," I said, pausing to collect my thoughts. "Donnie, you still there?"

"Yeah!"

"They have cameras all over that place. Somebody told me there are over two hundred fifty of them. Go find someone from security and ask to speak with the head guy. Tell them what happened and see if they'll review the videos, and while you're at it, have them look at the video from Thursday. Don't hesitate to tell them what I told you about my experiences last evening. Marty and I are going to clean up and we'll be there in a bit," I stated.

"Oh and Donnie … if you get a chance, text Mike and fill him in. I'll text Mark and tell him it might be best if he stayed clear of the track today. There's going to be a lot of Feds hanging around the track," I told him before ending the call.

"When TA gets back, give him a drink and a bath, he's washing out. Then after he's cooled down, give him a brushing," Donnie said to Lance. "I'm going to the administration offices and hopefully talk with someone from security and let them know what happened. I'll get back to the barn as soon as I can. Oh – and after he has cooled out, rub his joints down with the Bigeoil, please," Donnie asked.

"I wonder if I can use some of that Bigeoil on my right shoulder," Lance mumbled to himself. The liquid, used as a rub, is an anti-inflammatory and TA loved a good rub. Lance had used it before on his own sore joints, ignoring the "not for human use" warning label posted on the jug of gel.

Washing out for a horse, especially at post time, almost always ends in a poor showing during the race. It's like taking a five mile jog in a sauna and then being asked to sprint an additional mile. There just isn't enough fluid remaining in the body, and the musculoskeletal system shuts down. Luckily for TA, there was enough time to recover before today's Stakes Race.

As Lance and Towers Above passed through the gate, Lance looked at his horse and said, "Just nine more hours TA. Hang in there buddy. Let's win this thing and then we'll go smell some roses." And TA in his best attempt to speak, whinnied as loud as he could for all to hear.

CHAPTER 27

Just beyond the elevators, was TRC's trackside mobile TV broadcasting studio. There were no lights, no cameras and no action happening this early in the morning, but the television tent was perfect for someone who wanted to hide out for a bit. There was one lone occupant inside … someone definitely interested in keeping a low profile.

During the previous fall meet, Ahmad's uncle hid in that same spot for the first time, patiently waiting for the moment when an unsuspecting paddock employee would put down his tan all-weather coat. He wasn't disappointed as an unsuspecting employee soon arrived, took off his coat and left it – giving Ben the few seconds needed to make his move and grab the coat.

With that theft, Ben's track employee wardrobe was complete – he had everything needed to look like the others. He knew that the track uniforms never appeared worn or dated since employees only wore them twice each year – in the Spring and Fall. It wasn't hard to find a caramel sport coat to buy and embroider the track's WP logo on it. And even though he thought the ties sold at the track's gift shop were outrageously expensive, he bought a couple of them. The grey slacks came from Sam's Club. Accessories included an American flag lapel pin and a track name tag – both easily replicated to match what the actual employees wore. He'd also purchased an umbrella adorned with the track's logo – which he modified for this special and final day.

Counting slowly to three hundred, he peeked around the all-weather curtain to make sure the coast was clear. It was – and Ben hastily made his way to the main entrance.

He passed through the entrance, knowing that if all went as planned, it would be the next-to-last time he would enter the track facilities.

It was a half mile walk to his car in the employee parking lot, where earlier, he'd parked under a mature sycamore tree. Climbing into the driver's seat, he started the car, and cranked up the air conditioning. He wasn't alone in the parking lot. as by now, many of the track's food prep employees had arrived for work and were now heading to their respective positions.

"God that horse is beautiful, but he could be collateral damage. How many signals do I have to give them? God knows I've tried to spook the horse enough that the owners are worried," he mused, wiping sweat from his brow. "If they can't interpret my warnings … then that's not my fault."

There was still a little time before he made the 9 a.m. call to Jamil … Ben's mind wandered even more. In fact, he was laughing to himself and reflecting how blessed he was that everything had come together. The drama at the Horseshoe Casino the previous night was superb.

The interview in the *Wall Street Journal* with Rob Becker when TA was named the "Two Year Old Horse of the Year," had been spot on – and provided Ben with some additional guidance for his plan. Becker had been quoted on how he prepared before each Stakes Race, telling the reporter he liked to get away the night before and that a good game of blackjack relaxed him, taking his mind off the next day's activities. The article even included how much he liked the Horseshoe Casino … that in fact, it was now his favorite casino.

The scenario that Ben, Ahmad and Jamil couldn't be certain of, though, was whether the casino of choice that night would be the Horseshoe Casino in Indiana or downtown Cincinnati's newer Jack Casino Cincinnati. Ahmad was waiting in Indiana, while Jamil was in Cincinnati. If it was the Jack Casino, Jamil would have to search for Dr. Becker as there were several twenty-five dollar two-deck tables. The casino in Indiana had a smaller footprint but only one active two-deck twenty-five dollar table – which was where Becker found his open seat – very near to Ahmad.

Not only had Ben managed to spook Becker's horse twice that week, but he felt certain that by now, two of the three owners had to be questioning whether it was worth the risk of running their horse that day. Maybe they'd do right by Towers Above and scratch him. TA already had enough points to qualify for the Kentucky Derby. Either way, he was convinced more than ever that success was at hand.

It was 9:00 and time to call Jamil.

"Yes," Jamil answered, hoping his uncle would tell him everything was cancelled.

"I'm all set here. Your departure should be at 11:00 and no later. Remember, travel along I-75 and then follow I-71. Fly no higher than three thousand feet and be careful around the capital. If the winds are too strong, proceed directly to the stadium. It won't take long before you have company. Do you have any questions?"

224

Jamil hesitated a bit too long. "Jamil … did you hear me?"

"Yes," he answered meekly … and then there was silence.

Jamil wanted nothing more than to drive away from the airport and head west to be with his brother. They could join up and when they felt confident no one was looking for them, they would escape. With that thought in mind, he turned the key in the ignition and put the car in drive … then suddenly slammed his foot down on the brake pedal. The reality and consequences of what had already occurred hit home hard … there really was no turning back. He could turn himself in to the authorities, but he would still do prison time. The federal penitentiaries had more than enough inmates who would guarantee him a quick journey to see Allah. No, he had no choice. Turning off the car, he opened the driver's door and got out, heading towards the plane.

In the meantime, his uncle grabbed a sandwich and a cola from the back seat – settling in for a meal and a little nap before setting up his ambush prior to the Stakes Race.

He laughed at the unique quality of the moment, wondering how many people have the opportunity to know they're eating the last meal of their life?

"All thee, all thee … in come free," Ben thought.

CHAPTER 28

Donnie stood at the receptionist's desk waiting to see the head of security for what seemed an eternity to him. Finally the outside door opened.

"Connie, what's going on?" Ted asked the receptionist, as he removed his hat.

"Sir, this is Donnie, TA's trainer and one of its owners, He's here because ... well, I'll let him tell you."

"Thanks Connie. Hello Donnie, I'm Ted. Have we met?"

"Yes sir, we met last year when TA raced in the spring," Donnie replied.

Ted already knew that. How could anyone not know who Donnie was? He and the other owners of Towers Above had been on the cover of nearly every horse racing publication in North America and abroad. He still had the security video of TA and his entourage from the two-year-old's Stakes Race the previous year. But no one other than his boss and the track's Director of Racing Operations knew it existed. "So … Connie told me on the radio that there were some problems in the paddock this morning," Ted said questioningly to Donnie.

Donnie proceeded to give details surrounding the morning issues and the unknown man who so obviously spooked TA – and he also shared Rob's unsettling experience at the casino the previous night. Ted sat on the edge of his chair, seeming to show a genuine interest. And he was – except for the events at the Horseshoe – Ted already knew about that after receiving an e-mail alert from Homeland Security in the early morning hours. He'd also gotten a phone call from Tommy, Rob's new BFF.

The message read: *ALERT … Probable terrorist attack at any venues with expected attendance #s greater than 1K this weekend. All states are included! Special emphasis for the states of Indiana, Kentucky & Ohio – the threat level is high!*

The e-mail also included the photo of Ahmad at the casino along with picture of the Accord, and a video clip of Ben's rental car which had been retrieved from the American Legion's security camera. The message also pointed out that the terrorists were most likely home-grown and that all possible scenarios needed to be considered – and further pushed home the seriousness of the situation: *All flights into and out of D. Boone Airport are cancelled this weekend.*

Please note the following cover story for the airport closure: A sinkhole in the main runway cancels air traffic in and out of the D.Boone Airport. Damage is not significant and flights are expected to resume in 48-72 hours.

Specific events of note that may be affected: all events in central and southwest Ohio and events in Louisville and all of Kentucky.

The bulletin had Einstein's intelligence information embedded within it – all parameters of the existing evidence had been analyzed and the resulting data indicated the highest probability of an attack would occur in any of these urban zones.

Donnie finished chronicling events of the past few days and was silent as Ted picked up the phone. "Connie, get JC on the line and have him call me immediately please." It took less than twenty seconds before JC returned Ted's call.

"JC, I want you to gather up all the security footage for today from 12:00 a.m. until now and ... hold on a second."

"Donnie, I've got another call coming in and this phone doesn't let me take two calls at once. I'll be back in a second. JC, I'm putting you on hold." With that, Ted left the room and entered an adjoining office, closing the door behind him.

"Okay, listen up JC! I received a flash e-mail from Homeland Security this morning and there's a possibility that we might have some real shit going down here this afternoon. The government has shut down the airport – we also had some trouble in the paddock Thursday and again this morning. And ... one of the owners of Towers Above was involved in some unnerving events at a casino in Indiana last night. There are spring college football scrimmages all over the tristate area – and this is the highest threat level I've ever witnessed. Do you remember the rumors last year when TA raced here?"

"No, boss I don't recall," JC answered.

"Supposedly there was an incident in the barns – a stranger wandering around the horse barns carrying either a baseball bat or baton, depending upon who's telling the story. He was about to open TA's stall ... but got spooked by someone coming in. The guy then disappeared. We asked Dr. Becker if that report was true, but he brushed the question off. I want you to contact our IT people and have them go through video archives from the week that TA was boarded here."

Pointing out the urgency to this request, Ted emphatically said to JC, "Tell them I need answers now! I'm going back to finish up with Donnie. I'll ask him about that incident, too, but I doubt anything comes from it. Thanks." Ted returned to the other office where Donnie was waiting nervously.

"Sorry about the delay Donnie. I told JC to start reviewing video from this morning and Thursday – and now this may not be anything, but I was wondering if something happened last year when TA was here. Could there be something from a year ago that's connected to what's going on now?"

Ted watched as Donnie started to fidget in his chair. As a former Army Ranger and special operative, he knew he'd hit a nerve and could tell that Donnie was hesitant to talk about it. Ted had been hired after the last Challenge Cup races and was now strongly focused on upgrading security at the track.

Suddenly, Donnie buried his head in his hands. Again, experience made Ted pause and not press the issue. "Give him time and a little slack, then slowly reel him in," Ted thought to himself.

"Look, Lance was supposed to be at the stall that morning, but wasn't – and Juan had just entered the barn and was coming around the corner when he saw this guy opening the gate. When he saw Juan coming, the guy ran off … that's what went down that day. I didn't think it was significant at the time – and I didn't want the other owners to come down on Lance. I was worried they'd fire him … I mean, he knows this horse better than we all do. Are you thinking the guy today is the same one as last year?" Donnie asked, expecting an answer he didn't want to hear.

"Did the guy have a ball bat?" Ted gently asked. Donnie paused a good half minute. "It was a cane, a walking cane. God, I'm sorry … I'm so stupid!" Donnie could barely get the words out.

"Donnie … Donnie! Listen to me. I'd have probably done the same thing if I'd been in your shoes. I'm not one to tell you what to do or say, but thanks for being upfront with me. Why don't you head back to the barns and I'll get the videos from last year's races?" Ted said.

Donnie headed back to the barn.

It was Ted's turn to squirm in his seat. Suddenly he felt light-headed as bright rays of light started flashing in front of his eyes – he was going to pass out and quickly lowered his head towards his knees. His office couldn't get any smaller, he thought. He felt like the walls were pressing in on him and he couldn't catch his breath.

Panic attacks are like that.

After spending several minutes inhaling and exhaling deeply, Ted regained his composure, and grabbing a bottle of cold water from the mini fridge, started furiously jotting notes down on a legal pad.

The airport closure is understandable since it's only a two miles away from the track – now any potential air assault would be handled more easily by fighter planes patrolling overhead. Highway patrol officers would be pulled from their regular duties to reinforce Metro and track security. The bomb-sniffing dogs were already scheduled to be at the track for additional training in preparation for the crowds at the upcoming Derby.

All this was included in Ted's written notes – with an immediate call to action for every security agency involved. *"Call an urgent meeting with the team leaders and pass out copies of all photos, along with descriptions of the makes and models of the cars involved in the casino incident.*"

He picked up the phone one more time. "Connie, we need to call an emergency meeting. Now … and there are no excuses for anyone not attending. Also, tell the boss I'm on the walkie-talkie."

There was no way Ted would take the fall for what might happen on this day. There would be shared responsibility.

CHAPTER 29

Just slightly over three hundred miles north-northeast of Ted's location at the Kentucky track, the campus facilities of The Ohio State University were under lock-down in the pre-dawn hours. The vast complex of buildings would not harbor evil that day.

Together with faculty and staff, the university's security teams went room-to-room and lab-to-lab, clearing every floor – one at a time. Unlike their counterparts in the south – the university's security detection tools were state-of-the art – they were equipped with all of FLIR Systems infrared thermal imaging and threat detection equipment. Some of the graduate assistants protested when they were told to leave the facilities – but decided to not argue when the officer's weapons were unholstered. There was no attempt at secrecy ... people were texting all over campus and beyond that something was going down at Ohio State. If those same individuals had bothered to turn on the television or go online, they would have heard or read about the tornado warning and a heightened terror alert in central Ohio that weekend.

OSU's Don Scott airport was also shut down.

There weren't any excuses given for its closure – just an "OSU's Don Scott Airport is closed until further notice" statement released by university officials. Those high-roller alumni flying in their private planes to attend the spring scrimmage that day would be filing different flight plans now – as Port Columbus International Airport prepared itself for more air traffic. Television news was even speculating that the Air National Guard F-16s and F-35s from Stanton Air Force Base in northwest Ohio would cover the airspace over Columbus 24/7 for the next two days.

In the university's administration building, OSU's president and athletic director were huddled in the president's office, debating whether to postpone the spring scrimmage game or not. Also taking part in the discussion were the university police chief, the Superintendent of the Ohio Highway Patrol and Columbus's chief of police. Sitting silently at the end of the table was a liaison from the Governor's office.

OSU is a unique entity in and of itself. In addition to its moniker preposition of "The" before Ohio State University, the land on which campus buildings sit is owned by the state of Ohio, and the entity ultimately responsible for on-campus law enforcement is the Ohio Highway Patrol. Surrounding the university are roads policed by the city of Columbus law enforcement officials. During the

Vietnam campus riots in 1970, Ohio Highway Patrol troopers drove rioters off campus property and onto Columbus streets where they were met by Columbus's finest dressed in full riot gear.

Colonel Wallace "Wally" Robinson was the current Superintendent of the Highway Patrol – and in no mood to repeat history that day. He called the meeting to order and asked the OSU president if he'd made a decision about canceling the scrimmage that day.

"My decision is to proceed with the game, but it is contingent on your troopers being able to provide the necessary security," the university president responded. "If there is any doubt that they can handle the task, then I'll issue a statement postponing the day's events."

The Colonel had anticipated the challenge and gladly accepted. "I've already called up the Auxiliary Force and extended our shifts, and also issued a call for all off-duty troopers to report for assignment. The Special Response team is deploying as we speak. I've also coordinated with Homeland Security about how to best utilize our Fixed Wing and Helicopter assets. I've been informed that agents from Homeland are expected here within an hour."

The Colonel knew what was at stake on this day. The

potential of a hundred thousand or more fans, along with gate proceeds of easily over a half million dollars that the scrimmage would bring in, just couldn't be ignored. Future football recruits would be present and the budgets of the university's other NCAA sports teams were also dependent upon revenues from the game.

"We've all trained for these possible situations and I believe we're prepared," Robinson told those assembled in the room. "But for the record, I would like to defer to the Governor's representative for his opinion on what our decision should be." The Colonel slumped in his chair and waited for the final decision to be made. He knew the Governor had aspirations of political office beyond Ohio's borders and that Las Vegas had current odds of 20:1 that he would be the Republican nominee for President of the United States in a few years. There was no way terrorist threats would shut down a sacred Ohio tradition. Weakness and cowardice were perceptions to be avoided when seeking the highest office in America.

"Colonel, you give me too much latitude and responsibility when I speak for the Governor. He sends his regards and wishes he could be here this morning. He has the utmost faith in everyone's judgment concerning this situation," the liaison said. "The only thing I'll reiterate on his behalf is that all of you were appointed by him based on interviews and experience. You all indicated that you were fully aware of possible crises of this type – and each one of you accepted those possibilities when you accepted your position. With that in mind, he wishes you success in the event something unfortunate occurs today."

The colonel nodded in the affirmative while silently praising the Governor's aide for gracefully placing responsibility back on the appointees – but knowing nonetheless that the ultimate responsibility still rested with the Governor. "If there is no further business to be brought before us this morning then this meeting is adjourned and may God watch over our University today."

Now, somehow, the final responsibility rested with God!

CHAPTER 30

Dozens of meetings were taking place throughout the Tri-State region during the early hours on this potentially ill-fated Saturday. Ted's boss, Art, raced into the administration offices – shouting orders at Connie as he sprinted to Ted's office.

"Have you seen the news? Good God ... what the hell's going on?" Art demanded, grabbing the remote and turning on the television. Not given a chance to reply, Ted watched, cringing as Art cranked up the volume well beyond the setting needed for even the most hard-of-hearing. In addition to the news banners scrolling across the bottom of the screen, the anchor of the CBS affiliate was confirming what Ted already knew – first and foremost, there was a terrorist threat for venues in the Ohio Valley region. Topping off what was most likely going to be a horrific day, there was also a tornado warning issued for the entire state of Kentucky, and the Daniel Boone Regional Airport had been shut down – thanks to a sinkhole that opened up on the main runway. In this quaint Southern Kentucky region, these were huge news events by themselves – but combined – and on the same day?

"OK, so what the hell's going on?" Art repeated, glaring at

Ted, knowing full well that Ted was privy to some information that he didn't have. Again, not giving Ted an opportunity to respond, he shouted, "Well?"

"Boss ... turn the TV off and sit down. Please." Leaning against the edge of his desk, hoping to regain a necessary position of control, Ted went through the events of the morning. When he was done speaking, Ted paused long enough to give Art a chance to say, "We need a meeting pronto."

Anticipating this very action, Ted said to Art, "Boss, I took the liberty of having Connie make the calls and send text messages ... with your blessing attached."

And for a long moment neither man spoke.

"Art, if we are the target of an attack today – or tomorrow for that matter – I truly hope every one of us in the meeting this morning understands the gravity of the situation. Off the record, I talked with the federal agent, Tommy, who's been assigned to remain with Rob Becker. I know him. He feels of the two specific targets – the Ohio State Stadium and here in Kentucky at this track – his gut instinct leads him to believe that we are the primary target. But he also told me that NSA's current computer analysis has tagged Ohio Stadium as the number one target because of the sheer numbers of people who would be at the scrimmage game – and the effect it would have on the psyche of Americans if an attack did take place there."

Art started to interrupt, but Ted continued.

"I know, you're wondering why I would believe this agent. Well, frankly sir, I think terrorists feel that we are the soft target. Look ... we're a park-like setting. People walk their dogs on our grounds, for Christ's sake ... and their animals crap all over the property. People have picnics and weddings here, they can walk through the paddocks at all hours. The only remotely curious acknowledgement from anyone is the occasional 'do y'all need any help finding anything'?"

Pausing to organize his thoughts, Ted elaborated more on which venue he believed was the potential attack site. "People have no idea about our level of security ... we've had this argument for years as to whether we should be open and honest about it. You know, we always come down in accord with the experts who advise to never tip your hand – because as soon as you do – the bad guys start to find ways around your capabilities and technology."

Giving   Art time to process this information, Ted told his boss what he needed – and what he didn't need – from the teams, hoping to impress upon Art the importance of keeping the meeting under control and on task.

"Frankly, the last thing I need right now is for everyone to come in here today and suddenly decide they know all about security – and tell us that we need to do this or that. For me, having this meeting run on and on until Miss Appalachia sings the National Anthem at 11:30 a.m. … well, I just don't have the patience and we don't have the luxury of time. I need you to run a quick meeting. I'll have my security agenda outlined and what I intend to do with it," Ted said, handing Art the notes he'd drafted earlier to look at before continuing.

"Art, I need your trust and I need your vote of confidence. I know that's asking a lot, but if I don't get it – I swear I'll resign right here and now! If something happens today, I'm going to be blamed and hell … you're also going to be out of a job. Nobody promised this would be easy, but right now I don't need any political wishy-washy crap. All we can do is what we know is right – and that which we've been trained to do! It's imperative the meeting be in Executive Session and if it runs any later than 10:30, well I'm out of there. Have I left anything out?"

Ted left Art speechless … but only for a second!

"I really don't have much choice at this point. Don't think I'm not appreciative of what you do – but you and I both know this meeting is going to be pure chaos," Art told him. "Have the final outline of what you're setting up plus a list of our existing security capabilities on my desk in twenty minutes. I'll cover for you." Ted, heading to his office to finish compiling the list, was stopped once more by Art who added, "Ted, I sincerely hope you and that agent are wrong about an attack here or anywhere else this weekend."

* * *

Computers are a wonderful means of getting something done yesterday. As Ted sat at his desk and spoke his thoughts out loud, the computer recorded and dictated every word and sent it to a printer. After ending a sentence or thought, Ted said "stop." In less than five minutes, the computer had recorded and printed twenty copies of the security assets available throughout the grounds for the weekend.

One of the primary points in Ted's outline was threat detection … beginning with the word FLIR.

FLIR Systems, an American security company, manufactures and bundles a series of products used in combating terrorist threats. However, Ted was not going into specifics about the equipment his security staff should have possessed. That morning, when the Board of Directors did an online search for FLIR, they would be directed to the company's web site which elaborated on the company's assets – and they would learn that FLIR manufactures explosive, biological, chemical and radiation detection equipment.

What the website doesn't show is the anti-terrorism equipment, known and available only to those in the country who hold the highest level security clearance. Ted remembered that the last time he flew on an airplane, a TSA agent wiped his briefcase with a small piece of cloth, then disappeared for a few minutes – he knew the agent was running the cloth through FLIR's equipment that detects specific explosive residue levels.

"Anyone can read a webpage. They're going to want to know exactly what products we are using and the real answer is zero," Ted mumbled to himself.

Nonetheless, Ted was sure the Board would assume these were items that he'd procured – and indeed, he was in the process of purchasing some unique products that were currently in beta testing across the country and abroad. Since Ted had been recently hired to replace Captain Hanson as head of security, he and the track's Board of Directors had promised FLIR and the government that they'd protect any proprietary and confidential information about these products. He knew full well they'd pay enormous fines if any of this technology was ever compromised. The bottom line was that there was no way in hell Ted was going to reveal the track's lack of FLIR equipment inventory – and Art knew as much.

* * *

Entering the auditorium, Ted headed directly to the podium, putting on a lapel microphone and running a mic check. Pausing, he turned his back to the group of men and women now assembled in the auditorium seats.

Now, those anxiously waiting to hear what he had to say were the ones whose actions would determine whether he still had a job the following week. Those seated in the first few rows that were trained in reading body language would instantly see just how stressed Ted was.

Almost all of his security detachment was already in uniform – and half were armed. In the back of the room was a group of individuals in civilian clothing.

"Ladies and gentlemen, thanks for coming to this hastily-called meeting. I expect many of you are aware of the weather situation and that the airport has been shut down. I want to update you on another situation, and how all three relate to your job today and tomorrow. I would also very much appreciate that you not share this information with anyone. If you do, not only will you lose your job, you will jeopardize the welfare and reputation of this sacred institution."

He proceeded to chronicle the threats facing them throughout the weekend.

The proverbial "you could hear a pin drop" scenario was in play. If one of the track photographers had been taking pictures, the images would have shown mouths and eyes wide open in shock, beads of perspiration forming on some of their foreheads, and a general demeanor of panic and consternation.

Ted ended his update and instructions with a personal note. "Folks, as I already said, I have no idea what form of terrorist activity might occur this weekend. The only difference between yesterday and today is this might be the last day of our lives ... along with maybe hundreds of others. Every day people die unexpectedly from accidents, heart attacks and God knows what else! They just don't know that it's coming. Let's use our knowledge to our advantage."

Pausing a moment to let the fatalistic news sink in, Ted added a last caution. "Finally, I know I can't stop you from calling your loved ones to warn them – even if I were to confiscate your phones, I know you all could easily borrow a phone from someone else … even from a patron. If you do make a call, please realize your actions may tip off and postpone the terrorist's actions and will actually make it more difficult to stop an attack."

"Let's go do our job!"

"Team leaders, please hang around. We'll have another meeting in five minutes," Ted announced.

CHAPTER 31

Three separate security groups reported directly to Ted. Jim was team leader of the armed security group ... and the first person Ted pulled aside for specific instructions.

"I know you and your team still have questions. Let your guys know that after they're all in position, I'll be roaming throughout the entire track ... and I'll be in communication over the phone. I've assigned two non-uniformed men to you, Jim – Jamie and Hank – they'll also be able to communicate with the others by cell phone. Everyone on the special security team will be easily identifiable – they'll be wearing these ball caps with a special track logo, so if you see any men or women with these caps on, well – they're the good guys. Tell everyone on your team about these caps and also ... weapon safeties are off. Your team has new phones to use – these phones are pre-set to the same frequency, which is secure, and they also have a walkie-talkie function. There should be no hesitation – tell your men to challenge the slightest sign of abnormal behavior. Today, we're not worrying about our Ritz-Carlton brand of public relations."

Ted then turned to Ralph, who headed up the unarmed team of security officers – Ralph couldn't help overhearing Ted's discussion with Jim. "Do we get new phones too?" Ralph asked Ted – eliciting a quick smile. "Leave it to Ralph to break the tension with a sarcastic comment," he thought to himself.

"No, Ralph, you son of a …!"

Ted's message to Ralph was more low-key … but no less serious. "You and your men are still stuck with the old walkie-talkies – I'm way beyond budget with the new phones. Ralph, I need your group to act like it's a normal workday. If someone is coming after us, I want them to believe everything is status quo. Tell your crew to profile all they want, we're not being politically correct today. You're on the talkie now ... good hunting."

The last man Ted needed to update was Fred, who supervised the plain clothes security team. Fred had on his usual tan colored sport coat, grey slacks and white polo shirt – and all of Fred's fellow team members wore the same type of uninspired wardrobe – a uniform truly the epitome of "plain clothes." The one commonality of their clothing – which would be immediately noticed by any good tailor – was that every man's sport coat was one size too large. That was intentional though, as the larger jacket allowed the men to strap on their nine millimeter semi-automatic pistols, comfortably and inconspicuously. "Fred, usually your folks are right in the thick of it

... but not today. I need two of your men up on the hill, another two in back around the barns, and two more roaming the parking lots."

Fred wasn't listening. He was staring at the back of the auditorium where about twenty men and woman dressed as casually as his team, but ten times more GQ, were assembled. Ted looked in the same direction and said, "Those people are Feds and I wouldn't be surprised if some of them are CIA. They give a whole new meaning to the word secret. I'm your boss, but today they own you ... and your men. If you ignore their orders, the consequences are on you, not me." Driving home the import of this, Ted added, "personally, I wouldn't want to be looking over my shoulder the rest of my life. More will be arriving throughout the day, coming in from Atlanta, Chicago and St. Louis. Tell your men to ask for ID – and to respect their badge. I'm sorry Fred ... really sorry."

Finished with his briefings, Ted headed to the group in the back, ostensibly to introduce himself and the team leaders to their new interim bosses. Fred had no way of knowing that Ted was no stranger to the federal agents, and that in fact, he'd worked with a number of them in the Middle East.

Sinking into one of the auditorium seats, Ted closed his eyes and said a prayer before getting up and heading to the auditorium's doors. Usually unlocked, Ted made sure that on this day, the doors were now secured.

It was time to meet up with yet another group of agents who had come to help. Heading to the   doors, Ted approached the four men silently waiting just outside the doorway.

"Gentlemen, thank you for being here on such short notice. Here are your All Access badges – be sure to wear them at all times! It's time to take up your positions on the roof – the equipment is already in place. These secure phones have a walkie-talkie function – and there are only two people that can communicate with you over these phones. One is me, and my call sign is Adam. The other person is your number one boss, Tommy – his call sign is Talon. Both of us will be able to hear every communication that takes place."

He distributed the badges and phones before continuing.

"It's critical that you make contact with Talon before acquiring any target. Talon is the only person … and I repeat … the only person that can give you the go-ahead to take a shot," Ted cautioned the agents.

"Tommy and I will both do a radio check with all of you in

thirty minutes. Make sure you have your earpieces in. I hope and pray that nobody here has to use a weapon today. Oh – and memorize the image of this ball cap – anyone you see wearing this cap today is one of the good guys."

Done with the briefings, Ted left the auditorium, and headed back to his office to check in with JC and Art, worrying to himself, "Thank God Tommy's assets are arriving … but this venue's security is still too soft."

* * *

Calling out loudly to Marty to see if she was ready to leave, I was told she needed another ten to fifteen minutes to finish getting ready. That gave me time to strap on my holster and check the clip in my nine millimeter Glock.

The thought of carrying a weapon or owning one was foreign to me for most of my life. Years ago, my father had offered me his 22 revolver, but I declined. While on Naval Duty at Newport Rhode Island, I reluctantly joined some fellow officers at the shooting range where I was introduced to a 45 automatic pistol – that was not an experience I remembered fondly.

Besides being nearsighted, my wrists had stopped growing when I was twelve – and the pistol felt like it weighed fifty pounds in my hands. Even when I tried to mimic the stereotypical film detective and support my shooting hand with the other, I knew the target was safe from harm. My dislike for guns continued for many years, even after Marty and I, along with our children, walked in on a robbery in progress at our home.

Perhaps my aversion to guns started to diminish when I acquired a number of local law enforcement members as patients. Even though we were in close quarters in the treatment room, I understood that there was no way their weapons would be removed, even had I requested it.

Then one day, a local dermatologist was shot and killed by a disgruntled patient just a few miles from my office. The newspaper article didn't elaborate on a motive – but I doubted it was the first time a physician had been killed because he or she failed to resolve someone's health issues.

I suddenly realized that a Louisville Slugger wasn't enough protection in the event some head-case patient decided to burst past the ladies at the front desk. The realization that the only time the office was truly secure was when a police officer was in the office as a patient. That was what convinced me it was time to get a gun. After asking one of my law enforcement patients to recommend a good lightweight gun that would be easy for Marty and I to handle, I was told that a 38 revolver would meet our needs.

Shortly after that conversation, Marty and I headed to a friend's mountain home for a summer vacation ... with a 38 revolver carefully packed away in our luggage. Target practice was one of our activities at the cabin that week.

Hindsight being what it always is showed both of us that we needed far more than one week of target practice. I may have hit the target twice in ten shots that week – but Marty killed a three-inch thick Ponderosa Pine branch when the gun recoiled. If we hadn't been using hollow point bullets, perhaps the branch would have only been wounded instead of instantly becoming kindling.

Jarred out of my reverie by the sound of a door opening, I saw Marty coming around the corner. She spotted the gun. "You're not really taking that today?" she stated rather than asked.

"Why wouldn't I?" I answered tersely, now more comfortable and skilled in target practice than decades ago. Kentucky gun laws require a gun owner to place seven out of ten shots in a target's torso from a distance of seven yards in order to get a permit to carry – and I had that permit. After ten minutes of heated discussion, it was clear that neither of us was going to change our mind – and that she couldn't sway my decision to conceal and carry. As I put on my sport coat and checked its fit in the mirror, I couldn't help wondering if I could even make a torso shot today.

As we left the house, Marty couldn't resist a parting shot. "You sure you got everything you need Marshall Dillon?" I didn't bother to answer. Stopping short of the car, I turned back towards the house because I had forgotten something – our new companion.

Tommy wasn't in the house when we walked out the door, but suddenly emerged on the lawn, coming from the side of the sunroom, I realized he was on the phone with someone, somewhere, most likely getting the latest news … information I wanted to know. He got in the back of the car and began texting … I turned and just stared at him. He finally looked up and with a nod, effectively rebuffing me … and instead of giving me that update, he gave the nod for me to head to the track.

I had effectively become a chauffeur.

CHAPTER 32

It was late morning when we arrived at the track. Guest Services employees were clocking in for work and Ted had just finished up with his meetings in the pavilion. I dropped Marty and Tommy off at the south entrance for a very specific reason – one entrance had a posted *No Conceal and Carry* sign, while the other entrance didn't. Marty headed for the barns north of the paddocks, and I eventually sat down on a bench next to a paddock. I wanted to watch the jockeys mount their rides and proceed through the tunnel onto the track – I was also on the lookout for Len.

The paddock attendants were generally at their stations before 11:00 a.m. and I expected Len at any moment. I was always impressed by his demeanor and how good an ambassador he was for the sport – and I hoped the higher-ups at the track realized that.

I really wanted to pick Len's brain, especially since I still had no recollection of when and where I had crossed paths with the mystery man playing blackjack at the casino. "Maybe Len saw something that caught his attention in the past couple of years and will remember more than I do," I thought to myself. Len was a retired letter carrier from the U.S. Postal Service – and a people person, just like me. But where I might recognize an individual by their face or smile, yet struggle with the name, Len not only remembered the name and face, he could tell me if there were any distinguishable markings like a scar or beauty mark.

Wondering why Len still hadn't appeared, it suddenly dawned on me that given the circumstances, the morning staff meetings were going to run longer than usual. I was sure that all employees would be briefed about the situation and potential threats facing everyone today. It was a quarter past 11 when I finally caught sight of the workers heading to their posts.

Eventually, I spotted Len and got up, waving my arms frantically to catch his attention – but he didn't see me. I had to sprint to catch up with him.

"Len, wait up!" I shouted.

Len turned, recognized me and paused. "Rob, I don't have time to chit-chat today, I'm sorry but we've …"

"I know what you've got. I'm right in the middle of it. Just give me five minutes of your time and maybe you can help all of us with some answers … please," I pleaded.

I could see in his eyes that I needed to be quick with my words. The first of eleven races, including five Stakes Races that day, had a post time of 12:20 p.m. The horses would be coming through the north gates for Race One in a few moments and my time with Len would come to an abrupt end. I quickly gave him a short version of my previous eighteen hours, praying that Len would absorb at least two thirds of what I was saying.

"Len, you've got my cell number. I'm begging you, please ... in your spare moments ... before Towers Above comes into the paddock today, try to remember if there was anyone hanging around both paddocks when TA was schooling this year – or when he schooled and raced last year. Especially if it was a stranger to the track."

Calling on him to really concentrate, and knowing that he was good with names and faces, I gave him some further encouragement. "You know who the usual folks are who show up for racing meets. I'm going to leave a photo of the guy from last night – and if you recognize him, please let me know. I really appreciate your help." Giving his forearm a squeeze, I nodded goodbye. As I walked out, the horses were coming up from the barns, entering the paddock for saddling and the start of the first race.

It was not my intention to dump my problems on Len … he already had more than his share of issues to deal with. His wife was undergoing weekly chemotherapy for cancer, and I was pretty sure that after the Guest Services staff huddle that morning, he was worried that he might not be there for her after today.

Len started letting people with proper credentials in through the side entrance. I could see him glance down at the photo he'd placed on his chair every few moments. Bob, the attendant working with Len at the side entrance, suddenly pulled the caramel colored strap across, closing the entrance as Len sat down. "You alright, Len?" Bob asked.

Len wanted to answer "yes," but knew it was a lie – his heart was racing and signs of cardiac distress were evident. It'd been a while since he'd had an episode of angina – thankfully the nitroglycerine tablets were just a few inches away in the top of his ever-present cooler bag. He started to reach for the bag, but Bob was seconds ahead of him, knowing that Len had stents in his heart and he knew about the nitro. Bob also knew the drill … he'd had encounters with other individuals in cardiac distress and had been able to help. Seeing only the whites of Len's eyes now, Bob knew he had to act quickly – and placed the nitro under Len's tongue. It was now a matter of waiting for the medication to start dissolving in Len's mouth.

Within just a couple of heartbeats, the crushing feeling in Len's chest began to subside. Bob grabbed a cold bottle of water from the cooler and soaked a handkerchief to place on Len's forehead. Len's eyes quickly returned to normal and his heart rate began to slow down.

"You okay?" Bob asked. Len nodded in the affirmative. "How about heading down to First Aid if you're up to it?" Bob suggested. Len didn't answer, instead pulling his cell phone from his pocket. Scrolling through his list of contacts, Len touched the screen to dial a number.

I had barely arrived at the barn when my phone began to vibrate. "Len, I just left, what's going ...?" I didn't have time to finish my question as Len was talking in an agitated voice.

"Rob, you're not going to believe ..." Len paused to calm himself.

Some would identify Len's semi-conscious cardiac event as a

dream – others have defined it as an out-of-body experience.

"Rob, that picture you gave me … there was a young man here last year when Towers Above entered the paddock for some kind of Stakes Race for two year old Thoroughbreds. It's his eyes … I mean … the eyes are the same. The guy in your picture may look older, but strip away that goatee and I'll bet it's him!" Len said breathlessly.

"You better tell your friend he was here last spring. I gotta' go ..." The phone connection suddenly ended.

I found out later that Len spent the remainder of the day in the hospital.

"Tommy … it's Rob. My friend in the paddock just called and he's convinced that the guy at the Horseshoe last night was hanging around the saddling paddock last spring, during TA's Stakes Race. He said the guy didn't have a goatee then and ..." For the second time in two minutes, my phone connection was abruptly ended.

Tommy's first text was to NSA in Virginia … a few minutes later Ted's cell phone began to vibrate.

CHAPTER 33

Within minutes of Tommy's text to Ted, the photo of Ahmad at the casino was digitally altered for the final time. Several modifications were made, minus a moustache and chin hair, along with age variations, which resulted in a half dozen other possible photos of Ahmad.

Einstein had been busy as well, data-mining motor vehicle and driver's license records from Indiana, Kentucky and Ohio – looking for any driver's license photographs that bore a resemblance to the new Ahmad. Out of three dozen possible matches, Einstein narrowed the results down to two men who closely resembled the NSA's computer renderings.

The first person of interest was licensed to drive in the state of Ohio while the second was licensed in Kentucky. The Ohio driver had a first name of Samuel while his Kentucky counterpart was named Leonard.

Taking into account the resolution of the photos taken at the respective license bureaus, Einstein enhanced the images as much as possible. The results were confounding. Each time the photos were put through the rigors of his programmer's code, the end result produced the same word ... *Identical.* After a half dozen additional cycles, the seventh software run produced a different noun ... *Twins.*

Einstein simultaneously relayed the data to Tommy at the track and to the Homeland headquarters. Tommy took the photographs to the track's First Aid center where Len was waiting to be transported to the hospital's cardiac care unit downtown.

Showing the pictures to Len, Tommy didn't have to watch his face directly – the accelerated sound of the heart monitor was a head's up signal of Len's verbal confirmation and the positive ID – it was indeed Ahmad.

Tommy sent a text to his boss confirming the identification, knowing that Homeland Security agents would quickly be dispatched to each twin's home. Einstein also knew that other Federal agencies' respective IT groups would generate reports on income, health insurance, political affiliations, educational loans, employment history and of course ... any social media interactions. The world's largest democratic country whose core values embodied freedom from government intrusion had indeed evolved.

"First it was the Tsarnaev brothers at the Boston Marathon

and now identical twin brothers being terrorist threats ... the NSA had anticipated copycat attacks ... but perhaps not specifically one that involved identical siblings," Tommy thought, shaking his head.

Less than five minutes passed before copies of the driver's license photos and names of the suspected terrorists were transmitted nationwide and internationally. The information was also sent to network and cable television news organizations ... with an announcement that Homeland Security had raised the threat levels to *Severe.*

Time was running out and the NSA knew it – it was now time to enlist the public's help. Using the same psychology of those endless airport terminal messages about not leaving bags unattended, subliminally reminding travelers to report a piece of baggage without an obvious owner, news banners with the twin's names and pictures began to scroll across the bottom of television screens across the country. Every fifteen minutes, televised programming paused for a *We Interrupt this Program* detailed bulletin. It was the hope of the NSA and every other federal security agency that someone would come forward and identify the twins.

The citizens of the Heartland didn't disappoint.

It took less than an hour for a tip to come in, enabling the NSA to learn that Sam and Len were really Ahmad and Jamil, and that their names had been legally changed shortly after 9/11. The tipster also told authorities that the twin's uncle was their legal guardian. It had to be assumed he'd been supplying the Kool Aid in their formative years.

A search for each man's residence ended in less than thirty minutes – the addresses didn't exist. Except for their photos, all the information on each driver's license had been fabricated – and the uncle's home, now minus a battered front door, was vacant. None of the neighbors had seen him or the twins for several years. The uncle's name and picture was now also included with the twin's photos and identities on the TV news bulletins.

All the dots had been connected ... but unfortunately, the dot's whereabouts were still unknown.

I'd just left Donnie and Lance at the track, and was rounding a row of barns when Tommy almost collided with me. "We need to talk!" he said in breathless rush. All I could think was, "Wow, this is a first!"

"What I'm telling you, I swear if pressed, I'll deny that I ever shared it with you ... understand?"

"Yes, but ..." I said.

"No buts ... just listen. Homeland has identified three individuals. The two primary individuals are identical twins – and we don't know which twin is last night's John Doe. We also intercepted a suspicious phone conversation that took place last night in an area west of the casino. Agents recovered a cell phone that was attached to an eighteen-wheeler – the rig was pulled over by the Ohio Highway Patrol, just north of Cincinnati. Homeland's best information indicates that the Ohio Stadium is the primary target. The tipping point was John Doe's shoes that were left in in the rental car. The dirt samples from the shoes match soil composites that are common to the Olentangy-Scioto River basin in Columbus."

"And yet ... I don't agree," Tommy said.

Obviously needing to finish what he started, Tommy elaborated further. "There was some chatter originating from this track earlier today ... crazy stuff ... stuff that didn't make any sense. There was a thread of conversation about the 'Shoe – and whether that means the casino or Ohio State is anyone's guess at this moment."

"The bottom line is that Ohio Stadium is going to have more spectators than this racing oval today, and whatever form the attack takes, the impact terror-wise will be more devastating there than here! That's Homeland's opinion."

Not buying into that scenario, Tommy went on to say that he didn't agree with Homeland's theory – telling me that he said as much to the agency before getting a "duly-noted" response from them. "So, Doc … there are composite photos of all the bad guys that are being printed out now in the track's administration offices. There'll be enough copies for your partners and any other friends you may have here today."

Changing tack, Tommy said to me, "I've just one question for you. It's obvious that someone doesn't want your horse to race today – why not just scratch him? He's already qualified for the Derby field! Just parade him around the paddocks, make up some lame excuse to scratch him and race him the first Saturday in May," was his advice.

For one of the few times in my life, I was speechless. I didn't know if I was answering for myself or for Towers Above. I had watched our horse will himself to victory for three years – and

Donnie swore that TA craved the competition. If he was today's prime target, well ... there'd been numerous other opportunities to carry out an attack before today.

Finally pulling my jumbled thoughts together, I told Tommy. "I really appreciate that you're trusting me now. Most people probably believe a Thoroughbred or for that matter, any horse, is stupid. I used to believe that. I can't begin to tell you how wrong I was."

It was clear to me that Tommy didn't understand the world of horse racing – or the evolution of getting a horse to race day. I tried to explain it all. "When we start our prep for a race, we can tell that TA understands the process. Every day leading up to race day is choreographed. This morning he got his usual half ration of food – and right now he's in the stall mentally gearing up to race. I know you won't believe this ... but he's psyching himself up to run today."

I further explained to Tommy that TA would become confused if the routine and schedule was interrupted – and any sudden change could create problems for subsequent races. "We had that happen last year – we had TA prepped, but at the last second scratched him. He raced a month later and just narrowly won. No, Tommy, he's racing today. We can't risk any changes prior to the

Kentucky Derby."

I could tell Tommy still didn't quite comprehend.

"OK then, Doc … where I need you and your folks today is at the track entrances. I need eyes there in case one of the twins or their uncle tries to enter the facilities. Obviously you and Marty have an advantage in that you've seen what the twins look like."

Reaching into his bag, Tommy pulled out a couple of mobile devices and handed them to me. "I'm giving you these phones to use when communicating with me. They have a walkie-talkie feature." Digging in the bag again, Tommy then pulled out two of the new track-logo ball caps. "You and Marty need to wear these caps. It will help my men identify both of you and know that you're on our side."

Tommy turned to leave – but not before one final parting shot to me. "I know you're packing today. For God's sake … don't try to be a hero. Call me … please!"

Heading to the barns, I stopped – it was my turn for some final words – but Tommy was already gone. I called Marty, asking her to meet me outside the administration office. While waiting for her at the east entrance, I saw that the line of patrons extended down the hill, well past the building that housed the auditorium . Slowly approaching one of the security officers nearby, I innocently asked what the hold-up was. He didn't pause to look up, but sarcastically replied, "I don't know where you've been, but today nobody gets in here without having every bag, container or purse checked!"

"Protocol has finally changed," I mumbled.

"What's up with the hat?" Marty, who was coming toward me, asked.

"Put this on, please ... I'm in no mood for questions," I said testily. "Finally ... they're checking everything and at least wanding everyone at the entrances. They've never done more than random checks before – heaven forbid there's a long line and patrons are inconvenienced!"

Not quite done with my tirade, I said to Marty, "Nothing like a terror threat to shake things up! Can you tell me why it takes something like this to make folks do the right thing?" I asked, shaking my head in bewilderment. Marty knew from experience that nothing she said would make a difference – and wisely remained silent.

Now in surveillance mode, I remained at the east entrance – and Marty positioned herself just past the turnstiles at the south entrance. Typically, a large number of patrons would arrive on the grounds during the first two races, with a second wave of people entering during the fourth and fifth races. We would remain at our posts during those times. Marty and I would then head to the barns and give Towers Above his send off before the Stakes Race.

A sudden gust of wind swept through the area as I turned away from the entrance, now facing the paddock where the horses were being saddled for the first race. Track attendants were directing the horses, trainers and their accompanying entourage towards the stalls at the north end of the saddling paddock. Umbrellas were popping open everywhere, and I directed my gaze to the west. Tapping on the cell phone's weather app, I was immediately reminded that there are always environmental forces in play somewhere that no human being has ever been able to control.

CHAPTER 34

I was in the process of sending a text to Marty when track attendants began furiously racing to open the north gate. Horses that had been ready to run in the first race quickly exited the saddling paddock, led by their groomsmen.

At virtually the same moment, tornado sirens began to loudly wail … people were now scattering, running in every direction to escape and find safety. Some headed for the nearest exit, ignoring the pleas of Guest Services personnel to stay under cover where it was safest.

The main structure of the track facility had been built during the 60's recession and was structurally sound – having been constructed with pride, craftsmanship and materials that surpassed those which any modern-day architecture or building design might offer. It could easily withstand an F-5 tornado, but on this day, very few knew that.

Opening my iPhone's WeatherBug Radar application, I quickly saw one of the most bizarre weather fronts I'd ever seen. Closing the app, I then opened the Weather Channel's App. At that moment, the cell phone image was indicating the leading edge of a bow-like front that was just east of Lexington. An online weatherman characterized the storm front as a hybrid derecho.

"Damn weather forecasters ... don't they have anything better to do than spew strange weather jargon when all hell's breaking loose? What was the last one? Oh yeah, polar vortex ... back in 2014 and '15. That was another new term," I mused to myself. "Derecho ... sounds like a character in a Clint Eastwood spaghetti western. Anyone can see it's a bad-ass storm ... probably with tornados coming on the backside. Well, I'd better get Marty and take cover before this derecho arrives." I began running towards the south gate to find her.

No more than twenty yards in front of me stood the signature Clock Tower encircled by three Pin oak trees that had to be every bit of sixty years old, if not more. Thirty to forty feet up, on each tree, at a point where several branches veered off in different directions, there was bracing – similar to a wagon wheel – that was attached to the main trunk. Extending off all three wheels were a number of anchored cables that stretched to support divergent limbs ... making the apparatus look like a halo. It was obvious these trees were special. Visitors and patrons regularly posed in front of the majestic trees for selfies and group pictures – and I'm sure that more than one proposal of marriage was made under the bows over the years. During every meet, artists also paid homage to the Tower and the cluster of oaks, taking up positions in one paddock or the other – and nine times out of ten, the oak trees were part of their watercolor or oil creation. Over the years, I'd watched as people would pat the trees on their way to their seats ... or give it a soft caress as they left the track, as if they were saying, "Don't worry. I'll be back again in the fall ... take care of yourselves."

I was no stranger to severe storms – in fact, I'd had two previous encounters with lightening, once in the mountains of Colorado and the other when lounging in a glider on my front porch during my teen years – and this prepared my senses for what happened next.

On this day, my senses took a big hit – but nothing compared to the largest of the three oak trees and three unlucky bystanders – all three being in the wrong place at the wrong time. The strike of lightning sounded to me like an explosion ... the smell of burning wood quickly permeated the air ... and heavy smoke blurred the eyes of anyone nearby.

When my vision cleared, I saw steam and smoke seeping out of the trunk everywhere. Three of those huge limbs, each ten to twelve inches thick, had broken off from the force of the strike – two of them were now in the Riders Up paddock and the third was lying in the rotary between both paddocks. All three looked like a giant firework with a fuse that was still smoldering ... but hadn't yet ignited.

The three patrons were prone on the ground, no more than fifteen feet from the trunk. It was immediately apparent that one had been a conduit for most of the electrical energy released during the strike; he was lying on the ground unconscious. His right shoe had been blown off his foot, encased in a cloud of smoke two feet away.

I made my way as quickly as possible to him and began administering CPR. Within a minute, a track paramedic arrived and was yelling something at me – but I couldn't hear a thing because the sound of the blast was still reverberating in my ears. Quickly, he placed his hands on mine to stop me, waving me off with a throat slash motion – it was time to use an AED on the person. I backed away so he could do his job and help the unconscious guy on the ground.

Looking at the trunk of the injured tree, my eyes followed the path of the strike up to where the trunk split and even further up to where the cables had just minutes earlier held the huge branches in place. Now, the cables were a shredded mess, looking like someone's weird attempt to decorate with metal tinsel. What a shame, I thought … the oak tree was probably the first fatality at the track that day.

It wouldn't be the last.

* * *

Tommy had worked with Jamie for just over six months now. He knew Jamie had a two-year-old son and that his wife was near term with their second child. Not fully confident that Jamie's mind wasn't distracted with thoughts of his family, Tommy decided to put him on the parking lot detail. "There would be less chance of something going wrong out there," Tommy hoped to himself.

Jamie was working the parking lot aisles closest to the track, eventually extending his surveillance further out to the south end of the track's property. He stopped to chat with a track security guard who was directing traffic.

"Hey, how ya' doing?" Jamie asked, starting the conversation.

The guard just nodded his head. He was staring at the new logo ball cap Jamie was wearing, thinking how cool it was.

"What parking lot is that one?" Jamie pointed slightly southeast.

"That's the employee parking lot. Workers have passes to show ... that allows them to get in that entrance and park in that lot. Golf carts take the staff back and forth to the track," the guard replied.

His eyes caught by something, Jamie quickly turned to the west as a flash of lightening split the afternoon sky, appearing to strike the structures around the paddocks.

"Great, just great. I'm walking around during an electrical storm surrounded by some of the biggest trees in Kentucky! The only thing I'm missing is a two iron." Laughing to himself, Jamie finished the joke, "... because even God can't hit a two iron!"

Walking up and down between the rows of cars ... looking for anything out of the ordinary, Jamie peered in both the front and rear windows of each car. The wind was picking up. At first the gusts were about twenty-five to thirty miles per hour – followed by heavy bursts of rain – wind gusts now were reaching fifty to sixty miles per hour. He was soaked to the skin, and every time the wind rose, Jamie turned his back to it, grabbing on to anything that would help keep him from doing a face plant.

And then there was an eerie silence.

The rain and wind slowed. Jamie looked skyward and had no idea what he was watching because he'd never seen anything like it. And suddenly he remembered the movie *Twister.*

"Shit … that's a tornado forming!"

He tried to move, but this marvel of nature had him transfixed and frozen in place. He watched the clouds rotate slowly at first, and then begin to spin more quickly in a tighter circle. Somewhere between the ground and the clouds was the rest of the tornado, spinning invisibly. Only when it touched the ground would the tornado reveal its entire vortex. "Somebody's going to catch hell in a few seconds," Jamie silently commented to himself – grateful it wasn't coming towards him.

The rain began again, signaling that another weather cell was over the grounds of the track – and round two commenced with a clap of thunder. As he continued to head west to east, Jamie took comfort in knowing there were only a couple more rows to check.

Parked under a huge sycamore tree was an older model Camry and what appeared to be a man in the driver's seat. Jamie approached the car with caution, as he'd been trained to do. He walked past, twenty yards to the south of its location and then looped back. Now crouching, Jamie began a slow sixty-second count before proceeding further. He approached the Camry from the right rear, trying to avoid detection from the rear-view mirror.

At first, only the driver's eyes moved. His right hand slowly reached under the floor mat to retrieve a handgun. Jamie tactically moved closer. "Is this guy sleeping, did he have a heart attack or ...?" Jamie quietly questioned to himself. Reaching the rear of the car, Jamie made a fist and thumped the trunk a couple of times.

"Track security ... are you OK in there?" Jamie shouted, trying to be heard above the sound of the storm. He waited for a response, but the subject didn't move. He reached for his Glock and tapped on the left rear passenger window.

"Track security!" he again shouted.

The subject was wearing employee garb and he abruptly lurched in his seat, as if he had been suddenly awakened. The driver's side window rolled down and the stranger stuck his head out of the window and into the downpour.

"Sorry officer, I closed my eyes this morning to take a nap and obviously time got away from me."

Jamie was now at the driver's door and his eyes met the stranger's pupils straight on. Jamie's brain shifted into overdrive.

"It's him ... the uncle!" was his last conscious thought on this day.

The first bullet hit Jamie squarely in the sternum, and the second grazed his head above the left earlobe before ricocheting off his skull. Body armor absorbed the first shot ... Jamie felt himself being lifted and pulled before losing consciousness.

The security guard directing traffic turned towards the employee parking lot. "That sounded like shots ..." but then two more flashes of lightening were followed immediately by loud claps of thunder. The guard's train of thought shifted elsewhere.

Ben finished cleaning up the mess on the ground, and moved the car to a different parking spot two rows away before getting out and opening his umbrella with the 'WP' insignia imprint emblazoned on each panel. Checking to make sure he had his lanyard with the employee ID, Ben headed toward the track. As he approached the guard directing traffic, he paused. He'd recognized Jamie's facial expression a few minutes earlier. He'd seen this type of reaction before – it was one of those "I know you" looks, which meant he would no longer be just another track employee.

His cover was blown for the most part.

"Hey Richard, did you see anything going on in the parking lot a couple minutes ago?" the security guard asked while gazing at Ben's ID badge and name tag.

"I got a late start today … can't stop … gotta' get going," Richard responded. He took a deep breath of relief and walked towards the track's south entrance. Plan A had become Plan B … and he had a hunch the rest of the afternoon would continue in an ad lib mode.

CHAPTER 35

The derecho was heading southeast, now wreaking havoc on the South Eastern portion of the Commonwealth and continuing on into West Virginia and Virginia. Metro's finest had left the grounds with the three patrons who were felled by the lightning strike. Remarkably, all three were breathing.

* * *

An hour and a half had past and it was déjà vu time.

The horses in the first race were once again entering the saddling paddock. Post time was now 1:40 p.m. and Saturday's premier Stakes Race post time had been pushed back. The only sounds out of the ordinary were chainsaws gnawing away on the oak branches at the crossover path between the paddocks. Several carts were being loaded with remnants of the tree – destined to become lumber. The Thoroughbreds closest to the action were not a bit happy. They'd never been schooled to the sounds and smells of chainsaws – but clean-up had to be done. Sure enough, when it was time to cross the rotary and pronounce Riders Up, both paddocks pretty much looked like nothing had happened there that early afternoon.

The patrons were also re-entering the gates as Marty and I resumed our positions at our respective posts – but not before I got a dose of venom from my wife.

"Thanks for coming to help me. What if I'd been struck by lightning? That's how much you care about me! And by the way, I lost that stupid cap you gave me. God knows where the wind took it. I swear if this ever happens again … I'll … " Marty finally stopped yelling.

I turned and gave Marty an Atlanta Braves tomahawk chop motion. After so many years of bickering, we had developed a series of hand signals. The tomahawk motion meant zip it, and she did. I swear I even detected a slight smile cross her face.

Ted and Tommy began to check in with their respective staff and agents on the new phones. Everyone was safe and accounted for except for one person – Tommy hadn't been able to connect with Jamie – and Jamie wasn't answering his phone. The last communication was when Tommy texted the most recent pictures of the twins and their uncle – and that was a while ago. Being thin on agents, Tommy asked Ted if he could spare a couple men to help find Jamie.

Five minutes later, Tommy, Ralph and Gary were in a golf cart, driving to the south parking lot to look for Jamie. Tommy reversed Jamie's normal search pattern, going first to the farthest reaches of the track grounds to start his search for Jamie ... near the employee parking lot.

The security guard that Jamie had talked to earlier that day responded to Tommy's beckoning hand gesture.

"Has there been anyone walking around here during the past couple of hours?" Tommy asked. Tommy knew the best way to get information was to start with a broad and general question.

"Yeah ... there was a guy with a new logo cap, heading for that parking lot and later, there was an employee ... his name was Richard. It looked like he was late getting here today because he was in a hurry to get to the track. Why? What's going on?" the security guard asked. Tommy wanted to press forward to the parking lot ... but experience and intuition made him pause and ask one more question.

"Take a look at these pictures. Did your fellow employee

look like any of these guys? Take a good look now," Tommy said.

"Damn, this picture here sure looks like that guy ... Richard."

"What do you think? Are you fifty, seventy, or ninety percent sure that's this guy?" Tommy calmly asked while pointing at Ben's photo.

The guard was breathing a little quicker now – he knew what was at stake today. "Jesus ... is this one of the terrorists and I messed up? Damn it!" he said to himself. Tommy could read body language easily ... and saw the tension rising in the young man's demeanor.

"Son ... it's alright ... relax! Is this the man you saw a few minutes ago?"

"Yes sir. It is."

Tommy stepped away from Ralph and Gary, and sent a text to his boss. The text read: *The uncle is here ... on the racetrack grounds!*

Tommy motioned for Gary and Ralph to get closer. "Guys, this guard just identified the uncle and confirmed that he's somewhere inside the track's confines. Gary, do you have a maintenance chief that can get some tools out here?" Responding in the affirmative, Gary got on his phone and placed a call to his boss, while Tommy radioed Ted and told him to spread the word that the uncle – masquerading as Richard – was somewhere on the grounds.

Finally, Tommy walked over to the young security guard and put his arm around him. No words were going to console the guard – but Tommy and the others knew he hadn't screwed the pooch.

Heading to the parking lot, Tommy gave the men their instructions, telling them they would be looking for a car that had been running recently. "Each of you, grab one of these temperature guns. Any car that gives off any hint of a reading ... mark it in some fashion. I'm betting our subject's car will register positive."

The three men got out of the golf cart, sprinting quickly towards the employee parking lot. Just past the paved entrance, Tommy stopped to give final instructions to the security team.

"OK, this is what you should look for ... bear in mind that these cars should have been here since early this morning ... and we just had a downpour. Look for any grass that appears like it has recently been flattened down … or muddy tire tread marks on the grass between the parking rows. Anything you see that looks unusual, mark it with a handkerchief, hat, whatever you have on you. It shouldn't be hard to spot … let's spread out and get going."

Gary took the eastern portion of the lot, Ralph headed to the rows due south towards the track and Tommy started to scour the far western section. Gary, heading in the direction of the big sycamore tree, suddenly spotted something bright in the grass … right in line with the large tree … and headed straight for it. It was a maroon-colored ball cap, upside down in the grass. Picking the cap up and turning it over, Gary realized it was the exact style cap as he was wearing. He quickly called Tommy.

"Sir … this is Gary, I'm east of you and I've got something over here by the big sycamore tree."

"Roger that," Tommy shouted into the cell phone, changing course in an instant … now sprinting toward the tree and Gary. When he saw the cap in Gary's hand, Tommy quickly and with a heavy heart understood the situation.

"The cap has to be Jamie's … and Jamie is missing. Maybe

he came across Richard," Tommy worried to himself. Walking down the row a bit, Tommy spotted an area with matted grass – and immediately picked up the trail with more flattened, muddy grass on the opposite side of the paved path in between the rows of cars. Going two rows further to the west, the flattened trail suddenly stopped behind an older Camry sedan.

Walking to the front of the car, Tommy realized that this was the end of the road – they had found Richard's car, but needed a final confirmation. Taking aim at the car with the temperature gun, the reading showed the car was still warm … indicating recent activity … and the inside of the car was empty.

"Only one more place to check … the trunk," Tommy realized. The maintenance department hadn't come with the tools yet … and Tommy wasn't going to wait. "Give me the cap," he shouted at Gary. Covering his hand with the cap, Tommy made a fist and slammed it into the driver's side window … not only breaking the glass in the process, but also his hand. Two seconds later the door was open and the trunk lever was raised.

Tommy watched as Gary lifted Jamie's still body out of the trunk. An adrenaline rush prevented Tommy from feeling any pain … only a sense of dread until hearing Gary exclaim after checking

Jamie's pulse ... "he's alive!" Gary ripped open Jamie's shirt and immediately saw the bullet crater in the vest. It took a few seconds longer to unfasten the body armor – and realize that the vest had not been totally pierced by the bullet.

Tommy dropped to his knees in gratitude – and with significant pain now registering from his broken hand. Ralph had arrived on the scene, and was checking Jamie's head wound ... seeing no sign that a bullet had entered or exited the skull. "Gutsy move, sir. I'm guessing your friend has a fractured skull ... but hell, what do I know?" Ralph said to Tommy. In the meantime, Ted had been called and medical assistance for Jamie and Tommy was requested.

It took about six minutes for the track paramedics to arrive. Tommy and the other security men sat in the grass, waiting for an initial diagnosis on Jamie. The chief medic turned to the men and said, "His vitals are good ... I'm guessing a fracture and a concussion, but I'm not a neurologist ... sorry!"

"Hey Doc, do me a favor. You got anything for pain?" Tommy asked, holding up his injured hand. The paramedic carefully examined Tommy's hand, pushing gently on an area already swollen and red. Tommy didn't realize he could scream so loud. "Look, I don't have time to take a ride right now … you got a shot or a pill you can give me? Please Doc, damn it!"

As if on cue, the other paramedics turned their backs, attending to Jamie as the lead paramedic reached into what looked like a tackle box, pulling out a syringe and a vial of liquid. Taking their cues from the medics, Ralph and Gary also turned their backs. In two seconds, the syringe's contents had been injected, and in a just a few minutes, Tommy almost forgot that the hand was broken. "Cap the syringe and leave the vial!" Tommy ordered. The senior paramedic performed as told … he knew not to argue when someone has a gun.

CHAPTER 36

Several FBI agents had arrived on the crime scene, cordoning off the employee parking lot to begin their investigation and collect evidence. Gary remained at the scene, while Ralph and Tommy headed to Ted's office.

Ted took one look at Tommy cradling his right hand and shook his head.

"Jesus … you couldn't wait two more minutes? My guys were three hundred yards away and …" Ted wasn't given a chance to finish his chain of thought.

"They just carted off one of my men," Tommy stated angrily. "If it hadn't been for his body armor and the grace of God, he'd be dead."

"Clean this desk off and if you've got schematics of the grounds and every building that the son of a bitch can hide in, bring 'em out now … 'cause, Ted, you and I need to brainstorm. When we're done, get your team leaders in here … we're going to make sure everyone is on the same page. This useless fuck is going down!" Tommy promised with a vengeance.

The morphine was working … and so was Richard. Just a few minutes earlier, he'd been heading towards the Clubhouse … a building that ironically was only about two hundred yards from where Tommy and Ted were meeting.

Just short of the entrance, Richard spotted a ball cap on the ground next to the walkway. "I've seen that cap. That plain clothes guy had one," Richard thought to himself. He picked it up and put it in a pocket of his employee coat.

Richard assumed that by now they'd found his car and the body in the trunk … and that he was now a hunted man. He needed a place to think and unchallenged by anyone, went through the Clubhouse entrance and into the men's room. Richard knew he wouldn't attract any attention in the privacy of a stall, and could even gain a few minutes of peace and some time to think – and he needed a new plan.

First though, it was time to change his appearance. In the left pocket of his sport coat was a small tube of cyanoacrylate adhesive, along with a fake mustache made from his own hair. Putting his cell phone on the toilet paper dispenser, Richard opened a mirror app on his mobile phone's screen, and then carefully applied glue to the moustache. He placed it perfectly on his lip – looking in the mirror to make sure it was straight. Admiring his new debonair look, he took three more items from his pocket to complete his disguise: a pair of eye glasses that were befitting an older man and not too avant garde, another name tag – from now on, he was Dick, not Richard – and a new employee ID card to attach to the lanyard.

* * *

"It's gonna' be a special day today. We're probably going to see another future Triple Crown winner," Dick said to a track employee selling programs. The vendor stared at Dick for about five seconds before responding.

"Maybe … but I doubt it," the employee answered, while thinking, "I've never seen this guy around here before … must be a new hire." It wasn't unusual for employees to come and go during meets. Working for minimum wage in a job some people felt was beneath them wasn't an uncommon occurrence at the track. An employee would clock-in one day, and the next day, a different employee was there instead, ready to begin his or her new hire training. The employee followed the new guy to the exit with his eyes before resuming his alert status … never realizing he'd just missed an opportunity to be a Hero of the Month employee.

Dick headed for the 'Mountain', armed with several programs he'd just purchased.

Because Woodlands Park was built in the foothills of the Appalachian mountains, the natives had named a previously strip mined plateau, located a half mile from the track - the 'Mountain'. Race fans could park there and tailgate. If they wanted, they could descend 500 feet on a winding trail and proceed to enter the track for the live action.

Since Alcohol was abundant on the Mountain … by the fourth or fifth race, many of the younger patrons entering the track were more inebriated than those leaving.

Dick's plan was to sell the recently-purchased programs to patrons on the Mountain, hang out for the first few races … and then make his way back to the track to finish his mission.

"Hey guys, I'm Dick. I got hired yesterday and they directed me up here to sell programs. Where should I post up?" Dick said to an employee legitimately assigned to work the Mountain.

Nobody thought to question his presence that afternoon. They had more pressing issues to worry about.

* * *

Tommy and Ted were in deep discussion about Ben ... trying to anticipate his moves. "He's got two choices ... either he stays in uniform or he goes civilian. Agreed?" Tommy asked Ted, automatically assuming he was in agreement.

Ted wasn't so sure – and said so. "He's got us at a disadvantage. We have no idea what he's up to ... we have no hint of where he's going to act next ... and we haven't a clue as to when he's going to do it. I think he'll switch plans back and forth, depending on what he needs to do at any given moment."

Tommy suddenly realized Ted was every bit his equal in expertise. Then again, to the best of his knowledge, Ted wasn't high on a pain killer. "Damn, he's right ... I should have known that."

"Well, at least we're both in agreement that the big Stakes Race is probably his priority." Ted nodded his head in confirmation. "And if he's in the caramel colored jacket, the last place he'd want to be is mixing in with the trackside crowd ... at least until the seventh race because he'll stick out. So how many employees are on the grounds wearing caramel sport coats and how many of them have those all weather coats?" Tommy asked.

Ted realized just how vulnerable the track was at that moment. He had no clue as to who was actually present that day. Employees called in sick every day – staff was encouraged to cross train for other jobs, often working in different positions from one day to the next. Realizing he was close to having another panic attack, Ted quickly put his hands on the desk to steady himself.

Ted called his secretary. "Connie, call Jenny and tell her to bring the staff roster to my office. Also, get in touch with all the team leaders and tell them to get here – right away!" Glancing at the closed circuit television screen, Ted watched the horses break from the gate in the third race. He quickly realized time was slipping away and there was still no plan in place to identify and stop Richard. He picked up the phone and called Art.

"I've been waiting for your call," Art said to Ted brusquely. "Tell me you've found our rogue employee ... and that this nightmare is over. You know our reputation is taking a big hit today. Hell, the damn storm and this terrorist threat have knocked our attendance down by at least a third. I've talked with the governor and he's willing to send National Guard troops over ..."

"Art, Goddamn it ... will you shut it please?" Ted was

stunned that there was now silence, and quickly told his boss what he thought had to be done.

"Art, this is what I need right now. I need you to slow the race card down … I need an extra fifteen to twenty minutes between races, beginning with the fourth race. I don't want the tenth race to go off any earlier than 6:00 p.m.! It's 3:00 now … do whatever you've got to … but back things up," Ted exclaimed.

All Art could think about was how this would affect the track's television revenue. The tenth race was going to be a live national broadcast on this Saturday afternoon. Any delay would cut into prime time news on the east coast. Besides that, the last race of the day would have a post time close to sunset and darkness.

"Art, Art … did you hear me?" Ted shouted into the phone.

"Okay, Ted. I'll get it done but you sure as hell better finish this … today."

CHAPTER 37

Hypnotized by the threatening weather, Jamil was sitting in his plane on the airstrip, wondering what he was going to do. Every two minutes, he'd open the weather app on his smartphone again – hoping and praying that what he saw two minutes earlier wasn't actually real. Each time, the words *locating you* would appear on the screen. His uncle had warned him about using the cell phone ... but since he wasn't in the air yet, what was the harm in checking the weather?

Splashed across the screen once more was the same threatening weather front ... extending from the northern-most part of Lake Michigan all the way down to Arkansas. The bow in the line of the front was headed toward Indianapolis, and curving just west of Louisville – and then down the Mississippi River where it ended somewhere in Arkansas.

The phone display was filled with a significant number of directional cones and marked by colored shapes: circles, squares and triangles. Some were green, others yellow or blue – but it was the red symbols that worried him – he was especially concerned about the red triangles. There were thirty or more of them along the entire front. "That many tornado warnings ... this can't be right!" Jamil said to himself, checking the weather stats more closely to see if any tornados had touched down – and seeing that three had indeed touched ground west of Kentucky. "How can I fly in this weather?" he thought nervously.

Activating the forecast app's time lapse function each time he opened the app, Jamil could see where the front should be in the next hour. Finally after a dozen more weather checks over the next half hour, Jamil started the plane's engine ... deciding finally that he wasn't going to stick around and wait for the weather front to arrive.

The airstrip he was on was one of four such runways that his uncle had created on the 150-acre farm. Ben had been a pilot for over twenty-five years and knew how to create a runway. It took him two years to bulldoze and construct four airstrips, each crisscrossing in different directions. One main strip ran true north to south while a second main strip went east to west. A third strip was northeast to southwest, and the last, northwest to southeast. From the air, the strips looked no different than trails for all-terrain vehicles – which was Ben's intention – anything to confuse spying eyes.

The north-south airstrip was prime for take-off today as Jamil and Ahmad had cut the grass there forty-eight hours earlier ...

in preparation for the flight.

Throttling forward, Jamil began his roll on the runway, lifting off the ground at fifty-five knots, and heading south. Slowly climbing to two thousand feet, Jamil banked right until his heading read north-northwest ... gradually descending to fifteen hundred feet where he leveled off.

It was 9:30 a.m. – not 11:00.

"Screw it! If my uncle wants precision, then he should have flown the plane," Jamil mumbled aloud.

He was wearing a gas mask by choice – it was not one of the items his uncle had given him twenty-four hours earlier. The payload on the plane was just shy of fifty pounds and Jamil decided that if the weather prevented the Ricin from directly hitting the intended target, he'd at least have a chance to survive inhalation of any of the fine powder by wearing the mask. However, the mask would not be necessary after all. Jamil had now decided he was going to martyr himself, despite an earlier conversation with Ahmad.

The morning before the casino incident, both Ahmad and Jamil discussed the possibility of defying their uncle. Neither of them wanted to die – and God willing, Jamil would see his brother Ahmad in a few days – hoping somehow, they'd find a way to reunite with their father.

An hour into the flight, Jamil's cell phone began to vibrate. Seeing the number on the screen, Jamil took off his headset.

"Jamil ... you've taken off?" Ahmad asked.

Jamil lifted his mask and screamed into his cell phone. "Ahmad, why are you calling me? You know what can happen!"

"Brother please ... I beg you, listen ... there's not much time! They know about our plan. I stopped to gas up at a convenience store and there are news bulletins all over the television. If you're not airborne, get going. Jamil ... those plans we talked about ... there's no turning back now. I love you brother. I'll see you in heaven ... goodbye."

Jamil ripped the mask off his head in anguish. Placing the plane on autopilot, tears began to stream down his cheeks – he sobbed for five minutes and abruptly stopped. Anger now took the place of anguish.

He had to find a way to circumvent the advancing weather front – certainly there would be no other planes flying near him in these conditions. If he was going to be successful in reaching Ohio Stadium, he couldn't ride the eastern side of the front – he would have to go around it somehow. Working out the plan in his head, Jamil decided to head northwest and look for a clear opening. Then when the weather opportunity was right, he'd first head west, then turn back to the east and follow the front as it advanced through Columbus.

Jamil was right to be concerned about the phone call from his brother.

* * *

The NSA has a listening network of phony cell carrier towers. these fake cell towers, operated by the government, utilize 'Stingray' equipment. They literally steal mobile communications from cellular providers. They can function in real time, relaying live transmissions in times of crisis or threats. The Stingray network also records conversation that can be reviewed at a later time, or as needed – and in this instance – it was set to immediately transmit communications triggered by its geographic location, key words, threat levels and other factors. In fact, on this particular Saturday, all phone transmissions in and out of the urban regions of Ohio,

Kentucky and Indiana were active and in live function ... NSA had already captured an earlier conversation in close proximity to the race track.

Ahmad's call to Jamil was a badly-needed answer to the NSA analyst's prayers. They replayed the conversation over and over – their conclusions were that one twin was west of the Mississippi River while the other was still in the Tri-State region ... and possibly airborne. The pilot's target was unknown, but it was one that had already been statistically identified by Einstein.

Jamil was in Lexington's airspace when he saw his chance – a break in the storm about twenty-five miles northwest of Lexington. He throttled up and turned towards the opening in the heavens, confident in his skills as a pilot. After all, he'd completed nearly two dozen takeoffs and landings in the light sports plane he was now flying. That, combined with hundreds of hours of intense activity on flight simulator programs he'd downloaded to his computer, gave Jamil the confidence that he had the proficiency to fly almost any aircraft.

* * *

Americans innovate, the Chinese copy and Germans know

how to ... engineer airplanes.

The CTLSi light sports aircraft was Jamil's air chariot of choice. If he felt invincible in it, it was because he was flying in an aircraft that was fabricated with over ninety percent carbon fiber materials. Forgetting his transponder was still on, he was maneuvering at a low altitude and was confident that his plane was virtually invisible ... and could not be detected. Radar signals that struck the plane's surface would be absorbed by the plane's carbon fiber structure and would not bounce back to the point of origin. With over three hundred such planes flying in the states – this particular model of aircraft certainly gave the folks at Homeland Security a headache. However, the agency kept close tabs on the sales of this particular model aircraft and maintained detailed profiles of the owners.

The Great Recession of 2008 had been a great equalizer when it came to debt. Jamil's uncle, being the generous man he was, became a benefactor for another Kentuckian who was struggling to make his aircraft's payments and had to sell the plane ... and that's all the twins knew. As far as Homeland was concerned, Ben didn't own a CTLSi.

After completing the purchase of the plane, Ben made

frequent trips to the airport with Ahmad and Jamil … each twin taking turns and learning to fly the CTLSi. Once the grass airstrips on the farm were completed, the twins would fly from the airport to the farm … practicing touch and go departures and landings, along with procedures for cutting the engine and coasting from different elevations.

They learned how the plane would begin a stall at thirty-nine knots – which was around forty-six miles per hour. With their uncle as instructor and co-pilot, each twin practiced placing the plane close to stall speed. They did it repeatedly until it was tedious – but perfected. Their first engine stall was at fifty feet … to see how far the plane would coast and how much altitude it would lose. Once that maneuver was mastered, the level was raised to one hundred fifty feet, and finally to two hundred feet. Never once in their training did the uncle offer an explanation for the maneuvers they were learning. In fact, it was not until one month before the track's Spring Meet that they learned that the plane was equipped with a BRS – Ballistic Recovery System.

"Say what?" Jamil asked.

"Listen closely, both of you. I didn't tell you about this before for a reason. Behind the cockpit is a parachute – but it's not for you to use to evacuate the plane – instead, it drops the plane safely to the ground when deployed," Ben told his nephews.

He went into detail with the twins, explaining that the parachute was rocket-launched and upon safe landing, the chute would simply be repacked with a new rocket. He told his nephews that with a new parachute, the plane could fly again another day – "but that's not what I intend for you to do," he clarified.

Ben then revealed his horrific plan to Ahmad and Jamil, advising them that ideally on the day of the mission, wind currents would be low … and this would allow the plane's pilot to make a pass over the Ohio Stadium and drop the payload of toxic Ricin powder. Pausing to let that sink in, he continued, telling his nephews that the next step would be to reduce the plane's speed, and cut the engine and glide – just as they'd practiced so many times – but this time, they'd be stalling and gliding over the football stadium.

The final part of the plan would be dependent upon their piloting skills and a bit of luck, Ben said. "When you activate the BRS system, you'll have maybe a five percent chance of dropping directly into the stadium – I'm guessing the odds of the perfect conditions allowing for this scenario to happen are about … mmm … one in one hundred. But just imagine the panic that will ensue!"

he exclaimed.

"Do you both understand or do I need to repeat myself?" he asked the twins.

"Why would I even consider it with such low odds?" replied Ahmad.

"Because I'm guessing you'll have only one pass before a fighter jet will lock on to your plane – and the odds of them firing when you're over the stadium, resulting in stray fire or a missile flying into the crowd, are a plus for you – and what we need to happen in order to achieve our mission. You both knew going into this that you would be martyring yourselves. If you have any doubts, let me know and we'll end this now. I'll do it by myself."

"I'll give you one day to make your decision … know that I have loved both of you as if you were my sons. Let's call it a day and you can evaluate your feelings. Go and pray about your decision. I'll be here tomorrow at noon … if you're not here then … so be it," Ben said, heading to his car and driving away.

CHAPTER 38

Ahmad knew he'd made a serious mistake calling his brother, but he wanted to hear Jamil's voice again before starting the long drive to the mountains of Colorado. It was going to be an arduous and slow journey. After all, he was the tortoise and Jamil, traveling by airplane was the hare, and would arrive at his destination much faster.

Returning to his car, he placed the phone in the Faraday bag and searched the parking lot for a place to dispose of it. He noticed an eighteen wheeler parked at a service station across the street with hazard lights blinking. Within five minutes, the now-burned cell phone was attached to the undercarriage of the big rig – streaming its new location to Google and NSA. It was time to get going, Ahmad thought – and time for a new look. His electric razor would do most of the job, but a straight razor was needed to fine-tune his changed appearance. Not wanting to chance another trip to the same convenience store he was at earlier, Ahmad decided to head west to the next small town, some fifty miles away.

Forty minutes later, he eased into the farm town, looking for a drugstore and a motel. The pharmacist bagged his shaving cream, scissors and safety razor … and drew a map for Ahmad with directions to the town's finest one-star motel.

* * *

"Just fill out this registration form please," the motel clerk said.

Ahmad left the license plate information line blank. "Excuse me sir, if you wouldn't mind filling in your license plate number, I'd appreciate it."

"It's a temporary tag … I just bought the car. It's some long number … you know how those things are," Ahmad said, attempting to make the issue insignificant.

"I know, man, but I still need the number – it's a liability thing and my boss – well, you know," the clerk stated emphatically.

Ahmad grabbed the paper and pen from the clerk, walking angrily to the parking lot to get the number from the tag taped to the back window of the car. He was pissed … because now he'd have to put another temporary tag on the car in the early morning darkness.

The numbers had no significance as the tags were forgeries ... they could have been 1234567 or the reverse. He now had only two forged tags left, indicating they were from Colorado and Texas. He was unaware that some police officers had already unsuccessfully tried to photograph his temporary tags using License Plate Readers – an occurrence his uncle had anticipated and thwarted by using heavy stock paper for the tags ... with characters that were nearly impossible to read.

Approaching his motel room, Ahmad immediately noticed a gap at the bottom of the door – he knew that he wouldn't be the sole occupant of that room. Opening the door quickly to catch a glimpse of the uninvited guests, Ahmad was not surprised to see the mob of spiders and roaches that froze for a second in the daylight before scurrying back into the darkness. But where were the mice? Ahmad worried. He hated rodents and was going to rid the room of them. Sure enough, one raced along the baseboard and into the bathroom. "No way out ... always fatal," Ahmad laughed.

Five minutes later, the deed was done and Ahmad returned to his car where he sat quietly for a few minutes. Knowing that rodents travel in pairs, he entered the room a second time ... it took him less than thirty minutes to fully rid the room of uninvited vermin, excluding the roaches. Those he could live with.

The motel had cable TV … probably why it earned a one star rating. Ahmad turned the television set on, searching for CNN Headline News.

Ahmad froze.

Plastered across the screen was a picture of him and his uncle Ben … with a bulletin advising of the heightened terrorist threat level … and the terrorist's probable targets. He sat transfixed for fifteen minutes, watching the news. There was no sense in burning another cell phone. He knew Jamil was airborne and his uncle … well, he had no clue of his exact location. Ahmad assumed Ben was somewhere around the grounds of the racetrack, and while he and Jamil were fairly certain they knew Ben's target, he'd never specifically told either of them what his intentions were.

Draping a bath towel in the sink, Ahmad grabbed the scissors to begin the transformation. The process of shaving his thick head of hair was like the collection of new mown hay, except there wouldn't be any baling. He tackled the job first with scissors, then the electric shaver – which frequently clogged. After thirty minutes, it was time for the finishing touches using the razor and some shaving cream. Ahmad was quite proud of his barren dome – and his new look.

Adjusting his ball cap to get a tighter fit on his now bare head, he then put on a pair of Maui Jim sunglasses – thoroughly convinced he looked nothing like the guy whose face was all over the news. The next step was to switch out the temporary license tag on the car with the fake Colorado tag, then make his way to Allenspark, Colorado and the vacant cabin. It would serve as his home for a couple weeks. After the spring thaw, he'd get into yet another car using the Texas temporary tag… the last he'd need … before heading to the border and safety.

The cabin hideaway had been planned far in advance. Ben found a summer cabin, which had been closed and winterized last fall by its owners, to use as a temporary hideout … assuming it would be the end of April at the earliest before the owners returned to open the cabin for the season.

Earlier, in March, the trio had parked a Toyota 4Runner at the cabin – and Ben had stocked the vehicle with rations, thermal gear and a bolt cutter. The cutter would be used to snap the combination locks on a utility door, giving Ahmad access to the circuit breaker that controlled the well's water pump. Breaking into the cabin wouldn't pose a problem either. Since no one lived in any of the neighboring mountainside homes during the winter, no one would hear the sound of breaking and entering into the cabin. Turning up the cabin's electric heat and upping the owner's monthly utility bill wouldn't be noticed until the May billing cycle … and Ahmad would be gone by then.

Kicking back on the bed, Ahmad grabbed the remote and searched for the Weather Channel on the television. Besides the tornado warnings throughout the Ohio River Valley, he noticed that there was a winter storm warning for the front range of the Rockies. He might have to hike up the mountainside to get to the cabin … but he was also prepared for that eventuality.

Everything was perfect. It was 2:00 p.m., Central Time … and time for a quick nap. Closing the shades to darken the room, Ahmad failed to notice a group of exterminators gathering outside. It was only Ahmad and the cockroaches in the room now – but he could hear others obviously checking in to the rooms on either side of his. "Damn, who'd want to stay at this dump?" he thought as his eyes slowly closed for some needed rest.

CHAPTER 39

Colonel Murray received the call at noon Central Time. An agent from Homeland Security was calling from a secure cell phone, sixty miles east of Hays, Kansas – and speeding towards Hays at about one hundred miles per hour. He would be at Murray's facility in a few minutes and wanted Murray to assemble his troopers ASAP.

D-Troop consisted of twenty-five Highway Patrol officers who routinely saw action in illegal drug transactions and other nefarious activities – a dozen of them were off duty on this day. Murray called all the troopers in immediately – most likely causing concern to those on the ground and in the air who could see some two dozen troopers in their cars with lights flashing … coming from all directions and exiting I-70 just west of Vine Street in downtown Hays, Kansas.

Murray was aware of the high alert and suspected terrorist activity in the Midwest – after all, it was all over the news nationally. He wondered what that had to do with him … and why. He'd worked with the FBI on drug busts in the past, but had never been contacted by someone from Homeland Security.

"Unless this was going to be the mother of all drug take-downs or …. Nah, it couldn't be anything related to this terrorist shit," he thought.

Agent Tibbits raced past the stone fence posts that encircled many Kansas farmlands and pastures. He'd heard about them and how valuable they were.

People in the Heartland weren't shy about their values – and messages about some of the more compelling beliefs were posted on billboards for all to see. Nearing his destination, he drove past three billboards – each with one word of the final message: Adoption Not Abortion. He went past a fourth sign, this one with the message "Jesus is Real." He truly wanted to believe in this theology … but had become jaded from his dealings with Islamic jihadists in recent years – those who believed that Muhammad was the only true God – and were willing to kill and die for their beliefs.

"Why can't everyone accept the beliefs of others without committing savage acts on those who don't share their convictions?" while pulling into the parking lot of the Kansas Highway Patrol. He entered the building with a sense of urgency, flashing his badge in front of the camera zooming in on him. It seemed like an eternity before he was buzzed inside – and he didn't have time or tolerance for any delay. At long last, the door was unlocked and Colonel Murray was standing there to greet the agent.

"Welcome sir, what can we do for you?" Murray said.

"The name's Tibbits ... you're Colonel Murray?"

"I am ... what brings you all the way to Hays, Kans ... ?"

"How long 'till all of your men are here?" Tibbits demanded, cutting Murray's greeting short.

"Shouldn't be more than 45 minutes until the last one arrives ... and most of them will be here in twenty minutes," Murray replied. Becoming somewhat protective of his turf, Murray asserted himself. "I need to know what's going on in my territory."

"A little over an hour ago, one of three men believed to be part of a potential terrorist attack ... one we think will happen today, made a call from his cell phone outside a convenience store no more than fifty to sixty miles east of here," Tibbits said. "We tracked the call to that location – and found the phone attached to a disabled truck at a gas station across from the store. The clerk in the store gave us a positive ID of our suspect."

The agent went on to say that Homeland Security analysts determined the suspect was holed up somewhere within a hundred mile radius from where he made the call. He added that in fact, a tip was called in a short time ago by a clerk at the Prairie Vista motel who thought a man who had just checked into a room there is one of the guys he saw on the television news.

"Of course, he wanted the one million dollar reward immediately ... but that's not important right now. We need our suspect captured alive, even though we're ninety percent certain he's a decoy. We need to interrogate him about his twin brother and uncle before they carry out their plans," Tibbits added.

Tibbits told the Colonel that he needed the Kansas troopers to get into full body armor and prepare to deploy as quickly as possible, adding that FBI agents were on their way to the motel where Homeland Security had already worked with the clerk to access the rooms on either side of the suspect, which thankfully were vacant. "I also need eight of your men in civilian clothes in case the terrorist is watching. That sums it up ... any questions?" Tibbits asked breathlessly.

Murray was numb, literally numb from the agent's discourse.

He had a disc problem at L-4 and L-5 and the tension that was building up in his back was now causing the muscle fibers to spasm. As the nerve became more pinched, a hot poker-like pain pierced down his right buttock and leg, causing him to nearly collapse in pain.

"You OK, Murray?" Tibbits asked.

"I've got a disc problem that flares up now and then . . . no big deal, it'll be gone in a second." Murray sat down at a desk and picked up the phone to reach the dispatcher, asking her to call the men and tell them to double time it to the building.

Fifteen minutes later, all but five of the twenty-five troopers were gathered in the conference room ... and Murray turned the podium over to Tibbits. The remaining troopers would be brought up to speed by Murray as they arrived.

Agent Tibbits presented the troopers with the same rundown he'd given their Colonel – explaining how Kansas's finest would roust Ahmad out of his motel room. While standard protocol to flush someone out of a room was to use concussion grenades, smoke and tear gas, what Tibbits had in mind was more bizarre and definitely unconventional.

He told the troopers that the rooms at the Prairie Vista had paper thin walls – they were simply constructed of two by fours with drywall, and fire retardant insulation in between. The plan was to break through the walls ... two pairs of Murray's strongest men would each have hollowed out golf bags that instead of clubs, contained battering rams. Each team would be accompanied by two additional troopers who would enter the rooms on either side of Ahmad with the fake golf bags. Once inside, the men would unpack the rams and position themselves along the wall at the same exact spot on either side of Ahmad's room. On Tibbits' count, the men would then batter through the walls.

"Gentlemen, if this works the way I expect it to, once you're through the drywall and into his room, you'll throw your flash-bangs and tear gas canisters inside. I fully expect him to be armed. I have no idea if he has armor-piercing ammo. You know the drywall and insulation won't stop the bullets – and I know most of you have families," Tibbits told the troopers somberly. "I need to tell you what these terrorists are up to today."

The Homeland Security agent went into specifics with the troopers – about the Kentucky Stakes Races – and that one in particular was a qualifying race for the Kentucky Derby, and that over thirty thousand fans were expected at the track. He then told them about the spring football scrimmage at The Ohio State University – an event expected to draw more than ninety thousand spectators to the football stadium.

"I have no clue what mode of attack the terrorists intend to use and whether their weapons are biological, chemical or radioactive. There could be significant casualties," Tibbits said – then asking for eight troopers to volunteer for the impending attack on the room at the motel.

He further detailed logistics of the plan, telling the troopers that the rest of them would be positioned outside the front and back of the room, watching for the suspect to try and escape from the front door or bathroom window. He warned the troopers that this mission was classified … and that they could not talk about it – ever. "If you do, I guarantee that you'll never hold a position in law enforcement again … the weight of the federal government will exact its toll."

Seemingly unsure that he made his point, Tibbits shared his final warning. "One last thing, if you see me or any other federal agent do something you consider questionable … well you best have the good Lord on your side if you decide to talk about it. My agents will become your worst best friend and your betrayal will haunt you for as long as you live … however long that might be. Now, I'll give you five minutes to call your loved ones."

Ten troopers rushed to the podium to volunteer – more than what was needed. Tibbits could overhear troopers on their phones saying, "I love you so … so much" while attempting to gloss over the "what's going on?" questions. And then there were tears.

Ten minutes later, everyone was on their way to the nearby motel. They arrived in five minutes and began deploying. The FBI agents were already there and had placed listening devices in both rooms … there was no sound of movement coming from the room in between. The battering crews assumed their positions – and all troopers, with earpieces in place – awaited the signal to go.

"This is Tibbits," a voice sounded in their ears. "On my count … we start on three and go on one. Everyone ready?" A round of "check" followed in quick order.

Tibbits wasn't a religious man, but he did believe in a higher power. He wanted to believe in the Resurrection, but watching assholes like Ahmad pop up across the world, using their religious beliefs as a foundation for murder, and now this shit … threatening the Heartland, made a "Come to Jesus" commitment questionable for him. Nonetheless, he bowed his head and asked God to let his men be successful in their actions.

"Three ... Two ... One. Go! Go ... Go!"

Ahmad thought it was an earthquake at first. He bolted upright, spotting the metal piping that had pierced through the walls on both sides of his room. Suddenly there were explosions and blinding light, followed by burning eyes. He was having difficulty breathing, but managed to grab his gun and one clip. He could barely see anything, as he was taking aim at the holes in the wall and emptying the clip. Reloading, he pointed randomly at the opposite wall ... then reached into a pocket of his pants frantically searching for the pills that would put him out of his misery.

They were in the car.

He ran instinctively for the door to get to the car, knowing that once he bit down on the pills, he'd be on his way to heaven. In less than thirty seconds instead, Ahmad was face down on the ground ... it took only another thirty seconds to put Ahmad in the back seat of Tibbits' car, hands cuffed behind him.

The mission over and everyone unharmed, Tibbits radioed

his thanks to Murray and his men for a job well done from his car. He was heading south, followed by another car with three men dressed in brown khaki pants and Columbia shirts.

A third car was a quarter mile behind the first two.

"I'll be damned if this happens in my territory and I don't get to see how it ends," Murray muttered to himself, while trying to keep up.

CHAPTER 40

They're our neighbors in some cases ... or at the very least ... they live and shop in our communities. Their kids go to school with our kids. Most of the time, we never know their background – or what it is they do. They've obeyed orders without question and have done things very few others could or would be willing to do ... or would want to have made public. Any attempt to challenge the strong belief of these men and women that America is the only country capable of standing up for democracy and human decency would be futile.

They possess unique communication skills, but have no presence on social media.

If necessary, they'll use e-mail. Their language is nuanced and exclusive to them – and the message contained within their words is encrypted except when talking with one of their counterparts.

These are the unsung defenders of our country, tactically trained in subterfuge and counter-terrorism. They are America's true patriots.

* * *

Tibbits was taking Ahmad to the home of one of these patriots, a former Army Ranger ... just five minutes south of the motel. He'd been in touch with the retiree during his drive to Hays earlier that day, asking for permission – if all went as planned – to bring the prisoner to his farm where he could be interrogated. Knowing the gravity of the situation that was taking place in Kentucky and Ohio led the Ranger to ask, "Should I arrange for any enhancements? I wouldn't be surprised if he is thirsty." Tibbits gave the okay for the enhancements ... but responded in the negative about intake of any fluids.

Arriving at the farm property, they turned onto a county road and headed quickly towards the farmhouse. As they pulled in the driveway, the former Ranger was waiting to greet his fellow soldier. Tibbits got out of the car, accompanied by an agent who'd made the trip to the farm with him and Ahmad. Fifteen seconds later, the second car pulled up and the three military specialists emerged. Looking back down the drive, Tibbits saw a cloud of dust kicking up on the road he'd just traveled ... someone else was heading for the farmhouse.

"Gentlemen, we've got uninvited company coming, so let's get ready to welcome them," he said.

Murray pulled up directly behind the other cars, and as he got out of the patrol car, felt the pressure of cold metal against the back of his neck.

"Murray, what the hell are you doing here?"

"Goddamn it, Tibbits, you're on my turf ... you put my men in harm's way and yet you expect me to not see this to a conclusion. You can kill me ... go ahead, damn it, but I'm sure as hell not leaving ... at least not until this is over. You owe me that!"

"Let that crazy son of a bitch go!" Tibbits barked.

"Murray, I'm telling you right now – and I hope you remember what I said to your men. It applies to you as well. You're going to see some shit you might not like and so help me God ... if you ever give these men up – any of them – I guarantee that you're a dead man and that includes your family! Have I made myself clear? You can get in your car and drive away right now if you want!"

Murray refused to budge – he knew the situation and that this was not going to be a tea party. Tibbits wheeled around and entered the house, followed by his team, with Murray and the Ranger bringing up the rear. Once inside, the Ranger took the lead, steering the group down a flight of stairs to a room off the main part of a finished basement.

As they entered the room, the first thing they saw was what looked like a long diving board close to a far wall. The board had restraining straps at the bottom, middle and top of it. A garden hose lay coiled on the floor … attached to a water spigot. The board was slightly inclined at the feet, with the head rest tilted down.

Tibbits sat Ahmad down on a folding chair.

* * *

"Okay young man, tell us where your brother and uncle are. Where are they going and what are their targets?" Tibbits stated calmly.

Ahmad spit at Tibbits and missed. Tibbits had expected it.

"You can eat shit, I'm not telling you anything," Ahmad shot back at Tibbits.

"Look, I know you think we've got a lot of time to spend together, but we don't. Take a peek behind you. That's a board I'm going to strap you on. I know you think I'm going to water board you ... but that takes too long. Oh, you're going to get wet ... and then I'm going to slowly electrocute you."

"Get on with it," Ahmad said defiantly.

"So be it," Tibbits replied.

Water boarding was much more predictable. But boarding worked best when the subject was prepped several days beforehand. Loud music and sleep deprivation maximizes the effects of simulated drowning.

Colonel Murray's back began to tighten up again. He saw the antique crank phone now carried towards Ahmad by an agent. Murray was a country boy ... just like Tibbits ... and he knew how the game worked. He'd been a participant in many a "fish fry" with his father, who would crank the phone and dangle the hot wire into the pond. He'd then net the stunned catfish, only stopping when there were enough for a feast.

His spinal cord fired and his muscles began to spasm ... dropping him to the floor this time. "Damn it Murray, if this is too much for you, then leave," Tibbits barked.

"Tibbits, you can't do this! It's torture. Please stop now!" replied Murray.

"OK, Murray, I'll stop … for now … but what are you going to say to those thousands of people whose loved ones are lost to yet another terrorist act – especially when it comes out that we had access to information that could've prevented the catastrophe – but didn't act on it?"

Murray wanted to move his lips, but there were no words that came to him at that moment.

"I tell you what. Your neighbor – our host – is going to take you upstairs to the kitchen. I know he's got some fresh lemonade. You sit down and take a load off your back and we'll be up shortly," Tibbits stated calmly.

CHAPTER 41

After Murray left, Tibbits gave the order for his men to attach the cardiac leads to Ahmad's chest and ankles. Whether it was boarding or other types of interrogation, it was important to monitor the subject's vitals lest the body be stressed too much. Ahmad had almost as much hair on his chest as he once had on his head … Tibbits dry-shaved him which would most likely be considered torture by Geneva Convention standards. Finally, the board was tilted down and the restraints tightened up.

This was all on Tibbits.

Everyone slipped on a pair of muck boots to be grounded against stray electrical shocks. Turning the hose on, Tibbetts adjusted the stream to a fine mist, lightly spraying Ahmad from head to toe. When directed, the agent standing to the right began cranking the phone, while at the same time, placing the hot wire on Ahmad's right ankle. Tibbits applied the hot wire for only a quick second – he wanted Ahmad to feel just a tiny bit of electricity coursing through his body at first.

"Ahmad … how much did you enjoy that?"

Tibbits snapped his fingers and one of the other specialists handed him a dental instrument with a blunted metal tip. "Sure looks harmless ... huh?" Tibbits asked, dangling the tool in front of Ahmad to taunt him, while pulling surgical gloves on both hands.

"It's your lucky day – I'm going to give you the daily double. This thing in my hand is called a pulp tester. Did you ever see the movie *Marathon Man*? The producer and director of the movie wasted far too much money on dental equipment. Who needs a drill when I can use this dental tool? Hell, it's a fraction of the cost of all that other fancy dental crap! I place a little toothpaste on each tooth and some on the tip of this electric tester! Hell, the toothpaste contains titanium dioxide. Titanium, Ahmad, one of the most expensive metals on earth. It conducts electricity generated by the batteries that are inside this tool! First I rotate this dial up to this number ten here! Ya' see that number? Then I place it against each tooth ... one tooth at a time ... until we find the one that doesn't like electricity. I'm betting none of your teeth are going to be happy campers! What do you think?"

Ahmad didn't answer. He didn't need to – his eyes answered for him. Tibbits had seen that look of fear before. He touched Ahmad's right upper central incisor with the tip of the probe, holding it directly on the surface of the tooth for ten seconds. Ahmad's scream was deafening. He had never experienced that type of pain.

"Okay Ahmad, it's time for round two ... unless you want to talk?"

Tibbits placed the exposed wire on Ahmad's groin. "Make the call," he said, nodding to his associate, who started cranking the phone. He held the wire steady for a good five seconds while Ahmad twitched on the board. Checking Ahmad's EKG, Tibbits saw that the heart rate was only slightly elevated and there were no heart abnormalities.

"Ahmad, c'mon ... it's no disgrace to talk."

Ahmad bleated out an emphatic "No!"

Tibbits grabbed the dental instrument again and returned to Ahmad's mouth. This time he maintained contact with a different tooth for thirty seconds. Ahmad's blood pressure soared to 160/100 and there were three skipped heartbeats. Tibbits gave him thirty seconds to compose himself, before leaning down and whispering in Ahmad's ear.

"What do you think ... you're wasting electricity ... how about the truth?" Again Ahmad tried to spit at Tibbits. "OK, Ahmad, I've got plenty of juice."

Tibbits alternated between the torturous processes ten more times. Tibbits' associate motioned him aside, advising that Ahmad's blood pressure had spiked to 220/180 in the last three sessions and his heart rate was 175 beats per minute. Too much more, he said ... and Ahmad's heart might explode. Tibbits had to give it to Ahmad. The kid sure had moxie. Then his phone rang.

"Murray, what the hell do you want?"

"I just got a call from one of my troopers cleaning up at the motel. He said Ahmad's gun was filled with blanks. There were no bullet holes in the walls and the last clip on the bed also had blanks. And get this, the car's console had a couple of pills in it ... our forensics guy believes they are cyanide pills."

Tibbits hung up on Murray. He sat down and closed his eyes.

"Alright, think damn it. The kid didn't load his gun with blanks, and an identical twin brother wouldn't betray him. That meant the uncle wanted Ahmad to fail. And if he wanted the one twin to fail, would he do the same with the other?" Tibbits pondered these thoughts silently.

He called Murray back and quietly took the tongue lashing.

"Colonel, pipe down. Have one of your men bring Ahmad's gun over here, please, and tell him no one else needs to know. Also tell your people to seal off the crime scene. No media is allowed in. Did you hear me, Murray? Damn it, Murray, answer me!"

"Tibbits, I hear you. I'll call him with your instructions, but after this is finished, we need to talk. Is that a deal?"

"We'll talk ... make the call" Tibbitts said in frustration, ending the conversation and upon returning to Ahmad's side, saw that his blood pressure was not stabilizing. He turned to one of the other agents who was also a certified EMT. "What do you think?" he asked, nodding toward Ahmad.

"Maybe one more cycle, but after that I wouldn't chance it ... you'll have to give him a break," he replied.

Tibbitts leaned down and whispered in Ahmad's ear. "Listen

up Ahmad ... your time is almost up. I just got a call from the Kansas Highway Patrol and you're not going to believe this, but your gun was loaded with blanks. There were no bullet holes in your room ... you were firing blanks," he said, laughing lightly at the irony of it.

"That means your uncle really didn't care much for you after all. That's pretty shitty... huh?"

Ahmad's chest heaved slightly and he turned away from Tibbits. He gasped and said, "my hands ... please." Tibbits loosened the restraints and took off the handcuffs. Ahmad reached up to Tibbits and motioned him close. Tibbits had seen it before ... Ahmad was going to roll over on his uncle. "My brother ... Ricin ... Ohio Stadium. The tenth race ... two horses ... the one you think ..."

And then the EKG alarm blared!

Ahmad had flat-lined. Tibbits stepped back, leaving room for the specialist to begin CPR. After a minute, another agent rushed back in with a defibrillator fetched from the car. CPR continued on Ahmad. The defibrillator unit's recorded voice told everyone to clear, which was a good thing as both men were standing in water –

had they'd been touching Ahmad – there would have been three people down. No cardiac rhythm returned. The unit recharged and the voice said "Clear" one more time – again with no response. The team continued CPR, shocking Ahmad one last time. Knowing it was over, the specialist stood straight up … sweat was running down his face as he slowly walked to the corner of the room.

In the meantime, Murray had come downstairs to hand Ahmad's gun to one of the specialists before disappearing, heading back to the kitchen.

Tibbits didn't hesitate. "Sit him up," he ordered. Two specialists propped Ahmad up, watching as Tibbits reached into his holster, pulled out his Glock and began emptying his clip … reloading the live ammunition into Ahmad's clip. Examining both of Ahmad's hands, Tibbits saw that the right wrist was larger – that was his primary hand. Putting the gun in Ahmad's right hand … with the right index finger on the trigger, he placed the barrel against Ahmad's right temple.

Tibbits pulled Ahmad's finger backwards on the trigger.

The blast blew fragments of skin, bone, brain tissue and blood from the exit wound on the opposite side of Ahmad's head.

"Get a bag and load him in the trunk ... collect as much of this spatter as you can! We're going back to the motel," Tibbits told the team as he headed up the basement stairs. "Murray, get in your car. We're going back to the motel."

Five minutes, later the Ranger was once again alone in his farmhouse. He methodically put the board, hose, EKG machine and crank phone back in his safe room, and brought out the Clorox. The enhancement room in the basement would be first. Unfortunately, blood takes far too much time to clean up ... he decided to take a break instead and watch the Kentucky races on satellite television.

Post time for the day's feature race was just a few minutes away.

* * *

Everyone arrived back at the hotel fifteen minutes later – and during the drive, Tibbitts placed a secure call to NSA headquarters, giving them the information they wanted. His superior on the other end grabbed the phone.

"Listen up Tibbits, Ohio's threat is over ... I repeat ... the OSU threat has been eliminated. Nothing has happened yet in

Kentucky." Tibbits listened to the briefing about Ohio Stadium for nearly ten minutes.

Now he was mentally drained.

Back in the motel room Ahmad had reserved only a few hours ago, Tibbits directed the special agents to put the body on the floor between the twin beds, and reloaded the clip with more live ammunition. Making sure the two adjacent rooms were clear, Tibbets fired three shots in one wall and four in the other. Last, he placed the gun in Ahmad's right hand and slowly but forcibly bent the right index finger around the trigger. Checking the angle of Ahmad's body in relation to the wall, he fired a final shot. Powder burns were critical in forensics. The debris from the previous shot to the head was then scattered against the wall.

The next day, the local paper was filled with coverage about the valor of the Kansas Highway Patrol. There was a *What If* editorial that discussed possible scenarios had Ahmad not committed suicide. However, it was the tragedies in Ohio and Kentucky that dominated the front page. A television reporter actually speculated on what would have happened if the authorities had captured Ahmad earlier in the day … and whether the FBI would have been able to get information from the terrorist through enhanced interrogation methods.

Tibbits tied up any loose ends at the morgue, making sure the coroner was on board and would officially list suicide as the cause of death.

Finally at 10 p.m., Tibbits sat down for the promised talk with Colonel Murray. They argued with each other into the wee hours of the morning and finally agreed to disagree. But after dissecting all the day's events, and debating their philosophies, both agreed on one thing. Ahmad didn't die from the electric shock therapy, he died from a broken heart.

CHAPTER 42

As Jamil flew the plane through the darkened sky and out into the sunlight, he felt like a bullseye target was now painted on him. He kept glancing nervously above him and from side to side in the cockpit – not sure what he expected to see – but finally regaining control of his emotions. The weather front was now to his east and he banked right, heading in the direction of the front … hoping for some protective cover from the residual clouds trailing behind the storms.

He assumed that by now, he was a hunted man.

Jamil's uncle had created all the alternate scenarios he could imagine, based on the eventuality that their air attack plan had fallen apart. Jamil was free to choose another target if necessary.

Any terrorist flying on this or any other day would do so with a fatalistic acceptance that unlike 9/11, there would now be armed fighter planes dispatched by the U.S. Air Force to take down rogue aircraft in the skies. There would be no kamikaze maneuver reminiscent of Lt. Heather Penney … hoping to ram an unarmed

F-16 into a plane controlled by terrorists … for Jamil today. Strangely though, he drew comfort from the fact that he would most likely meet his God quickly and painlessly after his aircraft was annihilated by an air-to-air missile.

Reaching a bank of clouds, Jamil began to fly long oval loops while heading northeast … and then reversing course back to the southwest. The plane's altitude was two thousand feet – and Air Traffic Control began hailing Jamil as soon as he entered Indianapolis airspace. He refused to answer them. They could see the plane on their screens … but he was an outlier with no flight plan filed.

The transponder was still on … even though Jamil had intended to turn it off during takeoff. "As long as I remain in these clouds, I'll be invisible," he thought.

He was content to loop his way towards Columbus, knowing the storms were also headed in that direction … he prayed the front would hold together and not weaken.

At seventy-five hundred feet and fifty miles to the southeast, Southwest Flight 3474 was heading towards Jamil's position – the pilot unaware that a small plane would soon enter his airspace. The

737 was in a holding pattern and the pilot in a slow descent on final approach, awaiting clearance for a very late arrival at Indianapolis International Airport.

"Indianapolis Control ... this is Southwest 3474 ... my fuel level is critical. I need landing clearance ... please advise my options," was heard over the airways.

The Southwest pilot knew there was a chance he'd be told to divert south to Louisville ... but not southeast to the Cincinnati/ Northern Kentucky International Airport. His onboard weather radar showed that the storm cloud tops around Cincinnati were currently well over forty thousand feet. He had also declared an emergency when there was none – in reality, there was enough fuel, but the passengers were becoming restless.

"Southwest 3474 ... this is Indianapolis Control. Are you declaring an emergency?"

"Indianapolis Control ... this is Southwest 3474 ... I'm declaring an emergency." After landing, the pilot knew he'd be questioned by the FAA ... he'd deal with that issue later.

"This is Indianapolis Control ... turn one-hundred degrees

left and descend to twenty-three hundred feet. ILS has you …
ceiling is three hundred feet and winds are twenty-five knots
variable out of the north/northwest with gusts up to thirty knots.

"You are number one for landing on Runway Left two-three
… repeat … you are number one for landing on Runway L-two-three."

The control tower still had Jamil's aircraft on its screen …
and once again tried to hail him.

"This is Indianapolis Air Traffic Control hailing unidentified
aircraft … do you read me?"

"This is Indianapolis Control … unidentified aircraft heading
northeast at two thousand feet, please identify yourself."

Jamil was monitoring Indianapolis Control and realized that
he wasn't invisible. His plane's transponder was on and his plane
was still a blip on the air traffic control screen. "I'm an idiot," Jamil
said to himself while quickly switching off his transponder. Jamil
stopped his long loop – instead doing a one-eighty in the opposite
direction … and unknowingly placing himself on a collision course
with Southwest 3474.

"Southwest 3474 … this is Indianapolis Control … we have an unidentified aircraft heading towards you. I repeat … an unidentified aircraft is in your airspace! The pilot has turned off the transponder and the aircraft is off our primary screen … repeat … off our primary screen!"

"Initiate evasive maneuvers!"

Southwest 3474's pilot throttled up and began a quick ascent … too late!

Jamil quickly turned his aircraft to the west … too late!

Jamil never saw the Boeing 737. It's difficult to see anything when your plane is suddenly flipped upside down. He struggled to regain control and fought the yoke for another half minute. Righting the plane, Jamil somehow managed to level the wings. In another minute he'd regained control of the flight … and his bladder. "Damn jet-wash," he mumbled to himself.

* * *

"Jesus Christ … c'mon climb, baby … steady! Steady, damn it!"

Pete turned to his co-pilot. "You okay Jeff?" he asked his visibly shaken number two in command.

Jeff shook his head up and down. He also had experienced a bladder problem in those frightening seconds. "Did you see what it was, Pete?" Jeff asked angrily.

"Some kind of single engine sports plane, I think," Pete replied.

"Better call it in to Indy control. It's a damned good thing that alarm went off," Jeff shouted.

Jeff was referring to the 737's TCAS alarm system which sounds when an air collision is imminent. Instead of descending, for some reason Pete put the aircraft in a climb. Pete might occasionally tell a lie, but he was a man of faith … and at that moment, believed he had just been part of a miracle.

"Call back to the cabin attendants and see if our passengers are alright. I'm calling Indy control and telling them what happened," Pete advised Jeff.

Pete didn't need to call Indianapolis Control ... they were already watching Flight 3474's erratic flying on screen ... and knew the plane had just performed an evasive maneuver.

Ten thousand feet above Indianapolis, a USAF drone – with a live feed to Homeland and the NSA – was also watching. There were drones flying over every major metropolitan city in the Tri-State on this day. Even though Jamil's aircraft didn't have a set of electronic eyes on it at the moment, Indianapolis Control, Homeland Security and the NSA now knew what their adversary was flying that afternoon.

Homeland instantly ordered all air traffic in Ohio, Indiana and Kentucky to land immediately. The message was sent on all frequencies with Indianapolis Control having the responsibility for routing the majority of the planes to safe landings. The control towers at Louisville, Cincinnati and Columbus handled those planes entering their respective airspaces – all now flying below ten thousand feet – and in the FAA's B Category altitude level.

Jamil realized he was truly alone as he continued toward Columbus. "Why haven't they taken me out?" he wondered aloud. He mistakenly assumed it was due to his plane's carbon fiber structure. "They can't see me," he laughed.

If only he knew the truth, he might have lived. One of America's most protected secrets is its stealth technology … and conversely, its need to have the necessary reverse technology that enables the detection of aircraft with similar stealth capabilities. It wasn't an easy process … but became simpler today with the skies so empty. Jamil's plane was now the only aircraft detected, and on its way to Columbus, Ohio.

CHAPTER 43

After the events of 9/11, Ohio Stadium was classified by the National Security and Defense Intelligence Agencies as among the nation's tier one targets for terrorists. The two agencies were the precursor of what would become Homeland Security – and at that time, it fell to the NSA and DIA to develop a list of potential targets, and create and prepare for what-if scenarios across the country.

It was obvious ... given that the Twin Towers in NYC were destroyed on that fateful day and an earlier attack was made on the North Tower in 1993 ... that this particular site of land would always be a prime target for terrorists.

However, on this day, the potential for death, destruction and devastation was much more significant at Ohio Stadium. Whether it was a regular season game or the team's annual Spring Scrimmage event, an attack of any form on the Horseshoe could easily parallel the 1993 World Trade Center bombing and the kamikaze attacks of 2001.

In fact, the numbers of injuries and fatalities from the 1993 attack, as well as the attacks on the towers on 9/11, could easily be surpassed by an attack at The Ohio State University football stadium.

During any given weekend throughout football season, Homeland Security is responsible for monitoring terrorist threats – and ensuring the safety of spectators and players on college campuses across the country every Saturday. The agency turns around and does the same thing the very next day – as NFL teams play their games in packed stadiums. It's a demanding responsibility of the Homeland Security folks as there is no shortage of collegiate and professional sporting events in the U.S. ... events that draw thousands of citizens into the tightly packed stadiums or arenas on a given day.

Yet, Homeland Security can't launch fighter jets to circle above and refuel at every one of these venues each weekend of football season – it would be a logistical nightmare and an economic disaster. However, the agency knows what battles to pick ... which is why it decided to focus its primary attention on Ohio this particular weekend.

If there was to be an attack using explosive devices, the most significant propaganda gain for the terrorists would come from video and still photos of bloody bodies strewn throughout the stadium. If the attack was biological or chemical in nature, then videos of people retching, and covering their faces while gasping for air, would help advance the terrorist's cause … in their sick minds. The best most impacting attack by far, though, would be by radiation. Not only would there be immediate physical harm and human suffering, the lingering effects of radiation incurred by countless individuals who survived the attack would be newsworthy for months … even years. What a great psychological victory that would be for the terrorists!

The twins fully believed they would be celebrated worldwide for their actions … especially in Islamic communities … just as Bin Ladin had been. After all, that's what their father had written to them in an online encrypted message only forty-eight hours ago.

Homeland Security didn't believe in luck … and they were unsure as to why so many clues and tips about the possible attacks had fortuitously fallen in their laps this week. Einstein gave them a reality check, indicating in a report that whoever or whatever was running the suspected terrorist operations this weekend wanted Homeland to know exactly what the targets were going to be. Those who worked with Einstein agreed – and were grateful to have the supercomputer on their side!

The analysts also knew that if Homeland did successfully prevent or stop an attack, the terrorists would most likely still gain a measure of economic and psychological victory.

The Kentucky Thoroughbred track was also tagged by Homeland – but as the least likely primary target. This determination was driven more by the economies of horse racing – the agency believing that the business and horse racing connections with Saudi Arabian and United Arab Emirates business factions in Kentucky would preclude such an attack.

Tommy wasn't as sure ... he was still strongly insistent that the race track was a primary target on this weekend. "Whoever the masterminds are behind this, they seem to be sure that the majority of our resources are going to be vested in Columbus ... and that's what they want," he told his superiors more than once.

Tommy wasn't kept fully in the loop – Homeland intended to split its resources between the two venues close to sixty-forty. However, prayers would be equally distributed fifty-fifty.

* * *

In the early pre-dawn hours of Saturday morning, the U.S. Air Force had dispatched several of its fighter planes to the Midwest. There were two Boeing KC 135 military planes and two Boeing KC 46 Pegasus fueling tankers. The Pegasus tankers had just received their flight certification, and were dead-heading to their Ohio and Kentucky destinations ... carrying multiple teams of Air Force military personnel. Operation Noble Eagle was now underway with the military defense system NORAD-NORTHCOM in command of operations.

Accompanying the Pegasus tankers were two more teams of fighter planes – four Lockheed Martin F-22 Raptors and four Lockheed Martin F-35 Lightning II aircraft. All of the planes took off from the famed Area 51 in Roswell, New Mexico. Besides the standard military armament carried in these planes, these planes were equipped with highly-sophisticated weaponry systems – some of which first came into use during the Reagan era.

It was during Reagan's years in the White House that the *Star Wars* phenomenon first hit the big screen – and America's fascination with bizarre and out-there weaponry and battlefield platforms began. It wasn't just the average American who was intrigued – the U.S. military paid attention as well – and began to research and develop new technologies designed to help the

American military protect the country.

Could there be nuclear-driven technologies? Despite research on atom-driven engines conducted by General Electric years ago in Connecticut and Ohio, the Air Force eventually gave up on the concept of a nuclear-powered aircraft – that would have to wait until new technology was developed that would make the dream a reality.

But ... weapon systems were different. Perhaps a small nuclear reactor could be capable of generating enough energy to produce a laser weapon. Those dreamers of yesteryear ... whose imaginations were the genesis for all the Stealth weapons and their platforms ... would be proud of these newer Stealth fighters now heading east and carrying laser cannons.

In late 2014, the U.S. Navy publicly released information and a video about a laser weapon on social media. The weapon is described as having multiple beam settings – and it was implied that it was also capable of several levels of destruction. The demonstration videos showed the downing of a small drone and the disabling of a small raft-type attack boat, a boat not dissimilar to what Somali pirates were known to use as they terrorized others on the seas.

Nowhere else was it divulged that laser cannons had become a vital part of America's ground and aircraft weapons systems.

In a world where individuals still question whether the chicken or the egg came first, the people who contributed to the Star Wars initiative would readily reveal – if they were allowed to – that the stealth technology was developed first. Using reverse technology, our military also soon learned how to identify an adversary's stealth capabilities and gather information on weapons that would eventually be developed.

No weapon system remains impossible or secret forever.

* * *

Jamil had no idea his CTLSi aircraft was being shadowed – or that the tracking started immediately upon his departure from Southern Kentucky. The sports plane was being surveilled by a Northrop Grumman RQ4 Global Hawk unmanned U.S. aircraft that was attached to the Air Force fleet launched to the Midwest earlier in the day.

Homeland Security's toughest decision this weekend was whether to risk totally exposing its newest spy plane asset, the teardrop shaped Aurora T-3 and its look-alike mini drones. The only other choices were to rely on the old-school, but now modernized U-2 spy plane with sophisticated surveillance systems, or settle on an unmanned plane because of the extreme weather conditions. The decision was finally made – opting for two of the three choices. Primary eyes-on responsibility was tasked to the unmanned RQ4 aircraft – and a piloted U-2 would serve as a backup in the event of severe weather and extreme cloud tops.

The RQ4's air traffic control screens were more sophisticated than Indianapolis Control's radar screens. Homeland could modulate between the screens that showed all aircraft with transponders turned on – that in turn verified any corresponding flight plans that had been filed. The system could also switch over to a screen that identified aircraft whose pilots were flying carelessly, perhaps joyriding for a few minutes – or worse, in physical distress. Or ... like Jamil, their intent was illicit and designed to do harm.

The RQ4 lost Jamil briefly when he crossed through the weather front ... the system quickly recovered the plane's signature and watched as Southwest 3474 almost brought Jamil's aircraft down.

By now, a debate was raging at the Defense Department over

how they were going to bring Jamil down. Several agents wanted to bring the CTLSi down with a Pulsed Energy Projectile – a weapon relatively new to tactical warfare – some said it was like lightening in a canister. The small smart bomb would be dropped and detonate in close proximity to Jamil's plane. After it exploded, the expanding blob of energy and its sound, light and electromagnetic waves would shut down every one of the CTLSi's electronic systems. The engine would quit and Jamil would be forced to glide and land. The plane's payload would be preserved … with the worst case scenario being that a rural farm or community might suffer casualties.

Other agents argued that two of the fighters should fire their laser cannons and tear apart the CTLSi's tail section … making the plane aeronautically crippled but still maintain its functioning electronics. The terrorist could then fire the plane's rocket-propelled parachute … and the plane would descend harmlessly.

The agency's primary concern was which form of take-down would cause the most confusion for Jamil … and distract him from releasing the payload … whatever it was.

The debate raged on as Jamil crossed the Indiana-Ohio border.

POTUS, exasperated with the back and forth bickering,

finally forced a resolution.

"Gentleman, time is of the essence. We're going to bring it down in five minutes – and by the way, all of your concerns are valid. So I'll make this easy for you – I'm going to make the call – it's on me now.

Both methods are equally efficient as far as I can tell. You're still going to have a window of time when the terrorist is relatively free to make a decision about what to do with the payload. Right now, you still have another terrorist somewhere in Kansas, hopefully close to being captured and interrogated, and a third terrorist whose whereabouts are still not known and still unaccounted for!" POTUS told the indecisive national defense agency.

"Disable the plane by using the laser cannon and let the pilot deploy the chute. Once your people are sure that the parachute is working, buzz the hell out of him with your fighters and drop the EMP or whatever the hell your new bomb is … he won't be able to use electronics to deploy or activate his payload. Distract … distract … distract until agents on the ground get there and capture the son of a bitch. We've got to learn about their entire plan."

"Engage now, damn it!" was POTUS's last order.

CHAPTER 44

Jamil sighed as he crossed the Indiana-Ohio border ... nervous, but ready for what was going to happen today. He banked the plane forty-five degrees, along a route that would head northeast for seventy-five miles, until he made one more forty-five degree turn – this time heading southeast towards Columbus. He and Ahmad had flown this path as well as the direct path from Southern Kentucky up I-75 to I-71 in March performing trial runs. Jamil knew this particular route allowed him to avoid air traffic around Wright Patterson Air Force Base, as well as from Dayton's International Airport.

Once past the suburbs of Dayton, there'd be nothing but farmland below – that didn't matter today – the clouds were so heavy, no one would be able to see him. His presence could only be detected by the sound of the plane's engine bouncing off the clouds and the ground.

Or so he believed.

Now on autopilot, Jamil allowed his mind to wander. He was visualizing the small scale mock-up of Ohio Stadium and the geographic landscape and landmarks around it. The mock-up had been constructed by his uncle … and it helped Jamil familiarize himself with the campus without actually being in Columbus.

The plane's GPS would indicate when he was getting near the Olentangy River. He planned to follow the river in a southern direction when he was about fifteen miles north of the stadium … when he'd begin a slow descent in and out of the clouds. Once past the Lane Avenue Bridge, he'd slow the speed and begin a final approach, turning 180 degrees just south of Twelfth Avenue. He knew it was time for visual flying – and that the CTLSi was going to lose its protective cover of the clouds during the descent.

Jamil let his thoughts wander back to the plan – a plan that was crystal clear in his mind. As the plane began to cross over the athletic complex, just south of the stadium, Jamil would drop down to 100 feet … he could already visualize the look on the faces of the fans still tailgating outside the stadium. "At first, they'll have a skeptical 'What the hell is that guy doing?' look in their eyes," he told himself. "Then the horror will sink in … their faces will take on an 'Oh shit, it's another 9/11' look of terror!"

Jamil began laughing out loud and resumed his thoughts.

When the plane was about four hundred yards from the south end of the stadium, Jamil was going to drop even more ... down to thirty feet ... and begin evasive maneuvers. He was realistic ... anticipating that the Ohio Highway Patrol's fixed-wing aircraft or choppers would be in offensive positions, and would start to fire on him as he approached the stadium.

"They'll fire automatic weapons, and have sharpshooters positioned on the north and south stadium towers," Jamil predicted to himself.

"Once I start my approach, someone is going to notice and call in the fighters ... but they'll be too late. I'll punch it, go up and over the seats by the south end zone ... and drop the Ricin. I'll finish my mission by killing the engine ... glide, launch the parachute rocket and finally ... drop the plane into the stadium," Jamil promised, in deep reverie with his eyes closed.

Unexpectedly jolted out of his imaginings, Jamil opened his eyes to a sudden burst of what appeared to be a bolt of lightning exploding directly in front of the cockpit. The resulting shock wave caused the CTLSi to shake violently. "What ... what just happened?" he asked, blinded by the explosion. His brain swirled, trying to make sense of what was taking place. He was unaware that the plane was under attack by an F-22 that was now sharing airspace with his smaller plane.

It was eerily silent – and Jamil was still temporarily blinded when laser beams – this time aimed at the CTLSi's tail section – were fired by both F-35 fighters.

The nose of Jamil's plane tipped downward.

In quick succession, another group of explosions came from above and in front of the cockpit – the aircraft had been struck by "lightening in a can" ... twice.

"Shit, what was that? I gotta' look for a place to land," was Jamil's gut reaction.

The tail section was now hanging from the main fuselage of the sports plane and the CTLSi began a dive. Jamil instinctively activated the parachute launcher button and heard the rocket launch. Within five seconds, the parachute had contained enough air to fill itself and tighten its tethers to what remained of the plane. It was then that the Air Force dropped an EMP that exploded over the CTLSi.

Jamil was still at a loss when suddenly an F-22 appeared midair, seemingly hovering in front of the smaller plane – the fighter's nose pointing up at about 60 degrees, Jamil couldn't believe what he was seeing. The pilot in the fighter was repeatedly gesturing towards the ground – as if Jamil didn't already know where he was going.

Reaching behind to grab his backpack, Jamil opened it and retrieved his handgun. While his uncle had pre-loaded one clip of ammunition and included another two in the backpack, Jamil had also brought his own clips – something else he didn't share with Ben. Jamil was a fan of hollow point bullets – and if he was going down, he was going to take others with him in a big way. Removing the clip that had been loaded by his uncle, Jamil replaced that with his own – never realizing that his uncle had intentionally loaded the gun with blanks.

The plane was going down – and Jamil was helpless to do anything. The ground was quickly rising to meet the plane – and Jamil could see several vehicles with flashing blue lights on the ground waiting. There was no sense in dispensing the payload now ... there was nothing below worth killing. However, the flashing lights told Jamil that there was no shortage of federal agents and other law enforcement personnel just waiting to take him out.

Permanently.

He was dead wrong. There were plenty of law officers waiting – but they wanted him alive.

The agents and local police had specific orders – do not shoot to kill, only to wound the suspect. Direct orders were that if a shot was taken, "it damn well better not kill the subject!"

The CTLSi touched down on its nose and it became obvious to Jamil that the plane was stuck in that position. Quickly releasing his safety belt, he opened the door and jumped to the ground. Quickly surveying his surroundings, he realized he was alone … for the moment. He didn't know whose farm he had dropped in on and didn't care … at this point, Jamil needed cover and a good defensive position.

Seeing a thick grove of trees about four hundred yards away, he began running for cover, hoping to find a small creek or pond to help with his escape. It was no more than three minutes though before he heard the sound of motorcycles racing across the farmland … he situated himself behind one of the larger trees to take cover.

"That can't be motorcycles, Jamil," he told himself. You're an idiot. ... those are quad runners."

Raising his head slightly, he caught sight of eight quads traveling over rough rain-soaked fields, which also appeared to have been recently-plowed. The riders were coming at him in pairs from every angle and direction. They came to a halt about one hundred twenty-five yards away from the trees and dismounted ... taking protective cover behind the vehicles.

Jamil was ready for them ... "Okay, tell me how nice you're going to be. Tell me you just want to talk with me. Tell me I haven't broken any laws and everything's going to be wonderful ... you fuckers!" he thought to himself.

And sure enough, that was the first message to him. The second statement was unexpected and rocked Jamil to the core.

"Young man ... we had your twin brother surrounded in Kansas thirty minutes ago. He gave himself up and told us to tell you to do the same thing. C'mon ... make it easy on yourself. You and your brother won't do any time if you tell us what your uncle is going to do ... just give us the when and where," the voice on the bullhorn stated.

The agent who spoke those words had no idea he'd just lit Jamil's fuse – unleashing a pent-up anger that was so quick to rise in both twins. Jamil realized that those waiting for his response didn't know which of the twins they were talking to – he hadn't been called by either name.

Jamil was going to be Mustafa, his hero from the movie *American Sniper*. He'd seen the movie four times, silently cheering each time Mustafa sniped and killed an American soldier. This would be his holy moment now … and those hunting him would be on the receiving side of his vengeance.

The F-22 was circling above the action on the ground.

"Rufous, do you read me?"

"Roger that, Groundhog. I'm over your position," Rufous replied.

"Rufous" was the call sign for the F-22 pilot who'd released the flash-bangs that blinded Jamil for a while.

"You need some assistance, Groundhog?" Rufous asked.

"Rufous, do you have any more of that lightning in a can ordnance and if so … how much? I need a diversion. Over."

"Groundhog … I've got at least another seven or eight … how about you tell me when to drop? I'll set the detonators for ground only. You make the call. Over."

"Roger that, Rufous. Give me five minutes. I'll be back at you. Over."

"Rufous" was Col. Jack Zacharias of the U.S. Air Force. He had over a thousand flight hours behind the controls of an F-22. They didn't call him "Rufous" because he was a redhead … it was because every time he went into battle, his neck would turn red. His roommate at the Air Force Academy first picked up on this strange occurrence and told Jack the name fit because the neck of a rufous hummingbird also turns red – when it drives other hummingbirds away from feeders.

The Groundhog agent communicating with Rufous was Dan Shoemacher, a close friend of Tommy and a fellow graduate of the Citadel. Dan wanted one last chance to convince the twin to surrender.

"Ahmad … or is it Jamil? Why don't we end this right now? You don't really want to die. Son, look around you. It's spring, everything is coming alive again. It's a time to renew …"

Jamil determined the general direction the voice was coming from … and took his first shot, aiming at the left front tire of the quad runner. The tire exploded when the hollow point hit.

"That ought to shut him up," Jamil thought.

He shouted to nobody in particular, "My name's Jamil ... let's get it on, damn it."
Jamil wanted to honor his father at that moment.

"Rufous, close in on the target and engage in two minutes. Start the countdown."

"Engaging, Groundhog … you're on my count now."

As the second-hand on his watch slowly advanced, Dan gave the order for his men to prepare to advance the remaining one hundred twenty-five yards to the target.

"Twenty … fifteen … ten … five … four … three … two …

one. Now! Now ... Now!" he shouted over the radio.

From the corner of his eye, Jamil saw something fall from the sky and bury itself in the furrowed field some twenty five yards in front of him ... he was blinded for the third time that day. There were explosions and flashes of hot white light all around him, as he was knocked backwards onto his back. Bolting upright, he emptied the clip, aiming at no one in particular.

"You stupid fuck ... you just wasted your ammo," Jamil verbally chastised himself. He quickly loaded a second clip, peering from his position behind the tree ... searching for someone, anyone ... to kill. Detecting movement twenty yards to his right, he carefully took aim when suddenly, he felt a burning pain in his right thigh. Looking down, Jamil felt his right kneecap jerking and saw bone piercing through a gaping hole in his right pants leg. The leg buckled and he slumped to his right. One moment later ... the same thing happened to his left leg.

Unable to stand, Jamil crawled out from behind the tree, once again focusing on his target. He pulled the trigger nine times in succession.

Repeating the words he'd heard each time at the beginning of the *American Sniper* movie, Jamil screamed ..."Allahu Akbar."

Then, he pressed the automatic pistol to his right temple, pulling the trigger one last time.

"Rufous, cease fire. Good work … target is down … disengage."

The fighter planes broke away and headed north to Swanton Air Force Base near Toledo, followed by the Pegasus tanker and the RQ4 aircraft.

On the ground, Dan approached Jamil with his weapon drawn and gave him a hard kick to the ribs … there was no sign of life. Kneeling down, Dan felt for a pulse in the carotid artery … Jamil had succeeded in killing himself.

Holstering his weapon, Dan gently closed Jamil's eyelids. The gaping hole in Jamil's head caused him to turn away and he began dry heaving. "Why Lord … why can't you sort this shit out? Why must this go on and on? If I hear Allahu Akbar one more time and it's followed by yet another death …" His sorrowful plea ended.

Jamil would never know that Ahmad also died with one side of his head shattered and destroyed in the same manner.

Perhaps it was an identical twin thing.

CHAPTER 45

Ben had no idea how this Saturday day would end – but was certain that the events he'd set in motion left no room for turning back. His two nephews might be another story ... he'd done his best to make sure they would no longer be a menace to mankind. His thoughts turned to the start of his day several hours earlier.

* * *

Wondering if the severe weather projections had changed from the previous evening, he turned on his favorite local TV morning news program. Unfortunately the conditions had worsened.

Taking his morning cup of coffee outside, he sat down in the lounge chair for a few minutes ... waiting for the typical sounds of nature that accompanied his spring morning ritual.

He heard the chirps and tones of the song birds coming from the two mockingbirds that nested in a tree next to his patio. They sang in their mocking manner, drowning out the real chirps coming from the nearby robins, blue jays, cardinals and doves that started his morning. After fifteen minutes, Ben went back inside to watch the last of the morning news. The anchorman was talking about a recent geological event that was common in Kentucky – a sink hole – an occurrence that was one of the morning's top news stories. A geologist was explaining what might have caused it to open up underneath the airport's main runway.

It was time to leave, and Ben packed some food to carry, along with his nine millimeter handgun and five fully loaded clips, and any other items he thought he'd need during that day.

Now, nearly eight hours later, he was hawking race programs.

* * *

After introducing himself to the other staff on the 'Mountain', Ben set out to sell his programs while casually watching the two other employees he'd just met.

The two employees walked about thirty yards away from him and seemed to be in an animated discussion. "I may need to be prepared for something," Ben said to himself, after seeing the pair approach a Metro cop and engage him in a conversation … one that Ben couldn't hear.

He knew it was only a matter of minutes before he'd be challenged by the officer.

Reaching into his pocket, Ben removed three fake badges. Placing two of the forged badges back in his pocket, Ben put the third badge into the right-side pocket of his coat. Going about his business and avoiding eye contact with the officer heading in his direction, Ben bided his time, waiting for the interruption.

"Excuse me sir, is it Dick? I'm sorry to interrupt your sale, I wonder if I might ask …"

"No problem, Officer ... let me give change to this patron … thank you, young lady ... that's very much appreciated," Ben said to the woman who had given him a tip.

"Now ... what can I do for you, Officer?"

"You're new up here on the Mountain. When did you hire on?" the officer asked.

"I interviewed late last week and started yesterday … they had me doing concierge work up by the paddocks. Today, they asked me to move up here for the afternoon," Ben replied.

It was now a judgment call ... Ben tried to determine if the cop believed him. Did his story come across as legit? Had the cop bought it? Ben didn't want to burn his "get out of jail card" so soon ... and had to decide quickly whether to use it or lose it. The decision took no more than three seconds to make, after which Ben calmly said, "Officer, hold on a second ... we need to talk."

Ben pulled out the stolen badge he'd put in his pocket – it was an FBI security badge – the same badge that Jamie had proudly worn two hours earlier.

"I just got here a couple hours ago. I'm attached to the Knoxville office. I'm up here on the Mountain to watch for any unusual activity. Specifically, there have been rumors that a drone might be launched from here. Those two employees aren't supposed to know about me ... nor is anyone else," Ben calmly stated.

Reversing his conciliatory demeanor, Ben then stated in a demanding voice, "Now it's up to you to convince those guys that I'm legitimate. You screw this up ... I guarantee the only police work you'll find next week is in Pikeville! Have I cleared things up for you?" he asked harshly.

"Yes sir," the Metro officer replied sheepishly.

Ben dismissed him with a wave of his hand and resumed selling programs as if nothing had happened. In reality, he was taking several deep breaths, trying to calm himself. "Damn it, I wanted to save that badge to use later. I'll never know if I really needed to do it," Ben said desolately to himself.

The fourth race had just finished … the sixth race was slated as the first of five consecutive Stakes Races. Ben checked the program, figuring that post time would be in twenty-five minutes. He continued to sell programs while casually watching the approach path that snaked up the Mountain, looking for any unusual activity.

A half hour passed and the fifth race had yet to begin. Another ten minutes went by … and finally, the horses were entering the track.

Ben knew the reason for the unexpected delay. "You're looking for me … but you need more time," he said to himself. "So you slow the race card down … brilliant. I'd do the same thing if I was in charge," Ben thought. Ben also was sufficiently savvy about the world of horse racing – and knew that the Derby Prep Stakes Race still had to go off at a time that met the demands and schedule of network television. And, he laughed to himself, "You're going to have trainers and owners going nuts because you've screwed up their horse's schedules. Good luck with that!"

* * *

Every staff team leader was now at the administration offices ... Ted wasted no time getting to the point.

"Ladies and gentlemen, thanks for getting here so quickly. My people are now passing out enhanced photos of a man who is armed and dangerous. He already shot a Federal Agent on our grounds today." Ted paused to let that sink in, before advising the team leaders that the man was one of three suspected of being involved in terrorist activities today – and that there was sufficient reason to believe he was going to conduct some form of terrorist attack at the track.

Ted added that in fact, the man was already on the grounds, dressed as an employee attached to Guest Services, and last seen with an employee track identification badge bearing the name of Richard or Dick. "You've probably already noticed that today's race card has been delayed – we believe he intends to inflict a level of terrorism during the tenth race. I do not want any of you to try and be a hero … I repeat … do not be a hero. This man will kill you if confronted." He ended his report by telling the employees that if anyone sees Richard, they should immediately find a track security officer, a Metro police officer – or any other individual wearing the track logo hats designed for special law officers. "Most of these folks are federal agents," Ted again shared with the group.

Ted turned towards Tommy, and whispering loudly asked, "Is there anything you want to add?"

The effects of the morphine were wearing off, and Tommy was obviously feeling the pain in his broken hand. The throbbing was significantly more intense and the levels of pain racing throughout the hand were accelerating. Tommy started to stand, but slumped back into the chair … motioning for Ted to bend down so he could speak to him.

Tommy whispered, "We need to gain an advantage. First, any of the employees wearing the caramel colored all-weather coats should shed them. That's one less set of pockets he'll have to hide things in. Tell them to direct the team members that they know personally to invert the American Flag Pin if they're wearing it. I know many of your employees are ex-veterans and they'll strenuously object to this, but it's the best way to trip up our jihadist.

He won't be checking the position of lapel pins, but we will."

"Jesus … that's sheer genius! Why didn't I think of that?" Ted questioned of himself.

Ted then explained to the team leaders what Tommy had come up with and finished with an added warning. "Folks, there's not much time left between now and the tenth race … don't let this bastard spit in your face! That's what he's doing ... he's mocking you!

Let's find him and capture him! We can do this … dammit!"

CHAPTER 46

As the track's team leaders were leaving the administration office and the meeting with Ted and Tommy, a phone began to vibrate loudly. Recognizing the number, Tommy answered the call.

"Did the river reach flood level?" Tommy asked.

"If fifty-two feet is flood level … then, yes it has," the caller responded.

Tommy told the person, "Hold on ... I've got another call." A call was coming in from me, over the walkie-talkie. "Rob, I was heading down your way. I'll see you in a few minutes," Tommy said, ending my call and returning to the caller still waiting on the mobile phone.

"Danny, I got the flash message … what happened?"

"We never had a chance, Tommy. The kid was determined to martyr himself. Our sharpshooters took out his legs … he unloaded on us and then scattered his brains all over the cornfield. Now get this … he had two unused loaded clips, but when we inventoried the plane, there were several other unused clips … all loaded with blanks.

Danny went into detail about what else was found on the plane, telling Tommy that the HAZMAT team first suspected Ricin during its preliminary investigation of the payload, but quickly realized there was no threat. "It's nothing but fine salt granules coated with unscented talcum powder. There were a couple of cyanide pills too. I've racked my brain trying to figure out all the contradictions and still don't understand this jihadist's plans. It's like he was taunting us and saying, 'I'm going to scare the shit out of you Ohioans, but I'll really be faking you out.' Ha, ha, ha!"

"Tommy … are you listening?"

Tommy was multi-tasking. He was listening to what Danny was telling him while also filling a syringe with pain medication. It was half the amount of morphine he'd taken earlier … and Tommy needed to finish the injection.

"Sorry Danny, I dummied up this afternoon when breaking into a car. Instead of using a side kick to shatter the window, I used my fist. Now my hand is broken and I sort of bullied the paramedics into giving me some pain meds. I was just loading the syringe."

Tommy continued talking as he injected the contents of the syringe into a muscle. "I just got an update about the other twin. One of our guys, Tibbitts, is in charge of the operation in Kansas … where they captured Ahmad. They were getting ready to start the interrogation of him a few minutes ago. I'll let you know what I hear back."

Removing the syringe and capping it, Tommy told Danny he felt that the Homeland Security analysts were finally starting to listen and think he was right after all … and that the Kentucky race track is the real target. "I don't take any comfort in that, and the fact that we can't find the uncle only confirms my greatest fear. This race track has always been a soft target … although they've done an amazing job with their security preparedness for the weekend on such short notice."

"Christ, Danny …" Tommy added, "I wish you could be down here right now. The twin's uncle has me so twisted up in knots. Every move I make, he counters!"

"Tommy, it sounds like you're chasing a shadow … so quit chasing!"

"Damn it, Danny, stop messing with me!"

"Tommy … you need to stop trying to second guess his every move. Quit wondering where he'll be in fifteen minutes or a half hour from now … time is running out too quickly for that. Focus on what you think his intent is … concentrate your resources in that direction," Danny responded with sincerity.

Danny knew his best friend wasn't thinking clearly, and decided to pose a series of questions and answers for Tommy to focus on. The most crucial question was … what is the primary target? If the uncle is wearing an explosive vest … where would he accomplish the most carnage and have the biggest impact? Could the vest itself be a chemical or biological weapon? If he is carrying a firearm or grenades … then how would these possibilities all come into play?

He gave Tommy some time to digest all that before speaking again.

"Tommy, five races are over. The spotlight hasn't been turned on yet and I'm guessing he won't act until the national television feed goes live … and I mean network TV, not the cable horse racing channel. If the Derby Prep Stakes Race is the uncle's intended target of attack … then the most vulnerable time for the horses is going to be when they're at the starting gate and again at the finish line. And we know the winner's circle is a huge draw for the owners and bigwigs."

Danny had one more piece of advice for Tommy. "Before and after the Derby Stakes Race, why not shut down any entry or exit from the track itself? Do that and you'll effectively keep the uncle from moving in and out of those areas. That about taps me out, Tommy … I wish I could help more." Danny had run out of ideas.

"Thanks Danny … that's more than enough input. You're right … I've been spending too much of my time reacting. I'm headed down to the holding barn now … that's where the horses running in the Derby Prep Stakes Race are waiting for their walk to the paddock. The owners of the favorite, Towers Above, are there … maybe I can get some other ideas from them. I'll get back with you and … thanks, brother."

Tommy felt somewhat re-energized, even his mind felt fresher … and the pain in his hand was again starting to diminish.

Horses running in the seventh race were now being led to the saddling paddock. One of the few track courtesies Tommy knew was to never get in the path of a Thoroughbred – but waiting for the procession of horses to pass by caused a five-minute delay. It was precious time he couldn't afford to lose.

His phone was vibrating again as he reached the path leading to the barns ... it was another recognizable number, this time from Washington, DC, showing up on the screen. Tommy used the same code words he'd used thirty-five minutes earlier.

"Has the river reached flood level?" Any response other than fifty-two feet would have resulted in Tommy saying, "I'm sorry, you have the wrong number."

"Fifty-two feet" was correctly stated. It was Tommy's boss who filled him in about the Kansas operation. Tommy listened attentively and without interrupting ... until his boss told him that the gun's automatic clips were loaded with blank rounds.

"Repeat that again," Tommy said, following up with ... "you're shitting me."

"Danny told me the twin in Columbus ... well, investigators there also found clips that were loaded with blanks. Did you feed that info into the computer ... and if so, what did you find out?" Tommy asked.

"Einstein's conclusion is that there was sabotage ... a double cross ... that the twins were merely pawns and diversions for their uncle's activity. You were right ... the track is the primary target. I'm sorry I didn't agree with your suspicions about that earlier, Tommy."

Tommy's boss had one more bit of intel for Tommy to digest. "The twin who was interrogated started to tell the agents about what the uncle's target was. He reportedly said something along the lines of the 'target not being the one or it was the one' ... but he never finished the sentence. He died. Einstein is analyzing that statement, but at this moment we have no clue as to what it means. Good hunting Tommy ... stay in touch."

Rounding the curve in the dirt and gravel path, Tommy saw the barn ... but as he drew close, almost to the entrance of the barn, he came to an abrupt halt.

An Arab contingent was gathered around the first stall, chatting and casually observing their prized stallion. Two stalls down were Donnie, Mike, Marty and myself.

"Thanks for telling me there's a wild card entered in today's Derby Prep Stakes Race," Tommy said to me incredulously.

"What the hell are you talking about Tommy?" was my reply.

"The Arab-owned horse," Tommy replied. "Let me guess ... I'll bet that horse is TA's main competition."

"And if he is, what difference does it make, Tommy? I'm sorry ... that wasn't fair. Actually, we're not sure. Donnie did some research and we know that horse did win one prep race already. If he wins today, he'll have enough points to solidify himself in the Derby point standings and qualify for the first leg of the Triple Crown," I said.

I went further into detail, telling Tommy that Towers Above had not yet raced against that horse ... and that the horse's fractions had been impressive during his training on the Kentucky track. "He didn't race as a two year old ... and I'll admit he is a beauty. Our consensus is that as TA makes the turn to the finish line ... the Arab's horse will be right there with him."

Tommy listened, but didn't respond ... he felt there was no reason to give Rob anything else to worry about and decided to keep his thoughts to himself. Besides, he figured his thoughts were so bizarre ... no one would believe them.

Tommy couldn't stop his mind from racing, though. "I've got two Islamic terrorists who were betrayed by their uncle and he's probably the one who's been messing around and spooking Towers Above. If he had wanted to harm TA, there've been numerous chances to do something. His actions seemed more designed to discourage TA from competing on this day," he thought.

Trying to make sense of his jumbled thoughts, Tommy started to go over everything in his mind, point by point, coming to the conclusion that Towers Above was not the target. "He's ... what did the one twin say ... not the one or was it there's more than one? That might mean the Saudi's horse or the entourage is the intended target." Tommy was starting to believe again that he was right.

But was this a drug-induced conspiracy theory coming out of his pain-addled mind? "It's too absurd," Tommy told himself. "But they thought my theory about the racetrack being the prime target was not credible or believable either."

Shaking off his Rod Serling *Twilight Zone* moment, Tommy's mind returned to the pressing questions that initially drew him to the barn. He came over to where I was standing.

"Rob, I need your help. I know virtually nothing about horse racing or track protocol. I know the horses are paraded around the paddocks before they proceed to the track and on to the starting gate. After the race is over, where do the VIPs and the winning horse go?" Tommy asked.

"More to the point, Rob ... at what point is the horse and its entourage the most vulnerable?"

I wasn't surprised by his questions, because I had thought about the same issues. In fact, I'd actually gone through some scenarios with Donnie earlier in the day and now had some ideas I needed to share with Tommy privately.

"Let's walk for a minute," I said, being unexpectedly curt with Tommy ... but there was no time to waste. "Your hand is broken and you're stoned. What the hell is going on?"

"I'm fine, Rob and don't mess with me. I may have had a problem earlier but I'm in control now. Please give me your input ... I'm begging you ... please."

It had been over three years since the four friends and owners started their dream venture ... suddenly it came down to these final moments and having trust in a Federal special agent.

"Screw it," I said … and started telling Tommy my thoughts and recommendations on how to keep the horses and their respective entourage safe.

"This track is steeped in tradition … but, Tommy, we need to break tradition today. If you can convince the decision makers to send the horses straight to the track with their jockeys aboard, you decrease the odds of a pre-race attack. Following the race, have the award ceremony held someplace way out on the turf. Don't let them bring the winner anywhere near the patrons."

I extended my hand to Tommy, who shook it with his one good hand. Tommy turned, heading back to the administration building while pulling his phone out of his pocket to make a call.

Five minutes later, a voice loudly emanated from Art's office … one shrill question piercing the air for all the staff to hear.

"He wants me to do what?"

CHAPTER 47

Tommy couldn't let it go – something told him that his instincts were right – another horse was the target today ... not Towers Above.

On his way to the administration building to finish the discussion with Art, Tommy suddenly stopped and did an about-face, yelling for me to wait.

"Rob, can I borrow Donnie for a moment?"

"Sure, I said, calling out to Donnie, gesturing for him to come over to where we were.

"Donnie, how hard would it be to get the other trainers here for a few minutes?" Tommy asked.

"I can do it ... but we have to make it short. These folks all have a pre-race routine and you're taking valuable time from them ... they don't have much to spare," Donnie replied.

Five minutes later, Tommy was surrounded by a group of

eight horse trainers, a number of their assistants ... even some owners. The elite members of the Royal Family were tucked away elsewhere in one of the private areas of the track.

The trainers, attendants and owners had been briefed about the situation at the track earlier in the day. Tommy was aware of that ... but believed it wouldn't hurt to go fishing one more time.

"Folks, my name is Tommy ... I'm a Homeland Security agent. In a few minutes, today's feature race will start. If any of you have information ... have heard rumors or innuendo about anything or anyone involved with today's big Stakes Race, now's the time to speak up." Tommy knew the benefit of the pregnant pause rather than a lengthy diatribe ... but there was nothing but silence. He was disappointed but realistic. "Nothing ventured, nothing gained," he told himself, ready to head back to the administration building.

Within a few seconds, he heard a voice from behind. "Hold up ... sir. Please?" It was the assistant trainer for the Royal Family's horse that was running in the Stakes Race. "I'm Charlie. Can I walk and chat with you for a bit?"

"Sure," Tommy replied. "You can't give me up, okay?" the trainer said.

Again Tommy said "Sure."

"A half hour ago, I overheard my boss talking with someone on his phone about how he was going to do a late scratch if you guys didn't find the old man."

Tommy looked at Charlie with a blank expression on his face. "What old man?" he said.

"Ahmed … you know … the guy on the news … the terrorist dude! The guy has a history with the family." Suddenly, Charlie realized Tommy didn't have a clue about anything he'd just said. "The news is referring to him as Ben … we know him as Ahmed. He and the family go way back. If your men don't grab him before post-time in the tenth race, we're pulling our horse out of the race."

"Our horse is Ahmed's target!"

Everything that hadn't made sense earlier … suddenly and instantly became crystal clear. Tommy's entire body shuddered from the realization.

Pulling out his phone, Tommy placed an urgent call to Ted. "Ted … get down here now! I'm at the holding barn … and you better get Art and the Arabs on a conference line with us when you get here … all hell's about to break loose!"

Turning back to the trainer, Tommy thanked him for the information. "Charlie, I know it's not your decision whether your horse is scratched. Thanks for stepping up … your employer probably won't appreciate what you just did. I do and … thank you. We'll make this right for you somehow, but I think you better disappear now. Some tough discussions are going to take place."

Tommy returned to TA's stall. "Jesus Tommy, you're starting to be a pain … what now?" I demanded.

"Rob, point out the Arab Thoroughbred's trainer and then I'll be gone," Tommy replied.

"Look over my right shoulder, it's the guy with the traditional blue sport coat and grey pants. That's Peter McQuire. He's an ass, but knows his stuff. Good luck with whatever's going on. Just know that when you say black, he'll say white … that's his way with everyone."

Tommy stepped aside and began texting on his phone. No doubt checking in with his superiors, I thought.

Why wasn't Ahmed in the database, Tommy wondered. Each nephew had been unmasked – but what was Ahmed's history and why had it become dark?

He texted what he'd just learned to his superiors at Homeland Security in Virginia: *Ben = Ahmed? Who is Ahmed? Saudi family, here at the track, knows of him ... Why? Any info? Be quick!*

While waiting for Ted at the barn, Tommy could only speculate about why there was no intelligence on Ahmed. Every agent knew firewalls existed that prevented access to specific intelligence. For years, there was even talk about individuals who were connected to the Saudi Royal Family – individuals who had intimate financial connections with ongoing terrorist activities. He had read all 29 pages of the supposed Saudi government's connection to the 9/11 attacks which were released in 2016. However, he didn't have security clearance to see the un-redacted pages and their release only raised more questions about Saudi culpability.

Two minutes after sending the text, Tommy got a text back. The text read: *That information is for "Eyes Only." Access Denied.*

Suggest that you not pursue decisions on your own. Any decisions made must respect diplomatic protocol. Text or call before any decision is made. Your new contact is Kent – he is now your State Department associate and is assigned to this situation.

Maybe if Tommy's hand wasn't broken ... or if his young field agent hadn't been shot ... or a whole lot of other crap hadn't occurred in the last twenty-four hours, just maybe he would have followed orders.

Or not.

Tommy decided he'd be damned if he was going to allow Washington bureaucrats tell him how to deal with Ahmed. As far as he was concerned, he was looking for Ben, the terrorist uncle who was going to leave the grounds on this day – in handcuffs – or in a body bag.

Ted pulled up in a golf cart and Tommy briefed him.

"Let me take the lead in this ... please," Tommy pleaded. Ted gave him an affirmative nod. The agents approached the Arab stall, Tommy brushing aside some of their security people as he flashed his badge. Peter McQuire had an astonished look on his face as

Tommy and Ted stepped into what he considered his personal domain.

"Whoa guys, I don't know who you are, but you need to leave right now or I'm calling track security and having you …" He never finished his sentence.

"Don't bother," Tommy said. "Let me introduce you to my friend Ted … he's in charge of track security and again … you can call me Tommy. I just told you before, I'm with Homeland Security. I don't want to get in the way of your race preparation, but there's a rumor floating around among the track handicappers that you're going to do a late scratch. I'm not a horseman and I've got my own problems right now so I'll shut up and let you tell me that the rumor isn't true." Tommy stopped talking, clearly waiting for Peter's response.

"I can't tell you it isn't true … anything can happen up until the starting gates open and the horses are away. So you might as well buzz off … because I have nothing else to tell you," McQuire answered.

Tommy shook his head and mumbled to himself, "Becker was right, he's an ass."

"Ted, get Art on the speaker phone with the Arabs," Tommy said in a voice loud enough for McQuire to hear.

"Art, this is Ted. Tommy and I are with Peter McQuire and he won't give us a straight answer as to whether he's going to scratch Nidalas in the Grade One Stakes Race. I'm sure he's had a discussion with the sheikh about the situation here at the track, as well as the race itself. Sir, I can't emphasize enough how important it is that their horse run. The only reason we have the crowd we have today is because the fans view this event as a Challenge Cup caliber race." Ted paused to let that point hit home with Art, then continued on.

"You might also point out to the sheikh that even though their horse currently has enough qualifying points for the Derby, unless they run the horse in another race between now and early May, he could easily slide out of contention point-wise – and not be eligible to run in the Kentucky Derby.

"Hang on, Ted." Art could be heard in heated discussion with the sheikh, demanding to know why he was going to scratch the horse. Tommy heard Ahmed's name mentioned and then there were more garbled exchanges. "Ted, the sheikh is pulling his horse because we haven't captured an individual named Ahmed. He won't explain who this individual is … but there must be some connection between the Royal Family and the terrorist we can't seem to find."

"Art, this is Tommy."

"Yes, Tommy …? "

"Sir, I'm going to ask you to trust me with what I'm going to propose. But first, I'm ninety-nine percent certain that Ahmed is Ben. He's the one we've been searching for … he's walking freely around the grounds right now posing as an employee … with forged credentials in the name of Richard and a track ID badge on his coat."

Without divulging the confidence of the assistant trainer, Tommy told Art that he'd received credible information that Ben and the Royal Family had a previous relationship which soured … and that's why Nidalas became the target. Tommy offered to give the name of a contact at the State Department if the sheikh wanted to know more details. "I'd guess, though that neither the guy at the State Department or the sheikh would give up any information. And I bet Ahmed or Ben – whatever name he went by then – played a part in some sort of conflict between the Saudis and America surrounding 9/11 … and that information remains buried still to this day in some dark vault in Washington, DC."

Driving home what he felt was the most important and obvious consideration, Tommy advised Art, "You need to tell the sheikh that if his horse is the target – the moment he is scratched, Ahmed will disappear – but only for now. He'll show up at some other place, at some other time ... he still wants retribution and will go after it."

Tommy explained that scratching the horse from today's race was only postponing the inevitable. Ahmed most likely had the resources to travel to any other track in the United States where Nidalas would run and, in Tommy's estimation, would do just that. "It may seem like we're using Nidalas as bait at the moment, but I firmly believe we are capable of protecting the horse – and that today will be the last time Ahmed remains free to terrorize anyone."

Tommy was unaware that the sheikh had been in the room with Art throughout the entire conversation – and as he'd suspected, the sheikh had no interest in talking to anyone at the State Department.

For the next ten minutes, the sheikh met privately with the rest of his entourage to talk about the events that were taking place – and to make a decision about running their horse in the race. In the meantime, Tommy received another text from his new contact in Virginia, demanding an update on the Saudi family.

Tommy ignored the text.

This wasn't the first time he'd burned bridges before ... and hopefully this wasn't going to be his last intelligence operation. "Hell, it's pretty nice country here in the Bluegrass ... maybe these folks could use a man with my skills," he mused.

The ten minutes seemed like an eternity to the security team. Finally, Ted's phone vibrated – it was Art. "Ted, call Tommy over, I want both of you to hear the sheikh's decision and if you need to physically drag McQuire over to listen as well, you have my permission."

Tommy returned to Nidalas' stall, politely asking Peter to come with him. Anticipating a lack of cooperation from the trainer, Tommy had two state troopers with him – and upon Peter's refusal, they lifted the trainer off his feet, literally carrying him to where Ted was waiting.

"Art, we're all here now. Please put the sheikh on the line."

"Mister Ted and Tommy, I want to thank you for all you've done today. It is a shame that one of my citizens has put a damper on the festivities."

"Always the politician. Yeah ... yeah ... yeah. Blah ... blah ... blah. Jesus, cut to the chase," Tommy wanted to say, as his hand began to throb once again.

"Mister Tommy, I have a condition for you. I will have my horse run today if you will guarantee his safety. If you can't, then I will scratch Nidalas. Oh, and one other thing, if he runs and somehow your promise is not kept, I would like you to accompany me home and explain to the king what happened. Do we have a deal?"

It had been a difficult day, and Tommy's emotions were on a roller coaster ride that continued plunging downward. He'd been challenged and he'd been threatened ... there was no way his life was worth less than Nidalas'. But if he didn't accept the sheikh's terms, the resulting devastation would be as significant as the carnage he suspected Ben intended to wreak at the track. He also knew that if he failed to protect the sheikh's horse, his trip to the desert would most likely be a one-way journey.

"Sir … I accept your offer with one condition," Tommy stammered.

"And what might that condition be, Mister Tommy?"

"I want your trainer, Peter McQuire, removed from the premises and for someone else to be assigned to take his place immediately," Tommy answered.

"You bargain well, Mister Tommy … the assistant trainer will now take his place. Mister Tommy, good luck today … I say that because we know that Ahmcd is a very clever individual."

Tommy never knew why the sheikh gave in so easily. The sheikh had thrown his horse's trainer under the bus, losing him for any future Triple Crown races. Then again, Tommy didn't know that it was the trainer's idea to scratch the sheikh's horse … which is when the sheikh also determined that his current trainer was an ass.

CHAPTER 48

"Yo voy a vomitar," Ben said ... in obvious distress, one of his hands half-over his mouth, sprinting to a bathroom stall while slipping the restroom attendant a twenty dollar bill. Locking the stall door behind him, he began to fake the sounds of heavy vomiting, heaving, groaning – even pouring water from his drinking bottle into the toilet bowl to make the splashing sound that accompanies a bout of puking. His performance was worthy of an award ... the occupant of the stall next to Ben couldn't get out of the men's room quickly enough!

The attendant's eyes were still glazed over – it had been a long time since anyone gave him a twenty dollar tip. The Spanglish Ben spoke was perfect and as far as Eduardo was concerned, a fellow Latino was in that stall and obviously very sick. He'd leave the man alone and maybe check on him in a few minutes, and if lucky enough, coax another twenty from him. Ben pretended to heave one more time ... moaning for a minute or so longer. Eduardo slipped out of the bathroom ... he'd heard enough and was beginning to feel his stomach start to churn – he didn't want another twenty dollars that badly.

Still in the stall, Ben pulled out his mobile phone, logging onto the Thoroughbred App so he could watch live video from the track.

* * *

The only thing security guards found on the Mountain was the caramel outer coat Ben had been wearing all day. Every one of the coat's pockets was empty. The only indication he'd been wearing it was the name badge identifying him as Dick still attached to the coat's right pocket. There was no sign of Jamie's badge.

Tommy's walkie-talkie was squawking loudly. One of his fellow agents was trying to reach him. "Tommy, Tommy ... this is Ronnie, do you copy?"

"Ronnie, I read you ... go ahead."

"Tommy, we've got Richard's coat. We found it up here on the Mountain. I did preliminary interviews with the Metro officers and other guest services employees who were working up here. I showed them the photos of Ben and they all positively identified him. His appearance is changed, though. He has a moustache now and is wearing glasses – and that's not the worst part – he's got another badge."

"What the hell are you talking about Ronnie … what badge does he have?" Tommy demanded to know. "He's got an FBI badge," Ronnie explained. "I showed them my badge and asked if it was similar to the one he flashed. It was the same one," Ronnie said.

"Just a minute Ronnie … hang on, please. I gotta' think …"

Tommy shouted out a round of expletives. "Goddamit!" he finished … with Ted watching and trying to figure out what was going on now. Tommy replayed the events of the day in his mind – especially the moments when Jamie was found – and mumbled a barely audible "fuck."

Answering Ted's unspoken questions, Tommy explained that the security team just learned that the uncle had been working on the Mountain – and that he was now in disguise, sporting a moustache and glasses. "And Ted, he's carrying Jamie's FBI badge. I forgot to check and see if it was still in Jamie's pocket."

"Ronnie … would you ask those men if Ben had on the same type of logo cap that you're wearing?" Tommy asked, finally getting back to the walkie-talkie.

"Ted, the old man is probably carrying every identifier we have and is still wearing the track's logo sport coat. It's too damn late to change our garb and all the track's employees have been told to respect the logo caps in particular. If he shows the badge, nobody will get in his way. Let me check, though."

A couple minutes passed before Ronnie had an answer. "Nope ... no logo ball cap, Tommy."

Tommy took that in, and turned back to Ted with his thoughts. "I'm just thinking out loud here ... we've got fifteen minutes until the ninth race goes off. Then we'll have another forty or so minutes before the big race. The horses in the tenth will go directly from the barn out to the track ... right? So that narrows Ben's options for attack if the Saudi's horse is the target. And if I'm right, Ben doesn't know the paddock routine has changed."

"It hasn't been announced," Ted answered.

"I noticed during these Stakes Races that the horses have the same colored saddle blankets. The only difference on each is their post position number."

"They're known as a saddle cloth, but yes, you're right.

What's your point?" Ted shot back.

An idea for a ruse was formulating in Tommy's mind … and maybe it was crazy, but his other off-the-wall thoughts so far this day had worked. "If you have spare saddling cloths for the Stakes Race, why not send the horses scheduled for the eleventh race to the north end of the paddock and keep them corralled there before their race? The saddling attendants can carry the saddles and cloths down there and then start the saddling process."

Tommy shared his hunch with Ted that Ben was hiding somewhere on the grounds, watching the events at the track live from his mobile phone… pointing out to Ted that Ben most likely had no way of knowing or seeing what was happening around the paddock – or anywhere else on the grounds. That disconnect would lead to Ben's downfall, Tommy felt. "If he doesn't get tipped off about the ruse, maybe he'll come out into the open then and begin his attack … and we can pick him off. What do you think?" Tommy asked, fervently hoping this would be the case.

Ted put both hands behind his head, gazing skyward as if God was watching, waiting to give him the thumbs-up or thumbs-down signal to proceed with this course of action. Deep in thought, he said to himself, "God, I'm exhausted. This only works if Tommy's right and Ben is a lone wolf right now. They're too many savvy horsemen here who will recognize the substitute horses – it wouldn't take more than a minute for the buzz to spread throughout the grounds – then our scam would be over." Ted glanced at Tommy, whose eyes were pleading for the go ahead. "You know, if this window of opportunity is what Ben's plan revolves around and he gets wind of the switch … you know he'll probably disappear and we'll lose him."

Tommy didn't answer. He just continued to stare.

Ted knew there definitely was no time to waste. He had to get to the barns and convince the owners and trainers to allow those Thoroughbreds running in the eleventh race to become bait. Even more urgent, he'd have to convince the trainers of the tenth race – the million dollar Kentucky Pride Stakes Race – to buy into the ruse, with everyone involved understanding how important it was to keep their mouths shut about the bait and switch.

Nonetheless, Ted was going to buy-in to Tommy's idea, and told him as much. "You can help by having your friends Rob and Donnie start spreading the word to others at the barn. I know they're both trusted and respected. Let's get moving."

Tommy exhaled a huge sigh of relief. Hopefully this would be the plan that would finally take Ben down.

Texting his boss with an update about the new plan, Ted asked Art to give a heads-up to the track announcer and event handicappers ... hoping to avoid any screw-ups later. And Ted stressed, this was an urgent matter of security and that total confidentiality was expected of everyone. Art was asked to also contact the paddock workers, and one final group, the media. Ted knew they needed a miracle and shook his head, worrying – there were too many "what ifs" that could happen – and too many factors outside his control that needed to come together.

"Hey Ted, one more thought," Tommy said. "How about we have the Homeland Security operatives and other agents put their logo caps on backward when the horses for the tenth race come through the north entrance? I doubt that Ben would pick up on that if somehow he got hold of one of those caps."

"Go with it, Tommy, but he's a sharp codger and you'll only pull that stunt successfully once. But hell, why not? We're running out of options," Ted said.

Tommy sent a text to the other team members, advising them to wear their caps backwards – when suddenly he remembered Rob and Marty – they also had the logoed caps. Immediately he called Rob and told him the plan … waiting quietly on the phone as he heard Rob talking with Marty about the caps, and realizing there was an unnerving silence. This was not going to be good news, Tommy was certain.

"Tommy … Marty just told me she lost her hat in the storm. She wasn't in any mood to look for it at the time and she just gave me that 'WTF difference does it make at this point?' look. I'm sorry Tommy, but we just got the word about the switching ruse here in the barn. I've got to go."

"Damn…we get no breaks with this guy," Tommy muttered to himself, disgusted with Ben's ongoing good fortune.

"Ben … you lucky bastard!" Tommy screamed out in frustration.

"The SOB probably picked up her hat," he immediately thought.

Ted's cell phone began to vibrate. Seeing the caller was Art, he answered … reluctantly. He was given no chance to say hello, and holding the phone about eight inches from his ear, waited for the stream of profanities to end. Finally hearing Art ask, "Do you understand?" Ted brought the phone directly back to his ear. "Art, I understand. I knew the board of directors would eventually lay all of this at my feet. And yes, I know, as soon as today is over ... I may as well submit my resignation. You'll have it, but my severance package is going to be a damn good one."

Not quite threatening, but also not conciliatory, Ted advised his boss that if he didn't get fair treatment from the board, he would go directly to the media and tell them everything that had occurred at the track on this day. "It might help matters if you went to the barns now to help convince everyone to make this last-ditch plan work – because you can bet that your sweet ass is also on thin ice at this very moment."

"Give me your best odds," Art stated, somewhat more calmly.

"For what?" Ted answered back.

"Do we get this guy before he does something?" Art replied.

"God Art, I wish I could tell you ours are better than fifty-fifty, but the reality is, the odds are still in the uncle's favor," Ted despondently answered.

"This old man – he's good. He's been steps ahead of us all day and if I didn't know better – I'd say he's had special training. His plan has worked almost flawlessly. If it wasn't for Tommy and his crew, we'd be screwed. File that last thought away and when this nightmare is over, think about how his operatives did their jobs. Maybe it's time for new line items in the budget."

"Well, I guess we'll know in an hour or so ... I'm on my way," Art said dejectedly.

CHAPTER 49

It felt good to just sit. Ben was confident that he could safely hide out in the men's room stall – considerably large for a bathroom stall – undetected for a little longer.

He hoped the sympathetic look in the attendant's eyes – now that he was done "throwing up" – and some additional monetary exchange would provide a safe haven during his final moments of physical and mental preparation before the attack.

Taking off the logo emblazoned track sports coat and emptying its pockets, he lined up their contents on the floor while propping his umbrella in the corner. There was an order to what he was doing and how he would use those items. Some things he would keep and take with him, the rest he would simply abandon. But first … Ben needed to attach the suppressor to his automatic handgun. The last thing he wanted was to attract attention from the loud bang of his gun discharging – especially if those shots were at close range.

The next item placed in the keep pile was the FBI agent's security badge. It had already saved his ass once.

Staring at the logo ball cap, Ben was unsure … but then remembered that the guard he'd seen earlier in the employee parking lot was wearing a similar cap. Flashing back to when he left the Hill, he remembered seeing two men, dressed in similar fashion, walking towards him … both were also wearing the same ball caps. He had already decided that they were security agents of some sort from their dress, their athletic frames and now … the hats. Seeing those two men is why he left the Hill to find a new place to hide out.

"I've never seen this hat until today and only a few people seem to be wearing them," Ben thought, right before it hit him. "These damn hats are the identifiers! The spotters are using them to sort out their security detachment folks!" Ben smiled, shoving the hat onto the keep pile. His mobile phone was also added to the pile.

The next decision was whether to keep any of the three remaining fake name badges. The first two name badges – Dick and Richard – were now useless. He rightfully assumed that the security team had by now found his outer coat with the attached name badge of Dick. He was also pretty sure that the security agents were interrogating any employees unlucky enough to go by either name or variation thereof.

Ben decided it was too much of a gamble to try and pass himself off as a track employee any longer. "I'm sure by now that the officials are comparing employee's names with their assigned job locations – and that anyone not recognized is going to be challenged," he cautioned himself.

He would prove to be right again.

His final badge had everything to do with the world of horse racing – but nothing to do with the Kentucky track. This badge was a perfect counterfeit copy of the Challenge Cup name badge worn by officials during the Cup Races held in California the previous fall.

The name on the badge read Charles Davis III ... with his title emblazoned directly below: Events Chairman. Holding it in his palm for nearly thirty seconds ... as if it were a lucky charm ... Ben decided it was a keeper.

The last remaining items he brought out were the moustache glue, more facial hair and the RayBan sunglasses.

Ben began yet another metamorphosis.

The ninth race had just ended. It was time to get moving … his legs were starting to fall asleep from sitting for a good half hour. He braced himself against the stall door and tried to stand, but stumbled and fell against it. The sound of Ben's body hitting the door caught the attendant's attention.

Eduardo decided it was time to check on his amigo. "Estas bien? No necesitas un doctor? … si necesutas ayuda yo puedo llamar alguien por ti?"

Ben replied, "No es necesario. Yo siento major. No mas necesito decansar por unis vcinte minutis mas y depues yo voy intentar otra ves."

He didn't need a doctor and in fact, would be gone in a few minutes.

Cracking the door a bit, Ben handed another twenty dollar bill through the opening. The money and a smiling Eduardo vanished in an instant. Then, removing the vest he'd been wearing, Ben inspected the wiring connections and the arming mechanism. The compartments were still intact and no powder was leaking … he had no intention of committing mass murder.

If forced, Ben was prepared to ignite the powders hidden within the vest and turn himself into a large roman candle. The distraction might buy him a few extra needed seconds to eliminate his target.

His mission was based on a vendetta ... not the intent to inflict mass casualties on otherwise innocent people.

Putting the vest back on, Ben began to place items from the keep pile into various pockets – the last item, a wallet filled with hundred dollar bills, went into the left hip pocket of his slacks.

Removing a small knife from a pocket, he began to cut off the inside lining of his sport coat – quickly revealing another coat sewn inside – one emblazoned with the Challenge Cup logo.

After putting on the new coat, Ben was nearly ready. He sat down again and closed his eyes ... visualizing and rehearsing each step in his mind ... for the final time.

The plan was set ... and the details instilled in Ben's mind. The horses would proceed from the saddling paddock to the riders up paddock. Wearing the logoed ball cap, Ben would arrive at the entrance to the tunnel before the jockeys mounted their steeds. After showing the stolen FBI badge to the paddock attendant, he'd enter the tunnel, and casually walk to the end, well past where the outriders were positioned. It was there that he would wait as they picked up their mounts to lead to the track.

Continuing his mental review of the plan, Ben went through the sequence of horses that would pass by before the Saudi's horse. Towers Above was in the number one pole position … Nidalas had drawn number five. There were three others in between. After the number four horse passed by, Ben would slowly move forward towards the number five outrider, holding the FBI badge high in one hand. Hopefully he would pull up Nidalas – giving Ben the perfect chance to step forward and casually place the umbrella's tip against Nidalas' chest … and with a quick shot, unleash his deadly potion.

After taking the shot, Ben would reverse direction, heading back up the same side of the tunnel he'd just came down. Finally, he'd exit the East entrance and walk to the Uber taxi he'd hired to wait and take him to a restaurant in town. From there, Ben would walk three blocks north to where he'd parked a getaway car two days earlier.

It was time to make one last check on the phone's racing app and watch as the horses for the tenth race – the Kentucky Proud Stakes – began to enter the north gate.

Now, it was time to leave the sanctity of the men's room.

Ready to leave the stall, he heard the door to the men's room open – and could tell by the footsteps that two people had just come in. Quickly sitting on the commode, Ben pushed against the stall door with his feet to prevent anyone from entering. He also pulled out his automatic weapon, flipped off its safety and slowly chambered a round … just in case.

One of the men could be heard relieving himself at the urinal while Ben's neighbor in the next stall exploded into the toilet. "I can't take this kind of stress. I've got six grandkids and I'm sure as hell not going to play hero … even if this asshole terrorist is standing right in front of me."

The other finished his business, and was zipping up when he said, "these fake horses they're saddling down there aren't going to fool him. C'mon … hurry. We've got to get back to our positions."

Thirty seconds passed and both men were gone.

Ben picked up his mobile phone again … this time watching more intently. As they brought the horses into the second paddock,

419

Ben realized there was no close-up video. He stared intently at the number one horse, supposedly Towers Above. If anyone other than the owners knew what TA looked like, it was Ben.

"Those sons of bitches," Ben said quietly.

Loose lips sink ships.

CHAPTER 50

Ben could feel every muscle in his body tense up – intense anger was welling and he was trying to fight the impulse to strike out at anything or anyone within reach. All his intricate planning over nearly two decades ... when finally the opportunity he'd been waiting for availed itself, only to be snatched away at the last second. It was too difficult to accept.

Still on the mobile app, he watched as the horses passed through the tunnel and out onto the track, and heard the commentators' analysis of each horse and their respective jockey's history on the track and with the horse. But there were still no close-up shots of the horses heading to the starting gate. All of a sudden, the live video he was watching disappeared, but the audio remained ... an announcer told the audience they would be back in a moment for the start of the race.

When the video feed came back on, the horses were already loading into their positions at the starting gate.

It was during the lapse of live video that the actual horses competing in the tenth race entered the track from the far end –

through a gate where horses racing on the track normally exited at the end of a race. What Ben didn't see was Towers Above, Nidalas and the other horses entering … or mounted by their respective jockeys. Nor did he see the substitute horses unceremoniously led off the track … now awaiting their run in the eleventh race.

Race track tradition had been flipped on its head this day … unfortunately, though, the gamble failed to accomplish its intended purpose.

Ben wasn't the only one having a physical meltdown. Tommy was internalizing his own expletive-laden tirade, having convinced himself and others that Ben would strike during the parade to the post … yet nothing happened. He knew it would have been the most opportune time for Ben to get to the Saudi's stallion. Tommy's angst was so heavy and painful … he slammed his remaining good fist into the wall of the tunnel.

The ensuing pain was excruciating.

* * *

Ben began a series of deep breathing exercises, letting his arms hang limp from his body … this was his way of decompressing. Within three minutes, he was once again in control of his emotions – and working out in his head the next opportunity to exact revenge. "I can bide my time if Nidalas wins this race and advances to the Derby and then the other Triple Crown venues. The more successful Nidalas is, the greater the chance he'll go to more tracks to race and parade around in glory." Ben then remembered that the Owners Challenge Cup races would be held on this same track later in the year.

"Hell, that might even be an easier opportunity to shoot the stallion," Ben said under his breath. Standing again and pausing a moment before finally opening the stall door slightly, he made sure there was no one else nearby. As he quickly exited the restroom, he nodded to Eduardo … "Gracias," he said. Eduardo smiled. As he never got a good look at Ben when he first rushed into the restroom, Eduardo was unaware that Ben was sporting a new look. He took his broom, mop and bucket to the stall for the clean-up.

Opening the stall door, Eduardo was immediately stopped in his tracks by what he saw … it wasn't the signs of heavy vomiting. Instead, hanging from a hook on the back of the door was a man's sport coat emblazoned with the track's logo … it was in tatters. The floor was covered with hair and a tube of glue was next to the hair. He knew it was glue because of the strong chemical smell. In the opposite corner were three track employee name badges. Eduardo read the names – and realizing this was not good, immediately ran out of the restroom and onto the surrounding grounds, searching frantically for a Metro officer. He saw one not more than fifty yards away. He ran to the officer and grabbed his arm ... urgently telling him he had to come to the restroom. The obvious fear in Eduardo's eyes convinced the cop that something was seriously wrong.

Entering the stall, the officer looked around and picked up the two badges lying on the floor. That was all he needed. In less than two seconds he was on his mobile ... and just as quickly, Ted was sprinting to the men's room.

Pulling out his walkie-talkie, Ted shouted over the airways, "Tommy, do you read me? Tommy, come in ... Tommy, this is Ted." There was only silence.

"Tommy ... I'm at the men's restroom next to the entrance to the tunnel. Do you copy?" Ted repeated frantically.

Tommy, who was in tremendous pain, managed to activate his walkie-talkie and replied in a shaky voice, "Ted, this is Tommy ... please repeat."

Ted gave his location, knowing something wasn't right …
again telling Tommy to get to the men's room – immediately.

Quickly taking in the scene … Ted was amazed and yet not
so amazed at the same time. "So this is where you were holed up,
huh Ben? You prick!" Looking closely at the items strewn
throughout the stall, Ted knew what Ben had done. "You've added
more hair, you had another jacket sewn inside the sport coat … and
maybe a weapon. I bet Tommy was right. You were close, right here
on the grounds watching … somehow you figured out our charade."

Ted called the administration offices for a Spanglish
translator, who arrived within five minutes – he needed to question
Eduardo, who was standing somberly by the far wall. Distress was
written all over his face … it was obvious he understood the
seriousness of what had taken place in the restroom stall. Eduardo
had no idea that he hadn't screwed up, or that countless other track
employees and other individuals also messed up that day – most
through no fault of their own. "Will I be blamed for not identifying
the terrorist?" Eduardo nervously wondered to himself.

As Ted began to interview Eduardo, Tommy appeared in the
doorway … Ted could tell from the glazed look in Tommy's eyes
that he had taken yet another shot of morphine.

At that very moment, the speakers crackled with the announcement that everyone was waiting for, "The horses in the Kentucky Proud Grade 1 Stakes Race were off and running."

CHAPTER 51

Exiting the men's room, Ben flipped his ball cap around ... frustration had turned him into a gangsta. This flip of the cap mimicking that of the security team members – who earlier had been instructed by Tommy to wear the caps backwards as an identification measure.

Walking past the clock tower and the tallest of three oak trees that was still smoldering from the lightning strike earlier that day, he wearily sat down on a bench, needing to see the race on the track's big screen monitor.

Ben couldn't believe he'd been out-maneuvered ... he'd counted too much on the traditions so deeply steeped within the track culture, certain that the old school formalities would always prevail. Ben turned his attention to the finish of the race. The roar of the crowd escalated as the horses reached the final turn, each frantically heading for the finish line.

Two of the eight horses in the field were perfectly matched ... stride for stride. Their eyes were locked on the other, hearts pumping furiously and efficiently. Neither horse knew or cared about the physical demands on their bodies … why their hearts hadn't exploded or that their respective genetic lineage made that prospect a virtual impossibility.

They remained in fierce competition … one horse would head-bob for the lead and the other would quickly overtake his opponent and regain the lead. They were in sync … and yet they weren't.

One hundred yards from the finish line, both horses came together as one … now perfectly matching stride for stride and head bob for head bob. The patrons were mesmerized … half loudly cheering on their favorite, the other half frozen and unconsciously holding their breaths in anticipation.

Finally the intense duel between the two horses ended … and the crowd remained electrified.

And no one noticed – except perhaps the smoldering oak tree – that the bench was no longer occupied.

* * *

Donnie knew he was going to be repetitive again with their

jockey – but as the week progressed and the race took on a heightened significance – its importance couldn't be overstated. Pulling Joey aside, he reminded her that while the track appeared to be in good shape, it was still sloppy ... offering her some final words of encouragement and advice.

"You've got to start quickly and remember, he doesn't like a muddy course. The Saudi's horse will head for the rail ... you need to keep pace," he stressed. "You need to be near the lead when you reach the quarter pole. Settle in and keep pace with Nidalas through the half-mile marker ... then let TA go. This horse is the best we'll face all summer ... so let's finish the test today and be done with that group forever!"

Joey nodded her agreement to Donnie who gave her a leg up ... as Lance awaited the signal to head out.

It was time to go. Grabbing the lead shank, Lance led their horse along the path to the exit gate ... the redirected route onto the track for this race. As he guided Towers Above towards the opening, he couldn't help but laugh at the irony of the situation ... there was no doubt this would be the only time he'd ever lead a Thoroughbred to the start of a race through a gate normally used as an exit ... especially at this track.

"I hope someone is filming the grand entrance," Lance shouted, lifting his head to smile at Joey. She cracked a smile back, knowing that there were probably dozens of cameras trained on the procession of horses stepping onto the moist dirt and heading to the starting gate.

Joey had watched Nidalas work out all week, and was impressed with the stallion's confirmation and training fractions. His workouts had earned him the same odds pre-race as Towers Above. Now, which horse would break better? Which could take the most bumping and jostling … and didn't mind a little dirt and mud in his face?

It was time. Towers Above and Keep My Word were the first to be loaded into the starting gates, quickly followed by Cokeammo and Tiny Danzer. Next in were Nidalas and Fizz Ed. Last to load were Aisle Ofhay and Foursquare. Joey's good friend, Eddie, was aboard Cokeammo … he couldn't resist giving her some trash talk while the other horses loaded.

"Hey, Joey … you're going down today. If not by me, it'll be the Arab."

"Bullshit, Eddie ... the only thing going down is you. Oops, look out ... your horse is about to take a crap," Joey retorted.

Eddie's head snapped around to look ... the last thing a jockey wants is the horse taking a dump when the gates are about to open. Joey just smiled. It was time to go to work.

All the horses were loaded but one, Tiny Danzer, who was having a difficult time ... but with an attendant's final shove, he was in place.

Joey's left hand had a grip on TA's mane while simultaneously holding the reins. Towers had never had a bad start – and she didn't expect one today.

The gates flew open and Towers was away cleanly ... another flawless start. Cokeammo and Nidalas also broke well, with Cokeammo taking an early half-length lead on the rail ... and Towers and Nidalas on his outside flank.

The three horses reached the quarter-mile marker in twenty-four seconds. The only horse straining was Cokeammo – Joey had to give Eddie kudos. Either he truly felt he had enough horse to win on this day ... or he was unconsciously helping Towers win the race.

Joey kept TA two horses wide ... clear of any dirt that would kick up from the track. She continued to maintain a strong grip on the still-loose reins ... it wasn't time yet to make her move.

The time at the half-mile was forty-eight seconds, not a spectacular time, but the best the horses could do considering the sloppy track. Cokeammo began to tire, slipping into third place. Nidalas had the lead by a half-length ... the match race was on.

Joey tightened the reins and crouched even lower toward the saddle ... Towers immediately accelerated. Another furlong and her mount had pulled a length ahead of Nidalas. Glancing over her left shoulder, Joey saw that Nidalas showed no signs of tiring. There wouldn't be room to go to the rail – she didn't want to risk a bump and a subsequent inquiry. As Joey guided TA into the last three furlongs, she knew Nidalas would pull even because he was traveling the inside route.

She hated having to make the next decision ... to use the whip. She'd used it only once before on Towers ... when he raced as a two year old. It took a week before Towers easily accepted Joey's presence in the paddock ... and that broke her heart.

"Time to show him the whip," Joey thought.

She flashed the whip in front of Tower's right eye, quickly lowering it to his side without ever touching the horse ... the crowd couldn't see from her vantage point and had no idea that TA hadn't been touched by the whip. Towers surged a second time, then closed the gap again. Each time Joey raised and lowered the whip, Towers would widen his stride just enough to slightly pull ahead ... and each time Nidalas responded by pulling even again.

At three quarters of a mile, their times were one minute, eleven seconds and at the mile marker, one minute, thirty-four seconds. Both jockeys knew their horses were in a zone, but neither knew the fraction times ... and at this point, neither jockey had any control over the outcome.

Hunkering down even lower on TA's withers, Joey pressed her face into his mane. The final furlong would become a footnote in horse racing history. Joey saw the flash of light and assumed the finish line picture had been taken. Glancing to her left, she thought Nidalas was slightly behind.

TA's run-out continued for another three furlongs before finally slowing to a gallop. Directing her mount back towards the winner circle, anticipating the trophy presentation and an interview or two, Joey had no idea she'd be cool walking her horse for the next fifteen minutes ... directly alongside Miguel and his mount Nidalas. A decision as to which horse had won was going to be made by the track's stewards ... after review of the finish line video and pictures. The queasiness in Joey's stomach was a strong indicator she knew what the decision would be.

"Nobody likes ties!" Joey griped into the late afternoon air.

To top things, off the word *"Inquiry"* was now lit up on the tote board ... Nidalas' owners were certain their horse had been fouled.

CHAPTER 52

Tommy was probably the only person disappointed. The race was over and the horses would soon leave the track, and head back to the barns.

Nothing bad had happened.

"I may not get that son of a bitch this weekend, but my gut tells me we'll find him before Nidalas or Towers Above race again … that will be at the Derby," Tommy thought.

"Ted … this is Tommy. Do you read me?" Tommy was still down by the rail, unaware that there was a review of the finish … or that there had been no announcement yet of the winner.

Track officials hate dead heats and this race, with Derby qualifying points on the line that could affect other Thoroughbred's positions in the standings, meant making the right call that much more imperative.

Furthermore … there were millions of betting dollars in play … and those who placed bets had every right to see the finish line photo, even if it had to be magnified a thousand times.

Which is why a single winner was preferred.

"Go ahead Tommy," Ted answered.

"Why's it taking so long to clear the horses?" he asked.

"Tommy, we may be looking at a dead-heat finish. The officials have to take their time because ..." Ted said before being cut off mid-sentence.

"Jesus Ted, we've got a crazy terrorist on the grounds. Is there any way you can hurry up whoever makes the final decision? Those horses and their jockeys are sitting ducks out there. Can we get them off the track or something? Damn it ... anything!" Tommy screamed into the phone as he ran through the tunnel to the track office.

"Rooftop, this is Talon ... be on your toes. This is too perfect for a shooter. Remember, no freelancing ... you're acting on my call. Roger that, please."

Sniper by sniper, each marksman once again confirmed the

specific orders given to them. Making his way to the track office looking for Art, Tommy found Connie instead.

"Show me, show me ... where, where the horses exit the track after the race is completed," Tommy demanded of her, breathless from running – and from the pain now in both hands. Although Connie had no idea who he was, she knew that since he'd passed through a security check at the entrance, he was one of the team. Pulling out a map that showed the layout of the track, Connie pointed to the spot on the oval where the horses had just been thirty minutes earlier.

"Damn morphine ... I'm all fucked up," Tommy muttered.

"We may have fooled him before the start of this race, but I guarantee he's not fooled now ... damn, I've got to get more men down there," Tommy said to himself frantically. At the exact moment an older man, a Challenge Cup official, was engaging in race track chitchat with a Metro officer.

* * *

While no one knew for sure who the winner was, it appeared everyone had an opinion. Arguments raged between friends – even among patrons who didn't know each other – and who now would never be friends. Each claimed they'd the perfect view of the finish line and knew which horse, because of their birds-eye view, won the race. Fifteen years from now, there'll still be millions of fans swearing they were standing right at the rail, right at the finish line. They'd swear that …

The scoreboard lit up.

Results are official, it read.

Win: Number One and Number Five

Show: Number Four

The supposed foul had been disallowed.

The crowd's response to the decision would be described in Sunday's sports section of the newspaper as a collective loud groan.

* * *

With a lead shank attached to TA's halter, Lance cool-walked our horse over the dirt track during the time race stewards were still determining the race results. I was uneasy and would remain so until Towers was safely ensconced back in his stall. Impatient to hear the official announcement, I was sure there would be a single winner, as the advent of digital photography and enhanced resolution years ago had virtually eliminated the dead-heat dual race winner result.

But not this time. "Damn it to hell," I said, kicking angrily at the dirt on the track.

"Thank God Art had the winning horses moved to the turf to continue their cool down," I told myself. "A little more distance might make it slightly more difficult for a shooter."

Once the race was over and officially declared a tie, both horses received the customary track protocol – pictures – first with Nidalas and his entourage ... then with TA – Joey still astride – and the rest of our entourage. Finally able to dismount, she grabbed the saddle and crossed the dirt track, heading for the scales for the post-race weigh-in and subsequent interviews.

In the meantime, Lance, with TA in tow, was preparing to head to the main track and exit to the barns. Donnie and Mike, and Marty and I were headed to the presentation area to receive a trophy ... when something made me turn away from the group, shouting

Lance's name.

To this day, I have no idea why I felt the need to be at the exit to accompany TA and Lance from the track. Everyone has those moments when, for some inexplicable reason, they're compelled to take a specific action. Sometimes it's quite clear later that the decision was the right one. Other times, we simply admit, "Well, that was stupid … there was no reason to do that."

I told Lance I'd meet up with him shortly – first though, I wanted to reassure myself that the area was indeed secure. My first thought watching the two winning horses a couple of minutes earlier was that both were still vulnerable. "Perhaps the uncle is drawing a bead on one or both of them at this moment," I said to myself, shuddering at the thought … praying that the hundred yards before they reached the barn would be calm and safe.

Looking around, I saw two Metro officers on the path by the exit, both engaged in conversation with an older man wearing a Challenge Cup jacket, gray slacks and one of the security team's logo ball caps.

"Tommy's got this area locked up well," I said to myself – watching as the two winning horses advanced towards the exit –

drawing the attention of a swelling crowd. The only way off the track for the two champions was blocked somewhat by a throng of happy horse lovers ... and others who were angry with the race's outcome.

I heard shouts of congratulations coming from the crowd, while another patron – most likely someone who lost a significant amount of money – was belligerent, blaming me for having Joey supposedly "dump the race."

"Becker ... Rob Becker. We see you. What the hell happened today? Your horse sucks. Don't even show up at the Derby, you asshole!" That statement and others cascaded around me.

"Hey Metro ... you guys want to start making some room for the horses?" I pleaded, still concerned about the safety of Towers Above and Nidalas – and fully expecting that both officers and the other official would do something. The two officers responded, and started moving the crowd back – but not the stranger wearing the logo ball cap. That older man seemed oblivious to it all.

Nidalas was first to reach the exit gate, but instead of directing Nidalas through the opening, his groom started to circle the horse on the track – giving deference to Towers Above. I smiled in

441

response to the gallant act.

Towers Above stepped off the track, Lance slowly leading him past the gathered crowd. People reached out to touch our horse … and some were successful. Bathing in the adoration, Towers never flinched, even appearing to pause for photographs. I sensed that Lance was holding up Towers' trip to the barn … he too was basking in the limelight.

Finally away from the fanfare, I began walking with Lance and Towers Above back to the barns. I was clearly on an endorphin high … and the weight on my shoulders much less apparent. Tommy must have foiled the uncle, I told myself. "He did it … and the big show for the day is over," I said happily to no one in particular.

"Momma said there'd be days like this, there'd be days like this my momma said … momma said, momma said, momma said," suddenly burst from my lips. I walked another twenty yards, still singing away, before stopping abruptly.

"Jesus … Nidalas!" I said, chastising myself for forgetting which horse was the probable target … suddenly remembering the older man I'd seen just minutes earlier with the two Metro officers.

"That Cup guy is an old man and that's not how Tommy and his men are dressed. I've seen Tommy's men all day long and none of them are wearing racing gear," I said to myself – now clearly remembering there'd been no representatives from the Challenge Cup at the track at any time during the week.

"Shit. Nidalas is just now reaching the exit ..." I exclaimed, breaking into a sprint, while pulling out my semi-automatic.

CHAPTER 53

Sending the horses onto the track through the exit gate was a brilliant maneuver, Tommy thought. The glitch, though, was that there wasn't enough time to organize post-race crowd-control measures. There were no ropes or straps long enough to control the growing crowd that was converging at the exit gate. The patrons had been robbed of the traditional paddock experience – but they surely weren't going to be denied their up-close and personal opportunity.

By the time Towers Above made his way through the crowd, the mass of people was surging forward ... and the path by the track had become a sea of excited horse racing fans. Nidalas, who was still circling on the track, was becoming agitated. He was overheated, wanted water and his post-race bath. Trying to calm Nidalas, the groom began walking him towards the winner circle. In the meantime, the horses running in the last race of the day had just stepped onto the track surface.

"Jesus Ted ... where the hell are your people? We need help down here at the exit gate! Nidalas is a sitting duck out here and ..."

"Tommy, stop. Calm down ... I have a contingent of men on

the way," Ted responded in obvious exasperation.

* * *

I was still frantically sprinting towards Nidalas, and getting closer … my actions immediately drawing the attention of the agents on the rooftop.

"Talon … this is Rooftop. We've got a suspect headed for the track. He's pulling a weapon! Permission to take out the target?"

Tommy quickly turned toward the agent on the rooftop, asking for more information. "What's the target's position …?"

"He's ten yards from the track's exit gate … a weapon is visible and he's physically pushing people aside. Again … requesting permission to fire, Talon!"

Suddenly, Tommy saw the "suspect" less than ten yards from him. It was me, breathless from running and nearing the exit gate – not realizing I was about to be taken down. "Becker. Rob Becker … not one more step," Tommy shouted angrily.

"Rooftop, this is Talon. Hold your fire … the target is

friendly."

"Jesus Rob, one of my men on the roof was about to off you. Put that fucking gun away … Now!" Tommy screamed.

"Tommy … he's there at the gate. I know it's him. You don't have your guys dressed in Challenge Cup clothes … and this guy is twice your age! He's stalking Nidalas. It's the uncle … it has to be," I exclaimed, out of breath and visibly shaken.

"Rooftop, this is Talon. At the edge of the track, by the exit gate … do you see a man in a Challenge Cup uniform?"

"Talon … wait a few seconds, I'm looking. Talon, yes there is a man … but he's also wearing one of our logo caps. Do you roger that, Talon?" was the rooftop marksman's reply.

Part of Tommy wanted more morphine … being in pain and trying to process thoughts without a clear head was not usually a workable situation. Ignoring the pain, Tommy began to mentally visualize the roster of operatives he'd assigned to the track.

"Talon … we have the target in our sights. Permission to take the shot."

"Rooftop ... put your spotter on the phone," Tommy commanded.

"Spotter here, Sir ... waiting for your instructions."

"Is the target's cap on forward or backward?" Tommy asked.

"The hat's on forward, Sir," the spotter replied.

"Gotcha ... you son of a bitch." Tommy said excitedly.

"Rooftop ... if he gives even the slightest indication of drawing a weapon on anyone or anything, if he looks like he's going rogue on us – take the shot. I'm going to try for a snatch. We need to know if there are any more assholes here today. I repeat, you have a green light. Talon out."

Turning around, looking for me, Tommy quickly realized that I was gone again. "Goddamn it, Becker ... let us do our job," Tommy said to himself in frustration.

* * *

Arriving at the exit gate before the rest of the crowd, Ben saw several patrons, only a couple of Metro officers, and two older track security guards. Most of the patrons were still transfixed, staring at the big screen by the track, watching the replay of the race segment with the supposed infraction.

Ben knew he needed to position himself at the edge of the track … and for that to happen, he'd have to mingle with the Metro officers. But since he'd already done that on the 'mountain', he wasn't overly concerned.

No longer wanting to have the gangsta look, he turned his cap forward … he needed to look professional when he approached the officers. If challenged, well, he still had the badge.

"Hell of a race, huh guys?" Ben said to the officers as an icebreaker.

The officers responded with the typical Metro stare down, both eyeballing Ben from head to toe. There were no visible tells that he was a threat … and they both knew about the new logo hats that the federal security team was wearing. Hal spoke first.

"You're with the Challenge Cup … huh?"

"No ... not really," Ben responded, pulling out the FBI badge. "Figured I'd fit in better if I was dressed like this, in case that terrorist is close by."

That was all the explanation Hal needed to hear, nodding to his partner Charlie that Ben was okay ... one of the good guys. As luck would have it, neither officer had been given the message about the security team wearing their caps backward.

Ben knew if there was ever a time for patience, that moment was now ... with the realization that this was where he was going to die. The only thing he prayed for was that death be quick.

Watching as Nidalas drew closer in his approach to the exit, Ben slowly reached for his weapon. Then, as if the horse suddenly received a pardon from execution, Nidalas halted and turned away, letting Towers Above pass through the gate first. Ben didn't like the delay ... he wanted to get on with the plan. He quickly dismissed that thought, though ... again, accepting the need for patience. Removing the cap, Ben ran his fingers through his hair, and turned to survey the growing crowd.

Agents on the rooftop were snapping photographs in rapid

fashion … streaming them instantly to Ted and Tommy. Tommy was amazed at the resolution of the photos … grateful for the visual confirmation that their prey was here … only a few feet away.

Ted's men had arrived on the scene and were busy breaking up the crowd and dispersing it. Nidalas turned one more time … heading again to the exit gate.

"That's it. Keep coming – you won't suffer – it'll be quick," Ben quietly promised the horse.

Tommy's phone crackled again. "Talon, your friendly target is closing on the horse! He's pulled his weapon again … please advise quickly!" reported one of the rooftop shooters.

CHAPTER 54

Tommy brought me to my knees with a sleeper hold. He then flashed his badge to the patrons who had gathered during the brief melee.

Although slightly dazed, I wasn't quite ready to give up the fight. Getting up, I looked at the track and noticed Nidalas was still taking his cool-down walk and hadn't yet left the track … Ben was still standing by the exit gate, alive and well. My thoughts were racing – I was more determined than ever to end Ben's life once and for all.

I got up, and began pushing towards the exit with my gun in hand.

Breaking through the crowd, I was less then fifteen feet from Ben when I felt a piercing pain – like a hot jolt of electricity – in my right thigh. For the second time in five minutes, I was on the ground … and this time, blood was seeping from my leg.

"Talon … the target is down. It was a shot to the thigh. He's not going anywhere soon," said the rooftop shooter.

"Thanks Rooftop. Notify EMS of his location ... and tell them to move it ASAP! I'm almost at ground zero. I have the uncle in my kill zone ... this one is mine," Tommy said with vehemence and surety.

Despite the nearby commotion, Nidalas was ready to exit, making one last turn before being led to the gate.

Ben was watching closely, waiting for his opportunity ... it was now. Taking two steps forward, he raised the umbrella, pointing its tip directly at Nidalas' chest. The Metro cops were oblivious to what Ben was doing.

* * *

Ben had practiced this shot at least fifty times – the last time was one week earlier – with the victim being his rescue horse, Saladin. Reliving that day and recalling the events of that shot, Ben wondered if people understood the irony – that Saladin was Nidalas spelled backwards. Or that many books on world history referred to Saladin as the greatest Arabian fighter and leader ... ever.

Ben's weapon was a spring-loaded, eighteen-gauge needle attached to a hypodermic syringe that when triggered, would pierce through the protective thin layer of beeswax covering the tip of the umbrella. Once released, a bolus of Ben's purest Ricin, combined with specifically-calibrated Ringers IV solution, would discharge through the needle. The mechanism was propelled by the release of a CO_2 cartridge that was connected to the syringe. Experimentation with the various animal species helped Ben refine the mechanism, ensuring sufficient PSI and flow speed that would inject the solution directly into horse flesh in just half a second ... too quickly for a horse to react and escape.

Ben first began his research using mice, then rats and pigs. Saladin would be his final research subject for the syringe test ... before Nidalas.

Approaching Saladin seven days earlier, Ben imagined it was actually Nidalas he was going to inject. Saladin, patiently waiting for his daily treat, never stood a chance. Instead of giving the horse the expected treat, Ben triggered the syringe of Ricin, activated a timer and walked away ... it was important for Ben to know precisely how long it took for Saladin to die.

Each hour, Ben headed to his paddock to check on Saladin, leaving nothing to chance. The horse's last breath was twenty-five hours and forty minutes later.

* * *

Tommy, Ben and Nidalas came together in the same place and at the same time – Nidalas' chest a mere inch from the tip of the Ricin-laden umbrella – while Tommy's gun was less than a foot away from Ben's skull, aimed directly behind the terrorist's left ear lobe.

"Ahmed … Ben Slaughter. Don't even flinch or you die!" Tommy shouted.

Ben didn't flinch or turn around … he pulled the trigger mechanism inside the umbrella.

Nidalas reared up!

Tommy looked at the umbrella now lying in the dirt on the track. … his eyes immediately drawn to the tip of the umbrella and the large needle sticking out of it. Had it pierced Nidalas?

Turning around, Ben looked Tommy straight in the eyes … a weird smile of contentment flashing across his face. He began to reach inside his jacket and …

Tommy squeezed the trigger of his nine millimeter ... there was no sound because of the suppressor attached.

Ben's skull exploded into at least twenty fragments from the hollow point round that smashed through bone and tissue, his body crumpling onto the dirt surface of the track in a split second.

Now under tight reign, Nidalas stepped around Ben, heading to the holding barn where he and Towers Above would undergo the standard drug test to make sure there were no illicit substances in their bodies.

Retrieving the umbrella from the ground, Tommy directed the Metro police to cordon off the area around Ben's body, and called Ted, telling him to go immediately to the administration office.

It was over ... and yet it wasn't.

CHAPTER 55

With the umbrella still in hand, Tommy headed to where I was now receiving care from the EMS team. Flashing his badge at the paramedics, he asked who was in charge. "I am," Sonny confirmed.

"How bad is it?" Tommy inquired.

"He's lucky, it's a clean wound. He can move his leg … and whatever caliber bullet took him down missed the major blood vessels. We'll transport him to the hospital, they'll take care of his wound and I assume also give him a tetanus shot and some antibiotics," Sonny answered.

"Can you guys step back a moment? I'd like a word with him," Tommy asked assertively, in a tone that indicated "No" would be the wrong answer. The paramedics and Metro officers securing the area moved away, giving Tommy and I some privacy.

I didn't want to even look at, let alone talk to, Tommy … now crouched on the ground next to me.

"Rob, I know you're pissed and I would be too if it had happened to me. My guys had no choice ... they had to take the shot. We had the situation in hand and you just wouldn't give it up! Rob, if you want to go through special ops training, I can arrange it. I'll see you tonight."

Placing a hand on my shoulder, Tommy gave me a gentle squeeze of reassurance – then thanked the paramedics and started to take his leave.

"Sir, you should go to the hospital too ... that hand looks pretty nasty," the medic said. Tommy just nodded and headed to the administration building to meet up with Ted.

While walking to the Ted's office, he placed a long overdue phone call to the home office in Virginia – and before he could utter a single word, Tommy was verbally slammed to the ground by his superior.

"What the hell is going on out there? State has called you at least a dozen times and you haven't answered. You're fucked now." Tommy silently agreed.

"Now, how about that race? It sure was one hell of a finish

..." Tommy said to his boss in an appeasing tone.

"Shut up, Goddamn it, and just listen. At least the network television didn't show you blowing Ben's head off his shoulders," his boss came back with. Tommy knew he needed to update his boss on the sequence of events that weren't seen on TV.

"He got a shot off before I could stop him," Tommy explained over the phone, adding that Ben had turned the umbrella into a weapon. "He gave Nidalas a shot ... an injection of something. It was like the KGB hit in Great Britain years ago – and yes, I'm thinking Ricin."

Now in control of the conversation, Tommy continued his recap of the events. "Nidalas didn't go down and he left the track seemingly okay. I've got the umbrella and will turn it over to our forensics team in a couple of minutes ... I'd appreciate it if you tell the lab to rush the results ... or at least give us a speedy preliminary analysis! Everything depends on what the lab finds. If it's Ricin, the Saudi's horse could die in a day or two. Hell, I don't know how long it will take – you need to get your best Bill Nye-type scientists and computer geeks working on answers."

Tommy was out of breath.

"Jesus Tommy, you know I can't sit on this. I'm going to have to let the State Department know what happened – and if your assumptions are right – well this is going to be a full-blown cluster fuck," his superior warned.

"I know. But if you cry wolf and the lab comes back with nothing, then both of us will look like fools," Tommy replied.

"Okay Tommy, you've got a small grace period until we get some lab results, but I'm going to have to talk with the Secretary of State ... and he'll most likely give POTUS a heads up."

"Do what you have to do. You have my initial snapshot of the events. I'll get back to you this evening," Tommy replied curtly, cutting off the communication. His next call was to Ted and the other operatives ... informing them that the hostilities were officially over and ending the conversation with an all clear. The shooters packed up their gear and departed the rooftop – removing their caps – now a souvenir of the events of the day.

Tommy counted the total casualties at the track that day to himself. One fatality – Ben. Four injuries – Jamie, Rob, himself and Nidalas.

As he entered the administration building, he saw Ted and Art standing in the lobby waiting ... with huge smiles on their faces.

"Sorry guys – you need to wipe those smiles off your faces – we still have problems," Tommy revealed. "I need you to take me to the most secure office in the building ... one with no microphones or video equipment, please."

The next thing Tommy knew, they were all standing in the men's room ... with Ted locking the door behind them.

Tommy started to talk but was interrupted when Art's phone began to ring – it was the sheikh – asking for Tommy's cell phone number. Art was gesturing to Tommy ... who quickly understood the sign language and wrote his cell number down for Art.

"Okay, here's the number," Art told the sheikh. "Well, that's all. How's Nidalas doing? It sure was a great race!" Art said to the sheikh exuberantly. After a couple more minutes of conversation, the call ended ... no more than thirty seconds passed before Tommy's phone rang.

"Hello ... how high is the water?" Tommy said, knowing full

well that it was the sheikh calling him.

"Mr. Tommy, you know I have no answer to that question. I want to thank you for all that you did today. Nidalas thanks you and our kingdom thanks you. I'll be leaving in a couple of days and would like you to be my guest for a month so I can reward you appropriately. You know I can make this happen with your country's consent … of course."

Tommy framed his response very carefully.

"Sir, I very much appreciate your invitation … today's situation has many loose ends that still require my attention. May your horse run well in the Derby … and please extend my best wishes to the king." The sheikh again thanked Tommy and with a final admonition, said, "I'm very pleased these events today did not result in an unfortunate situation for you."

Tommy managed a "you betcha" before the sheikh hung up.

Turning his attention back to Art and Ted, Tommy laid everything out for both men … their facial expressions becoming grimmer the longer he talked. Art posed the first question.

"If you're right and Nidalas dies ... do you think the Saudis will go public?"

Tommy replied, "I have no idea. This is now in the hands of the State Department – I imagine that POTUS has already been informed. It's a political football game now. Since it happened in our country, we'll end up not only apologizing ... but spending a lot of money making amends. Hell, the Saudis will probably end up with twenty or thirty of our most advanced fighters ... who knows?"

"Art, I'll tell you one thing, Ted has done one heck of a job here with the limited security budget he has to work with – but your track is still nowhere close to where it should be when it comes to security and safety. I know how much you love your Ritz Carlton twenty-first century formalities and your ivy-covered stone buildings ... but you and your power-driven Thoroughbred owners need to beef up security to the maximum here."

Tommy stopped to gather his thoughts – and to give Art time to digest what he'd just said – and he wasn't done yet. He felt the need to drive the message home even more – and reinforce just how serious the security issue was.

"It's not a matter of racing fans being inconvenienced – trust me, they'll eventually accept your changes. You've got a wonderful venue ... and the patrons aren't stupid. They see the lax security and after today, if you don't show them that you've upped the level of protection, they won't come back – and you'll lose more than revenue – you'll lose fan loyalty."

There was total silence. The bathroom may as well have been in outer space – it was that quiet. "Ted, we'll talk more and Art, thank you for all the cooperation today."

Neither said a word. Both of them were staring at the umbrella still in Tommy's hand – and the large needle sticking protruding from the tip.

CHAPTER 56

Tommy texted the forensic team: *Meet me outside the administration office; it's next to the riders up paddock.*

When he left the building, the team was already there waiting. Tommy handed the umbrella over to them, noticing that the few remaining patrons were leaving the grounds now that the last race was over. The day was done … nightfall was near. Tommy called me. Recognizing the number on the screen, I handed the phone to Marty … I wasn't ready to make peace.

"This is Marty, who's this?" she asked tersely.

"Marty, this is Tommy."

"You've got a lot of nerve calling. He doesn't want to talk to you!"

"Marty, I know but since my hand is broken hand and I'm heading to the hospital, I thought I'd stop in and see Rob while I'm there. Look Marty, you can say "No" if you want … but I'll bypass all protocols if I have to."

"Hold on Tommy." Two minutes passed before she returned to the call. "OK! He caved ... said to come on up when you get here."

Driven by one of his agents, Tommy arrived at the hospital, circumventing the reception desk and heading directly to the treatment admission area. "Sir you can't be in this ..." a hospital employee started, attempting to prevent Tommy from going further.

Stopping her in mid-sentence, Tommy put his badge and a forged FBI identification card on the desk. Hovering over his left shoulder was the driver ... also flashing a badge.

"I'm only saying this once," Tommy said in a tone that invited no dissent. "I'm invisible as far as you and this hospital are concerned. There will be zero records, no patient file, no entries or treatment notes. If you call security, I'll have you fired. I want X-rays taken of my hand and wrist, and I need a diagnosis. I'll wait in Dr. Becker's room while the radiologist or on-call orthopedist reads the radiographs. Have that person come to Dr. Becker's room when ready to give me a report on my hand ... and this entire process better be quick. Oh ... and tell the doctor to bring enough pain pills for a week. Are we clear?"

The admitting secretary, now thoroughly intimidated, nodded yes – and within fifteen minutes, Tommy's hand had been X-rayed, and he and his driver on their way to my hospital room.

As Tommy walked into the room, Marty got up to leave. "Marty, please stay," I beseeched. "I'm begging you." She stayed.

Tommy spoke first. "Rob, I take full responsibility for my sniper taking the shot. I was two yards away from Ben when you were hit – and I wanted to take Ben alive, before he shot Nidalas. Unfortunately he still shot Nidalas, but not with a gun. Ben made a weapon out of his umbrella and injected something, probably a poison into Nidalas' chest. We don't have any lab work yet, but I expect Nidalas to die."

I was filled with mixed emotions … wanting to rip the IV out of my arm and leave. I instantly thought, "what if Towers Above had been Ben's target instead of Nidalas?" Tears began welling in my eyes over the thought.

"Tommy, this shit has to stop … it has to end!" I said in frustration.

"I do need to thank you for watching over Marty and me … and Towers Above. I'm sorry for almost screwing everything up … and I have a favor to ask."

A nurse, wearing more badges than General Patton, marched into the room … interrupting me before I could ask for the favor. She stared hard at Tommy, who finally turned in her direction, and said. "You've got to be the head floor nurse – and judging by your demeanor, you're about to tell me what's broken. Let me guess, the doctor was too much of a pussy to come and talk with me himself." The nurse's stern demeanor relaxed into a big smile.

It was obvious that Tommy was spot-on with his characterization of the doctor and she was enjoying his interpretation of the situation. Behind her back was a dry erase board which she brought out, drawing the anatomy of the human hand and wrist on it, and pointing at two specific bones – bones I rightly assumed were the ones broken.

A nurse's aide also entered the room, carrying a large stainless steel bowl filled with ice and very little water. Placing it on a table, the head nurse asked Tommy to sit, gently lowering his hand and wrist into the ice bath to reduce the inflammation.

For the next four hours, Tommy soaked his injured hand, while regaling Marty and I with stories from his past – and the highs and lows of some of the covert operations he'd participated in. My eyes were glazing over and so were Tommy's. Finally, Tommy was "discharged" and as he prepared to leave, the nurse gave him the name of an orthopedic hand specialist … and a quick peck on the cheek.

"Rob, you'll be out of here tomorrow. I'll be in touch," Tommy said, squeezing my hand. With a parting kiss to Marty and a hand shake for me … Tommy was gone.

I had totally forgotten the favor I wanted to ask of Tommy.

CHAPTER 57

The federal agents wasted no time ... several of them converged upon Ben's farm that evening looking for information and clues. They began sifting through everything, and collecting evidence they needed, even though Ben and his twin nephews were dead. There was good cause ... the agents felt certain that eventually, there would be copycat attacks.

Several items were recovered from the search and seizure: castor plants, a prototype of the Ohio State University Stadium and its surroundings, aeronautical maps, eighteen-gauge needles and hypodermic syringes, letters from Ben's brother Omid pre-dating 9/11 – and perhaps the most compelling and useful of all – Ben's diary.

The diary provided agents with a well-written blueprint of Ben's terroristic mindset and his battles parenting the twins, with daily postings of their activities starting after 9/11. It was a mother lode of information, providing the agents with a documented timeline that would otherwise have taken them months or years to figure out ... if ever.

The agents went to the school the twins attended to try and find additional clues to their behavior, but it was a dead end. The boys had no friends … as identical twins, they were each other's best friend and confidant and needed no one else in their lives.

Throughout the night and well into the next day, Tommy received several status updates from the federal agents by text – and with each new text, he thought aloud, "if only they had listened to me from the start."

The remainder of time was spent soaking his hand, alternating between ice water and a hot Epsom salt solution. Early Sunday morning, he received a phone call from the office of the orthopedic specialist and was told "Dr. Nasser will make a special trip to his office and will see you at 3:00 P.M. to set your fractures and place your cast – and we only take MasterCard and VISA."

"Great, just great … the best orthopedic hand specialist in Southern Kentucky is an Arab," Tommy thought sarcastically.

Arriving a half hour before his appointed time, Tommy again went through the badge and fake FBI credentials scenario … adding a new wrinkle. Placing his weapon on the reception counter, he told the physician assistant to go and get the doctor.

When Dr. Nasser appeared, Tommy steered him to a corner of the reception area.

"Doctor, there will be no health history taken, or signing of a HIPAA acknowledgement form. Simply call me Mr. Invisible. Here's a digital copy of my radiographs and I want it back. I don't give a flying fuck about political correctness or your beliefs – and that includes your religion," Tommy told the physician … leaving no doubt from his body language that he was dead serious.

Continuing, still in a somewhat threatening demeanor, but talking in a calm tone, Tommy reinforced his expectation of anonymity to the doctor. "If you value your career in America and want to continue as you are, you'll do what I say. If you don't, then be prepared to look over your shoulder for a long time. You never know when I or some of my friends will pay you or your family members a surprise visit. Are we clear?"

One hour later, Tommy left the office in a cast extending up to his elbow – and enough pain medication to last a while. The cast was removable and would allow Tommy to still soak the hand and wrist in Epsom salts.

At this point, Tommy felt as if he was walking above the clouds. If he'd been in his home state, it would have been a definite Rocky Mountain High moment for him.

* * *

Marty and I left the hospital Sunday afternoon.

"Damn hospitals ... they always keep you past noon so they can tack on another day to the patient's bill," I said to Marty.

She laughed for the first time since I'd been shot. "How do you really feel, Marshall Dillon?"

"I feel like my leg was caught in an escalator ... not that I really know what that would be like! I know these crutches are going to be a pain in the ass. Let's head out to Donnie's farm and see how Towers is doing."

Seeing Marty and I heading to his stall, Towers' ears tilted up and straight forward – and with his usual horse whinny hello, approached me to nuzzle – and search for treats. Quickly relenting, I gave him the peppermint candy he knew was hidden in my pants pocket.

"God Marty, I hope he never grows up."

It took just a few hours before realizing that life had returned to normal. Donnie was at the farmhouse and Juan was cleaning out stalls. Nearby was a late model Camaro convertible … the radio on and the volume cranked to the maximum. "Is that Juan's car? I wonder where he got the coin for that?" the ever observant Marty said. I had no answer … but was wondering the same thing.

Donnie was in his office and rose quickly to give us both a hug. Stepping back, he said, "Show it to me."

I laughed and dropped my pants while saying, "You're not going to be able to see the bullet holes."

Marty smiled at our antics, saying, "Even Miss Kitty wasn't allowed to see that kind of stuff."

Frivolity aside, it was time to get down to business. Donnie rehashed the race for me as he remembered it from his vantage point in the stands – while also sharing Joey's summary – furlong by furlong. Having missed the race because of Ben, I admitted how disappointed I was – especially not seeing the end of the race and especially the battle at the finish line between Towers Above and Nidalas.

None of this was new to Marty – she decided to head outdoors and chat with Juan instead. She was very curious about his new Camaro – how could he afford an expensive car like that when his previous car was a 2006 Toyota Corolla? She learned nothing from him, though, except that she wasn't very good at interrogating!

For the next hour or so, Donnie and I went over Towers' training schedule for the next few weeks leading to the Kentucky Derby. "It's a shame we probably won't face Nidalas again. I wonder how competitive future races would be if he was an entrant?" I said.

"That horse has to have the X factor … and what the hell are you talking about Rob?" he asked, clearly confused by my last comment. I'd totally forgotten that Donnie was unaware about the umbrella that was altered into a weapon – or what I'd learned from Tommy the night before. I told Donnie about all the events that had transpired at the track, leaving nothing out. Suddenly, I realized I had taken all the air out of the room.

Quickly changing the tone of our conversation, I asked Donnie for his prediction on the Kentucky Derby.

"I think everything depends on our horse's post positions, as well as the weather conditions. If Churchill's track isn't sloppy like it was here yesterday and Towers isn't in the number thirteen hole or another outside position, he'll win going away," Donnie said with conviction.

I hadn't smiled that freely in over three days.

CHAPTER 58

The result of Nidalas' post-race urine test was normal. The effects of the Ricin had begun, but there was no indication yet of anything amiss in Nidalas' body.

Ricin is a cytotoxin and will cause red blood cells to agglutinate – an interesting process for scientists to observe on a microscope slide as the red blood cells clump together. Without a microscopic cytology examination, the only visible physical symptoms in Nidalas would have extreme agitation and diarrhea – and though still minimal, he was starting to exhibit both issues.

Nidalas' grooms were not unfamiliar with equine disease and had worked with sick horses before ... but the blood in Nidalas stools and his coughing indicated a different, possibly more serious condition. Nidalas' trainer made an urgent call to Mike's Equine Veterinary facility ... the staff responded immediately. Managing to get Nidalas up on his feet, they loaded the horse into an ambulance, transporting him quickly from the track to the veterinary hospital.

During the transport, Nidalas collapsed – at which time the equine attendants started an IV to give Nidalas much needed fluids and nutrients. The lead attendant radioed ahead to Mike, offering his best guess diagnosis and telling Mike he didn't think the horse had colic – one of the most serious of equine illnesses. When Nidalas arrived at the facility, Mike ordered a battery of tests, including blood draws and laboratory analysis of his saliva and stools – and adding every type of anti-viral medications into Nidalas' IV solution that he felt could help the horse.

Mike dictated his initial findings into an iPad. *"Nidalas is running a fever and is extremely dehydrated. Blood is present in the stools and saliva. Respirations are raspy and shallow. I've ordered a full GI series of films. I don't believe it is colic. Intravenous fluids were begun during transport and seem to have had a stabilizing result because Nidalas has not defecated since arrival. My differential diagnosis varies: a virus of unknown etiology, food poisoning, or poisoning with a substance of unknown origin.*

Calling me, Mike said, "I have a very interesting patient that was just admitted. He's one sick animal and his name is Nidalas. Have you heard anything from Donnie?"

"Jesus Christ Mike, you're screwed! The terrorist at the track injected Nidalas with some type of poison."

"Oh my God ... thanks Rob!"

"Mike. Mike. Mike ... are you still there?" I realized I was left holding a phone with no one at the other end.

Going into his office, Mike locked the door behind him and sat down – with a sudden comprehension that he was in a no-win situation. He knew he was going to lose his patient ... that Nidalas was going to die. He also knew he'd be blamed for Nidalas' death and that the Saudis would make the connection between him and the Four Horsemen's Farm. He doubted there was any bigger conflict taking place in Southern Kentucky at that moment.

The decision on how to handle the matter quickly became crystal clear to Mike.

Picking up the phone, Mike called another equine veterinary facility. Forty minutes later, Nidalas was enroute to that facility, along with his lab results and radiographs. He was pretty confident that his facility – and his long-time friends – had just dodged a bullet.

It was somewhat ironic that at the same time Nidalas was about to be admitted to the new vet hospital, the feds' official lab report confirmed that Nidalas had been injected with Ricin. The report concluded that as this particular composition of Ricin was so pure and concentrated, there was zero chance of survival – and every highly-trained cytologist the agency consulted with agreed.

Everyone at the federal level was also in agreement over another concern – the impact of this information, if made public, would raise international tensions to another level. Even though the terrorist Ben was an ex-Saudi national, America would be blamed for Nidalas murder. Headlines of the Middle Eastern newspapers would boldly proclaim, *American Terrorist Kills our Champion Thoroughbred.*

* * *

Upon arriving at the second veterinary facility, instead of being admitted, Nidalas was unexpectedly transferred to a waiting van, the van's logo indicating it was from the Saudi horse farm. The Saudi's had reversed course again. Now their horse was heading to the airport to travel back to the Middle East with the sheikh and his entourage. The sheikh was unaware, though, that a local newspaper reporter who covered equine news was watching the drama unfold. The reporter, Alexis, took photographs and video of an obviously-ill Nidalas staggering onto the jumbo jet.

It wasn't by chance that Alexis saw the dramatic events unfolding in front of her eyes. Upon returning to the newspaper office late Saturday – after covering the races at the track that day – she found a package that had been delivered by courier sitting on her desk. Inside was a two-inch thick envelope of papers filled with hand-written entries spanning nearly twenty years.

The newspaper office was in a state of chaos. Two-thirds of the Sunday paper had been put to bed, but the front page and sports sections were still on hold. It had been a busy Saturday news-wise. Reporters were hustling to finish their articles about the terrorist attacks, the tornadoes that had touched down in Kentucky and Tennessee and the fake sinkhole that had shut down the airport.

Alexis had to delay reading the contents of the package she'd received … after all, she was on deadline and already an hour behind. After finally submitting her copy for editing, she turned her attention to the package – tearing off the wrapping and reading the first few entries. Her attention was immediately captured. Alexis skimmed several more pages before flipping to the last entries. Her face was flushed and white light was dancing in front of her eyes. "I'm not going to faint," she told herself, while quickly lying down on the floor and taking deep breaths.

Five minutes later, Alexis was in the office of the newspaper's editor, Pete – who thankfully was still working. Plopping the papers on his desk, she had just one thing to say. "Pulitzer!"

Quickly scanning through the pages the same way as Alexis, the skin on his face suddenly turned ashen. "Holy shit--get back down to that racetrack now!" was all he said.

* * *

Knowing his story would be buried by the American government after he died, Ben made sure that someone – a person with a reputation of the utmost integrity – would learn his version of Saturday's events – and what led up to it. Ben made sure that the *Lexington Clarion's* reporter Alexis, who covered horse racing news, would get a copy of his diary.

* * *

The President of the United States and members of his Cabinet were huddled at Camp David, along with heads of the CIA, FBI, DIA, and NSA. They'd spent more than four hours in somewhat contentious debate over what the nation's response to the situation should be.

Tommy's boss, who headed the CIA, prevailed with his solution. He'd been told by Tommy that the poison shot through the altered umbrella happened in a split second ... so quickly that Tommy doubted anyone had a picture or video of the incident.

Quoting Tommy, his boss told POTUS and the others assembled, "Even if there is a video or photos of the so-called umbrella attack, the Saudis will perform an autopsy on their horse when they get home. They know it's their ex-national who attacked Nidalas ... but they have no proof or evidence to show the media since we grabbed the umbrella immediately after the shot. Everyone will debate the umbrella incident – and if the Saudi's accuse us of Nidalas' death, we'll plead ignorance about the umbrella and deny we even have it."

It was the old Grassy Knoll, second shooter in Dallas, conspiracy scenario about the Kennedy assassination.

Tommy's boss ended his proposed solution by stating, "Of course, we'll sympathize with their loss ... if the Saudi government even makes a public statement."

By straw vote, two thirds of the cabinet agreed to this solution ... and POTUS gave his thumbs up approval. Members of the Cabinet were dismissed, while the heads of the various intelligence groups remained at the President's request.

POTUS began to speak again – and there was no doubt about how serious he was.

"Tell our operatives in Kentucky to tie up all loose ends there related to this situation. By now, the horse has probably shown up at a veterinary hospital. I don't care what your agencies have to do. If it's money they want, then pay them for their silence. Make sure your agents get signed waivers ... have it made crystal clear that if anyone 'talks,' well ... accidents happen in this country every day. Make sure they understand that 'bad luck deaths' are contagious and can spread to their relatives as quickly as a cold can!"

The message was quickly sent and just as quickly, rumors in Southern Kentucky began to melt away like a typical Kentucky snowstorm.

Mike successfully negotiated a settlement of a half million dollars. His staff didn't know it, but there would be some huge Christmas bonuses come December.

As was handled post 9/11, information about the events of this first Saturday in April at Woodlands Park would become classified and stamped *Top Secret*. All physical evidence and information from this day would join with other Saudi materials that were still sitting in darkness in some vault, somewhere, since 9/11.

CHAPTER 59

It was early Monday morning when Tommy landed in Washington, DC … heading directly to his office at Langley to meet with his boss.

"Hell of a job you and your men did," Stan said, shaking Tommy's good hand. "Too bad the Arab horse had to take the fall," he added, intentionally not mentioning the recent meeting with POTUS. Tommy didn't answer … deep in thought about a fellow agent's report he had received by text late Sunday evening. The text was brief.

Nidalas and Saudi entourage have departed for home.

Tommy had expected that Nidalas would be shipped home and wanted to know when he had departed. He also knew that once the jumbo jet took off from a suddenly sinkhole-free airport – he was a marked man. After all, he'd failed to protect Nidalas … the sheikh had already warned Tommy that the price he'd pay would be his life.

But Tommy wasn't going to make it easy for the sheikh.

"Stan, I need to go dark. How soon before I can get new papers and ID ... and a makeover?"

"What the hell are you talking about?" he asked Tommy.

Tommy went into detail about his conversations with the sheikh, filling in the gaps and explaining the not-so-veiled threat if Nidalas was harmed by Ben. He could see the stress and worry lines in Stan's face ... and knew his boss understood the critical nature of this matter. Stan knew the likelihood of Saudi Arabia sending its own agents – agents of the same ilk of the CIA to New York or DC ... even directly to Kentucky to exact their revenge – would be high.

Tommy's thoughts were wandering in a similar fashion – speculating it wouldn't take long for the leader of the Saudi General Intelligence Presidency, also known as GIP – to determine the true cause of Nidalas' death before dispatching Saudi agents to find and dispose of Tommy.

Stan placed a call to his assistant, saying, "Andrea, we need a new identity and relevant paperwork for Tommy. Call downstairs and see if they can get this process started right away – Tommy can head there now."

"Boss, there's one last thing I want to do before this all gets locked away somewhere. I want to arrange a get-together with the key players from the events of this last week, including a civilian, Dr. Rob Becker. Can you set it up for some time next month in Hays, Kansas?

"I don't see why not," his boss acknowledged. "You'll still be a little black and blue then, but our people will know why… and they'll be the only ones who will."

Ready to learn about his new identity, Tommy headed several floors down in the agency headquarters, and was met at the elevator door by the best plastic surgeon CIA money could buy – a surgeon well compensated for his service – and for his silence.

"Follow me please," the surgeon said with no pleasantries and no introduction by name. Tommy had heard rumors there was a surgical facility on campus … rumors that were now confirmed. Entering the examination room, the surgeon closed the door, giving Tommy a detailed overview of the surgical procedures – and their expected results.

"This is what we're going to do. You'll get a nose job and a facial lift of both cheeks; we'll fit you with contacts that will make your inter-pupillary distance and eye color different. I want you to start growing a goatee and also change your hair color a little … just enough that it still matches the beard and moustache. You'll wear non-prescription glasses when you're out in public for the remainder of your life. You'll have a Jack Nicholson look … are there any questions?" the surgeon asked Tommy – in a demeanor that invited none.

Tommy felt like he'd been kicked in the groin – he knew he shouldn't say anything … but nonetheless wanted to argue over the changes that were going to happen to his face. Tommy's appearance was his identity and it represented what he'd accomplished in his life … he was proud of all that and felt the new appearance would take that away from him.

He felt that part of him was dying, and in one sense, it was.

Finally gathering his wits around him, Tommy asked, "When do we begin?"

"Did you eat or drink anything this morning?" the surgeon asked. "Yes," Tommy said.

"Then after midnight, don't eat or drink anything. You'll get a complete physical today, and your surgery will be at 6:00 a.m. tomorrow," the doctor of anonymity stated. "If you have no other questions, my staff will start your physical now ... and please don't bother asking their names. Are you ready to begin the new you?"

Looking around the examination room, he quickly saw what he was looking for – a mirror. Standing in front of it, Tommy stared for a moment or so before giving himself a silent goodbye. Turning away from the mirror, he said to the surgeon, "Let's get this started!"

The next four days were both emotionally and physically demanding on Tommy – the surgeon was unaware of Tommy's significant morphine usage since Saturday – and Tommy continued in his blissful state after his surgery. Once the bandages were removed, a cosmetologist visited Tommy twice a day, to help him with grooming ... then teaching him to use his non-dominant hand to get a decent shave. The biggest adjustment for Tommy, though, was the soft contacts – he'd never had contacts before and it was difficult not only learning how to put them in, but adjusting to the difference the contacts made in his inter-pupillary distance.

Slowly but surely, the swelling and purplish-green bruises faded and the new Tommy emerged. The metamorphosis was nearly complete.

CHAPTER 60

It took Alexis an hour to track down Abdul in Dubai …
finally connecting with him Monday afternoon by cell phone.

"Abdul, this is Alexis in Kentucky …"

"Hello my friend … it's a bit late for you to be calling me.
How can I help you?" he asked.

"How soon can you or someone that's already in Riyadh get
to the airport? Hold that thought … it might not be Riyadh. Let me
back up and start over. Abdul, Nidalas was loaded aboard one of the
sheikh's jumbo jets and the plane took off about 3:00 p.m. my time.
Nidalas is gravely ill, Abdul. I can't tell you any more than that …
but I need you or someone else there wherever the plane lands,
confirming that Nidalas gets off the plane and what his condition is.
If you help me with this story and we win the Pulitzer Prize, you'll
be highly rewarded."

"Alexis, let me get in touch with one of my sources. Can I
reach you at the number you're calling from?" "Yes," Alexis
answered.

Retreating to a quiet place in her home, Alexis continued to read Ben's diary – her editor was also going through Ben's account of the events – and she was determined to keep up with his pace. Perusing a two-inch thick diary that read like a novel – while also taking notes and developing leads to follow and investigate – was a challenge. It required concentration and lots of caffeine ... and an overnight reading marathon to complete.

Unable to get in touch with her editor by phone – all she got was his voicemail – Alexis was unwilling to delay her investigative efforts. She decided to head south on I-75 to visit Metro Police headquarters and request a list of the officers who were at the track on Saturday ... and more specifically, those who had been in close proximity to Nidalas.

Knowing that the horse had been poisoned by Ricin could pose a problem – people may already have been told to not talk with media – but if forced to use the Freedom of Information card, Alexis knew she would. Luckily, the federal agencies hadn't yet restricted the local police department, and she was told that a list of officers and where they were stationed at Woodlands Park on Saturday would be ready the next morning.

Her next stop was the track, going first to Guest Services –
where she was immediately turned down, told that any request for
names and phone numbers of employees violated confidentiality
and that she would need a court order to gain access to the
information. Undeterred, Alexis then went to the administration
offices and asked to speak with the person in charge of the track's
audiovisual department. A few minutes passed.

"Hi, I'm Rod, what can I do for you?"

"Hello Rod. Can I have access to the video from Saturday's
Stakes Race – including from when the horses left the barns and
stepped onto the track – and also as they left the track to return to
their respective barns after their stop at the test barn?" She believed
in a broad brush style of questioning first, and then if necessary, she
would narrow her requests down accordingly.

Although appearing willing to cooperate, Rod knew that the
exit footage of Towers Above and Nidalas had been scrubbed. He
also knew that any video she'd see wouldn't include the umbrella
attack.

Ted's orders had been very precise.

Accompanying Alexis to a viewing room, they watched the

492

requested video together for the next forty minutes. The video included the time when the dead heat winners were pacing back and forth while their owners awaited the official decision. Everything Alexis had asked for was there … except for the footage at the time both horses exited the dirt surface. The video only showed the horses making their final approach to the exit when suddenly the video skipped to a path a few feet past the rail.

"I could've watched this on YouTube," Alexis said heatedly. "Where's the video of Nidalas leaving the dirt surface?"

Rod gave Alexis a stunned, incredulous look. "You just saw all that I have." Alexis glared at Rod … but he didn't flinch. She turned and left the room as Rod said, "Thanks for stopping by, glad I could help."

On Tuesday morning after a restless night at one of the local motels, Alexis went back to Metro headquarters … this time she was led to a room occupied by one of the detectives.

"Good morning Alexis, I'm Detective Nelson … call me Larry. The Chief told me that you'd be coming by for some information this morning. He said you wanted a list of all the officers who worked at the track on Saturday … am I correct?"

Alexis nodded in the affirmative.

"Well, I've got a map of Woodlands Park and marked the positions our officers worked in, as well as their names, but I need to ask … why do you want this information?"

"Larry, I have a source who told me that someone trackside on Saturday injected poison into one of the two dead heat winners either before or after the Stakes Race. I wonder if any of the officers observed anything out of the ordinary … perhaps any suspicious activity anywhere that both of the winning horses had been."

Larry swallowed hard, his mouth suddenly dry and out of saliva. Pausing only briefly, he reached across the desk, and passed the map with markings of where the Metro officers were assigned to Alexis. The map was marked by Post-It notes handwritten with the names of the officers and their respective stations on that day.

Alexis focused on the marked entrance and exit areas, asking Detective Nelson if she could interview the officers who had manned each location. It took the detective only a minute to see that both men were due to start their shift within the next hour. She then asked, "Do you have a problem if I interview both officers this morning, if they're willing?"

"No, I don't," Larry said – putting her in a vacant office to wait – checking in with her several times until the officers arrived for their shift. Larry gave them a heads-up on who she was and what she wanted – and both officers were amenable to being interviewed.

"Officers, thank you for agreeing to meet with me. I know your time is valuable … so I'll get right to the point. The other day when Nidalas was entering or exiting the track – either before or after the Stakes Race – do you remember seeing anyone standing near the horse, holding an umbrella in his hand?"

The officers' eyes opened wide – each looking at the other in dismay, as if both had just been caught with their hand in the forbidden cookie jar – but looking directly at Alexis and simultaneously answering "Yes." Sounds of nervous laughter and obvious tension filled the room briefly … the officers now feeling as if the heavy load they'd carried for the past three days had been lifted from their shoulders. They confirmed to Alexis the events that Ben had written about in his diary – including his intent to harm Nidalas. Neither man had a clue that the diary even existed.

"What happened to the umbrella?" Alexis asked.

They told her that the federal agent who took Ben down had picked up the umbrella and left the vicinity immediately. Alexis asked both men if they would agree to a video interview with the same questions, and if they would also be willing to submit to a polygraph test – each officer once again giving permission. Alexis asked a final question of the men, "Did either of you consider telling someone else … a higher authority like your boss or a track official, about what you observed?"

"Almost as soon as the federal agent disappeared, taking the umbrella with him, another agent showed up and cordoned off the crime scene," one of the officers told her. "Then he told us that we had seen nothing … and that any loose lips would incur serious consequences! It was a message that chilled both of us to the core," the other officer stated.

Alexis thanked both men for their help as they left Detective Nelson's office, turning off the recording device that was in her purse on top of Nelson's desk. "It never hurts to have something to fall back on in case someone changes their mind," she mused to herself.

"I only need to hear from Abdul now," Alexis thought. She

again called her boss – this time, finally getting through – and bringing him up to speed. He told her to get back to the office immediately so they could strategize.

The story would break. It was simply a matter of when.

CHAPTER 61

Mike called Donnie Sunday evening, sharing the information he had concerning his near-patient earlier in the day.

"You're shitting me, Mike ... Rob never mentioned Ricin!" Donnie exclaimed.

"No, I'm not ... it's true."

"Wow, I have no words for this except to start praying. Thanks for calling."

Mike replied, "No problem, Donnie ... talk to you tomorrow. Bye."

Donnie sat there in a trance ... saying a prayer for Nidalas, when it struck him ... what if this had happened to Towers Above? What could or would Mike do to save TA?

Suddenly Donnie flashed back to earlier discussions about Mark and the genetically engineered compounds he was developing.

He hit redial ... Mike immediately answered.

"What did you forget?'

"Well, if what you just told me had been about Towers, not Nidalas, and you knew he'd been poisoned with Ricin, what would you do? I mean ... could you save him?"

"Good question, Donnie," Mike said. "If I knew it was Ricin, the sooner I was aware of it ... the better it would be. I'd sedate Towers immediately and put him in an induced coma. Then I would do two things." Mike paused briefly.

"I'd start blood transfusions and I'd start filtering his blood ... somewhat like dialysis. The sooner you get the red blood cells that are clumping together out of his system, the better his chance of survival. The key to this is a speedy diagnosis. It's my understanding that they flew him home, unfortunately he was never admitted to the Equine Hospital here. I give his chances of survival at no more than five percent."

"Is blood type a problem with horses?" Donnie asked.

"Yeah, Donnie ... it's a crap shoot. The first transfusion is probably going to be okay … but after that – unless you have specifically broken down the horse's blood type to the nth degree and have a perfect donor match waiting – there are just so many other variables to consider. Even with potential donor horses immediately available, a second transfusion could produce so many antibodies, causing an anaphylactic reaction … shock would set in and the horse would die!"

"Jesus Mike, this is so sad. Thanks for the info. When are you coming out to examine Towers?"

"Tomorrow morning. TA is doing fine … now it's on to the Derby! Talk to ya' later. Donnie I have to go," Mike said, in an obvious rush.

"Wait, please! I have one more question. Have we typed TA's blood and do we have a donor horse?"

"I knew that question was out there somewhere," Mike said. "You always were a doctor wanna-be! The answer is yes and you'll never guess who tipped me off to set up the protocol."

"Damn it Mike, I don't know," Donnie responded laughing … but not wanting to play Twenty Questions.

"It was Mark. Way back, he told me to do it ... back when we were breeding our Triple Crown creation. Okay ... bye now."

The phone connection had been cut off.

* * *

The tires of the jumbo jet had barely touched ground when the horse transport ambulance moved onto the tarmac.

Nidalas had blown past Ben's timeline and was still alive ... but barely!

If Nidalas could have spoken, he would have said, "Please, just give me some more new blood! I don't want to die! I don't care if I ever race again. I still have so much to do – new blood. Please!"

The attendants removed Nidalas from the plane, quickly placing him in the ambulance. The hospital staff was anxiously awaiting his arrival ... after which, he went directly to the equine ICU where dialysis and transfusions began.

From the time Nidalas had left Kentucky, someone had been

on the ball.

After being in critical condition for several hours, something appeared to stimulate Nidalas ... his eyes opened for the first time and just as quickly, they closed again. Another IV was started ... it was now time for Nidalas to sleep. While the lab techs continued to draw blood samples, it was nothing more than protocol – the veterinary team already knew what they were dealing with.

Abdul's good friend, Halim, was at the airport when the sheikh's plane landed. He watched through binoculars as Nidalas was taken off the plane ... there were so many people moving at Mach speed – and he knew that Nidalas was gravely ill – but still alive. He texted this information to Abdul, who in turn, updated Alexis.

Halim didn't wait for the ambulance to leave the airport. Heading for the hospital, Halim clocked in and put on his scrubs ... soon he would have a first-hand look at the magnificent racing machine.

* * *

Wednesday, four full days after the Stakes Race, the Saudi

government held an emergency press conference.

The king's spokesman stepped to the podium, announcing the death of Nidalas at 7:40 a.m. Saudi time that morning. He went on to explain the cause of death, making no mention of the assailant. The announcement only said that a poisoning had occurred in America the previous Saturday at Woodlands Park.

The U.S. State Department went immediately into damage control.

America was now branded a *Terrorist Nation* by many worldwide news publications and by several world leaders. The Soviet Union had a field day with the information.

POTUS called an emergency meeting of his cabinet, the various chiefs of U.S. intelligence agencies, and representatives from both the House and Senate Intelligence Committees.

There were no notes or recordings taken during the meeting.

"Ladies and Gentlemen, thank you for coming on such short notice. The Saudi report is false!" POTUS advised the collected group.

There was an audible and collective gasp of surprise from those gathered in the room.

"As we speak, Nidalas is still alive ... although barely. The kingdom officials flew him home last Sunday. If he'd remained in the United States, the horse would be well on his way to recovery. Our agent in the field there believes he still has a chance to survive ... and said he is battling valiantly to live. Our agent also told us that Nidalas is a unique horse, one of a kind – and his only equal on or off the track is Towers Above. I know some of you are not horse racing fans ... so I'll stop this discussion now to let you see the events of last Saturday's race."

The video took about three minutes before POTUS resumed the briefing.

"I intend to issue the usual condolences and the vice president is leaving for Riyadh as we speak to hand-deliver our apologies to the king – and any members of Congress who want to fly to Saudi Arabia are free to do so. In fact, we have another flight leaving from Dulles in six hours. I would expect my friends from the Commonwealth of Kentucky to also be on board."

The president further informed his captive audience that there was going to be a significant payback exacted from the U.S. government. "I fully expect that the Saudi king will give the VP a list of demands in compensation for their country's loss. I anticipate they'll want at least a significant number of our latest Stealth fighters. The sons of bitches have been banging on us for over three years to get their hands on our new weapons systems."

Before any of his staff could ask about a similar appeasement for Israel, POTUS advised the group the matter had been addressed. "I spoke with the Israeli Prime Minister and we're sending them the same type of fighters – but double what we give the Saudis – and with a much higher level of technology.

POTUS had one final point to make before dismissing some of the group … that the country's official position on the identity of the perpetrator would be one of ignorance. "We are going to deny any knowledge of the person or persons involved in the attack at Woodlands Park. So far the domestic press has not blown the lid off any of this … I know they're digging for information, but our intelligence agencies have done a stellar job plugging the leaks."

The president would come to learn just how wrong he was – and that in fact, a Pulitzer-winning story would soon be the front page story in the *Lexington Clarion* – and picked up by every major news source in the country.

"Thank you again … intelligence chiefs, you're not dismissed. Please remain seated." POTUS' Chief of Staff started closing the door, rushing all of the other agency heads out of the room.

"OK, which of you bastards knew about a black operation known as Project Withers … and who the hell is this person Mark and what's his role in the project?"

* * *

Three weeks passed and each new blood sample drawn from Nidalas showed less clumping of the red blood cells, until finally … there were no more clumps. The Director of the equine ICU said it was time – and the team slowly brought Nidalas out of his induced coma. There was no instance of immediate eyes opening or a sudden whinny. It was twenty-four hours before his legs even moved. The intubation tube was taken out and Nidalas was again breathing on his own. The transfusion line was removed and the dialysis line disconnected. His eyes opened and he tried to stand … but couldn't since he was still in restraints.

It was truly a miracle from God.

Out of the shadows of the room emerged a non-member of the ICU team – a man who nonetheless had been directing the treatment and recovery of Nidalas.

A hush fell over the room as the stranger spoke.

"It's time to lower the table and help our patient stand. I'm sure he's hungry!"

Halim lowered his mask below his lips and casually removed his iPhone from his pants pocket. No one noticed him snapping pictures. He then shouted in Arabic,

"Let's give it up for our American friend, Mark!

Everyone was busy celebrating ... and too busy to notice Halim. He forwarded his photos to his contact in Virginia ... but not to Abdul.

EPILOGUE

It was a beautiful fall day in southern Kentucky. The leaves on the Oak trees had already fallen off, arborists debating whether the April lightning strike or the early fall freeze was the culprit.

Towers Above easily won the Triple Crown, and had trained for the Challenge Cup Classic to be held later this day ... he was the overwhelming favorite to duplicate the success that American Pharoah had in 2015.

Woodlands Park had been so successful in hosting previous Cup races that those who decided the venue rotation brought the Cup back to Southeastern Kentucky.

On this particular Saturday, patrons were told to arrive early – and to expect tight security measures.

Walk-through metal detectors, similar to those in airports, had been installed. Over the summer months, horse fencing had also been installed around the entire grounds of Woodlands Park. The fencing was electronically monitored – and any animal or object that crossed the property lines would immediately set off an alarm at the newly-expanded security office.

The security officers were now highly-trained, top-notch professionals.

The old-guard conventional, unarmed security team still existed at Woodlands Park, but their role was minimal … and their presence more for sentimental tradition. After all, the old style traditionalist image still had to be maintained.

Ted and Art were still employed at the track … believe it or not.

F-22 Raptors had replaced the F-18 Hornets and were flying cover over the track on this day. The expense of their protective services was now a line item in the budget.

The same type of security expense was also on the accounting books at The Ohio State University.

As a result of the incidents at the Kentucky racetrack that fateful Saturday in April, sporting venues throughout America began enhancing their security measures and protocols. Even my favorite school, the University of Cincinnati, had installed walk-through metal detectors at its Nippert Stadium.

The cost of tickets at the track had increased to help pay for enhanced security; however, Cup officials also realized that their profit margins could be reduced somewhat.

Ted's assistant, Lanny, was in his office. As he waited for Ted, the reunion in Kansas which never came to fruition came to mind. "The only thing certain is change," Lanny mused.

"C'mon. It's time to go and meet old friends," Ted said, sticking his head through Lanny's doorway.

Woodlands Park's guests on this day included Colonel Murray, Agent Tibbitts, and Tommy's good friend and fellow agent, Danny. Additional guests included Dr. Rob Becker and the latest Pulitzer Prize winner from the *Lexington Clarion*, Alexis Russell ... all were coming together in the track's Directors Room to view the race, enjoy a sumptuous feast – and reminisce over the events several months earlier. There'd be no Arab presence in that room on this day.

There was the usual pomp and circumstance opening Cup

ceremonies, followed by singing of the National Anthem – and this year, there was also a live video message from the President carried on the track's big screen and all other televisions throughout the track grounds.

"Ladies and Gentlemen ... welcome!"

"This year has been a very trying one for sporting venues across our country. I especially extend my thoughts and prayers to everyone present today at Woodlands Park." I also want to extend our county's best wishes to our Arab friends. Their horse, Nidalas, deserved to be at the track today."

"Let's all bow our heads for a moment of silence and reflection."

After thirty seconds of silence ... when all eyes returned to the screen, POTUS was gone. It had been somewhat irreverent in the Director's Room as the president spoke ... Lanny making silent gagging motions the whole time. Ted and Art were doubled over in silent laughter, as were the CIA agents securing the room.

It had been nearly seven months since I'd last seen Tommy ... and had no clue as to what had been happening with him during that time. Entering the room, I shook hands with Art and Ted, and looking squarely at a third man standing with them, said, "Hello. Who are you?"

Ted thought my question was hilarious. Lanny, with his surgically-altered face stoically answered, "I'm the Ghost of Christmas Past and your worst nightmare!"

I literally froze in my tracks, recognizing the voice, but the face ... that face? "Who the hell are you?" I blurted out.

"Well, you see ... I made this promise to protect a horse named Nidalas and I've had a little work done."
The stranger was pointing at his face.

"Jesus Christ, Tommy – holy shit – it is you!"

We embraced.

As expected, Towers Above swept to victory in the Classic a few hours later ... his future secure and now destined for a stud barn and patron tours. Our group had no intention of duplicating other stud farms lax security protocol. Visitors would pass through a metal detector and if need be, would undergo a pat-down by security officials ... and there would be guards posted every few paces in the stud barn.

Finally, all present and involved in April's tragic events sat down for a seven-course dinner.

Everyone had the opportunity to speak and share their memories. Alexis was the first person at the dais to speak ... still amazed how life had changed because of one simple package delivery.

Murray wanted to rant about torture on that Saturday in April but refrained from doing so. Instead he speculated that it could have occurred in Kansas. Tibbitts just shook his head.

At last, it was Lanny's turn to talk. He lifted his glass of wine and proposed the strangest, most righteous toast I'd ever heard.

"Y'all probably won't like what I'm about to say." Everyone nervously laughed, many even wondering who he was.

"This toast is for Ben!" There was total silence and looks of confusion on their faces.

"If that SOB, God rest his soul … yes, that's right, whatever God you believe in … if he hadn't done what he did, there could have been thousands of casualties this past spring. He left enough clues that even the comically-inept Inspector Jacques Clouseau could have predicted where the attacks were going to occur. His true intent that day was not to harm any one specific person. His target was the Saudi ruling class that had personally harmed his family. The terror that is sweeping the world was birthed on Saudi soil. It's on the Saudi's shoulders and until that country's rulers decide to truly end the ongoing conflict, we all must be prepared for the evil that has befallen us to continue!"

"To Ben," Lanny said, raising his glass.

It took a few minutes for the words to sink in, then one by one, glasses were raised by all seated around the table … and there wasn't a dry eye in the room.

Deciding to break the doom and gloom, I raised my glass for a toast. "This is for Juan, TA's groom – at least he used to be – wherever he is now! I hope he hasn't blown all his race winnings yet and is happy with his new Ferrari convertible. I saw him driving it on a YouTube video … he was somewhere in South America."

There was instant laughter.

Rob silently toasted one other person – and one other large animal.

There were persistent rumors that Nidalas was alive ... that his lungs were severely scarred from the effects of the Ricin ... but that he still had bursts of speed doing a couple of furlongs on the race track.

Most of all, if he was still alive, there'd be nothing wrong with his genetics or his desire for a toss in the hay with a pretty lady. That meant that sometime in the future, history would repeat itself. It always does!

And then there was Mark.

Mark never returned my phone calls or e-mails after the events of that fateful April day – I know Mike clearly found that suspicious. When asked about it, all Mike would say to me was, "there's no way Nidalas could have survived unless ..." but he never completed the thought or sentence.

I had my own theory on how Nidalas may have survived ... once Nidalas was loaded on the plane heading to the Saudi homeland, transfusions and blood filtering were started immediately. The Saudis were prepared for any contingency.

"So here's to you Mark or 007 ... or whatever name you go by now," I said silently. "This toast is for you, wherever you are. God Speed ... and salutations."

It was time to move on.

Made in the USA
Lexington, KY
23 March 2017